Over the Top

To Those Who Served in the War to End All Wars, 1914–1918

Over the Top

Alternate Histories of the First World War

Peter G. Tsouras

and

Spencer Jones

FRONTLINE BOOKS, LONDON

Over the Top: Alternate Histories of the First World War

This edition published in 2014 by Frontline Books,
an imprint of Pen & Sword Books Ltd,
47 Church Street, Barnsley, S. Yorkshire, S70 2AS
www.frontline-books.com

ISBN: 978-1-84832-753-5

CIP data records for this title are available from the British Library

For more information on our books, please visit
www.frontline-books.com, email info@frontline-books.com
or write to us at the above address.

Printed and bound by CPI Group (UK) Ltd, Croydon, CR0 4YY

Typeset in 11.75/14 point Adobe Jenson Pro by JCS Publishing Services Ltd,
www.jcs-publishing.co.uk

Contents

Illustrations

Maps

Plates

Chapter 1   *Der Tag*: The Germans Decision to Go East in 1914

ix

All plates are supplied from the private collections of Dr Spencer Jones and Peter Tsouras.

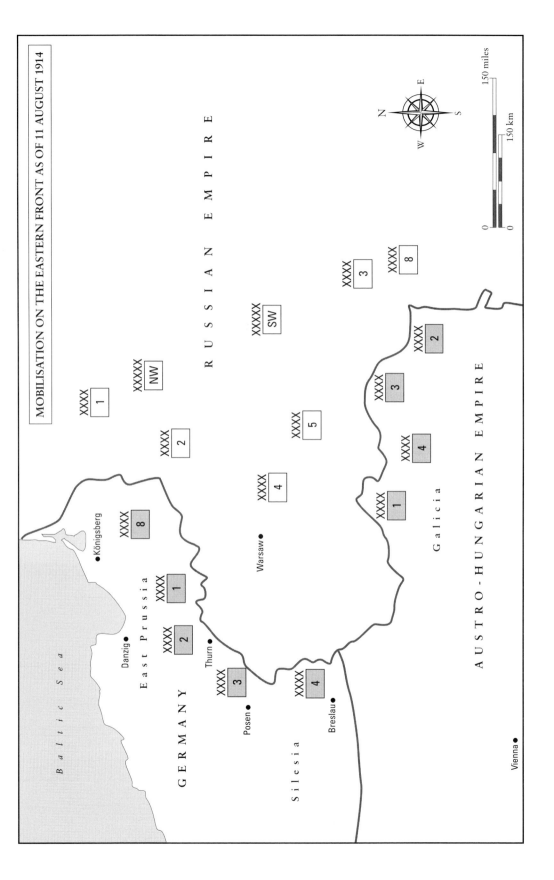

MOBILISATION ON THE EASTERN FRONT AS OF 11 AUGUST 1914

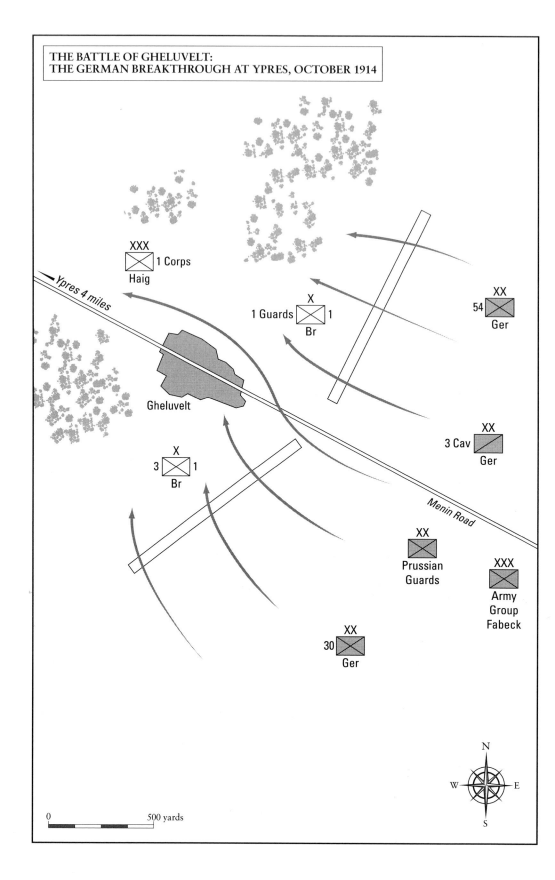

THE BATTLE OF GHELUVELT:
THE GERMAN BREAKTHROUGH AT YPRES, OCTOBER 1914

XXX
1 Corps
Haig

Ypres 4 miles

X
1 Guards ⊠ 1
Br

XX
54 ⊠
Ger

Gheluvelt

XX
3 Cav ⊠
Ger

X
3 ⊠ 1
Br

Menin Road

XX
⊠
Prussian
Guards

XXX
⊠
Army
Group
Fabeck

XX
30 ⊠
Ger

N
W E
S

0   500 yards

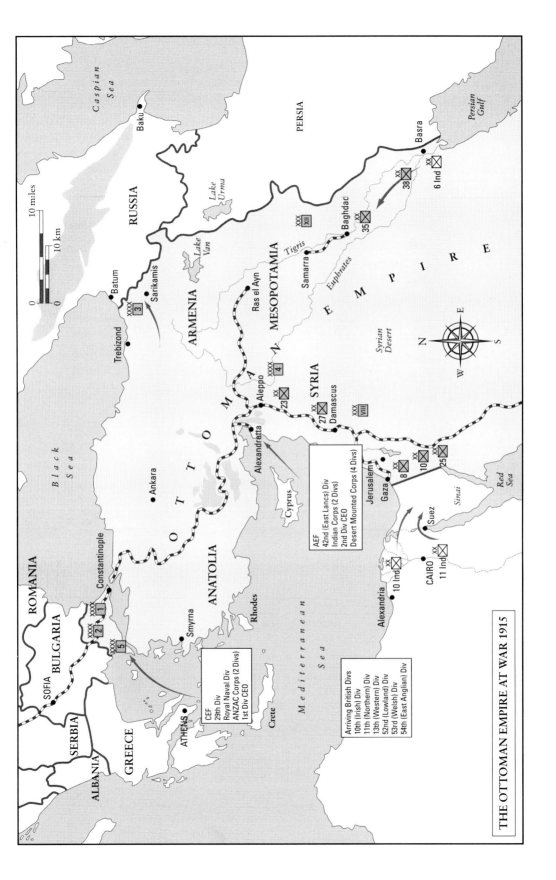

THE OTTOMAN EMPIRE AT WAR 1915

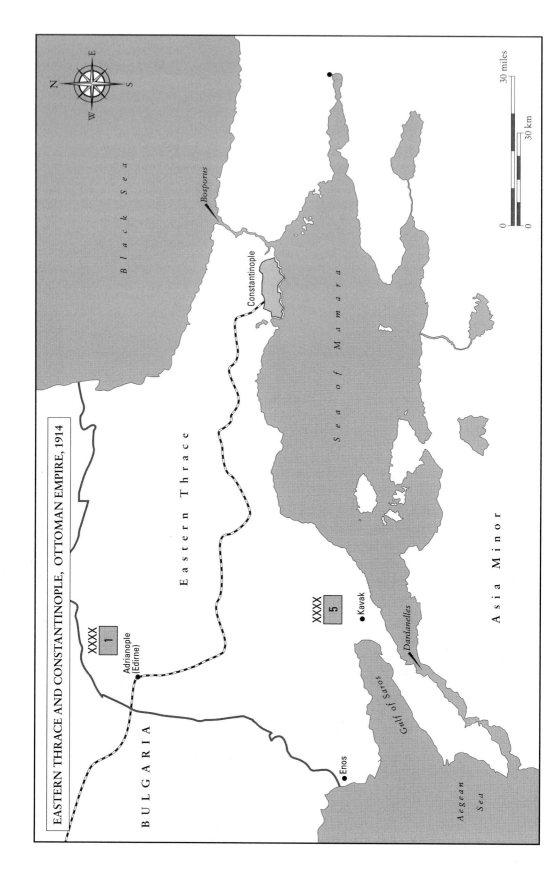

EASTERN THRACE AND CONSTANTINOPLE, OTTOMAN EMPIRE, 1914

N E W S

Black Sea

Bosporus

Constantinople

BULGARIA

Eastern Thrace

Adrianople
(Edirne)

XXXX
1

Sea of Marmara

Gulf of Saros

Enos

Dardanelles

Kavak

XXXX
5

Aegean Sea

Asia Minor

30 miles

30 km

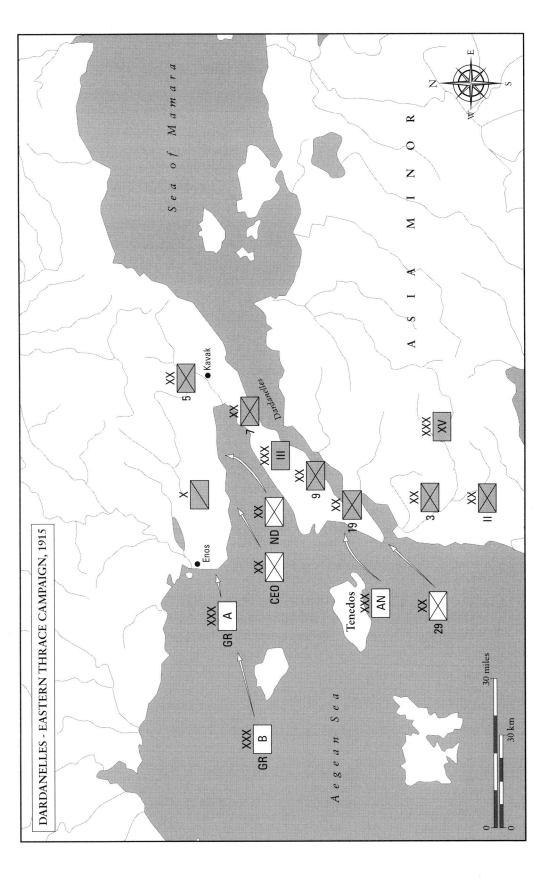

DARDANELLES - EASTERN THRACE CAMPAIGN, 1915

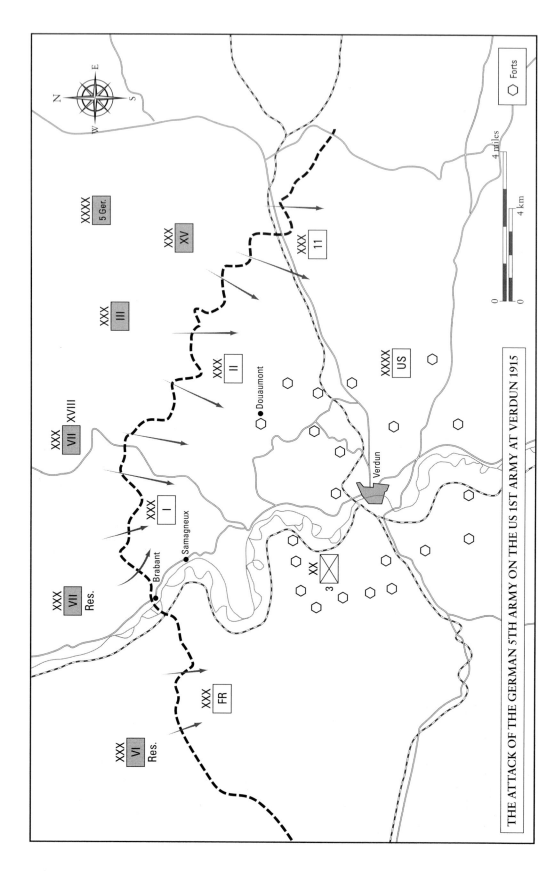

THE ATTACK OF THE GERMAN 5TH ARMY ON THE US 1ST ARMY AT VERDUN 1915

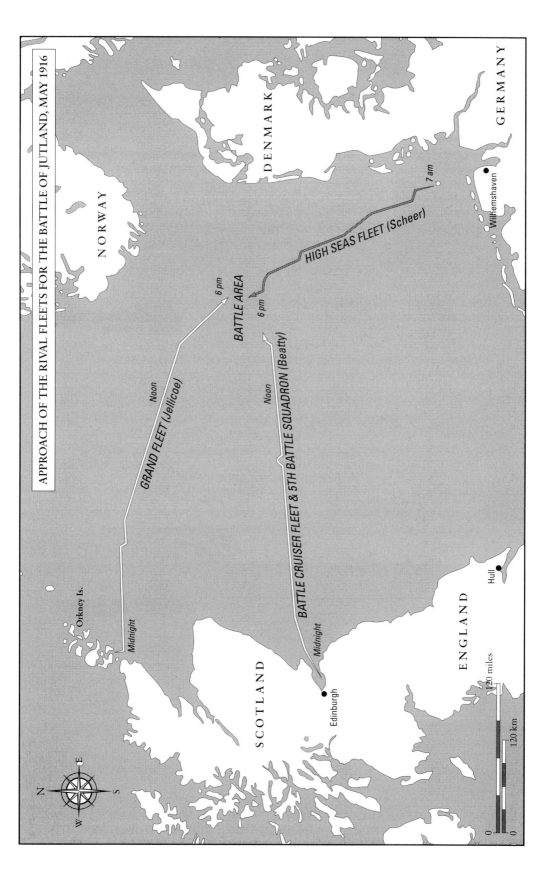

APPROACH OF THE RIVAL FLEETS FOR THE BATTLE OF JUTLAND, MAY 1916

NORWAY

DENMARK

GERMANY

Withemshaven

7 am

HIGH SEAS FLEET (Scheer)

6 pm

BATTLE AREA

6 pm

GRAND FLEET (Jellicoe)

Noon

Noon

BATTLE CRUISER FLEET & 5TH BATTLE SQUADRON (Beatty)

Orkney Is.

Midnight

Midnight

Midnight

SCOTLAND

Edinburgh

ENGLAND

Hull

120 miles

120 km

N
E
S
W

0

120 km

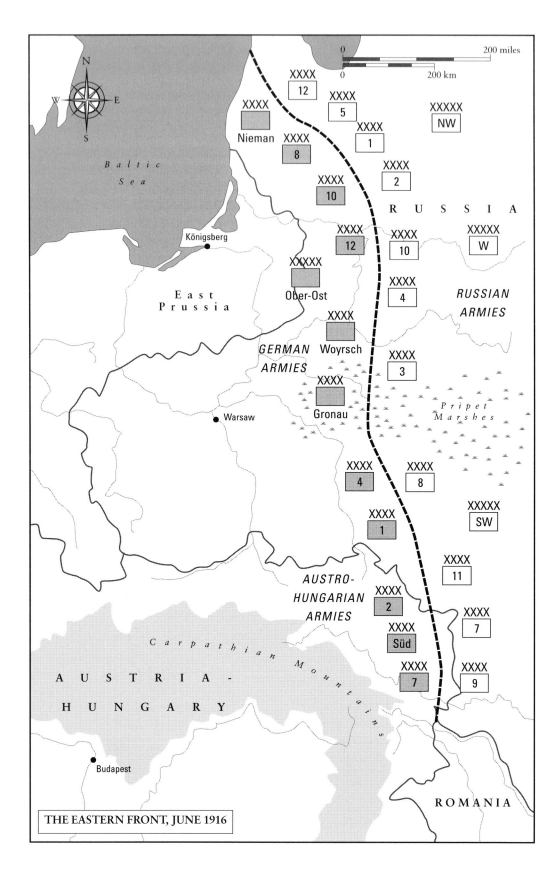

THE EASTERN FRONT, JUNE 1916

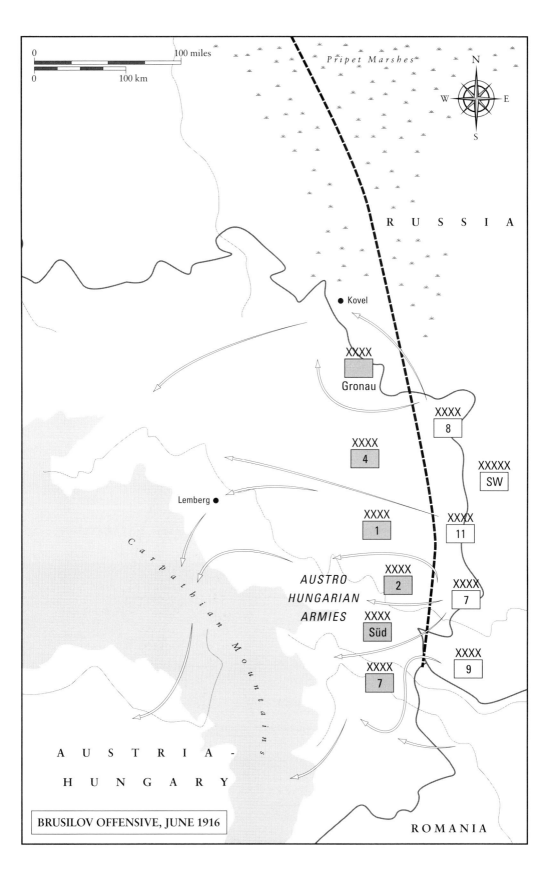

Pripet Marshes

N
W   E
S

R U S S I A

● Kovel

XXXX
Gronau

XXXX
8

XXXX
4

XXXXX
SW

Lemberg ●

XXXX
1

XXXX
11

C a r p a t h i a n   M o u n t a i n s

*AUSTRO
HUNGARIAN
ARMIES*

XXXX
2

XXXX
7

XXXX
Süd

XXXX
9

XXXX
7

A U S T R I A -

H U N G A R Y

0 ————————— 100 miles
0 ————————— 100 km

BRUSILOV OFFENSIVE, JUNE 1916

R O M A N I A

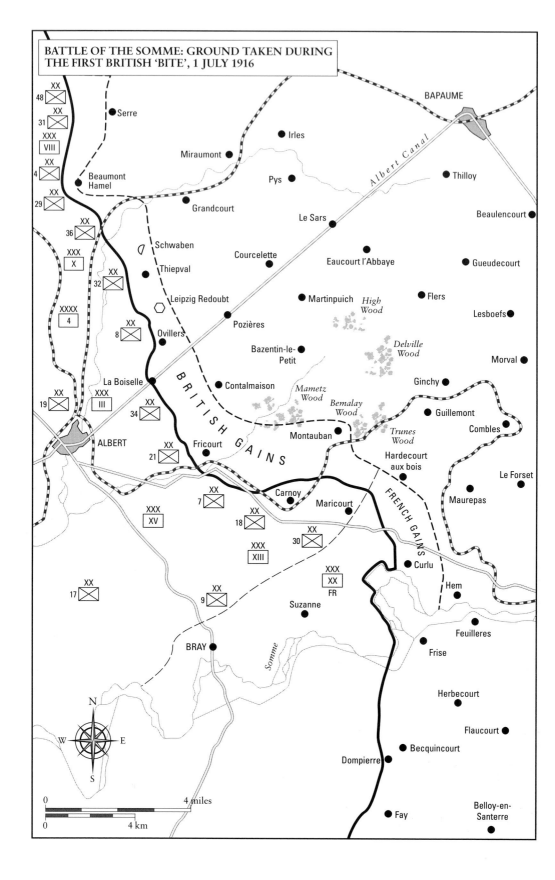

BATTLE OF THE SOMME: GROUND TAKEN DURING THE FIRST BRITISH 'BITE', 1 JULY 1916

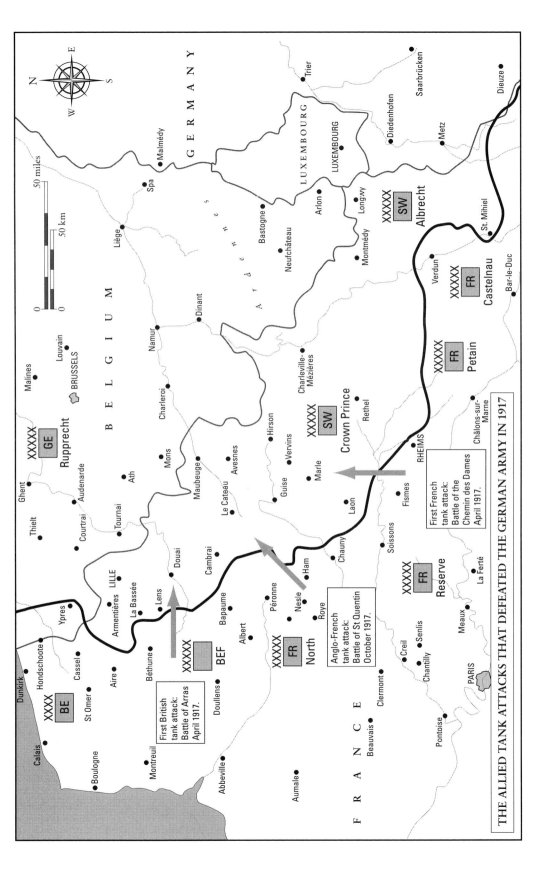

THE ALLIED TANK ATTACKS THAT DEFEATED THE GERMAN ARMY IN 1917

First British tank attack: Battle of Arras April 1917.

First French tank attack: Battle of the Chemin des Dames April 1917.

Anglo-French tank attack: Battle of St Quentin October 1917.

Contributor Biographies

Stephen Badsey PhD MA (Cantab) is Professor of Conflict Studies at the University of Wolverhampton, UK and a Fellow of the Royal Historical Society. An internationally recognised authority on military history and military-media issues, he has written or edited twenty-five books and more than sixty-five articles, his writings have been translated into five languages and he appears frequently on television and in other media.

Spencer Jones is Senior Lecturer in Armed Forces and War Studies at the University of Wolverhampton. He currently serves as Regimental Historian for the Royal Regiment of Artillery. His previous publications include *From Boer War to World War: Tactical Reform of the British Army 1902–1914*, *Stemming the Tide: Officers and Leadership in the British Expeditionary Force 1914* and *The Great Retreat of 1914: From Mons to the Marne*.

Stuart Mitchell is currently working towards his PhD at the University of Birmingham, tackling the process of learning in the British Army during the First World War. He is also Secretary of the Centre for War Studies at the University of Birmingham and a member of the British Commission for military history as well as the Institute for Historical Research.

James Pugh holds a BA (Hons) in Contemporary Military and International History (Salford), an MA in International History (Wales), and a PhD in Modern History (Birmingham). He is currently a visiting lecturer with the University of Birmingham, specialising in air-power studies and the history of the First and Second World Wars. His thesis explored the conceptual origins of the control of the air in Britain between 1911 and 1918. He has also written on air-power leadership and doctrine.

Peter G. Tsouras is a retired army officer and a retired senior intelligence officer for the National Ground Intelligence Center and Defense Intelligence Agency. He has written extensively on the Second World War and is a leading author of military alternative history to include *Disaster at D-Day*, *Gettysburg: An Alternate History*, *Stalingrad: An Alternate History*, and the *Britiannia's Fist Trilogy*, as well as six anthologies. He is the author and/ or editor of twenty-eight books and forty-five articles, and writes a regular column, 'Forgotten History', for *Armchair General Magazine*. His *Scouting for Grant and Meade: The Memoir of Sergeant Knight, Chief of Scouts, Army of the Potomac* will appear in 2014.

Introduction

The Great War was just that – great beyond all experience. It remained the Great War until madness a generation later forced it to become merely a numbered war. Nevertheless, one must go back 2,400 years to find another such inter-civilisational war that was so devastating to the spirit of the age – to the Peloponnesian War (431–404 BC). As the flower of Athens died in the quarries of Syracuse or with throats cut on Goat Creek, so did the shining youth of Europe die in the mud of the Somme, the charnel house of Verdun, and across the vast distances of the Eastern Front.

Four great empires were destroyed by the war: the Austro-Hungarian, the German, the Ottoman, and the Russian empires all fell during or shortly after the conflict. The war culled the European peoples of some of their best and brightest. The survivors sought meaning in the conflict and christened it the 'war to end all wars', hoping that the sheer cost would dissuade nations from future struggles. But the Great War did not end war; in fact it only seeded monstrous tyrannies in Germany and Russia and laid the foundations for a vaster, even more destructive war between 1939 and 1945. Its name even changed, from the Great War to merely the First World War, the precursor to the Second World War, and so slipped from historical prominence.

Yet history did indeed pivot upon the Great War, setting the stage for all that followed in the twentieth century. Where a spirit of optimism prevailed before the war, the aftermath was a pall of dispiriting, morale-sapping despair at the enormous waste. The colonial subjects of even the victors lost much of the awe with which they had beheld their rulers. If not more important, the centre of gravity of Western civilisation had shifted to the United States, along with much of Europe's wealth, the treasure of empire spent on war. Thus, whilst America enjoyed the 'Roaring 1920s', the devastated economies of Europe were wracked by shortages and strikes. At the same time, the war sowed, like dragon's teeth, the predatory tyrannies of communism, national socialism, and Japanese imperialism that would convulse the rest of the century.

All this need not have happened in just the way it did. Nothing was preordained or inevitable. Europe was not subject to some god curse pronounced from the Oracle of Delphi. History does not roll down some prearranged grove. It rolls all over the place. It is contingency writ large, subject to vast and ever-shifting influences. It most resembles a kaleidoscope in which every turn of the tube presents a new picture, with no two ever alike.

In the years after the First World War there was a degree of public interest in 'counterfactual' history that explored the alternative possibilities of war.[1] For example, Winston Churchill's influential history of the conflict, *The World Crisis*, offered the reader a tantalising series of potential turning points. With verve so typical of the author, *The World Crisis* outlined several key moments when greater vision or determination might have swung the war to Britain's advantage, including a successful Gallipoli operation, a decisive Battle of Jutland or greater ambition in the use of tanks. The idea was carried further in Bernard Newman's popular novel *The Cavalry Went Through*, in which a dynamic young British officer rises to command the army on the Western Front and achieves a dramatic breakthrough by employing innovative operational methods.

However, the outbreak of the Second World War abruptly ended interest in First World War alternative history. For a variety of reasons, not least commercial considerations, modern authors have been reluctant to explore the decisions of 1914–18. This is unfortunate, because the history of the Great War especially begs the question: What if? The student of the war cannot help but plead as the drama unfolds, 'Save yourselves, you fools!' More importantly, the reader cannot help but notice all the decision nodes where the resolution to take a particular course of action balanced on a knife's edge and could as easily have gone one way or another. Follow those plausible

---

1   For a full discussion of First World War alternative history literature, see Stephen Badsey, 'If It Had Happened Otherwise: First World War Exceptionalism in Counterfactual History', in Jessica Meyer (ed.), *British Popular Culture and the First World War* (London: Brill, 2008), pp. 351–68.

roads not taken, and history changes exponentially. Suddenly, the war is racing off in different and unexpected directions.

To describe these new directions, the arts of the historian and storyteller must be given full play. Writing alternate history (more accurately 'alternative history') must follow rigorous rules to create plausible scenarios. Author, historian, strategist and soldier Ralph Peters has described the 'Five Pillars of alternative history', in Frontline's recent *Disaster at Stalingrad: An Alternate History*. They are worth summarising here for there is no more perceptive analysis in the requirements of writing for this new genre.[2] Good alternate history must have:

A compelling, convincing vision. 'If the alternative-history does not grip us with logic – the recognition that this could have happened – the entire structure falls flat . . . We have to be captured by the recognition that, yes, but for a few matters of happenstance, the author's vision might have come to pass, changing history.'

Historical and technical knowledge. The writer must know 'what has happened down to the "sub-atomic" details'. He must also grasp 'why things happened and how slight alterations in events or personal relations might have led to very different outcomes'. He must also 'know what soldiers can do and won't do' and also know 'not only what political leaders are supposed to do, but what they actually end up doing'.

Grasp of character. 'Alternative history doesn't work if the author doesn't understand the actual personalities of the figures he enlivens on the page – or human complexity in general . . . [T]he actions men make and the actions they take must be grounded in their actual psychology and mundane circumstances.' Characters must 'make credible decisions based on the different developments confronting them'.

Writing ability. 'In alternative history, the focus should be on events and characters presented in transparent prose that never calls attention to itself. The writing should be so clean and clear that it disappears, leaving only the author's vision . . . Even when' addressing 'infernally complex situations or arcane technical details, the writing is a spotless window that lures the reader to look deeper inside'.

---

2 Peter G. Tsouras, *Disaster at Stalingrad: An Alternate History* (London: Frontline, 2013). Peters uses the word 'alternative', which is a more accurate word than alternate. Unfortunately, 'alternate' was first used colloquially and then simply stuck, another triumph for the teaching of English usage.

Storytelling ability. 'Writing ability and storytelling are often confused with one another, but while related involve separate talents and skill-sets . . . The novelist/storyteller . . . is a literary Dr. Frankenstein, struggling bravely to create not only a living being, but an entire living world . . .', choosing 'from an infinite number of possibilities, the unique combination of body parts that will spring to life for the reader. The non-fiction writer declares, "It's a fact." The novelist cries, "It's alive!"'

The reader will have to judge whether the contributors to *Over the Top* have successfully crafted these five pillars to support their stories.

The Great War has always been dominated by images of the Western Front in the popular imagination of the British, French, Germans, and Americans. Yet, numbers of men even greater than those fighting in France and Belgium were fighting in other theatres where the opportunities were more fluid – the Eastern Front, the Balkan Front, and the Arabian provinces of the Ottoman Empire. Half of our stories address these theatres and the obscured, yet vital, contributions of the Russians, Austrians, Greeks, Turks, and Arabs. How would the war have changed had the Germans not attacked France but turned their main thrust against Russia; had the Russians thoroughly defeated the Austro-Hungarians; had the Greeks joined the Allies at Gallipoli; or had the British severed the communications of the Ottoman Empire at Alexandretta?

The war in the west is not neglected. The BEF was especially vulnerable at Ypres in 1914; Jutland begged for a more decisive outcome; technological solutions to the stalemate in the trenches were plausible earlier than they were actually realised; and there were alternative plans in place for the Battle of the Somme in 1916 that could have changed the nature and perhaps outcome of the fighting. The possibility of earlier American intervention in the war – entering in 1915 rather than 1917 – is also explored.

Although separated from the modern reader by a full century, the First World War continues to generate controversy and interest as the great event upon which modern history pivoted. It is hoped that the ten scenarios presented in this volume focus the reader upon the immensity of that event and the roads not taken that could have led to a far different world.

Notes

As we have marched down one of history's roads that was not taken and into an alternate history of events, that history requires references in the form of endnotes that reflect its own literature – the memoirs, histories, and other accounts that it would have generated. These have been added to the real references. The use of these alternate reality notes, of course, creates a risk for the unwary reader who may make strenuous efforts to acquire a new and fascinating source. To avoid frustrating and futile searches the alternate notes are indicated with an asterisk (*) before the number.

Peter G. Tsouras,
Lieutenant Colonel,
United States Army Reserve (ret.)
Alexandria, Virginia

Spencer Jones, PhD
Stourbridge, West Midlands

1

Der Tag

The German Decision to Go East in 1914

Peter G. Tsouras

If any man represented the genius of the German General Staff system in July 1914 as Europe stumbled toward war, it was General Hermann von Staab, Chief of the Railway Department. Upon his expertise and that of his department depended Germany's ability to mobilise against its encircling enemies and maximise its advantage of interior lines.

That expertise was superior to that of either France or Russia, Germany's two main enemies. The Railway Department, upon receipt of mobilisation orders, would prove the worth of the thousands of officers assigned to making sure Germany's eight wartime armies and over two million men assembled, moved, and deployed faster than the French or Russians.

> It was an incredible feat of organization. To move a single army corps – and there were fifty-six of them in the German Army – required 6,010 railway cars: 170 for officers, 965 for the infantry, 2,960 for cavalry (troopers and mounts), and 1,915 for the artillery and support troops. They would be organized into 280 trains, all moving at precisely fixed times at exact intervals. So detailed were the German Army's mobilization plans that the number of railroad cars that could pass over any given bridge within a given time were, for safety's sake, determined in advance.[1]

The entire mobilisation required eleven thousand trains.

Staab and the rest of the German Army were now aware that *Der Tag* – 'the day' – was approaching with the speed of an out-of-control train. *Der Tag* was that moment when all the pent-up fears about the encirclement of Germany would be lanced, that everything the German nation had planned and prepared for would be set in motion in one tidal, emotional release. All across Germany every soldier in his garrison and every reservist in his home waited in expectation as the clouds of war gathered over Europe. They waited for the telegrams of *Kriegsgefahrzustand* – the announcement of imminent danger of war, the trigger for mobilisation. *Kriegsgefahrzustand* 'put German railways under full military control; inaugurated martial law and military censorship; cancelled all leaves, returning troops to their garrisons, strengthened frontier defenses; and suspended postal traffic across the border'.[2] *Kriegsgefahrzustand* was the cocking of the gun. All that was left was to pull the trigger with the mobilisation order itself, which could be issued two days after the *Kriegsgefahrzustand* measures had been taken.

All the great powers of Europe were spinning out of control towards war. It had all come out of nowhere. Serbian fanatics had engineered the murder of Archduke Ferdinand, heir to the throne of the Hapsburg dual monarchy of Austria and Hungary. And now the Austrian government was determined to use that as pretext to destroy the Serbian kingdom and absorb its territory, despite Emperor Franz Joseph's astute observation that it was a country only of goat droppings, plum trees, and murderous people. Russia, already humiliated by the Austrians in the Bosnian Crisis of 1908, had decided enough was enough and announced its support of fellow Slavs in Serbia. Unwisely then, the Kaiser had declared Germany's full support of Austria, which in effect subordinated German national security to petty Austrian territorial aggrandisement in a region in which no one's national interests, except the Serbs, was threatened. The late 'Iron Chancellor', Otto von Bismarck, had observed correctly that the entire Balkans were not worth the bones of a single Pomeranian grenadier.

Unfortunately, the situation was about trigger an automatic sequence of events that would lead to the war that no one wanted. The problem lay in the organisation for war of the armies of the great European powers, with the exception of Britain. The Napoleonic Wars of a hundred years ago had instilled the concept of a 'nation in arms', armies swollen to unprecedented size because they had the entire adult male population as a military resource. Peacetime armies became training vehicles for the large number of men that would be conscripted for short periods and then sent into the reserves. This mass of reservists would then be called up to reinforce and expand the regular armies in times of war.

Germany, with a population of over seventy million, had to call up only 50 per cent of its eligible males to man a peacetime army of 840,000, while France – with only half that population – had to call up 85 per cent to reach a peacetime strength of 770,000. The Austro-Hungarian Empire with fifty million people found that it could support a peacetime army of 450,000 while Russia, with a population approaching two hundred million, put almost two million men in uniform. The mechanism of their wartime expansion, upon which all war plans were based, was a complex mobilisation plan. That in turn relied upon an increasingly dense system of railway lines to transport masses of reservists to their depots where they would be equipped, then transported as organised units to their assembly areas. At the same time formations, both reserve and regular, along with mountains of supplies, would be moved to the frontiers to be prepared to attack or defend as various war plans dictated.

For the Germans, timing would be everything. It was upon this basis that the Chief of the General Staff, Count Alfred von Schlieffen (CGS from 1894 to 1905), had devised the plan for war against both France and Russia. The operative assumption was that Russia would take at least six weeks to mobilise, while the French would be much quicker off the mark and be able to amass their armies on the German border within a shorter time. Here, he thought, was the weak joint in the Franco-Russian alliance. He reasoned that if Germany mobilised faster than both France and Russia, it could knock France out of the war quickly and then turn its victorious armies to the east to meet the Russians. It would be a close-run thing, and he devoted his life to creating and honing the plan that would eventually bear his name. It called for the Germans to mass seven of their eight armies to face France. It was to maximise that window that the German Army had poured vast resources into the railway system and the precision of the mobilisation planning and execution. It needed every minute. Franco-Russian joint military planning called for simultaneous attacks on Germany on M+15 (fifteen days after mobilisation).

Yet the Franco-German border offered too little space and bad terrain for such a decisive campaign. Schlieffen then looked beyond those borders to the flat plains of Belgium, which would provide the ground for the crushing manoeuvre, the envelopment of the French left and Paris itself, thereby trapping the French armies against the other German armies along the

Franco-German border. There was only one problem with the plan: violation of Belgian neutrality would bring the British immediately into the war to protect the Belgian and French Channel ports, natural points of embarkation for an invasion of England. Schlieffen dismissed the small but lethal British Army as of little account in the manoeuvres of millions and gave no thought to the wider implications of fecklessly making an enemy of the British Empire. The British had been driven from the continent before by Napoleon, only to gather new allies and wear down and finally defeat France. They had lost little of their patient tenacity.

In its final form the Schlieffen Plan was allocated seven of Germany's eight armies, numbered one through seven; the remaining 8th Army was left to cover the Russian border. The 1st, 2nd, 3rd, and 4th armies, numbering 840,000 men, would form the great wheel through Belgium. With supporting and line-of-communication troops, this force numbered over a million men. The remaining 5th, 6th, and 7th armies, numbering another 520,000 men, would defend the Franco-German border against the inevitable strong French attacks to liberate the lost provinces of Alsace-Lorraine. The 9th Army would be maintained as a strategic reserve in central Germany to be assembled from various units around an existing army headquarters to move to either front as necessary.

It was a gamble that the long Russian mobilisation period would allow the Germans to crush the French and then turn their entire army east. It was all based on the calculation of a slow Russian mobilisation. That was a serious German intelligence failure. The Russians had worked diligently to streamline their mobilisation process and, despite a much less dense and efficient railway system, would be able to spring a major surprise on the Germans by being able to invade East Prussia with their 1st and 2nd armies, with over 400,000 men against the 170,000 men of the German 8th Army, long before the Germans expected to finish off the French. The only problem was that, unlike Germany, Russia's mobilisation would be a phased one. The railway system could not handle the mobilisation of all the Russian reserves at the same time. Formations would be continuously fed forward in waves. That meant that the initial blow would not have the full might of the completely mobilised Russian Army. Dissipating the Russian blow further was the fact that their other four armies in Poland were all facing the Austrians.[3]

The single-mindedness with which Schlieffen fixed Germany's fate to this plan was very dangerous. His predecessor, the great Feldmarshal Helmuth von Moltke (1800–91), had said, 'Plans are nothing; planning is everything.'

The emphasis on planning imbued operations with flexibility at all levels, which fixation on a single plan simply threw away. Despite Schlieffen's emphasis on this plan, which he was never truly satisfied with, the German General Staff did not allow itself to become brain-dead to the vagaries of fortune. Exercises were conducted that featured events that would throw the railway mobilisation off track, such as accidents and more importantly changes in strategic direction. There was even a war plan for mobilisation solely against Russia which was regularly exercised, though this plan never received the emphasis of the Schlieffen Plan.

So it was that Captain Sigurd von Ilsemann, a junior aide-de-camp to the Kaiser, was surprised to learn of this Russian variant on his advance visit in late 1913 to Staab's headquarters in preparation for a possible inspection by the Kaiser a few months later. Staab explained that they were about to conduct a staff exercise of the mobilisation plan against Russia. The captain was evidently surprised; he had been aware of only the Schlieffen Plan against France. Staab explained that though the Schlieffen Plan had had priority, there was an equally well-organised and exercised mobilisation plan to point the German armies east.[4] Tall and handsome, as were all of Wilhelm's aides, the thirty-year-old Ilsemann was also shrewd and intensely devoted to His Majesty. The Kaiser's visit would be cancelled, but Ilsemann tucked that piece of information away. His family had estates in East Prussia as well as his native Lüneburg in Lower Saxony, so war against the Russians was of more than professional interest to him.[5]

Ironically it was the Kaiser himself, Wilhelm II, who had reservations about the Schlieffen Plan and war with the British. He was a man of occasional brilliant insight, albeit well hidden by his Anglophobia, bombast, and reckless statements. He was the grandson of Victoria and well acquainted with his British cousins. His determination to match and surpass them had made him all too aware of their power.

Right now, as the war clouds gathered and darkened, his immediate problem was with his current Chief of the General Staff, General Helmuth von Moltke, the nephew and namesake of the great field marshal. The man upon whom the Kaiser had depended to command Germany in the life-and-death struggle against its surrounding enemies was a hollow nonentity.

The Kaiser had no one to blame but himself. Wilhelm II was obsessed with the illusion of the power of outward continuity. He had been so alarmed when Alfred Krupp, the founder of the German arms industry and the giant Krupp cannon factories, died with no male issue to carry on the name that he pushed through the Reichstag a single exception law that permitted whomever married his daughter Berta to take the Krupp name. It was not hard to find a broken-down aristocrat to throw away his name for a stake in the Krupp empire.

So it was with the Chief of the General Staff. His fate was to bear the same name as his legendary uncle, the field marshal and military genius who had organised the Prussian Army for its string of victories that created the German Empire. Von Moltke the Younger, as he came to be called, was appalled when the Kaiser announced to him in 1906 that he was to succeed Schlieffen as Chief of the German General Staff. He had worked diligently if unimaginatively as the great man's assistant as quartermaster general, but the thought of taking all that responsibility unnerved him. He had even told the Kaiser, 'I do not know how I shall get on in the event of a campaign. I am very critical of myself.'[6]

The Kaiser brushed that aside. He seemed to think the Moltke name alone had a magic quality. That sentiment in this case was not shared by Moltke, who had clearly taken to heart Socrates' admonition, 'Know thyself'. Moltke's constant air of melancholy was so palpable that even Wilhelm dubbed him *Der trauige Julius* – 'Sad Julius'.[7]

The Moltke name had been more of a curse, depriving him of the solid military background vital for someone who would direct Germany's armies in war. He had spent the first ten years of his service as aide-de-camp to his illustrious uncle, followed by the same position for the Kaiser himself for another five years, which required him to attend not only to the Kaiser personally but to accompany him on his restless travels. Despite subsequent troop commands from regiment to division (1896–1904), he still remained in close attendance on the Kaiser. His appointment as Schlieffen's deputy in 1904 'was met with incredulity' in knowledgeable circles.[8] That impression was echoed by foreign attaché reports which rated him a lightweight, such as the Austrian comment that 'He is a complete stranger to the activities within the General Staff.'[9] What really alarmed his contemporaries was his obsession with spiritualism and the occult under the domineering control of his wife. More than anything else they were concerned that 'he was a religious dreamer [who] believed in guardian angels, faith-healing and similar nonsense.'[10] Instead of taking this to heart, Wilhelm was more concerned with a candidate with whom he was familiar and comfortable, so much so that the addressed him with the familiar *du*. He said, 'General von der Goltz has also been recommended to me, whom

I don't want, and also General von Veseler, whom I don't know. I know you, and I trust you.'[11]

By 30 July the strain on Moltke's brittle personality was beginning to tell. It was not a propitious time to lose faith in oneself. Moltke was desperate for proof of Russia's mobilisation. Over a week ago, the tsar had ordered a partial mobilisation, but still Moltke had no tangible evidence, so well had the Russians kept their mobilisation secret. The same day the French armies were ordered to close on the border, based on misleading information that the Germans had mobilised, and yet the German Army had not even received its premobilisation order.[12] The Reichschancellor, Theobald von Bethmann-Hollweg, refused to authorise the order until there was definite proof that Russia was mobilising. That came from a telegram from Count Frederich Pourtalés, the German ambassador to St Petersburg. He emphatically stated that the Russians had already begun their mobilisation. The same day German Army intelligence had concluded that Russia's mobilisation was 'far advanced'. Compounding Moltke's shock was the news that the Austrians had decided to only pursue their war plan that involved Serbia and not the one that included Russia.[13] Only twenty Austrian divisions would be facing the four Russian armies along their mutual border. Germany would feel the full brunt of a Russian attack that would be able to divert more forces from the Austrian front. Moltke had pleaded with the Austrians to cancel their campaign against Serbia and concentrate on Russia. Unfortunately, the Austrians fecklessly had become obsessed with the petty spoils in the Balkans.

The chancellor realised that the next step was unavoidable. He then telephoned the Kaiser and read him Pourtalés's telegram. Wilhelm arrived quickly to sign the *Kriegsgefahrzustand* order, which was to be operative as of 3 p.m. It would take only two days from that point for mobilisation itself to begin. That same day, with the Kaiser's approval, Bethmann-Hollweg sent two fateful telegrams. The first was to Russia demanding that it halt its mobilisation or Germany would defend itself. The second was to France demanding that its government clarify its position on its own mobilisation. By noon the next day, when the Russian deadline had passed, the Russians had not responded, and the French reply stated tersely that: 'France would act according to her interests.' The French deadline passed at 2 p.m. Berlin time without any further clarification. By 4 p.m. the mobilisation placards were beginning to go up all through France.

Bethmann-Hollweg still shrank from recommending mobilisation to the Kaiser. Nevertheless, he had the day before addressed the Bundesrat and got its unanimous approval, but in a fateful remark stated, 'If the iron dice must roll, then God help us.' He had become a prisoner of the Schlieffen Plan, which required that mobilisation be followed immediately by war. Germany must violate the sovereignty of both Luxembourg and Belgium for the right wing of the German armies to envelop the French as well as declaring war against France. At the same time war would have to be declared against Russia.

The German naval minister, Admiral Alfred von Tirpitz, was aghast at how poorly the plan had been thought out from the diplomatic and international law perspective. He almost shouted at the chancellor, 'We will be seen as the aggressor in the eyes of the world but more importantly in the eyes of the British, who are the only ones in position to do something about it. And that, Herr Chancellor, is a great deal.'

Moltke came to the chancellor's defence and said, 'They have only a contemptible little army that we will easily throw into the Channel.'

Tirpiz glared at him. 'I will have a little more trouble with the Royal Navy.' His irony was lost on Moltke. He went on to say that both Italy and Romania were bound to come to Germany's aid if it were attacked. Those obligations would not be operative if Germany declared war first and attacked.[14] The defence minister, General Erich von Falkenhayn, was more concerned with the immediate realisation that Russian mobilisation was further along than anyone had expected. German reconnaissance reported parts of its order of battle as it observed the Russian 1st and 2nd armies massing on Germany's eastern frontier. He pressed the chancellor to recommend mobilisation to the Kaiser. At 5 p.m. Wilhelm signed the order in the Charlottenburg Palace in Berlin. Falkenhayn remembered that both the Kaiser and he 'had tears in their eyes'.

Moltke left immediately so as not give the Kaiser an opportunity for second thoughts even though it had been announced that a critical message from Germany's ambassador to Great Britain, Baron Karl Max von Lichnowsky, was being rushed over personally by the State Secretary for Foreign Affairs Gottlieb von Jagow. Moltke had barely reached the General Staff headquarters when he was recalled. It was as if a bomb had gone off in the palace. Instead of tears there was near jubilation. In the time he had been gone, Lichnowsky's telegram had completely reversed the entire strategic situation. It stated that 'Sir Edward Grey [British foreign secretary] had just called me upon the telephone and asked whether I thought I could give an assurance that in the event of a war between Russia and Germany whether we should not attack the French. I assured him that I could take the responsibility for such a guarantee and he will use this assurance at today's Cabinet meeting.'[15] Jagow interpreted this as Britain's guarantee of French neutrality. Wilhelm was visibly relieved and exclaimed, 'Now we can go to war against Russia only. We simply march the whole of our army to the east.'[16]

'Your Illustrious Uncle Would Not Have Given me Such an Answer'

Moltke nearly had an aneurism as he listened to the Kaiser, supported by Tirpitz, Bethmann-Hollweg, and Jagow, state he was willing to halt any movement against France in exchange for French neutrality. According to an observer, 'This gave rise to an extremely lively and dramatic dispute . . . Moltke, very excited, with trembling lips, insisted on his position. The Kaiser and the Chancellor and all the others pleaded with him in vain.' He insisted that mobilisation once set in motion could not be altered; the Schlieffen Plan was now automatically going to happen. There was no plan to mobilise solely against Russia. At this comment, Captain von Ilsemann sucked in his breath. What had the Chief of the Imperial General Staff just said? How could he possibly be ignorant of the Russian plan Staab had briefed him on?[17]

He listened as Moltke went on that it would be suicidal to do anything else. Already, he said the 16th Infantry Division had crossed the Luxembourg border. Wilhelm would have none of that. He immediately sent the order to halt the division. Moltke argued that the railway route through Luxembourg was vital. The Kaiser shot back, 'Use other routes.' It was an amazing performance. The bombastic, highly strung Wilhelm was now the soul of common sense, refusing to be dragged along behind a plan that was clearly being overtaken by events. Moltke's response was near to hysteria:

Your Majesty, it cannot be done. The deployment of millions cannot be improvised. If Your Majesty insists on leading the whole army to the East it will not be as an army ready for battle but a disorganised mob of armed men with no arrangements for supply. Those arrangements took a whole year of intricate labour to compete, and once settled it cannot be altered.[18]

He took Falkenhayn aside to say privately that 'he was a totally broken man, because this decision by the Kaiser demonstrated to him that the Kaiser still hoped for peace.'[19]

The Chief of the General Staff continued to plead, but Wilhelm remained adamant. He said, 'Your illustrious uncle would not have given me such an answer. If I order it, it must be possible.' He emphasised his decision by ordering champagne to be uncorked.[20] Bethmann-Hollweg and Jagow were busy drafting the German acceptance of the British offer. Moltke was now visibly losing control of himself. Suddenly he put his hands to his head. 'Such pain,' he murmured. Then he collapsed. The household physician was called, but all he could do was pronounce Moltke's death, probably due to a stroke. To add more chaos to the moment, Lichnowsky's follow-on telegram arrived. Apparently, Grey's comments had not had the backing of the Cabinet. He had merely been talking through his hat, an appalling act of fecklessness for the British foreign secretary. It would not be until 11 p.m., though, that a succession of clarifications had completely removed any doubt that the British were not going to broker anything that would ensure their neutrality or that of the French.

There is a Way Out

A thoroughly resigned Wilhelm then said to Falkenhayn, whom he had appointed to succeed Moltke, 'Now you can do what you want.' All this time Ilsemann had been in rapt but silent attention. His junior position precluded his participation in these conversations. To do so would be a violation of strict German military decorum. Yet he remembered at this moment a story told by the elder Moltke of the Franco-Prussian War. It seems that a Prussian major had been sent on a mission but in accomplishing it he ignored an even greater opportunity. The Crown Prince had tongue-lashed him for this failure, but he replied, 'His Majesty made me an officer to obey my orders.' The prince shot back, 'His Majesty made you an officer to know when to *disobey* your orders!'

The general bowed and was just about to turn away. Ilsemann stepped forward. 'Your Majesty, there is a way out.' Every eye turned to him. So desperate were the men in the room that they were willing to clutch at straws – decorum went flying out of the window.

'The attack against France is not set in stone, Your Majesty. Last year I visited the Railway Department of the General Staff in preparation for your inspection which was subsequently cancelled. They were exercising the mobilisation plan against Russia.' There was a moment of stupefied silence, then everyone started talking at once. The Kaiser jumped up and started pacing.

He stopped and said, 'But the French will still attack us in the west.'

Falkhenhayn added, 'We are just back where we were.'

A cooler head, General Baron Moritz von Lyncker, chief of the Prussian military cabinet, suggested: 'Gentlemen, I think it would be prudent to ask General von Staab.' He was summoned immediately to the palace from Potsdam.

No one was more surprised than Staab to receive the summons. Falkenhayn quickly filled him in on the situation. The Kaiser looked at him with all the nervousness of man whose wife had gone into labour twelve hours before. 'Can it be done?'

Without a pause, Staab replied with great confidence, 'Your Majesty, I can put a million men in four armies on the Russian border in ten days. We have a plan for just that and we exercised it just last November.' He saw Ilsemann and nodded to him. 'The good captain here visited the Railway Department just as the exercise was beginning.'

It was Tirpitz who spoke next. 'Your Majesty realises this is a priceless gift. Germany will stand the aggrieved party in the eyes of the world. This does not require us to declare war on anyone first or to attack anyone first. Most importantly, by respecting Belgian neutrality it seriously lowers the risk that the British will enter the war, and it will oblige Italy and Romania to enter the war as allies.' The prospect of not having to slug it out with the Royal Navy filled him with incredible relief. In comparison, Tirpitz viewed the Russian Baltic Fleet as prey.

Falkenhayn added, 'We can depend upon a French attack, but if it can be confined to the Franco-German border, we can hold them off while the decision is achieved in the east. We have spent years preparing the region for defence. The geography is perfect for it, and we have intelligence that the French war plan, Plan XVII, will throw the bulk of the French armies there. If the French invade Belgium to outflank us, it is they and not us who will have to deal with the British, who have guaranteed its neutrality. In any case we will be able to stand up the 9th Army, our strategic reserve, in central Germany to cover Belgium if that happens.'

The Kaiser was so immensely relieved that he could even assay a joke. 'Yes, then it will be the Belgians who request German assistance to resist the French invasion. I can always offer the Belgian king refuge in Germany.'

Again Tirpitz spoke. 'British neutrality is crucial for Germany to fight and win this war. A neutral Britain will not interfere with our importation of vital war materials. I must remind everyone here that this country cannot feed itself without very large imports of food.' His naval background with its emphasis on technology and material made him far more conscious of the effects of a cut-off of vital imports should the Royal Navy blockade Germany.

The Iron Dice Roll

Staab was as good as his word. Eleven thousand trains sped east, bringing the four German armies to the border of Russian Poland in the ten days he had promised. All were in place by 11 August. The 8th Army shifted north to open land north of the ninety-mile-long (145 km) Masurian Lakes. The immensely powerful 1st and 2nd armies with almost 600,000 men marshalled from Torn south of the lakes. The 3rd Army concentrated east of Posen and the 4th Army east of Breslau. Staab had indeed delivered his one million men to the east. These four armies hung back just far enough from the border so that Russian cavalry reconnaissance would not detect them. The Russians had made the mistake of sending all their reconnaissance aircraft to the Austrian border, which further blinded them to the secret massing of the German armies. The Germans now found that the configuration of the border offered them significant operational and strategic advantages. The part of Poland that Russia swallowed again after the end of the Napoleonic Wars formed a salient, with Prussia to the north and Austrian Galicia to the south. In the northern centre of the salient was the Polish capital of Warsaw, a major transportation hub for the Russians as well as Lodz in the middle, the main Russian supply and logistics base for any war with Germany. Both sides faced a limiting logistics problem. The Russian railway gauge was wider than the German. Either army penetrating the other's territory would be reduced to the logistical capabilities of the horse-drawn Napoleonic era during initial operations. The Germans, however, had the advantage of an efficient railway service that could immediately begin to reconfigure the wider Russian gauge to take German locomotives and railway carriages.

On the diplomatic front the Germans had pledged not to violate the neutrality or attack France. Jagow had formally informed the British that Germany would do everything to avoid war in the west and that it had concentrated most of its strength against the Russians due specifically to the provocation of the Russian mobilisation, which had preceded the Germans' own mobilisation. All of this simply let the air out of the momentum for war. British participation in the Triple Entente was provoked by fears of Germany's designs in the west. Britain had historically been the strategic balancing wheel of Europe, frustrating attempts by any power to dominate Western Europe. The necessity for such balancing diminished the farther east events moved. It just about evaporated on the Polish border. In Berlin the strategic decision had been made to not be the first to declare war. These events left the French almost frothing at the mouth. They saw a priceless opportunity to attack Germany now that most of its armies had been sent east, egged on by the Chief of the General Staff Joffre and the War Minister Viviani. Their own mobilisation was almost now complete and the time for agreed-upon joint offensives with the Russians was almost upon them. There was the feeling in the face of growing British hesitation to go it alone. In this moment of tension the luckless Austrians were now to play a decisive part. On 12 August two Austrian armies invaded Serbia.

A flurry of last-minute negotiations went nowhere in the next two days. The French and Russians used that time to confirm that they would begin simultaneous offensive operations against Germany on 15 August. On midnight of the 14th the Russian and French ambassadors delivered their declarations of war. Hours later, French and Russian cavalry divisions invaded Germany in East Prussia and Alsace-Lorraine. To the shock of the British, two French armies invaded Belgium in the Ardennes to swing around the heavily fortified German border. King Albert of the Belgians immediately called upon the British to fulfil their treaty obligations to defend the neutrality of his country. London dithered. The British interest in Belgium's neutrality had been only because whoever controlled its ports had a springboard to invade the British Isles. Clearly, the French in the Ardennes were not such a threat.

The French were making much of the iron law of necessity, much as the Athenians had when they invaded Sicily in 415 BC. Nevertheless, they maintained that they had no wish to take any Belgian territory and would not advance into the heavily populated Belgian heartland along the coast. Finally, the British Cabinet hit upon a solution that would demonstrate their support for Belgium without going to war. They deployed Royal Marines to Antwerp, to be followed by I Corps (two infantry divisions and one cavalry brigade), all with strict orders to stay away from the French. The French understood this 'wink–wink–nod–nod' situation and confined themselves to the Ardennes.[21] Unfortunately for them, the Germans committed their strategic reserve, the new 9th Army, to the Ardennes as well. The Germans could not have wished for better defensive ground and stopped the French cold in the wooded mountains. The French found themselves throwing at great cost wave after wave of infantry against the German division holding the vital road hub of Bastogne. The valiant defence of that minor Belgian town thrilled the German people and became legend.

To the south, the three German armies held the lunging French at bay, leaving heaps of red-trousered corpses in front of their numerous machine guns. But it was in the east that the attention of the German people was fixed. The Germans had waited for the Russians to attack into East Prussia. While the 8th Army fixed the Russian 1st Army north of the Masurian Lakes, the German 1st and 2nd armies enveloped the Russian 2nd Army. It was a complete Cannae, the great battle of 216 BC in which Hannibal had utterly destroyed Rome's finest army by envelopment. Hardly a man of the 200,000-strong Russian Army escaped. At the same time, the German 3rd and 4th armies crossed the border, aiming for the Russian logistics centre at Lodz fifty miles away. Not only a logistics centre, Lodz was 'the 'Manchester of the Russian Empire's huge cotton industry'.'[22] To the south, the Russians had given the Austrians a bloody nose in Galicia, stopping their bungled offensive dead and then throwing them back. Those victories drew the Russian gaze in that direction, and almost too late they tried to divert their 4th Army to the defence of Lodz. At this point the Russian railways served them well. They got enough of the army there just in time on 20 August to prevent advance German units from seizing the city. Newly mobilised Russian divisions began to arrive at the front to stabilise the defence of the city. Still, by the time the bulk of the two German armies arrived, the Russians would still be heavily outnumbered. To the north, the victorious 1st and 2nd armies were on the outskirts of Warsaw. Its fall would seriously disrupt the Russian railways.

Rennen von Kampf

The German steamroller seemed to be crushing everything in its path – except at Gumbinen in East Prussia. There another one of the Kaiser's 'social' promotions led to disaster. The commander of the 8th Army, General Maximilian von Prittwitz, had been a personal favourite of the Kaiser, but the man's incompetence was apparent even to Moltke, who repeatedly tried to get him removed. Against the imperial favour, his protestations of Prittwitz's professional ineptitude had been fruitless. Making the situation worse was the fact that his Chief of Staff, the other half of the German command team concept, was equally inadequate. The only man at army headquarters who seemed to have his wits about him was the operations officer, Lieutenant Colonel Max Hoffmann, by accounts a young military genius. Even he, though, could not shore up the situation after Prittwitz had lost his nerve when his advance corps had unwisely attacked the Russian 1st Army, commanded by General Pavel Rennenkampf, unsupported and got whipped at Gumbinen just inside the German border. It was a remarkable Russian success considering Rennenkampf's tactical timidity.

Prittwitz's solution was to withdraw all the way back to Königsberg on the Baltic coast as Rennenkampf cautiously followed. With the heartland of the Hohenzollern house threatened, Wilhelm came to his senses and agreed to Falkenhayn's demands for Prittwitz's dismissal. In his place, the retired general Paul von Hindenburg was appointed. Hoffmann was promoted to Chief of Staff, thus creating a command team that would be considered a model of effectiveness for the remainder of the war. Nevertheless, the crisis created by the panic had resulted in the detachment of General von Kluck's 1st Army from the drive on Warsaw to the defence of East Prussia. The irony was that it was completely unnecessary. The Hindenburg–Hoffmann team turned the retreating 8th Army on its heel and in a classic envelopment trapped half of the Russian 1st Army, inflicting 150,000 casualties. The shattered remnants fled back across the border, closely pursued by the 8th Army. In the lead was Rennenkampf himself, who fled so far that the incredulous Russian North-West Front command requested confirmation, only to discover how far Rennenkampf had outdistanced his command. By that time, even his own staff could not conceal their contempt for the man they now called 'Rennen von Kampf' or 'run from the fight'.[23]

Rennenkampf was only one example of the rot in the Russian Army. Despite a weeding out of incompetents after the Russo-Japanese War and 1905 Revolution, the army was just not good enough to fight the Germans, who in contrast operated with a breathtaking boldness, ability, and efficiency. Hindenburg pointed to an example of Russian ineptitude when he wrote in amazement how the Russian signals continued to send messages *en clair* without any attempt to use cyphers. Another fateful indicator was that one regiment of Rennenkampf's army used 1.5 per cent of the Russian ammunition production for 1914. The strain of war would quickly reveal how inadequate the rest of Russia's war production base was. It says something about the Austrians that the Russians were so clearly superior against them. Despite that, the Russians were paying for having concentrated so much force against a secondary enemy.

The Russian high command (Stavka) was beginning to panic. So crushing had been the German victories of mid- and late August that they cancelled out the equally impressive Russian victories over the Austrians. All reinforcements were now being sent to defend the Polish salient. Although Russian divisions were arriving in waves, it was not enough to affect the German numerical superiority on that front. Two new Russian armies were committed: the 10th to replace the shattered 1st Army facing Hindenburg and the 4th to defend Warsaw and Lodz. It was not enough. The Germans, by moving the bulk of their armies to the east, had established an immediate numerical superiority that continued to gobble up Russian reinforcements as they arrived – a result of their phased mobilisation. On top of the numerical superiority, the Germans were working at such a higher level of overall efficiency that one German soldier was the equivalent of half a dozen Russians or more. By the middle of September, both Warsaw and Lodz had fallen and the reeling Russian front was on the point of collapse despite its reinforcements from the Galician front. The only thing that saved them was that the Germans had to pause to let their exhausted troops rest as Staab's Railway Department expedited the conversion of the Russian-gauge railways.

In the west the French offensive had also paused in the face of sustained and bloody failure. The British remained neutral, a condition that was reinforced by the generally accepted position that Germany had had this war thrust upon it and that no British vital interests were at risk. There was also a reawakening of the old sense of British–German solidarity born of more than a hundred years of alliances against French ambitions. World opinion quickly followed that lead, the United States being the most supportive of Germany's situation, reinforced by its large German-American population. It was President Theodore Roosevelt, nearing the end of his second full term, who offered his good offices for peace negotiations based upon a return to the *status quo ante*. His reputation from forging a peace between Russia and Japan in 1905 had made him a man of serious international standing. The British Cabinet unanimously supported such a move – to the outrage of the French, who had resurrected the term 'perfidious Albion' and injected it with a new venom.

Yet the logic of the appeal resonated. None of the belligerents had sunk so much blood into a war barely two months old that they felt they had to fight on to redeem it. American diplomacy had been quietly sounding out the belligerents before Roosevelt made his offer. The ground had been prepared. Germany, with unexpected adroitness, eagerly accepted the American mediation first, dumping the onus of refusal on the French and Russians. Grudgingly, they accepted Roosevelt's recommendation of an immediate armistice. The peace commissioners met in The Hague and there hammered out the Roosevelt Peace, as it was commonly called. In the end, the *status quo ante* was generously interpreted.[24] The chunk of Russian Poland that the Germans had taken was made into an independent Kingdom of Poland with a Hohenzollern prince on the throne and the unspoken understanding that it would be a German client. The armies evacuated the new Polish state in stages, except certain German forces which were to train the new Polish Royal Army and dispose of masses of surrendered Russian materials. In 1916 the presence of these forces was formally recognised in a status of forces agreement.

The Russians were in no position to protest. Their defeat had been followed by an attempted Bolshevik revolution which was only staved off by the abdication of the tsar to be replaced by the young tsarevich Aleksei. His haemophilic disability tortuously placed him under the control of the most brilliant of the Russian ministers, Pytor Stolypin,[25] a man who had barely escaped assassination in 1911. He was considered the most dangerous of all the tsar's ministers by the Bolsheviks because he was creating an independent peasantry as a bulwark of the throne by breaking up the village collectives. Under his guidance, Russia was finally able to develop as a constitutional monarchy and continue its rapid industrialisation. Seeing the hopelessness of their revolutionary efforts, the surviving Bolsheviks eventually dissipated into a small remnant of malicious cranks. One of their leaders, named Vladimir Lenin, died of syphilis in Switzerland, forgotten and obscure.[26]

As a pro-German buffer state, the new Kingdom of Poland effectively insulated both the Germans and Russians from their traditional rivalry for the next twenty years. The French retreated into the reality of the situation. With their only possible ally on the continent no longer available and their temporary entente with British thoroughly discredited, they came to accept the state of affairs of German predominance in Europe. Yet that logic worked for the interests of France by breaking the alliance system that had produced the German paranoia of encirclement in the first place. Germany's attention would be occupied not with France but with the disintegration of the Austro-Hungarian Empire, whose performance in the short war had utterly discredited itself.

Europe gave an immense sigh of relief as the war concluded. Although there had been a million casualties in the two months of fighting, life resumed its normal course. The West's sense of optimism and progress actually increased, oddly enough spurred on by the fact that an even longer and more devastating war had been so responsibly avoided. Among those most relieved was Wilhelm, known now to his people as the *Heldkaiser* – the hero emperor. It is no wonder then that at the wedding of Colonel Sigurd von Ilsemann in 1925, to a lady-in-waiting to the empress, the Kaiser himself stood as best man. When the Kaiser died in 1940, the entire nation grieved for a man that had led them through the fire to a secure and prosperous future. Germany had indeed found its place in the sun.

The Reality

The German General Staff did indeed have a war mobilisation plan directed at Russia which it regularly exercised until 1913 despite the priority given to the Schlieffen Plan. The irony was that General von Staab was never consulted during the tense showdown between the Kaiser and Moltke. The latter was aware of the Russian variant of the mobilisation plan but had neither the moral courage nor imagination to raise it as a possible alternative when the misleading report from the German ambassador in London upset the mobilisation applecart. Indeed, as the Kaiser said, his uncle would have given him a different answer. The plausible basis for Moltke suffering a fatal stroke was the belief of his wife that that confrontation with the Kaiser and his chief ministers had indeed caused a minor stroke in her husband. He was never the same man. Following his relief after the Battle of the Marne, his health rapidly declined and he died in 1916.

For his part, Staab only learned of the showdown in the Charlottenburg Palace after the war. He was so outraged at the insult to his Railway Department that he wrote a book, *Aufmarsch nach zwei Fronten: auf Grund der Operationspläne von 1870–1914*, to show that he could have moved four German armies with a million men to the eastern border in ten days. Given his remarkable feat of putting seven German armies with almost two million men on the French and Belgian borders in a similar period, one can only take him at his word. Ilsemann was an actual aide of the Kaiser, went with him into exile, and continued to serve him until his death in 1940. The Kaiser was his best man at his wedding in 1925 to a lady-in-waiting to the empress.

His fictitious intervention at the critical moment was the catalyst for Staab to be consulted. It is conceivable that someone around the Kaiser would have known of the Russian variant. Yet no one did – or did not want to contradict Moltke – and upon that silence, history took the long and ruinous path: the war that nearly broke the back of Western civilisation and unleashed the lethal bacilli of communism and national socialism upon the world, political pandemic movements that fouled the twentieth century and caused the deaths of two hundred million human beings.

The Schlieffen Plan was based on the serious miscalculation of the Russian ability to mobilise. It was adopted as the priority plan in 1905, the very year that Russia was convulsed by defeat in the Russo-Japanese War and the following abortive revolution. Serious reforms were made in the Russian Army thereafter, including its mobilisation plan, which the Germans appear to not have taken into account in the years following 1905. Yet the phased Russian mobilisation plan was vulnerable to a rapid mobilisation of the German armies in the east. Such a plan would have put an enormous mass of manoeuvres on the border, against which the Russians would have had to commit their forces piecemeal as they arrived, ensuring their defeat comprehensively. This situation had the clear potential to result in the early defeat of the Russian Army. Such a strategic turn by Germany would have allowed it to follow Tirpitz's advice to not be the first nation to declare war but to let the enemies of Germany assume the role of aggressors, a neat juxtaposition of the onus that Germany actually incurred.

Notes

1 Daniel Allen Butler, *The Burden of Guilt: How Germany Shattered the Last Days of Peace, Summer 1914* (Havertown: Casemate Publishers, 2010), p. 188.

2 Sean McMeekin, *July 1914: Countdown to War* (New York: Basic Books, 2013), p. 309.

3 *First Lieutenant Dwight D. Eisenhower, *Mobilisation Plans of the Great Powers in the Late European War* (Fort Leveanworth: Command & General Staff College Press, 1935), p. 77.

4 Barbara Tuchman, *The Guns of August* (New York: Macmillan Co., 1962), p. 79.

5 *Oberst Sigurd von Ilsemann, *Aufzeichnungen des letzten Flügeladjutanten* (Frankurt: Goertz von Berlichingen & Soehne, 1929), p. 32.

6 Butler, *The Burden of Guilt*, p. 139.

7 Ibid.

8 Ian Senior, *Home Before the Leaves Fall: A New History of the German Invasion of 1914* (Oxford: Osprey Publishing, 2012), p. 37.

9 Annika Mombauer, *Helmuth von Moltke and the Origins of the First World War* (Cambridge: Cambridge University Press, 2001), p. 50, cited in Senior, *Home Before the Leaves Fall*, p. 37.

10 Mombauer, *Helmuth von Moltke*, p. 52, cited in Senior, *Home Before the Leaves Fall*, p. 38.

11 Mombauer, *Helmuth von Moltke*, p. 56, cited in Senior, *Home Before the Leaves Fall*, p. 38.

12 McMeekin, *July 1914*, p. 307.

13 Ibid., pp. 289, 317. The French forces in North Africa had already been ordered to France on the Tuesday of that week, 28 July 1914.

14 *Hans Wilhelm von Essbach, *Aufzeichnung Tirpitz* (Munich: Webber und Söhne, 1991), p. 177.

15 Karl Kautsky, Count Max Montgelas and Walter Schücking (eds), *Deutsche Dokumente zum Kriegsausbruch*, vol. 3 (Berlin: General Staff, 1919), document 562, p. 62.

16 McMeekin, *July 1914*, p. 342.

17 *Major General Sir Frederick Maurice, *The Indispenable Man: Captain Sigurd von Ilsemann* (London: Charing Cross Publishers Ltd, 1932), p. 211.

18 Tuchman, *The Guns of August*, p. 79.

19 Christopher Clark, *The Sleepwalkers: How Europe Went to War in 1914* (New York: HarperCollins, 2013), p. 531.

20 Ibid.

21 *Henry Wilson Smith, *Italian Diplomacy in the Period of the Alliance System* (New York: Empire State Press, 1955), pp. 290–2. There was more than one 'wink–wink–nod–nod' employed at this time. The Italians were loath to honour their agreement with Germany and so informed France. They managed to vacillate until the war ended.

22 W. Bruce Lincoln, *Passage Through Armageddon: The Russians in War and Revolution* (New York: Oxford University Press, 1994) p. 88.

23 Ibid., p. 77.

24 *Quentin Roosevelt, *The Great Peacemaker: Theodore Roosevelt at Dumbarton Oaks and The Hague* (New York: Hamilton Publishers, 1928), pp. 399–404.

25 *Aleksandr V. Dragomirov, *Imperial Savior: The Life of Piotr Stolypin* (London: Blackfriars Ltd, 1932), pp. 355–7.

26 *Alger Hiss, *Bolshevism: A Forgotten Footnote in History*, State Department Monographs in History Series (Washington, DC: Foreign Service Press, 1944), p. 339.

2

Vormarsch!
The Breakthrough at Ypres, 1914

Spencer Jones

A Season of Opportunity

The opening phase of the First World War was defined by fast-moving campaigns and ferocious battles. In August 1914, both France and Germany put their carefully crafted pre-war plans into action. The French Plan XVII called for an all-out offensive into the occupied provinces of Alsace-Lorraine. Unfortunately for France, disaster followed as courageous but poorly led French troops fruitlessly attacked well-prepared German fortifications. French casualties were horrendous and the gains non-existent. Whilst the French Army was bleeding to death on the border, the Germans launched the infamous 'Schlieffen Plan'. This ambitious operation called for a massive, multi-army offensive that would crash through neutral Belgium and then swing south-west into France like the arc of a giant scythe, outflanking the French armies on the border and racing on to encircle Paris. It was hoped that this bold gambit would defeat France in just six weeks, allowing the Germans to transfer their forces to face the Russian steamroller in the east.

In contrast to the disasters of Plan XVII, the Schlieffen Plan began promisingly. Belgium, trusting that its neutrality would spare it, was poorly prepared for the German invasion. The much-vaunted Belgian fortress system imposed a brief delay on the German advance but proved no match for the specialist siege guns which the invaders were able to deploy. By the final week of August the Germans had cleared much of Belgium and were marching across the border into France. Fierce clashes with the recently arrived British Expeditionary Force (BEF) delayed the advance but did not stop it.

September began with German armies surging south-west towards Paris, forcing British and French forces into the 'Great Retreat' that carried them across the river Marne and beyond. Yet at the moment when German victory seemed inevitable, French commander Joseph Joffre sensed an opportunity. His intuitive reading of the battlefront told him that the German offensive was losing steam, that its men were reaching the tipping point of exhaustion and that the nerves of its commanders were fraying. Reorganising the French forces under his control, Joffre prepared for a counterattack that would hurl the Germans back and leave the Schlieffen Plan in tatters. He perceived a perfect target for the counterstroke: the German 1st and 2nd armies had allowed a sizeable gap to develop between them. If Allied forces could drive into that space then the German armies would be isolated from one another and defeated in detail. In coordination with attacks along the rest of the front, Joffre resolved to target the weak spot with some of his best troops. To this end he hurled the small but elite BEF and the French 5th Army into the breach.

The result was the Battle of the Marne, which raged between 6 and 12 September. Joffre's operational vision was masterful. His counteroffensive surprised the Germans and created panic amongst their General Staff. However, the fog of war and the friction of battle slowed the Allied advance, whilst the tactical prowess of the Germans meant that they evaded encirclement and instead conducted a fighting retreat back to the north bank of the Aisne. Allied victory was strategically decisive – the Germans were forced to retire some sixty miles in six days and Paris was saved – but it did not translate into the complete destruction of the German armies which Joffre had hoped to achieve. Instead, German forces were able to form a strong defensive line which resisted a British assault at the Battle of the Aisne (13–15 September). Exhausted by the efforts of a month of constant fighting, both sides entrenched and considered their options.

The lull was deceptive, for this was a season of opportunity. Joffre was the hero of the hour and the French press began to speak of the 'miracle of the Marne'. His next challenge was how to drive the Germans from French soil entirely. Recognising that a direct frontal attack on the German lines would be costly and ineffective, Joffre sought fresh options. The northern flank offered tantalising possibilities. Aside from German forces conducting siege operations in Belgium and cavalry screening the siege lines, there were few enemy forces on this front. Furthermore, the Belgian Army was clinging on in the besieged port of Antwerp and desperately requesting support. Joffre envisaged an Allied offensive in the north that would turn the flank of the entrenched Germans to the south, link up with the Belgian Army and liberate Brussels. His vision was shared by the British commander Sir John French, who devised an effective plan to redeploy the BEF from the Aisne to the Flanders front, intending to drive onwards to relieve the siege of Antwerp. The scheme seemed rich with possibilities.

Yet the Germans were also planning their own offensive. There had been a change within the General Staff. Chief of the General Staff Helmuth von Moltke (known as 'Moltke the Younger' to differentiate him from his famous uncle of the same name) had been made the scapegoat for the defeat on the Marne and had been replaced by the ruthless Erich von Falkenhayn. Even though the Schlieffen Plan had failed, Falkenhayn believed that the war could still be won in the west. He proposed adopting a defensive strategy in the east and concentrating fresh forces for a renewed offensive against France. Like Joffre, his eye was drawn to the northern flank. There were good reasons for an attack here. A German victory would turn the Allied flank, crush the last vestiges of Belgian resistance and, most importantly, would allow the Germans to drive on and capture the Channel ports and rupture the BEF's supply chain.[1] Victory in Flanders thus held the possibility of eliminating both of France's western allies at a stroke.

Both Joffre and Falkenhayn resolved to launch major offensives in Flanders. Neither side was fully aware of the plans of their opponent. The opening weeks of the campaign resembled a vast meeting engagement. Both sides sought to advance, but the greater weight of German manpower gave them the battlefield advantage. Allied hopes of relieving Antwerp were soon dashed. The city was indefensible and the Belgian Army decided to evacuate the port and retreat west to link up with the Anglo-French armies. However, even with these reinforcements the British and French advance into Flanders could make no progress against numerically superior German forces. By mid-October the tide of the battle had clearly swung in Germany's favour. Outnumbered and outgunned, the Allies found themselves fighting an increasingly desperate defensive battle to hold onto what territory they possessed.

Dreams of liberating Brussels were soon forgotten and attention was instead focused on the defence of Ypres, the last free city of Belgium. Beyond its symbolic importance to the Belgians, Ypres was a strategically vital communication and transport centre. Good-quality roads ran from Ypres to all nearby towns and cities, including the Channel ports of Calais and Dunkirk. Control of the city was the key to control of the Channel. Both sides were aware of the stakes. The Allies resolved to defend Ypres at all costs whilst the Germans were determined to smash through the Allied lines and capture the city. The Battle of Ypres had begun.

The Battle for Ypres

The terrain around Ypres defined the decisive battle that was to follow. The vast majority of Flanders was flat, wooded terrain, dotted with small farms and villages. However, east of Ypres lay a ridgeline that provided an excellent defensive position in the otherwise level countryside. The soldiers of the British Expeditionary Force found themselves holding this crucial line against the impending German assault. Much of the ridge was covered with wood-land and marshy ground which greatly aided its defence. Yet there was one weakness in the position: the ridge was traversed by the broad Menin Road which ran directly to Ypres. Cutting through the broken terrain that covered much of the ridge, it offered a rapid and direct route to the strategic city.

However, standing directly astride the road stood Gheluvelt, a small village with a pre-war population of just over one thousand people. Any drive towards Ypres had to pass through the hamlet. Recognising the strategic importance of the Menin Road, the British had made Gheluvelt the linchpin of their defences.

The village was held by some of the finest troops of the elite British Expeditionary Force. Lieutenant-General Sir Douglas Haig's well-trained I Corps was charged with defending the sector. He placed his best formation – 1st Division – to cover the road. The front line at Gheluvelt was held by the crack 1st Guards Brigade under the command of Brigadier General Charles FitzClarence VC, a formidable Irishman who had earned the nickname 'The Demon' for his energy and aggression.

The soldiers in the line were 'Old Contemptibles' who had proved their fighting prowess at the battles of Mons and Le Cateau in August 1914. All the men were volunteers and had thus benefitted from longer, more-complex training than the mass conscript armies of the continental powers. The British had placed special emphasis on marksmanship. The pinnacle of a soldier's training was the 'mad minute' exercise. Lying prone, the rifleman was required to fire fifteen aimed rounds at a target three hundred yards distant within sixty seconds and expected to score hits with at least twelve of his rounds. Passing this exercise was considered the mark of a soldier, but excelling at it was the mark of a good one. As a result experienced riflemen were capable of firing twenty shots per minute or more.[2] In 1914, British infantry were able to produce such an intense volume of rifle fire that the Germans sometimes mistook it for machine guns. Many German attacks had been brought to a bloody halt by the sharpshooters of the BEF. A German survivor recalled that the accuracy and intensity of British fire 'bordered on the miraculous'.[3]

However, although undoubtedly elite, the BEF was very small in comparison to the mass armies of the continent. The stresses of the fighting from August to October had reduced its numbers further and reinforcements were few and far between. The experienced veterans amongst its ranks could not be easily replaced. The BEF had not been created with an attritional war in mind. It had been characterised by one officer as 'a rapier amongst scythes': a nimble and sharp weapon that was deadly when wielded with skill, but which could not parry away the heavy blows of its opponents indefinitely. At Mons and Le Cateau the BEF had delivered stinging ripostes to the Germans and then slipped away before the counterstroke landed. Unfortunately, locked into the defence of the vital city of Ypres, the BEF was bound to the spot and given no room to manoeuvre. Faced with relentless German pressure, casualties mounted, ammunition dwindled, and the rapier was close to breaking point. The official historian Brigadier General James Edmonds recalled that on the eve of the German breakthrough, 'the line that stood between the British Empire and ruin was composed of tired, haggard and unshaven men, unwashed, plastered with mud, many in little more than rags.'[4]

The position at Gheluvelt reflected these problems. On paper, Fitz-Clarence's Guards Brigade was four thousand men strong, but in reality the brigade had been reduced to less than half that number. With his manpower so heavily reduced, FitzClarence had to commit his entire force to the front, leaving precious few reserves. The only reserve troops that could be spared were just under five hundred battle-weary men of the 2nd Worcestershires. This meant that the British line was hard but brittle. If the Germans achieved a major breakthrough they would have a virtually open road to Ypres, which lay four miles behind the front.

In late October the Germans carefully assembled a specialist force of infantry, cavalry, and artillery to crash through the thin British line. The German spearhead was made up of the experienced 30th Division, 54th Reserve Division, and 3rd Cavalry Division, plus overwhelming artillery support, including the mighty siege guns that had pounded the Belgian fortress system into rubble.[5] In total the assault force outnumbered the British defenders by a factor of almost four to one. This powerful formation was placed under the command of Max von Fabeck, whom Falkenhayn tasked with breaking through the British line at Gheluvelt and surging onwards towards Ypres.[6] Falkenhayn himself retained control over immediate German reserves, including lead elements of the elite Prussian Guards Corps. These troops were held in readiness to exploit any breakthrough.

Whereas the British had an advantage in the quality of their rifle fire, the Germans had a clear advantage in their powerful artillery. Plentifully supplied with ammunition, the German gunners were able to keep up an almost constant fire on the British position. As a precursor to an infantry attack, the guns were capable of an unprecedented rate of fire, producing devastating bombardments that ripped apart trenches and their occupants with terrifying ease.

After several days of see-saw combat along the entire Ypres front, Fabeck's forces had spent 30 October in careful preparation for a decisive offensive. Artillery spotters had crept forward into no man's land and carefully registered their targets. Infantry had been briefed on the terrain and opposition in front of them. German cavalry had been told to prepare for a rapid advance to exploit any breakthrough.[7] Fabeck ended his orders for the day with a single word that captured the mood: *Vormarsch!* ('Forward!')

There was an air of destiny about this moment. Kaiser Wilhelm II himself was due to visit Falkenhayn's headquarters on 31 October. He would be present to witness the great breakthrough that was about to occur.

Breakthrough at Gheluvelt

Cold and dismal rain soaked the British line throughout the small hours of 31 October. Desultory German shelling and the regular crack of sniper rifles ensured that none of the defenders slept easily.

Gheluvelt itself was a hive of activity. The chateau served as a headquarters position and was a communications nerve centre. Telephone lines ran from the chateau to the front line and also to 1st Brigade HQ, which occupied a nearby farm. Signallers and engineers had worked through the night to ensure the lines were functioning and that replacement cable was available for the inevitable breakages caused by shelling. At 5.45 a.m. the communications staff contacted the front line to enquire about activity in the sector. All reported that the front was quiet. The staff at the chateau relaxed somewhat and prepared to forward their report to higher command.

One of the officers stepped outside the chateau to take in the cold autumn air. He checked his watch: 6.00 a.m. He looked up just in time to see the British front line disappear beneath a murderous rain of high-explosive shells.

The German artillery spotters had done their work well. Their guns had been carefully ranged and the fire plans had been worked out in unprecedented detail. Hundreds of artillery pieces launched a bombardment that possessed devastating synergy. Mighty 15-cm siege howitzers opened the attack, hurling high-explosive shells that plunged into the British trenches and blew them apart. A survivor recalled that the shells 'made the earth rock as in an earthquake'.[8] With their defences destroyed by the howitzers, the British had little shelter from the fire of field guns. These lighter pieces swept the ground with a storm of shrapnel, inflicting scores of casualties on the defenders. Longer-ranged weapons zeroed in on the rear areas, placing a curtain of fire that prevented both evacuation of the wounded and reinforcement of the front. The British defences were simply torn apart by this weight of metal. Trenches were reduced to a 'broken and bloody shambles'; machine-gun pits were demolished, communications collapsed and the surviving defenders were left deafened and stunned.[9] No one on the British side was certain how long the bombardment lasted. A veteran remembered: 'Time seemed to stand still; an hour was a day under this torture.'[10]

After what seemed like an age, the German bombardment lifted from the front and began to search the rear areas of the British position. Grey-clad infantry began their advance against the shattered line. Bitter experience had taught the attackers not to underestimate their opponents, but surely no one could have survived such a barrage?

The zip and whine of rifle rounds answered the question. The German front line shuddered as a fusillade ripped through its ranks. This was to be no walk-over. British troops still lived amongst the ruins of the trenches. Rallying around surviving officers and veteran NCOs, the 'Old Contemptibles' prepared to face the German onslaught. Ferocious close-range fighting followed as the Germans advanced on the desperate defenders. The artillery

27

had caused such destruction that it was difficult to talk of a front line. The shell-cratered landscape was wreathed in smoke and cordite fumes added to the sense of dislocation.

However, the attackers soon sensed that there was something different about this engagement. Although still accurate, British fire was not as rapid as usual. There were distinct lulls in the shooting that allowed the Germans to crawl or dash to better positions. The defenders were hampered by a poorly made batch of ammunition that had been delivered to the front line the previous day. The magazines were misshapen and did not feed the bullets through correctly. British soldiers cursed their ammunition as their breeches jammed on the faulty rounds. Many were forced to load one bullet at a time as if using weapons from an earlier era. Others seized the rifles of fallen Germans and made use of them until the ammunition ran out. There were even some accounts of soldiers hurling rocks in sheer desperation.[11]

Despite this crippling disadvantage the British line put up a tremendous fight. But for all their heroics, the task was ultimately hopeless. The Germans were too many and the British were too few. Enterprising attackers infiltrated through gaps in the shell-cratered line and outflanked the defenders. Others pushed further into the British position, cutting off any possibility of retreat and blocking reinforcements. Surrounded, many British soldiers fought to the last man and were overwhelmed at the point of the bayonet. To take a single example, by the end of the day's fighting the 1st Queen's (Royal West Sussex Regiment) mustered just two officers and thirteen men from a paper strength of one thousand soldiers.[12]

The British line, splintered and broken, finally gave way under the remorseless pressure. German attackers pressed forward past khaki-clad bodies and wrecked artillery pieces, and found, to their surprise, that there appeared to be no forces of any substance behind the front. British stragglers and rear area troops exchanged fire with the Germans but were without leadership and fell back when pressed. Gheluvelt had been reduced to a burning ruin by the bombardment and was virtually undefended. A handful of British troops clung on in the grounds of the chateau to the east of the town, firing from windows and doorways at the triumphant German infantry. However, the village itself was soon in German hands. The road to Ypres itself was all but open.

News of the breakthrough spread slowly. The telephone system had collapsed under the bombardment. Runners carrying hastily scribbled messages disappeared into the fire and smoke and were never seen again. In the race for information the Germans were a step ahead. A smoke-stained messenger arrived at Fabeck's headquarters to inform him that Gheluvelt was in German hands and the road to Ypres lay open. Fabeck immediately ordered the 3rd Cavalry Division to follow up the successful attack and exploit the confusion in the British defences. Sensing that a decisive breakthrough was possible, Fabeck requested support from the Prussian Guards Corps. He received a positive reply signed by the Kaiser himself. The military and cultural elite of the German Army would strike the blow that would crush the hated English once and for all.

There were no such reserves available to the British. At the front, Charles FitzClarence worked desperately to rally stragglers and re-establish some form of defence. 'The Demon' had earned a reputation as a superb horseman in the Boer War and he needed all his skill as he galloped down forest tracks and across the bullet-ridden battlefield. He was 'the soul of the defence'.[13] Surviving officers and men responded to his rallying call, even though all were exhausted and many were wounded. FitzClarence had sent messengers back to higher command informing of them of the crisis at the front, but as the man on the spot he had no time to wait for further instructions. He was organising the 2nd Worcestershires, the sole British reserve battalion, when disaster struck. A single bullet – probably a stray shot – hit FitzClarence in the chest and killed him instantly.[14]

The death of FitzClarence meant that Major Edward Hankey, the commanding officer of the 2nd Worcestershires, was left without orders. After the war he admitted that he 'knew nothing of the general situation'.[15] However, it was clear that his battalion was in the midst of a full-scale military disaster. Hankey remembered that 'Parties from various regiments in the 1st Division [majority of whom were severely wounded men, and all of whom were completely exhausted by the constant bombardments and massed attacks on their line] having been driven in by overwhelming odds retired actually through the ranks of the Battalion, even warning them that it was impossible to go on, and that it was murder etc. to attempt it.'[16]

By this point enterprising German troops were beginning to infiltrate around the flanks of the Worcestershires. Wounded survivors stumbling past the thin khaki line warned that a mass of German reinforcements were advancing along the Menin Road. Reluctantly, Hankey gave the order to withdraw, sending runners to the rear to try and establish contact with divisional command. Falling back, the Worcestershires had to pass abandoned equipment, disabled artillery pieces and a stream of retreating men. One officer remembered that 'the area behind Gheluvelt presented a scene that to the onlooker seemed to exhibit every element of disaster.'[17] German artillery harried the fugitives remorselessly and the air was thick with grey smoke from shrapnel bursts.

The situation was critical and the British urgently needed a firm hand to impose some form of order. None was to be found. FitzClarence lay dead, the other brigade commanders were caught up in localised combat, and the telephone lines had collapsed. In a desperate attempt to formulate a response, the commanders of 1st and 2nd divisions, Samuel Lomax and Charles Monro, held a crisis conference at Hooge Chateau behind the lines. The concentration of staff cars parked in the grounds outside attracted the notice of a German reconnaissance aircraft. Within half an hour a salvo of German high-explosive shells smashed into the farm buildings. Lomax was mortally wounded, Monro was knocked unconscious and remained seriously concussed for several hours, and the majority of the assembled staff officers were killed.[18] At the moment of crisis the British chain of command had simply ceased to exist.

By now news of the disaster had reached BEF commander Sir John French. In his memoirs he described this moment as 'the worst' of his entire life, writing that 'the last barrier between the Germans and the Channel seaboard was broken down, and I viewed the situation with the utmost gravity.'[19] His perception was accurate. At a fraught meeting with Sir Douglas Haig the two planned how to halt the German onslaught. There were defensible lines to the west but the army needed to be rallied before it could even consider holding them. Having discussed the situation, French left in a staff car, racing at breakneck speed to seek aid from Allied forces, leaving Haig to face the immediate crisis. Haig's two divisional commanders had become casualties and he had no reliable means of communicating with the surviving brigadiers. With bloodied and broken troops retreating past his headquarters, he resolved that desperate times required desperate measures. He would ride out to the front and take personal charge of the battle.

Many witnesses recall seeing Haig riding down the Menin Road followed by his staff officers. Haig was not a naturally charismatic leader but he carried a gravitas that gave men confidence. The fugitives on the road began to slow, and then stop. These were professional veterans and only needed an example of leadership to make them stand their ground. It seemed as if Haig would provide that precious guidance and stave off disaster. But fortune did not favour the brave on this black day.

The Germans had been shelling the Menin Road throughout the battle. The sharp *crack* of shrapnel bursts was so regular as to become monotonous.

But now a different sound had joined the roar of the artillery. The ominous *whomp* and *whoosh* of heavy howitzer shells signalled that the Germans had turned their biggest guns on the retreating troops. Known as 'Jack Johnsons' after the famous American boxer, the high-explosive shells detonated with dreadful concussive force, flinging huge plumes of dirt into the sky and sending men diving for shelter.

Haig did not have the luxury of seeking cover. He had to set an example for his men and that required enduring the bombardment with silent and unflinching courage. No one would doubt Haig's valour during his ride to the front, but it cost him his life. One moment he was sitting astride his horse in the centre of the road, giving instructions and rallying men around him. Seconds later he had disappeared in an eruption of earth, flame, and blood as a howitzer shell slammed directly into his position.

With Haig dead the British disaster was complete. Junior officers and NCOs were powerless to stop the retreat. German artillery pounded the survivors as they stumbled westwards towards Ypres. Closing in behind them were triumphant German soldiers, led by the fresh 3rd Cavalry Division. The road to Ypres was open and no one and nothing was left to oppose the German advance.

The British defeat was almost total. The breakthrough at Gheluvelt fatally destabilised the entire British line. Concurrent with the drive on Ypres, German forces widened the breach, turning north and south to outflank and destroy the British positions there. The rupture rapidly grew from a small hole to a devastating chasm. Within hours the entire BEF was reduced to a disordered retreat. German cavalry and lorry-borne jaeger infantry mounted a relentless pursuit of the routed army. Lead elements raced ahead, seizing bridges and capturing hundreds of British soldiers. By mid-afternoon the cavalry had reached Ypres itself. Regiments of the Prussian Guard arrived to secure the position in the early evening and the city was firmly in German hands by the end of the day.

The scale of German victory should not be underestimated. The BEF had ceased to exist as a cohesive force. A huge gap had been ripped in the Allied lines that exposed the flanks of the Belgians to the north and the French to the south. The road and rail network of Ypres was now under German control and the Prussian Guard Corps was poised to exploit the advantage.

Falkenhayn was a calculating man, not given to hyperbole, but his headquarters was thick with the euphoria of victory on the evening of

31 October. He raised a toast in honour of the Kaiser and delivered a simple assessment of the day to his monarch: 'Your Majesty, the English army has been destroyed.'[20]

Retreat and Pursuit

Sir John French was a 'soldier's general' who cared deeply about his men and had a keen sense of their morale. In early September, alarmed at the exhaustion of his soldiers after the Great Retreat, he had proposed to the British government that the BEF be withdrawn from the line for rest and refit.[21] On that occasion he had been brusquely overruled. This time, recognising that ministers in London would not understand the crisis at the front, he chose to act first and inform the government later. Despite the bitter protestations of the French and Belgians, Sir John withdrew the shattered remnants of the British from the line and retreated towards Boulogne. His intentions were twofold. Locating his army near the Channel ports would allow timely reinforcement from Britain, but perhaps more pertinently it would also allow swift evacuation if the Allied line collapsed. Sir John was a pragmatic commander. If the Allies were defeated, Britain would need all its soldiers to protect its own shores. There was no purpose in allowing what remained of the regular army to be uselessly sacrificed in France.

The French took a decidedly different view of the British 'betrayal'.[22] The twin blows of the breakthrough at Gheluvelt and the withdrawal of the BEF left them facing an operational crisis. A major gap had appeared in the line but redeploying troops to fill it was tremendously difficult due to the loss of the transportation hub at Ypres. The situation was especially critical for Belgian troops to the north, who were now in grave danger of being encircled and trapped against the coast. Withdrawal was the only option available to the Allied armies. The loss of British forces made it imperative that the front was shortened to prevent further German breakthroughs. On 1 November, Joffre gave the order to fall back.

The situation required rapid movement of the kind that had characterised the Great Retreat of August. However, the circumstances were very different. Flanders was known for its autumnal rains and the first week of November was sodden with precipitation. This turned the lesser roads of the area to mud and hampered the movement of heavy equipment. Many retreating soldiers, already exhausted after a month of fierce fighting, found themselves at the end of their endurance. The blow to morale fell heavily on the Belgians who were abandoning the last free city of their country to the invaders. The French Army also felt the mental strain as they retreated further into their own country, joining throngs of civilian refugees who crowded the roads. A British journalist remembered that 'The whole countryside was a mass of burning villages . . . Hundreds of mangled wounded lay unattended on the roads.'[23]

The Germans were less affected by the weather. Control of Ypres allowed them to make use of the well-developed road network of the area, which benefitted from paving and drainage. Falkenhayn took full advantage and launched a vigorous pursuit. The British, who had marched away first, were largely beyond his reach. However, exhausted French and dispirited Belgian formations were constantly harried by cavalry and jaegers. The elite Prussian Guards were at the forefront of the pursuit. German morale soared as they advanced ever deeper into France.

The Allies had enormous difficulty breaking free from the German pursuit. Joffre had hoped to avoid a repeat of the large-scale loss of French territory that had occurred in August. However, despite some courageous rearguard actions and local counterattacks, his troops were simply too tired and too demoralised to break contact with their tormentors. Thousands of Allied soldiers were captured or simply went missing on the harrowing retreat. Joffre's original plan for a relatively short withdrawal gave way to a much larger retreat to the south-west. The withdrawal to the south left Calais isolated and the town was soon cut off and besieged. The port was defended by a ragtag mixture of French territorials, Belgian stragglers, and Royal Marines. However, the garrison was dependent on a tenuous naval supply line that became a magnet for U-boats. Furthermore, the defenders could do nothing against the German siege guns which were systematically pounding the port. After a fortnight of increasingly desperate resistance, the survivors were evacuated by the Royal Navy under the cover of darkness.

By mid-November, with the recuperating British at Boulogne on the left, the new Allied line ran in a south-easterly direction to Bethune. Everything to the north of this line fell into German hands. The new Allied position was dreadfully weak. The Flanders front had stretched approximately sixty kilometres from the Channel coast to Ypres; the Boulogne–Bethune front was closer to a hundred kilometres and was held by considerably fewer troops due to the disastrous losses suffered on the retreat. The British forces at Boulogne had had time to dig in and the French had worked feverishly to fortify their positions around Bethune, but the bulk of the line in-between only existed on paper. Some areas of the front were held by nothing more than cavalry screens or desperately overstretched French territorial units.

Whilst the Allies struggled to form their line, the Germans were experiencing problems of their own. The rapid advance into north-eastern France and the lunge for Calais had caused the army to outrun its logistic network. German troops were elated at their success but physically exhausted by the pace of operations. Furthermore, the winter of 1914 was one of the coldest on record. Falkenhayn had no choice but to wait while his staff set up logistical bases in the newly conquered territory. Nevertheless, it was clear that Germany had won a great victory. Mobility had been restored to the front, the Allied armies had been smashed, and the Channel ports were in German hands.

1915: Consequences

1915 was a bleak year for the western Allies. The Belgian Army had been effectively destroyed by the defeat at Ypres. The force had always relied upon its courage to make up for its limited training, but the bitter retreat from its homeland shattered its morale. It had suffered high casualties and had been forced to abandon most of its equipment and stores. The surviving divisions, reduced to mere skeleton formations by their losses, were further weakened by spiralling desertion rates as exhausted soldiers sought a way to return home to Belgium. In December 1914, commander-in-chief King Albert I informed his allies that his force existed only on paper and announced his intention to withdraw it from the fighting, retaining it only as 'an army in being'. It would play no further part in the war.

Meanwhile, across the English Channel the British were faced with a strategic nightmare. The destruction of the regular BEF and the loss of Calais caused panic in Whitehall. Lord Kitchener, the Secretary of State for War, had held back British forces from France in August 1914 due to fears of a surprise German invasion. Faced with far greater dangers in January 1915, he was forced to retain a large portion of British forces on the south coast in anticipation of a German cross-channel attack. Territorial divisions were rushed out to Boulogne to reconstitute the BEF, but these formations suffered from limited training and inadequate equipment. Their inexperience would cost them dearly in the battles of 1915.

The need to secure the coast and reinforce Boulogne meant that schemes to take the offensive against the Ottoman Empire were abandoned. There was no prospect of sending out British divisions to a peripheral theatre when there was a grave threat lurking across the Channel. Similarly, the Royal Navy insisted on retaining its full strength in home waters, which eliminated the possibility of a naval attack on the Dardanelles. The Middle East became the preserve of the Indian Army, which, lacking the resources to prosecute a vigorous offensive, was forced to concentrate on the defence of Egypt and the Suez Canal. The passivity of the British had the baleful effect of disappointing pro-Allied neutrals such as Italy and Greece, whilst simultaneously bolstering Turkish morale. Growing Ottoman confidence resulted in a series of ambitious offensives in 1915. Although these only achieved limited military success the damage to Britain's imperial prestige was severe.

With its western allies crippled, France was left alone to face the German onslaught. Still reeling from the bloodletting at Ypres, with the line overstretched and the defences at Bethune outflanked, the French struggled to hold off the renewed German attacks that were unleashed along the front between January and June 1915. The symbolic fortress of Verdun was cut off and besieged, with the German siege lines beating back all French attempts to relieve the beleaguered garrison. Elsewhere, the Second Battle of the Aisne ended in a German victory and allowed the attackers to advance on Paris once more. Meanwhile, the paper-thin Boulogne–Bethune line was driven in during a dramatic fortnight in May 1915. The heroism of the French soldiers could not make up for the dire operational and strategic position which the army faced. The French fought stubbornly and even won a handful of local victories, but there was to be no 'miracle' in 1915 as there had been a year earlier.

Facing defeat on all fronts, Britain and France looked desperately towards Russia to redress the balance. Falkenhayn's victory at Ypres meant that the Western Front had priority for German reinforcements, leaving only a handful of divisions in the east to stiffen the spine of the Austro-Hungarian Army. Lumbering Russian offensives crashed into these relatively weak Austro-German lines and made steady, albeit costly, progress. But the Russian steamroller was a slow and unreliable machine at the best of times, and the inability of the Allies to supply Russia's faltering economy due to the Ottomans' closure of the Black Sea route greatly diminished Russian offensive capability.

In June 1915, with the Western Front crumbling and the government in disarray, France made unofficial approaches to Germany regarding a potential armistice. Holding a dominant position, Germany made clear that it expected France to accept the humiliating terms contained within the so-called 'September Memorandum'. These demanded the annexation of huge chunks of territory from France – including the Channel ports – and included a provision to leave it economically crippled. Belgian independence would be completely extinguished as the country was to be formally annexed into the German Empire.

The latter half of 1915 would be defined by a mixture of ferocious combat and equally savage politicking. Whilst Allied armies fought and died at the front, politicians who favoured peace clashed spectacularly with those who argued for continued resistance. The victors would reshape Europe in 1916.

The Reality

Historically, the Battle of Ypres was a decisive German defeat. Falkenhayn launched a series of costly frontal attacks against the Allies in a vain attempt to break through to the Channel ports. The assaults gained some ground but only at a high cost in lives, and by the middle of November the Germans had been fought to a standstill.

The defeat at Ypres meant that the pre-war German strategy to win a swift victory in the west before turning against Russia had collapsed. In a reversal of pre-war planning, the General Staff decided to adopt a defensive posture on the Western Front and concentrate on defeating Russia. The strategic consequences of this decision were profound, as the failure to defeat Britain and France in 1914 locked Germany into a two-front war that steadily eroded its military position.

However, things could have been different had Falkenhayn realised how close he had come to breaking the British line at Gheluvelt. The repulse of the German attack of the 31 October was a remarkable feat of arms. German forces had smashed through the British line and captured Gheluvelt by midday. Whilst trying to formulate a response to the disaster, British commanders Lomax (CO, 1st Division) and Monro (CO, 2nd Division) were hit by German shelling as described in the scenario, thus breaking the chain of command at a critical time.

At this point, Charles FitzClarence seized the initiative. Acting without orders, he commandeered the last British reserves – the 2nd Worcestershires, a unit over which he had no formal authority – and launched them into a counterattack against the Germans occupying the village. The attack took the Germans completely by surprise and routed them from Gheluvelt. Although the Battle of Ypres continued until 22 November, the fight for Gheluvelt was Germany's best opportunity to break through the British line.

This scenario makes several changes to the history. In reality, the first German attack on 31 October was repulsed and a second bombardment was ordered, which allowed the follow-up to break through. To allow a swifter German advance I have made reference to a batch of faulty ammunition: this batch was actually delivered on 29 October and proved a serious detriment to the British riflemen on that day. In the story, any hope of a British counterattack is snuffed out with the death of FitzClarence; he was actually killed by a stray bullet on 12 November 1914. The death of Douglas Haig is entirely my own invention, although historically Haig did ride down the Menin Road towards the front on 31 October and was at risk of being hit by German shellfire. I have also given the Germans some formidable forces for exploitation in the form of the Prussian Guards Corps. Historically, the Guards were still arriving around Ypres on 31 October and would not be ready for action until the second week of November.

It is unlikely that Sir John French would have withdrawn in the manner described in the story, but it is not impossible given his desire to do so in September 1914. The consequences for the French would have been disastrous. The French Army suffered appalling losses between August and October 1914. Severe losses in November – plus the defeat of its Belgian and British allies – would have left France in a dire strategic position in early 1915.

Notes

1 Graeme Chamley Wynne (trans.), *Ypres 1914: An Official Account Published by Order of the German General Staff* (London: Constable & Co., 1919), p. 11.

2 Spencer Jones, *From Boer War to World War: Tactical Reform of the British Army 1902–1914* (Norman: University of Oklahoma Press, 2012), pp. 92–4.

3 Jack Sheldon, *The German Army at Ypres 1914* (Barnsley: Pen & Sword, 2010), p. 262.

4 James Edmonds, *Official History of the Great War: Military Operations France and Belgium 1914*, vol. 2 (London: Macmillan, 1925), p. 304.

5 Intelligence Section of the General Staff, American Expeditionary Forces, *Histories of Two Hundred and Fifty-One Divisions of the German Army which Participated in the War 1914–1918* (London: London Stamp Exchange, 1920), pp. 48–52.

6 The force was known to the British as *Army Group Fabeck*. In total it consisted of six divisions and over seven hundred artillery pieces.

7 *Max von Fabeck, *The Victory at Ypres* (Berlin: Herzog Press, 1918), p. 81.

8 John Lucy, *There's a Devil in the Drum* (London: Faber & Faber, 1938), p. 220.

9 G. Valentine Williams, 'First Ypres 1914: The Turning of the Tide', in John Buchan (ed.), *The Long Road to Victory* (London: Thomas Nelson & Sons, 1920), p. 18.

10 Lucy, *Devil in the Drum*, p. 221.

11 *Cyril Falls, *The Tragedy at Gheluvelt* (London: E. Arnold, 1933), p. 112.

12 Edmonds, *Official History*, vol. 2, p. 317.

13 John Terraine, *The Ordeal of Victory* (Philadelphia: Lippincott, 1963), p. 121.

14 *Andrew Thorne, *Simply Splendid: The Life of Charles FitzClarence VC* (London: Cartwright & Son, 1924), p. 305.

15 Spencer Jones (ed.), *Stemming the Tide: Officers and Leadership in the British Expeditionary Force 1914* (Solihull: Helion, 2013), p. 254.

16 Ibid., p. 255.

17 Edmonds, *Official History*, vol. 2, p. 318.

18 A.H. Farrar-Hockley, *Death of an Army* (London: Arthur Baker, 1967) p. 165.

19 John French, *1914* (London: Constable & Co., 1919). pp. 252–3.

20 *Fabeck, *Victory*, p. 206.

21 The National Archives, WO 33/713, John French to Lord Kitchener, 30 August and 31 August 1914.

22 *Victor Huguet, *The British Betrayal: A French Indictment* (London: Cassell, 1927), pp. 175–87.

23 Phillip Gibbs, 'Battle of Dixmude', *Western Australian*, 27 October 1914.

3

Kitchener of Arabia

Stephen Badsey

Kitchener of Khartoum

His calendar in the War Office in Whitehall showed that it was Friday 18 December 1914. Sifting through the papers on his desk, Horatio, Lord Kitchener, His Britannic Majesty's Secretary of State for War, noted with a grunt that today a formal British protectorate over Egypt had come into force. So, Egypt was no longer part of the Ottoman Empire, that great rotting relic of past Turkish glories still ruled from Constantinople. It was an empire that included not just Turkey itself but the whole great swathe of Arabia, stretching eastwards from the Suez Canal through Palestine and Syria, then southwards taking in the whole of Mesopotamia and the desert vastness of the Arabian peninsula, all the way to the Indian Ocean. For Kitchener, Arabia would be the next great battlefield.[1]

The Ottoman Empire had entered the Great War because of a secret treaty signed with Germany on 2 August 1914. 'So much for secrecy in the Levant!' thought Kitchener. What his network of spies and contacts throughout Arabia could not find out could easily be bought for money or favours in Constantinople, or in Baghdad.[2] The Ottomans had entered the war when, after a series of provocative incidents, on 28 October their navy had bombarded the Black Sea ports of Odessa, Sebastopol, and Feodosia, belonging to their old enemy Russia. The declaration of war by Russia, France, and Great Britain that had followed on 4 November had been just a formality. The Ottoman response of declaring a *jihad*, or holy war, against the Allies had produced singularly little reaction among their own peoples, or among the Muslim troops and peoples of the British and French empires. Instead, the British had landed the 6th (Poona) Division from India unopposed at Basra, as the start of a painfully slow advance up the river Tigris into Mesopotamia.[3] Kitchener estimated that Major General Sir John Maxwell's 10th and 11th Indian divisions, now fully formed in Egypt, should be enough to hold against a Turkish attack on the Suez Canal. The much greater problem was that the Ottoman entry into the war had severed the main line of supply and communications through the Black Sea between the Russian Empire and its French and British allies. The British government should have appointed him ambassador to Constantinople back in 1910 when they had the chance, Kitchener thought. He would have put an end to all this nonsense with the Germans! Now, if the Black Sea route to Russia could be reopened, he could put that right. He might even just save little Serbia, hard-pressed though it was.

The formality of the British protectorate over Egypt was of little matter to Kitchener. In reality, the British had controlled Egypt since 1882, including officering the Egyptian Army. Kitchener himself spoke Arabic, and he had passed as an Egyptian when in disguise. In 1898 he had commanded the combined British and Egyptian army that had smashed the Sudanese at Omdurman and recaptured Khartoum. His active military service went back to 1870 and the Franco-Prussian War, when he had volunteered as an ambulance corpsman with the French. He had gone on to serve in most of the Levant, including Cyprus, which he had mapped early in his career. After Omdurman, he had faced down a French attempt at Fashoda to interfere in British rule over Sudan, risking a war with France to do so. Sent to South Africa in 1899 alongside Field Marshal Lord Roberts – little 'Bobs' who had died of old age and pneumonia only last month visiting his beloved Indian troops in France – he had rescued the disastrous British campaign against the Boers, ending the South African War of 1899–1902 by annexing the two Boer republics to the Crown.

Kitchener was now sixty-four years old. Having achieved his last great ambition of commanding the Indian Army, in 1914 he was ending a lifetime of imperial service with the post of consul general (effectively governor) for Egypt. In Cairo, he had shared a palatial house with the commander of the Egyptian Army, Major General the Honourable Julian Byng, an aristocratic, tough, and experienced cavalryman known to all as 'Bungo'. He was Field Marshal Earl Kitchener of Khartoum and Broome; 'K of K' – and to the British 'K' never meant anyone else, just as a century before 'the Duke' had only ever meant Wellington. The double 'K' monogram adorned the stately home that he had bought at Broome Park near Canterbury. Music hall songs were sung about him, and china plates and mugs were sold with his face on them. No British public figure was more popular, or more of an imperial legend.

Kitchener reached for the latest report from Maxwell's headquarters in Egypt, assessing the Ottoman threat to the Suez Canal. 'The only place from which a fleet can operate against Egypt is Alexandretta. It is a splendid natural naval base.'[4] The report's author was one Lieutenant T. E. Lawrence. Always on the lookout for promising officers, Kitchener made a note of the name. Alexandretta, that was the key. The small and almost unnoticed Turkish port in the eastern Mediterranean was barely a hundred miles from Cyprus (which the British had also just annexed from the Ottoman Empire, having governed it in practice since 1878). Kitchener knew better than most just how ramshackle Ottoman rule over Arabia had become. 'A great deal depends on the attitude of the Arab tribesmen,' he had told Sir Edward Grey, the foreign secretary, on 5 December, but Baghdad, five hundred miles from Basra along the Tigris, was 'an open city of 150,000 inhabitants – the garrison consists of a weak division of probably bad troops'.[5] Kitchener also knew all about the men now ruling the Ottoman Empire, the 'Young Turks' of the 1908 palace revolution who hoped to modernise their country. They cared far more about Turkey than about Arabia, and increasingly they had come to accept that the vast expanses of desert and palm trees might not be worth keeping in the future, even if they could.

Kitchener hated politics and politicians even more than he hated the cold of the London winter. Meetings of Prime Minister H. H. Asquith's new War Council were meant to decide strategy, but they were achieving nothing because no one could agree on a plan. Despite the high political office which he now held, Kitchener had insisted on keeping his job as consul general for Egypt, and because he was a serving field marshal he was still eligible for a military command. In July 1914 he had been in London only to receive his earldom from King George V, and had been about to take ship for Egypt again. But with war breaking out in Europe, Asquith had appealed to him to take the War Office position, which had been vacant since April after a political fiasco over Ireland which had nearly brought down the government, causing the fall of Colonel J. E. B. 'Galloper Jack' Seeley as Secretary of State for War, and nearly that of Winston Churchill as First Lord of the Admiralty.[6] Asquith should have given the War Office back to Lord Haldane, the brilliant political lawyer who had created the British Expeditionary Force (BEF), the Territorial Force of part-time peacetime volunteers, and much more besides. However, in the atmosphere of August 1914, Haldane's known admiration for – of all things – German philosophy had ruled him out.[7] The Chief of the Imperial General Staff (the army's professional head), Field Marshal Sir John French, had done the decent thing in also resigning. But at least on the war's outbreak French had been given a proper job as commander of the BEF, which had been sent to the continent. Kitchener grunted again, with approval: Johnny French was a difficult man to work with, but he knew how to do his duty.

To Kitchener, Asquith's appeal to take the War Office had been direct and simple: in their hour of trial his country and its people once more needed a hero, and he would never let them down. The problem was that, despite the all-powerful Royal Navy, the British Empire had gone to war against Germany without having an army to speak of. By continental European standards the BEF was tiny. It had been badly knocked about before playing its magnificent part in stemming the tide of the German invasion of France, and it was crying out for reinforcements. The first troops of the Territorial Force, who would ordinarily have needed months of training, were already in action alongside the BEF regulars.

Kitchener had agreed with his new Cabinet colleagues that the war would be long and hard, lasting perhaps three years. He had called for a volunteer New Army, and both Britain and its empire had answered his call. By the end of August one hundred thousand men had volunteered, and it would be half a million by the start of the New Year. The recruiting posters were everywhere, including Kitchener's pointing finger telling the men that he 'Wants You!' The first of the New Army divisions – the 'K-1' divisions, they were calling them – would be ready to be sent overseas by spring 1915. Volunteers from Canada were arriving in Britain, and more from Australia and New Zealand were training in Egypt, under the odd name of the Australia and New Zealand Army Corps or ANZAC. It was a worldwide phenomenon unprecedented in military history. Half a million men were volunteering to go to war, because K of K had summoned them to do their duty.

In October, the hard-pressed BEF had also been reinforced by four Indian Army divisions: an Indian Corps consisting of 3rd (Lahore) Division and 7th (Meerut) Division, and an Indian Cavalry Corps consisting of 1st and 2nd Indian cavalry divisions. That had been mostly because of the work before the war of General Sir Douglas Haig, now one of French's subordinate commanders with the BEF, from back when Haig had been

Chief of Staff in India a few years earlier. But putting Indian troops into a European war had been a stop-gap, and the sooner they were out of France the better. Already, over seven thousand Indian soldiers had been killed or wounded, in what one of them described ominously as 'this cold hell across the black water to which our British Sahibs have sent us'.[8] In Kitchener's view, the complex balancing act that was the British Empire did not include breaking faith with its Indian soldiers by getting them killed by the Germans. Nor did it include those Indian soldiers, many of whom revered their British officers, getting too close a look at the darker realities of British society.

Although Kitchener did not admit to mistakes, he also knew that appointing General Sir Horace Smith-Dorrien as Johnny French's other subordinate commander had been an error: the two men just did not trust each other. The problem was that Sir John French was in the wrong job. His replacement as Chief of the Imperial General Staff, General Sir Charles Douglas, had died from overwork in October while trying to make the New Armies a reality. Kitchener had chosen a pliable nonentity, Lieutenant General James Wolff Murray, for his successor. At least Kitchener had an old and trusted subordinate, General Sir Ian 'Johnnie' Hamilton, helping with recruiting at the War Office. Hamilton was also the British Army's expert on amphibious landings, having pioneered the techniques and training before the war.

Kitchener re-read the draft of a letter he was writing to Johnny French at BEF headquarters: 'the German lines in France may be looked on as a fortress that cannot be carried by assault and also cannot be completely invested, with the result that the lines may be held by an investing force whilst operations proceed elsewhere.'[9] Kitchener had seen too often what happened when under-trained and badly equipped troops were thrust into action. It would be at least two years before his New Army divisions were ready to beat the Germans on the Western Front. So before then, what was the best use of them, and of any other troops that he could find?

There was the last of the good divisions that Kitchener had formed by bringing home the regular battalions from all over the empire, the 29th Division. Winston Churchill had contributed a Royal Naval Division made up of sailors and marines, and the irrepressible Churchill would be bound to get involved in the fighting somehow. In October he had led the Royal Naval Division on a brief and unsuccessful excursion to preserve Antwerp from the Germans, and had even tried to resign from the Cabinet if only Asquith would give him command of the troops there! With a Cavalry Corps of three divisions already serving with the BEF – with old Bungo in command of the new 3rd Cavalry Division, Kitchener noted – an Indian Cavalry Corps of two divisions was not going to be of much use. The Western Front would be dominated by artillery and combat engineering for the foreseeable future. So, where would cavalry be most useful?

Kitchener thought about his days as commander-in-chief in India, when Haig as his inspector general of cavalry had introduced the new tactics and methods that he and Johnny French had pioneered in Britain. Unlike any other cavalry in the world – except for the Japanese and the Americans, and they didn't matter – the cavalry of the British Empire were equipped with the same rifles as the infantry, and were trained to charge rapidly to capture a position and then hold it dismounted. Even more importantly, years of hard experience campaigning in the desert and the veldt meant that British Empire troopers knew how to keep the horses alive and fit for battle in the most unpromising terrain.

Generals, soldiers, sailors, plans – it was all starting to fit together. Britain did not even have one proper army, but now by a conjuring trick Kitchener would create two. What if he took command of the Indian Corps and Indian Cavalry Corps taken from the Western Front, plus the Indian and ANZAC infantry in Egypt, the Royal Naval Division, and the crack 29th Division? Against the weak Ottoman Turkish divisions spread thinly throughout Arabia that was the beginnings of a powerful force. For the time being, Kitchener's job in Whitehall was done. The best service he could give his country now was to resign, go back to Egypt and beat the Turks, opening up the Black Sea route to Russia. Then he could return in a year or so, in triumph as so often before, to take command in the field of his New Army divisions, which by then would be well enough trained to take on the Germans, and so win the war. But it all hinged on the amphibious landings, on the cavalry, and on Alexandretta.

Alexandretta

On the very day that Kitchener was deliberating, 18 December 1914, at Alexandretta itself events were taking place that would convince Prime Minister Asquith and the War Council of the wisdom of his plan. Frightened officials in Alexandria were informed that a British warship had been sighted out to sea just to the north of the port, and had landed an armed party of sailors. The British had torn up the rail track, isolating Alexandretta from

Constantinople, and derailed an arriving train. The officials, with their small military garrison and no warships, had hardly expected the Great European War to reach as far as them. The artillery pieces from Alexandretta's obsolete fortress had been dismounted at the war's start and sent elsewhere. The strongest Ottoman forces, the fourteen divisions of the 1st and 2nd armies, were on the European side of the Bosphorus in Thrace. They were waiting for an expected attack by Bulgaria, which had been the main enemy in the First Balkan War of 1912–13. Bulgaria had then been attacked by its own allies, Serbia and Greece, in the Second Balkan War of 1913, enabling the Ottomans to seize back Adrianople, but the threat was still there. The best quality Ottoman formation, the 5th Army, of six divisions, was guarding the southern approaches to Constantinople including the Gallipoli peninsula, in case the British or French attempted to break through the Dardanelles by sea. Constantinople's attention was fixed on the Russian Caucasus, where the 3rd Army of eleven divisions and two cavalry divisions was launching its great offensive at Sarikamis against the Russians. This was an ambitious encirclement planned along impeccable German General Staff lines, and modelled on the recent German triumph at Tannenberg in August.

By far the weakest and least well-equipped Ottoman formation was the 4th Army under Djemel Pasha (with the German Colonel Werner von Frankenberg as his Chief of Staff). This had only XII Corps of two divisions in Mesopotamia, and VIII Corps of five divisions in Palestine and Syria, mostly facing the Sinai desert. That left only 27th Division at Damascus and 23rd Division at Aleppo. The damning postwar assessment by Paul von Hindenburg (in 1914 commander of German forces in Eastern Europe) was that "The protection of the Gulf of Alexandretta was entrusted to a Turkish Army which contained scarcely a single unit fit to fight."[10]

Kitchener's eyes were drawn to Alexandretta because, along with its importance as a harbour, Alexandretta was also the hinge of Ottoman strategic communications by land between Turkey and Arabia, including Mesopotamia and the Levant. Alexandretta was the southern terminus of a minor branch of the incomplete main rail line from Constantinople. In 1914 the main line ran with some breaks through to Muslimie Junction, only a few miles north of Aleppo. At this critical junction the line divided, with one branch going south through Damascus and Amman, with a further branch through Jerusalem, and the other going east to the railhead at Ras-el-Ayn, the gateway to Mesopotamia, where far to the south the line joining Samarra and Baghdad had only just opened that year.

North of Alexandretta there were two critical gaps in the main rail line, totalling about twenty-five miles, through the Taurus and Amanus mountains, where the route was impassable to wheeled transport. Rather than negotiate the Amanus gap with pack animals, it was actually faster for travellers and supplies to be routed down the Alexandretta branch line. They would then strike out eastwards across the lower slopes of the Amanus range to the open plain, covering the sixty or so miles inland to Muslimie Junction across country. With all the gaps and problems of the line, and the bureaucracy of a diverse and dissolute empire, military reinforcements and supplies from Constantinople could take two months to reach Baghdad or Jerusalem. Enver Pasha, the Ottoman minister of war, confided to his German allies that 'My only hope is that the enemy has not discovered our weakness at this critical spot.'[11]

Enver's hope was in vain. British war plans going back to 1906 included an attack from Egypt supported by amphibious landings at Haifa or Alexandretta, accompanied by possible support from the Arab tribes. But the British understood that the greatest Ottoman fear, other than a renewed attack from the west by Bulgaria or the other Balkan states, was that the British could use their formidable command of the sea to attack Constantinople through the Dardanelles narrows. British plans before the war had considered a landing on the Gallipoli peninsula to force a passage through the Dardanelles narrows and on to Constantinople, but only as part of a much larger campaign involving several fronts.[12] Even at worst for the British, a landing at Gallipoli would provoke a strong Ottoman response, tying down more of their best troops.

The first British warship to appear off the coast at Alexandretta – the appearance on 18 December that so panicked the town's officials – was the light cruiser HMS *Doris*, one of a small naval flotilla with seaplanes based in Egypt and sent out from Alexandria to gather intelligence on the Ottoman dispositions. Next day, the *Doris* landed another shore party which drove in a Turkish patrol, blew up a railway bridge, wrecked a railway station, and cut the telegraph wires. The ship's captain also sent an ultimatum, backed by the threat of a naval bombardment from the *Doris*'s 6-in guns against which Alexandretta had no defence, that its officials should surrender all warlike stores and engines.

The Ottoman officials' surprising response was to offer to destroy the two locomotives lying within the port's radius, if the British would oblige them with the explosives and demolition experts to do so. On disembarkation of the British shore party with its gun-cotton, the torpedo-lieutenant in charge found himself faced with prevarication. 'While they were delighted to comply, their honour and that of the Ottoman Empire meant that they could not be seen to collaborate with the enemy,' the lieutenant told his shipmate E. V. Kinross. So, the officials argued, the lieutenant must not place the charges himself, and since no one else was trained or competent to do so, the thing could not be done. 'I began to feel', the lieutenant complained, 'that they might not be entirely sincere.'[13] After several hours' negotiation, the solution was found: for that one day the lieutenant must be formally transferred to the Ottoman Navy. This accomplished, Turkish cavalry rounded up the locomotives and brought them into Alexandretta, where the British party duly destroyed them, after which the *Doris* sailed away.[14]

In London, this almost incredible story was repeated as proof that the Ottoman Empire was on the verge of collapse. As the New Year began, the War Council discussed many plans for the future, and Alexandretta kept appearing as an option, particularly favoured by Churchill. On 2 January there came an appeal from the Russian government for the British to make a military demonstration of some kind against the Turks. This was the last element for Kitchener to make his plan a reality. He spoke first to the king, as was his right as a field marshal, then went to BEF headquarters and talked the matter through with French and his subordinates. Only then did he speak to Asquith, followed by Churchill.

On Wednesday 13 January, Kitchener presented his plan to the War Council. Any public concerns over his giving up the War Office would be met by returning French to his old post of Chief of the Imperial General Staff; Colonel Seeley, who had been acting as a staff officer at BEF headquarters, could also return to be Secretary of State for War. Haldane would be the real power, with Seeley as the figurehead, something to which Seeley loyally agreed as long as he could take the outward credit. Douglas Haig would take over command of the BEF, which Kitchener knew he badly wanted, and in return Kitchener wanted Smith-Dorrien and Byng together with Hamilton for Egypt. Kitchener also wanted the Indian Corps and Indian Cavalry Corps, along with the 29th Division, the 42nd (East Lancashire) Division which had already been marked for Egypt, and the Royal Naval Division. They could all reach Alexandria or Cyprus in under two months' time if the government requisitioned as troopships four big ocean liners waiting idle in British ports for want of passengers because of the risks of an Atlantic crossing in wartime: the RMS *Olympic* and the sister ships RMS *Mauritania*, RMS *Aquitania*, and RMS *Lusitania*. Supported by a substantial Royal Navy presence, led by the battleship HMS *Queen Elizabeth*, the pre-dreadnoughts

HMS *Agamemnon* and HMS *Lord Nelson*, and the battlecruiser HMS *Inflexible*, with these troops Kitchener would make his first landing at Gallipoli, followed by a second landing at Alexandretta. This would leave the Royal Navy's Grand Fleet at Scapa Flow weakened against the potential threat of the German High Seas Fleet. But Churchill was not only confident that the Royal Navy could cope, but volunteered himself to go out to Egypt as the senior government representative and Kitchener's political adviser.

There was one remaining major obstacle for Kitchener to overcome: the French. In 1912, as part of the Entente Cordiale agreements, Britain had accepted that Alexandretta and the whole of Syria were a French sphere of influence. The French were utterly opposed to any British military action that might jeopardise this agreement. On 22 January a high-ranking diplomat, François Georges-Picot, a former consul in Beirut and ardent champion of Syrian independence under French tutelage, came to London to insist that Alexandretta would be French, not British. With him was Alexandre Millerand, the French minister for war, with a further demand that all British troops should be sent to France and nowhere else. The attitude of the French commander-in-chief General Joseph Joffre was that of course British soldiers were useless when compared to his own magnificent troops, but nevertheless France demanded from the British government as many of them as possible, and quickly. As with the Royal Navy facing the High Seas Fleet, there was a real chance that weakening the BEF on the Western Front could present the Germans with the opportunity for a successful attack. But Kitchener, with both Asquith and Churchill behind him, was not to be stopped. Millerand and Joffre huffed and puffed, but at last accepted the situation. Georges-Picot's deep suspicions were partly allayed by the undertaking that, when captured, Alexandretta would be placed under French control. To protect their own interests, and to keep an eye on the British so that there should be no misunderstanding between allies, the French agreed to provide for the venture a corps of two infantry divisions, the Corps Expéditionnaire d'Orient or CEO, together with a substantial fleet of transports and warships, including some pre-dreadnoughts.

From Gallipoli to Aleppo

The timing of the War Council's agreement on Kitchener's plan on 13 January could not have been better. Within days, news had reached London that the ambitious Ottoman 3rd Army envelopment of the Russians at Sarakamis had fallen apart in the winter snows and been heavily defeated. On 4 February an attack by the Ottoman VIII Corps on the Suez Canal line was also crushingly defeated by 10th and 11th Indian divisions and fell back through the Sinai to Gaza. This episode convinced Kitchener that the Suez Canal was safe, and that he could use his troops gathering in Egypt for the planned landings, starting with Gallipoli. On 18 February the combined British and French fleet began a bombardment of the Turkish forts on the Gallipoli peninsula, in the expectation that this would reinforce the Ottoman perception that the Allies planned to force their way through the Dardanelles.

While Kitchener with Churchill's help gathered his forces at Alexandria, Sir John French in Whitehall made sure that all ran smoothly, with Haldane's help behind the scenes. Asquith's government confidently rejected in March a Russian demand that Constantinople should be handed over to them when it was captured. Asquith also had confidence in Haig as the new BEF commander. Lacking the Indian Corps, Haig cancelled a proposed attack by the BEF at Neuve Chapelle in support of a French attack on Vimy Ridge. Well known for his stubbornness, Haig was adamant that no British attack would take place against the Germans until his arriving Territorial Force and New Army divisions were quite ready, probably in the early autumn.

Joffre was furious once more, although slightly mollified when on 22 April the expected German counterattack came at Ypres, including the first large-scale use of poison gas on the Western Front. A much stronger and better-prepared BEF helped the French inflict a severe defeat on the Germans, driving them back as far as the otherwise unimportant village of Passchendaele. On the same day, Russian forces captured the key town of Przemysl from the Austro-Hungarians on the Eastern Front, and began a major offensive in the Caucasus. In Mesopotamia, in the 'miracle of Shaiba', the 6th (Poona) Division, now under the newly arrived Lieutenant General Sir John Nixon, shattered a counterattack by the Turkish 35th Division aimed at driving them back into the sea. Everything seemed to be swinging the Allies' way.

Meanwhile, on the docks and in the harbour of Alexandria, all was chaos as Kitchener and his staffs worked to prepare their landing forces. With the naval bombardment of the Gallipoli forts already in progress, Hamilton was alarmed to find crates and boxes stencilled 'Constantinople Expeditionary Force'. Kitchener let the blunder stand; knowing that he could not keep the presence of his forces secret, he chose the other option by intentionally letting the Turks and the whole world know where he would attack and why.

Across the southern Mediterranean and the Levant, and as far away as India and South Africa, the call went out that K of K needed ships and craft of all descriptions to come to Alexandria, to sail under the protection of the Royal Navy, and to be paid in gold. 'Kitchener from the Mediterranean and Egypt,' Haig commented with rueful admiration, 'Wherever he is, by his masterful action he will give that sphere of operations undue prominence in the strategical picture.'[15]

On Sunday 25 April, with both Kitchener and Hamilton watching from warships, Smith-Dorrien led the landing boats of the Constantinople Expeditionary Force ashore at Gallipoli into a lethal hail of well-prepared Turkish fire. The 29th Division landed at the southern tip of the Gallipoli peninsula on designated beaches that were barely more than cliff-faces, the 1st Lancashire Fusiliers famously winning 'six VCs before breakfast' in the face of murderous fire. 'The trenches on the right raked us and those above us raked our right,' recalled one officer of the battalion, 'while trenches and machine guns fired straight down the valley. The noise was ghastly and the sights horrible.'[16]

Meanwhile, the Royal Naval Division made a brief diversionary landing to the north before re-embarking and joining in the real landings. Between this and the 29th Division beaches, the ANZAC divisions landed at what later became equally legendary as 'Anzac Cove'. The French 1st Division of the CEO landed on the mainland to the east of the Dardanelles narrows. In a matter of hours, in the gullies and crags of the peninsula, the entire landing force had been pinned down only a few miles inland by a brave and resolute Turkish defence. It was grim war, but the continuing threat to Constantinople was enough for Kitchener for now, holding the Ottoman 5th Army in its place; the British had never intended this to be anything more than part of a larger strategy. There had been hopes that Gallipoli by itself would be enough to prompt intervention by other countries, but as Hamilton – who had exhorted the Australians to 'Dig, dig, dig until you are safe!' – noted with disgust in his diary, 'The landing has been made but the Balkans fold their arms, the Italians show no interest, the Russians do not move an inch to get across the Black Sea.'[17]

Leaving Smith-Dorrien to manage the fight at Gallipoli, Kitchener and Hamilton returned to Egypt to ready the first wave of the Alexandretta Expeditionary Force (AEF). This now consisted of the two divisions of the Indian Corps, the 42nd (East Lancashire) Division, and the 2nd Division of the CEO, plus the 2nd Mounted Division from the Territorial Force, renamed the Yeomanry Division on its arrival in Cyprus. For the Allies, the strategic timing was now critical, including the few weeks remaining before the onset of the blistering heat of the full Arabian summer.

To emphasise the fragility of the brief Allied advantage, at the start of May a great German offensive at Gorlice-Tarnow drove the Russians back on the Eastern Front. But against the Ottoman Empire the story was different. The Russians scored a further success in the Caucasus, while Nixon resumed his advance up the Tigris, forcing the two weak Turkish divisions back. On 19 May a substantial Ottoman counterattack at Gallipoli, meant to sweep Smith-Dorrien's troops off the peninsula, was heavily defeated. Italy, more impressed than Hamilton realised, had signed a secret treaty to enter the war on the Allied side at the end of the month.

On Friday 14 May the War Council met and gave formal approval to the second phase of Kitchener's strategy, including the dispatch by the ocean liner fleet of six further infantry divisions, three of the Territorial Force and three of the New Army.[18] In fact sending these divisions was a bluff: they were still very raw, badly under-equipped, and would be unfit for combat for some months. But what leaked to the Turks was the dispatch of a powerful British strategic reserve assembling at Alexandria, threatening to reinforce either Maxwell or Smith-Dorrien. The result was to pin both 5th Army at Gallipoli and VIII Corps facing the Sinai in place. By now, rumours of Kitchener's intentions were flying around London. The chief military correspondent of *The Times* noted privately, 'I hear of mad schemes for him joining Nixon via Damascus and plunging into the centre of Asia Minor.'[19]

The Times's information was almost correct. On Sunday 23 May, the very day that Italy entered the war on the Allied side, troops of the 42nd (East Lancashire) Division rowed ashore to start an unopposed landing just north of Alexandretta. A delighted Churchill pointed out to all he could that it was also the anniversary of his ancestor the Duke of Marlborough's victory at the Battle of Ramilies. The local authorities promptly surrendered to the British, who equally promptly handed the town except for its port facilities over to the French under Georges-Picot.

Three days later Maxwell's 10th and 11th Indian divisions arrived to threaten Gaza unexpectedly from across the Sinai, and started to shell the Turkish positions. In Mesopotamia the Turkish XII Corps was already retreating before the 6th (Poona) Division, which reached Amara on 3 June. With their 3rd Army barely holding the Russians in the Caucasus, their 5th Army defending Gallipoli, and their 1st and 2nd armies facing an increasingly hostile and confident Bulgaria and Greece, there was no military response that the Ottomans could make. The 27th Division at Damascus was rushed north by rail to help the 23rd Division defend Aleppo. But it was more than two weeks after the first British landings that both divisions started a tentative advance towards Alexandretta. They found a well-prepared defence by the Indian Corps and 2nd Division of the CEO, dug in along the lower ridges of the Amanus mountain range that protected Alexandretta to the east, their fire augmented by artillery and offshore naval gunfire, including the 15-in guns of HMS *Queen Elizabeth*. The Battle of Alexandretta, fought on Friday 18 June (the anniversary of Waterloo, as Churchill politely explained to Georges-Picot in his terrible French) was a one-sided massacre.

The Ottoman defeat acted as a signal to the Arab leaders, with whom Kitchener had kept in close contact. Across the peninsula a major revolt began, with Bedouin horsemen raiding out of the desert, hitting supply routes and the rail lines from Aqaba to Amman, and from Samarra to Baghdad. Meanwhile, at Alexandretta harbour and across the nearby beaches, the frantic unloading of the second wave of the AEF continued, using anything that could float and carry horses and men.

None too soon, by 28 June, what was now named the Desert Mounted Corps under Major General Julian Byng was ready to begin its advance: the 1st and 2nd Indian cavalry divisions, the ANZAC Mounted Division, the Yeomanry Division, and the composite 1st Spahi Regiment as a token French contribution. Byng had forty thousand horsemen with just over sixty miles to cover, against the few reserves that the Ottoman VIII Corps could assemble, between them and Aleppo. 'A remarkable sight,' enthused one British regimental commander, 'ninety-four squadrons, all hurrying forward relentlessly on a decisive mission – a mission of which all cavalry soldiers have dreamed.'[20]

It was a wild ride, in which the cavalry's horses far outdistanced their artillery and supply vehicles. The Australians were particularly impressed by the Indian lancers' method of 'harpooning' enemy infantry with a single thrust as they rode past. Although some Ottoman battalions or batteries put up a brief resistance, most broke and ran. On 1 July, the first Indian troopers clattered through the streets of Aleppo, and within two days Byng's soldiers were holding the town and its environs in a solid dismounted perimeter, with the Australians and New Zealanders sitting on Muslimie Junction. A week later, to the astonishment of the tiny local garrison, the Yeomanry Division, who had followed the rail line eastwards, arrived at Ras-el-Ayn. When next morning, Friday 9 July, Kitchener entered Aleppo in triumph, Arabia was lost to the Ottoman Empire forever.

Hamilton's already great admiration for Kitchener overflowed at this astonishing feat of arms. 'He is the idol of England, and take him all in all, the biggest figure in the world,' he wrote.[21] Hindenburg added his own praise for Kitchener's identification of 'this critical weakness at the Gulf of Alexandretta', adding that, 'If ever there was a prospect of a brilliant strategic feat, it was here,' in a campaign that 'made an enormous impression on the whole world, and unquestionably [had] a far-reaching effect on our Turkish Ally'.[22]

Kitchener's victory certainly helped the Allied cause with Bulgaria, Greece, and other neutral Balkan countries that were wavering in their choice of sides, and did much to hearten hard-pressed Serbia. But in truth, with the fall of Aleppo, Kitchener's campaign had shot its bolt. The same mountains and ramshackle rail system that prevented the Turks reinforcing Arabia also posed massive difficulties for any proposed Allied offensive northwards, while neither the British nor the French had any interest in dismembering Turkey itself. The Anglo-French landing at Gallipoli could achieve nothing without other countries joining in, and was a strategic dead end.

The critical issue now was whether the Turkish government, facing the strong possibility of an imminent attack by Bulgaria and Greece as well as Russia, would decide to cut its losses while it still could. Any peace with the Allies would mean the Ottoman Empire accepting the loss of Arabia, and the opening of the Black Sea route to Russia, allowing the British and French to concentrate their forces within Europe, against Germany and Austria-Hungary. The world now well knows the decisions taken in Constantinople in June 1915, and their consequences down to the present day.

The Reality

This account follows the informal rules and conventions of accurate counterfactual history as developed since just after the First World War, and which I have helped codify.[23] The modern name for Alexandretta is Iskenderun, lying in Turkey close to the Syrian border.

Quotations from real people are all genuine, including the views of Kitchener, T. E. Lawrence ('of Arabia'), Haig, and Hamilton, although in some cases the dates and the context have been changed. The assessments of the vulnerability of Alexandretta from Enver Pasha and Hindenburg appear in Hindenburg's postwar memoirs. François Georges-Picot was the leading French opponent of British involvement in Alexandretta and Syria, although he did not accompany Millerand to London on 22 January; he was later one of the authors of the Sykes-Picot Agreement on the future of Arabia. Of others mentioned in passing or in the end-notes, Francis Aylmer ('Frank') Maxwell, nicknamed 'The Brat', was a prominent ADC to Kitchener earlier in his career, but by the First World War he had moved on and held various field commands, being killed in action as a brigadier general in 1917. Colonel J. E. B. 'Galloper Jack' Seeley, Secretary of State for War 1912–14, was a highly controversial figure, but it is likely that he would have agreed to serve again as a figurehead for Haldane. In reality, after serving at BEF headquarters he commanded the Canadian cavalry brigade on the Western Front 1915–18. Sidney Reilly (not his real name) was a legendary British spy of the period, but had no direct connection to Kitchener or to the Ottoman Empire. Captain E. V. Kinross and HMS *Torrin* are famously fictional.

A British landing at Alexandretta was debated and rejected in London over the winter of 1914–15 because of strong French political opposition, the risks to the Western Front and the Grand Fleet as described, and the shortage of available trained troops. The idea remained a British strategic option up to the end of the war. Real events up to early 1915 took place as described, including the comic-opera raid on Alexandretta by HMS *Doris*. But Kitchener gave up his position as consul general in Egypt in January 1915, and the various command changes described, which would have greatly improved the British management of the war, are fiction.

The War Council of 13 January 1915 approved a purely naval bombardment of the Dardanelles forts, so starting the real and disastrous Dardanelles campaign. The naval bombardment began on 18 February and the Gallipoli landings, commanded by Ian Hamilton, began on 25 April. The *Lusitania* was sunk on 7 May while making a commercial passenger crossing of the Atlantic, but the other liners mentioned were all used as troopships to help transport the raw British reinforcement divisions to Gallipoli between June and August. The British made a number of premature and unsuccessful attacks on the Western Front in 1915, starting with Neuve Chapelle on 10 March. Kitchener died when the armoured cruiser HMS *Hampshire*, on which he was travelling to Russia, sank in the North Atlantic on 5 June 1916.

What was briefly known as the Constantinople Expeditionary Force was rapidly renamed the Mediterranean Expeditionary Force, or MEF, otherwise its forces for the historical landing at Gallipoli are given correctly. The forces potentially available to create the Alexandretta Expeditionary Force are also historically accurate. The Indian Corps remained on the Western Front until late 1915, and the Indian Cavalry Corps remained there until early 1918, when its troops were sent to Egypt to join the real Desert Mounted Corps. The composite French 1st Spahi Regiment was also attached to the Desert Mounted Corps in 1918, for political reasons.

What actual decision the government in Constantinople would have taken in June 1915, faced with this fictional scenario, is beyond my ability or willingness to guess.

Notes

1 For many of the details of Kitchener's thinking and planning at this time, see the vivid account by his long-serving senior ADC, *Frank Maxwell, *Twenty Years a Brat* (Edinburgh: Blackwells, 1922).

2 For Kitchener's spy network and its exploits see *Sidney Reilly, *Dust and Ashes: A Life in Espionage* (New York: Citizen Cain Press, 1930) pp. 201–62, and of course *T. E. Lawrence, *The Last Pillar of Wisdom* (Oxford: Oxford University Press, 1926).

3 6th (Poona) Division, like the 11th Indian Division and the 12th Indian Division, was an infantry division of the Indian Army, structured in 1914, like all such divisions of the Indian Army under British rule with three infantry brigades each of three Indian battalions with British officers, and one British Army battalion, plus artillery and additional troops who might be either Indian or British.

4 Quoted in James Barr, *A Line in the Sand: Britain, France and the Struggle that Shaped the Middle East* (London: Simon and Schuster, 2011), p. 15.

5 Quoted in George H. Cassar, *Kitchener's War: British Strategy from 1914 to 1916* (Washington, DC: Brassey's, 2004)', p. 50.

6 The 'Curragh Mutiny' of April 1914 was a real event as described, but any explanation (assuming one is even possible) is outside the scope of this narrative; see Ian F. W. Beckett, *The Army and the Curragh Incident 1914* (London: Bodley Head, 1986).

7 For the British Army reforms under R. B. Haldane (later Lord Haldane) as Secretary of State for War, 1906–12 that created the British Expeditionary Force (BEF) and the Territorial Force (unofficially known as the Territorial Army, which became its official name in 1922) see Edward M. Spiers, *Haldane: An Army Reformer* (Edinburgh: Edinburgh University Press, 1980). The

BEF was composed of six infantry divisions and a cavalry division, and was Britain's field army, capable of deploying to Europe or almost anywhere else in the world. The Territorial Force was a reformed part-time volunteer militia intended chiefly for home defence but which in 1914 was asked to volunteer for overseas service.

8 *Paramjit Singh, *The Sikhs in the Great War*, trans. Martin Wright (Delhi: Congress Press, 1922), p. 31.

9 Quoted in John Terraine, *The First World War 1914–18* (London: Papermac, 1984), p. 60.

10 Marshal Paul von Hindenburg, *Out of My Life* (London: Cassell, 1920), p. 294.

11 Quoted in Hindenburg, *Out of My Life*, p. 294.

12 See Yigal Sheffy, *British Military Intelligence in the Palestine Campaign 1914–1918* (London: Frank Cass, 1998), pp. 23–6.

13 *Quoted in Captain E. V. Kinross, *From HMS Doris to HMS Torrin: My Service in Both World Wars* (London: Jonathan Cape, 1945) p. 81.

14 This account is based on C. F. Aspinall-Oglander, *Military Operations: Gallipoli Volume 1: History of the Great War based on Official Documents* (London: HMSO, 1929), p. 53.

15 Gary Sheffield and John Bourne (eds), *Douglas Haig: War Diaries and Letters 1914–1918* (London: Weidenfeld & Nicolson, 2005), p. 170.

16 Captain Harold Clayton, 1st Lancashire Fusiliers, quoted in Peter Hart, *Gallipoli* (London: Profile, 2011), p. 135.

17 General Sir Ian Hamilton, *Gallipoli Diary Volume 1* (London: Dodo Press, 2010), p. 159.

18 The infantry divisions were 52nd (Lowland) Division, 53rd (Welsh) Division and 54th (East Anglian) Division from the Territorial Force, plus 10th (Irish) Division, 11th (Northern) Division and 13th (Western) Division from the K-1 contingent of the New Army.

19 Letter from Charles Repington to Andrew Bonar Law, reproduced in J. A. Morris (ed.), *The Letters of Lieutenant Colonel Charles à Court Repington* (London: Sutton, 1999), p. 244.

20 Quoted in David R. Woodward, *Hell in the Holy Land: World War I in the Middle East* (Lexington: University Press of Kentucky, 2006), p. 195.

21 Hamilton, *Gallipoli Diary Volume 1*, p. 161; ironically Hamilton was Scots, and Kitchener had been born in Ireland, but the use of 'England' in this way was usual for the time.

22 Hindenburg, *Out of My Life*, p. 295.

23 See Stephen Badsey, 'If It Had Happened Otherwise: First World War Exceptionalism in Counterfactual History', in Jessica Meyer (ed.), *British Popular Culture and the First World War* (London: Brill, 2008), pp. 351–68.

4

The Queen of Cities Beckons

Peter G. Tsouras

Phocaea (Φώκαια), on the coast of Anatolia, 18 June 1914

Three-thousand-year-old Phocaea was dead. This Greek city in the Ottoman region of Smyrna lay silent save for the last of the looting Turks. Here and there houses burned, others lay smashed, belongings strewn through the street amid the bloating corpses.[1]

A week before, Charles Manciet, a French archaeologist, had been working out of this prosperous town. He was especially happy to be here because ancient Phocaea had founded his own home, Marseille (Massalia), in 600 BC, making it the oldest city in France. The affection between colony and mother city was ancient: in 132 BC the Massalians had successfully pleaded with the Romans not to destroy their mother city. Now sons of Marseille would again be on hand when disaster arrived.

On the 11 June panicked Greeks from surrounding villages came streaming into Phocaea desperate to escape by sea from the marauding bands of Turks that had sacked their homes. The next day these bands descended upon Phocaea, beginning seventy-two hours of looting, wanton destruction, and murder. The local police stood aside but acceded to Manciet's demand, and that of three other Frenchmen, to put guards on their homes as they ran up the tricolour of the French Republic. The four Frenchmen were able to shelter nine hundred Phocaeans from the horror, a small replay of 132 BC. By the end of the week, Manciet would write,

> We read . . . that order had been established, and that, in the regions of
> which we speak, the Christians have nothing further to fear, neither for

themselves, nor for their possessions. This is not a vain statement. Order reigns, for nobody is left. The possessions have nothing further to fear, for they are all in good hands – those of the robbers.[2]

This atrocity was no breakdown of law and order. It was official policy of the Ottoman government, and orders came directly from the highest authorities in Constantinople. A nationalist coup had overthrown the sultan in 1908, led by the *Genç Türkler* (Young Turks), whose political arm was the Committee of Union and Progress (CUP). They had drunk in the ideas of their German friends on ethnic purity and concluded that the Turkish people could never realise their potential if the Anatolian heartland of the Turks was also home to many millions of minorities, primarily Christian Greeks, Armenians, and Assyrians (Arab Christians). They were seen as a disloyal element that would stab the Turks in the back when the inevitable pan-European war began. The Turks had to strike now to both eliminate that threat and to purify Turkey. Phocaea was not alone. All throughout Anatolia similar acts had begun, especially along the Aegean and Black Sea coasts where the Greeks were most numerous and in some areas, an outright majority. The young men were separated out, put into labour battalions, and worked to death. Their families were sent on death marches into the interior. The weak and the elderly perished in the heat, whilst children and young women were sold into slavery and forced to convert to Islam.[3]

There were deeper reasons for the violence. The greater energy, ambition, technical knowledge, and education of their Christian subjects served as a constant reproach to the Turks. One Ottoman general put it into words when he said that they felt this land would never be truly theirs as long as a single Greek tavern remained on the docks at Smyrna.

Villa Ariadne, Knossos, Crete, 23 July 1914

The black car stopped by the shaded stone wall covered with blue and white morning glories, the Greek national colours. The man who got out from the back seat was pleased at the sight, a good omen, he thought. Eleftherios Venizelos, the prime minister of Greece, had been called back to Athens by the king, but he wanted to pay his respects to Sir Arthur Evans, the owner of Villa Ariadne, before he departed. Evans was the great English archaeologist who had revealed the splendour of Minoan Crete to a delighted world. That discovery had been a gift of added pride to the people of Crete, whom the other Greeks might say had enough pride already. They were a people sensitive about their honour and good with any weapon, particularly cold steel – not a good combination for the ill-mannered or the enemy. That Venizelos was a native of Crete himself made Evans dearer to his heart. With war looming in Europe, he was allowing himself a brief indulgence to see Evans.[4]

Evans was waiting for him in the garden with its young palms and pines and a headless statue of the Emperor Hadrian sulking in forgotten and slighted splendour. Evans had built the villa in 1906 to be his home and headquarters while he excavated right next door the great ruins of Knossos: the labyrinth of the Minotaur, the House of the Double Axe, the palace of Minos himself, first creator of the rule of the sea, the fabled thalassocracy. You could feel the history here in your bones, and if you were a Cretan, it ran deeper than your marrow and plumbed the soul.

Evans did not grudge the time from his work. Venizelos had been a generous patron, both of his pocket and the government's. 'It is an unexpected honour.' Not so unexpected, for his staff had already set the table under a pine with coffee and the inevitable honey-drenched pastries; the bees of Crete were generous with their golden bounty. They sat for a while, listening to the last songs of the nightingales, and chatted about the digs.

Venizelos put down his cup, and said, 'I expect you'll be staying in England because of the war. It will be a pity to see the work here suspended.'

Evans's head jerked up as he spilled his coffee. 'War, what war?'

'The great European war that is coming, my dear professor.'

'I cannot believe it will come to that. Cooler heads will prevail, surely.'

'Professor, I think the occupants of the palace', he nodded off towards the ruins, 'may have thought the same thing. Did you not find evidence of a great conflagration, the giant pithos jars in the basement magazines roaring from the burning olive oil in them, millions of litres you estimated? And it came in spring when a strong south wind would blow the flames almost horizontally. That is where the deepest scorch stains were, if I remember.'

'Yes, yes, but that was long, long ago.'

'Indeed, a long time ago, but the constant we are dealing with is human nature. It has not changed. There are men in the chanceries of Europe who value other things more than peace, I fear. I can see it all now. The Austrians are bent on destroying Serbia; the murder of the archduke was only an excuse. Because of some territorial greed, the alliance system will drag all of Europe into war.'

In office only three years, Venizelos already had a respected reputation in European diplomacy. He had been a leading force in the liberation of Crete from Ottoman rule, which had propelled him into office as prime minister by an overwhelming vote in the parliament. He was a great liberal, pushing through laws that would bring Greece into the modern world and improve the lives of the people. His party had been overwhelming elected, especially in those areas of northern Greece that the Greek Army had liberated from the Turks and Bulgarians in the Balkan Wars of 1912–13. He had been the engineer of the Balkan League of Greece, Serbia, Montenegro, and Bulgaria that had crushed the Ottoman armies on every front and tore from the Sublime Porte almost all of its remaining territory in Europe. All of these Balkan peoples had bitter memories of the almost four hundred years they had suffered under the Turkokratia. Aggrieved at obtaining less than it thought it deserved, Bulgaria had subsequently attacked its former allies and was severely drubbed in the Second Balkan War. The Greeks were reminded of their old saying that the devil was a Bulgarian. Even so, Bulgaria retained a strip of coastline on the Aegean Sea bounded on the west by the Nestorios River from Greece and on the Evros from Turkey.

Greece had doubled its territory and population in the wars, and Venizelos was a national hero. Of course, he had had a serious confrontation with Crown Prince Constantine, commander of the Army of Thessaly. The prince wanted to strike the main Turkish force further west, but Venizelos had to order him to seize Thessaloniki, the second city of the Ottoman Empire that the Turks, led by Sultan Murad II, had conquered from their ancestors in 1430.[5] It was the economic centre of Macedonia, the real prize of the war. Luckily the prince followed orders promptly because the Bulgarians arrived to their most bitter disappointment one day after the Greeks. Constantine had become king when his father, King George I, was assassinated as he rode through the city.

Venizelos's great ambition was the redeeming of all the Greek lands and people still under foreign rule. There were priorities: the Italians ruled the Dodecanese Islands, and Britain had Cyprus, which it had appropriated as its price for saving the Turks in the Crimean War. These were benign conditions, however, compared to the condition of those three and half million Greeks still under Turkish rule, mostly in Anatolia along the Aegean and Black Sea coasts and in Eastern Thrace. That population almost equalled that of the Greek state itself. For three thousand years their ancestors had lived there. And it was there that the classical civilisation first flowered. It was intolerable for every Greek that these lands remained unredeemed. That redemption was embodied in the concept of the *Megali Idea* or 'Great Idea', the gathering in of the Greek lands into a neo-Byzantine state surrounding the Aegean. Of this, Venizelos was the most eloquent and passionate champion.

Within the *Megali Idea*, though, was the great dream of planting the cross once more on the dome of the Hagia Sofia (Holy Wisdom) Cathedral in Constantinople. Mehmet the conqueror had ridden into it, his horse's fetlocks soaked in blood, to order its conversion into a mosque. The loss to the Greeks of their God-guarded 'Queen of Cities', the focus of a thousand years of imperial glory, had been a wound to the heart that would not stop bleeding. Its fall on Tuesday 29 May 1453 had made Tuesdays such bad luck that Greeks tried to avoid any serious business on that day. Laments on the fall of the city had filled Greek folk music.

> They took the City, they took Salonica
> They took St Sofia, too, the great monastery
> Which has 300 semandra and 62 bells
> For each bell a priest, for each priest a deacon.
>
> A dove came from heaven: Stop the
> Cherubic, and lower the Sacred Vessels,
> Priests, take the Sacramental and you candles blow out.
> For it is the will of God the City should fall to the Turks.
>
> Our Lady was disturbed and the icons tearful.
> Hush, Our Lady and you, icons weep not,
> With the passing of years and in time she'll be yours again.[6]

Yet there was more than dreams to its redemption. As in the days of Byzantium, its location brought power by controlling the connection between the Black Sea and the Mediterranean. It was where Asia and Europe met. Its possession would make the Greeks a power to be reckoned with.

All of this Evans knew, but Venizelos did not speak of it now as he bid the Englishman goodbye. But it was constantly on his mind. He was haunted by the line, 'With the passing of years and in time she'll be yours again.' Destiny seemed to call. Had he not played the vital role for his own native Crete and the doubling of the *patritha*, the fatherland, in 1912–13? Like a great statesman, he thought many moves ahead. The coming war would be the godfather of the redemption.

The Royal Palace, Herodou Attikou Street, Athens, 28 July 1914

Venizelos was on his way to the palace for the audience he had requested. Although he was head of the government, the king had enormous influence on policy. For the Cretan, this just made life difficult. He mulled over the contradiction posed by the royal family – the royals were essentially Germans. They had never married into the native Greek people, though they had become devoutly Greek Orthodox in religion. They found their brides in Germany or Russia. Constantine had been trained as a soldier in Germany and held a marshal's baton in the German Army; George, the Crown Prince, had actually served as a German officer for a while. Yet the family spoke English among themselves and had a decided Anglo orientation. Although the public thought the king's German wife pulled him towards Germany, she was more favourable to Britain. She was the sister of the Kaiser, but she was also the daughter of Queen Victoria's daughter Victoria and her mother had instilled in her very British attitudes to fair play and common decency. She was also not on speaking terms with her brother, who had made it known how unhappy he was that she had converted to Greek Orthodoxy without his permission. She actually got along much better with Britain's George V and Russia's Nicholas II.[7]

The king was stunned as Venizelos laid out in detail the intelligence reports of the widening horrors radiating out from the Smyrna region. Particularly graphic were the reports of survivors of Phocaea. Most damning of all were the eyewitness reports of resident Westerners – the Frenchman Manciet, the American consul in Smyrna, as well as reports from some of Queen Sophia's own German relatives. Berlin knew what was going on and was appalled, though not enough to question their close military relationship with the Ottomans. Yet Constantine recoiled at the thought of Greece going to war alone against the Ottoman Empire. It was one thing to do so when Greece was part of a larger alliance, with the Ottoman Army not as well trained and armed by the Germans as it was now. It was another thing to go it alone.

Venizelos said, 'When you led the Army of Thessaly into the invasion of Ottoman territory in Macedonia, you issued the general order that the army would fight a knightly, chivalrous war. How long did that last, Your Majesty? How many massacred Greek villages did you have to ride through before you rescinded that order with another – "Kill them all!" You could not have restrained our men had you tried. It is a hundred, no a thousand times worse now. Greek people are being slaughtered like sheep.'

'It would be suicide, prime minister, to go to war alone, and we would not help our people across the Aegean.'

'Then, Your Majesty, we must have allies. We have talked about the consequences of the murder of the archduke. General war is coming. We must attach ourselves to whatever side will help us redeem the lands in Asia Minor.'[8]

Constantine added, 'I have just received a telegram from the Kaiser asking my intentions should war break out. The man is endlessly tactless as well as indiscreet and stated that Germany had secret treaties with Bulgaria and the Ottomans. If Greece did not join Germany, she would be treated as an enemy.'

Clearly that angered the king. While he thought Germany was the greater power, he said, 'I have replied that Greece will remain neutral.'[9] The king was working himself up. He said:

It is extraordinary. Does [the Kaiser] take me for a German? And, because he has given me a German Field-Marshal's baton, does he imagine that I am under obligation towards him? If that is so, I am ready to return the baton at any time. Besides, he seems to forget his geography and that Greece, twenty-four hours after she had declared herself Germany's ally, would be reduced to cinders by the Allied fleet. What folly! Whoever heard of such things? No. We are Greeks, and the interests of Greece must come first. For the present, at any rate, it is imperative that we should remain neutral. But as to joining Germany, such an eventuality is and always will be an impossibility.[10]

This was not what Venizelos wanted to hear. Neutrality was not compatible with the golden opportunities that beckoned to fulfil the Great Idea. He would see what he could arrange. The enemies of Germany might be able to offer a great deal for Greece's help. Might that entice the king? It would take a certain amount of manipulation to bring the king around, and Venizelos would not scruple at the means. Already the horrors of Phocaea had been leaked to the press. That would ignite an incandescent fire storm of public opinion. His party also whispered maliciously that Queen Sophia was pushing her husband towards Germany. Venizelos just hoped that it wouldn't burn out before his plans came together. Still the king was adamant: Greece would remain neutral.

If the Price is Right

As the Battle of the Marne hung in doubt, Venizelos moved without the king's approval to assure the Allies that Greece would support them if Turkey entered the war on Germany's side as long as they could guarantee the neutrality of Bulgaria. The timing of his assurance meant that he wanted it known that Greece stood by them even in their darkest hour. To his surprise, the Allies refused. British Prime Minister Asquith stated that the Allies did not want to extend the war to areas still at peace. Venizelos fumed. Did they not understand that there were secret treaties that would bring the Ottoman Empire and Bulgaria into the war as German allies?

There matters stood until the Turks did Venizelos an extraordinary favour. They joined the war as a German ally in November. The British soon thereafter bombarded the forts at the mouth of the Dardanelles. Venizelos had not just fallen off the olive cart: the meaning was clear that the British were going to force the straits and take Constantinople. He wondered why they had so foolishly showed their hand. Nevertheless he was delighted when the British requested that Greek liaison officers be sent to Malta, where the operation was being planned. The Greek officers pointed out the difficulty of overrunning the narrow and rocky Gallipoli peninsula. The British ignored them. How could one take Turks seriously?

Nevertheless, things started to look up for Venizelos's plans. British Foreign Secretary Grey pledged that if Greece entered the war against the Central Powers, Britain would immediately cede Cyprus and actively support a Greek expedition to land at Smyrna. Without consulting the king, and he was not obliged to do so as head of the government, he offered an army corps of three divisions as well as the Greek fleet to support the upcoming Gallipoli operation. He presented this as a *fait accompli* to the king and laid out all his arguments in forceful and compelling terms. Finally he reminded him of the ancient prophecy that was being spoken of everywhere throughout the kingdom – that Constantinople was founded by a Constantine, was lost by a Constantine, and would be redeemed by a Constantine. He was referring to Constantine the Great who had built the city and Constantine XI, the martyred emperor, who had died in its defence. 'Your Majesty, the role of Constantine XII is yours if you will play it.' Constantine was clearly moved and could only say, 'Very well then, in God's name.'[11]

Venizelos's triumph was immediately spoiled when he exited the king's presence only to find that Major General Ioannis Metaxas, the acting Chief of the General Staff, was waiting there to tell him that he was resigning because he would have no part in the prime minister's hare-brained schemes. Metaxas was a known Germanophile from his military training in that country. The king again wavered and called a royal council to lay the matter before it. The council voted against Venizelos, who then resigned on 6 March. In his place, Constantine appointed the pro-German Dimitri Gounaris.

The Miracle-Working Icon

The strain was so great upon Constantine that his health collapsed, and he was prostrated with pleurisy and pneumonia. He hovered near death for two weeks as huge crowds gathered outside the palace.

> A warship was sent to Tinos to bring the miraculous holy icon of the Virgin and Child from the shrine of Panayia Evanghelistria to the royal sickroom. Thousands of other sick people had been cured by it before, and perhaps it would do the same for the apparently dying King. By the time it was brought to him, he had already been given the last rites. With his ebbing strength, he venerated the sacred image and fell into unconsciousness. Late that same evening he rallied. The icon remained beside his bed, until he was pronounced out of danger a week later.[12]

> Venizelos received a summons to the palace. He was ushered into the king's bedchamber. Constantine thanked him warmly and asked him to sit. 'I have asked you here to tell you how deeply wrong I have been. While I hovered near death, there came to me a vision of the Panayia. She said, 'It is time you restored me to my City. Then she put her hand on my brow and I felt a deep peace come over me. She showed me the cross upon which the word "Nika" glowed in gold.' Venizelos looked wide-eyed at the icon next to the king's bed and crossed himself. He would light a candle at the nearest church on the way home.[13]

That day both Gouranis and Metaxas were dismissed as the king asked Venizelos to form a government. He made a formal offer to the British of a Greek corps and the Greek fleet to aid in the Gallipoli operation. Staff talks had already been going on in Alexandria since December with the headquarters of the Allied expeditionary force being assembled in Egypt. The Greeks had made it known immediately that attempting to fight up the rocky, narrow Gallipoli peninsula was asking for trouble. As tactfully as they could, they pointed out that the British naval bombardment the previous November had alerted the Turks to the landings and they were rushing in troops and building fortifications. The peninsula was already heavily fortified because of the Greek threat during the Balkan Wars. Greek analysis placed 35,000 men in the garrison with another 25,000 from the Turkish III Corps able to quickly reinforce it. The III Corps, commanded by the much-respected Estat Pasha, had the finest reputation in the Ottoman Army and was the only corps not to shatter in the Balkan Wars. One of the Greek officers said that he fought Estat Pasha at the siege of Ionnina and that the man knew trench warfare. 'He is an adversary worthy of respect.'[14]

They also pointed out that the powerful Ottoman 1st Army of eight divisions was stationed in Eastern Thrace, the European hinterland of Constantinople, primarily to defend against the Bulgarians.[15] If Bulgaria joined the Central Powers, that large force would pour reserves into the battle for the Gallipoli peninsula.

Ottoman 1st Army[16]

I Corps
   1st Division, 2nd Division
II Corps
   4th Division, 5th Division, 6th Division
IV Corps
   10th Division, 12th Division
20th Division
1st Cavalry Brigade

A Greek colonel stated, 'Thus, you will fight your way slowly uphill on a narrow front where you cannot manoeuvre. All the advantages are with the defender. He can constantly replace his losses from 1st Army. He has grabbed you by the belt and immobilised you.' At the back of the briefing room, a small, slight, blond lieutenant named Lawrence had been paying keen attention.[17] The captain sitting next to him was equally attentive. But unlike Lawrence, Captain Richard Meinertzhagen, seconded from the Indian Army, was a huge, broad-shouldered man. He radiated lethality like a Bengal tiger. Where other officers might carry some sort of stick, he toyed with a knobkerrie, a native southern African weapon. It had a handle like a mace but the end was a solid piece of heavy hardwood. 'I like to get in close and bash in some heads,' Meinertzhagen grinned. Lawrence smiled and said, 'If you are close enough to bash them, you are close enough to shoot them.'[18]

The British commander, General Sir Ian Hamilton, was taken aback by the vehemence of the Greek position, but he heard them out. Hamilton had the reputation for being an intellectually curious and open man. He listened as the Greeks recommended that the landings at Gallipoli be only a feint to draw in Turkish reserves. Then the main landings would take place further west on the Gulf of Saros, to cut off Gallipoli. From there, the Allied forces could strike east to cut off the Turkish forces that had moved into the peninsula and then lunge north straight towards Constantinople. The Greeks made their case with excellent maps of the landing areas and Eastern Thrace that were far more detailed than anything the British had.[19]

By mid-February there had been only one change in the situation. The British Secretary of State for War, Field Marshal Lord Kitchener, had written of it to Winston Churchill, First Lord of the Admiralty. 'The Turks have evidently withdrawn most of their troops from Adrianople and are using them to reinforce their forces against Russia . . .' The Turks had been able to shift forces from their European border, which was now secured by the not-so-secret treaty with the Bulgarians, heavily underwritten if not guaranteed by the Germans. Of those eight Turkish divisions, there were only four and a cavalry brigade. This was an enormous relief to Hamilton. It reduced the risk to the operation. Eight Turkish divisions would surely overwhelm three Greek ones. However, now that there were only four (I and II corps), it was likely that the Greek corps could contain them and starve the Turks in Gallipoli of any reinforcements.[20]

At this point, things became awkward. Hamilton had been informed by the Foreign Office that the Russian tsar had very pointedly told the British ambassador that under no circumstances would Russia accept Greek troops in Constantinople. The Greeks were not to be allowed to interfere with Russia's centuries-old determination to control the straits and thereby secure access to the Mediterranean. Nicholas also stated that King Constantine was not to be permitted to enter the city after the British had taken it. Given that Russia was suffering severe reverses at this time and making no effort with its Black Sea Fleet to assist in the British operation, these were arrogant demands. Yet, the British had to be mindful of their major ally. It was Hamilton's problem: how to use the Greeks but not let them into Constantinople. Nothing was ever easy.[21]

Nevertheless, Hamilton realised that the Greek Army (*Ellinikos Stratos*) would be vital to the mission. By all accounts, it had performed professionally in the two Balkan Wars and was a largely veteran force. There were five corps, lettered A through E, with fourteen divisions. In several divisions one of its three regiments was an *Evzone* regiment. The *Evzones* were elite shock and mountain troops who had proved their skill and valour in the Balkan Wars and were distinguished by their traditional white kilts. There were also three regiments recruited specifically from Crete. By 1915 the Greek Army comprised forty-one infantry regiments of which there were thirty-three line, five *Evzone*, and three Cretan.[22]

In addition there were three special battalions raised in Crete referred to as *gendarmerie*, an elite paramilitary organisation with the native Cretan taste for cold steel. They had been modelled on the Italian *carabinieri* and earned a high reputation for re-establishing civil order in their own island after the collapse of the Ottoman administration and during the occupation of Thessaloniki after its capture in 1912. With their baggy black Cretan trousers, the *vraka*, and their blue jackets, these tall men were as striking as they were fierce. No taller race lived in the Mediterranean except in the mountains of Montenegro. It had been a great honour to be selected, and the Gendarmes took only the very best. With full mobilisation, Greece could put three hundred thousand men into the field out of a population of 4,733,013 Greeks. The Greek Royal Navy (*Vasilikon Náftikon*) was also a welcome addition with five battleships, one armoured cruiser, one light cruiser, fourteen destroyers, fourteen torpedo boats, and two submarines. Two new battleships built in the United States were in the process of being delivered. There was also a small Army Air Corps of three squadrons:[23]

Army Corps A, HQ Athens
    1st, 2nd, 13th infantry divisions
Army Corps B, HQ Patras (Peloponnesus)
    3rd, 4th, 14th infantry divisions
Army Corps C, HQ Thessaloniki (Macedonia)
    10th, 11th, 12th infantry divisions
Army Corps D, HQ Kavala (Thrace)
    5th, 6th, 7th infantry divisions
Army Corps E, HQ Ionnina (Epirus)
    8th, 9th infantry divisions[24]

Hamilton almost envied the national homogeneity of the Greek Army; the Allied forces he commanded were anything but uniform. The only British Army division was the new 29th, made up of imperial battalions gleaned from the Indian Army. The only other British division was not even an army unit – it was the Naval Division, composed of sailors for whom there were no ships. Then there was the ANZAC (Australia and New Zealand Army Corps) of one fully Australian division and one of a mix of units from both countries. Finally there was the French component – Corps Expéditionnaire d'Orient, thrown together from regular troops, Zouaves, and Senagalese. None of these troops had conducted any division-level exercises.[25]

In striking contrast, the Greek A Corps' 1st and 2nd divisions, slated to support the British, had a record of well-fought victories in the recent Balkan Wars, and its veteran reservists were now filling out its ranks. The mobilisation was underway and would be complete in seven days. B Corps in the Peloponnesus was designated as the reinforcement for the expedition to follow in less than a week. Army Corps C and D would defend the border with Bulgaria. The new E Corps in Epirus would remain in reserve for contingencies or possible assistance to Serbia.

Bulgaria was the wild card in the theatre. Defeated in the Second Balkan War and stripped of much of its territorial spoils from the previous war, it had many grievances, mostly directed at its former allies Greece and Serbia who had been awarded territories won by the Bulgarian sword. It had remained neutral after Turkey declared for the Central Powers. If Bulgaria did not join the Central Powers, German support of the Ottoman Empire, particularly through the Danube River, would be blocked. Before the war the Germans had helped to re-equip and retrain the Ottoman Army. Thousands of German advisers had brought a new efficiency to the warriors of the Sublime Porte.

Once the war began, the Bulgarian road then became a strategic necessity for both the Germans and the Turks. For that reason the Germans had floated the Bulgarians a huge loan, and the Turks had made a secret treaty of alliance with them. The British were trying to counter these influences by offering lavish bribes to every possible Bulgarian official. In the Balkan Wars, the Bulgarians had been able to mobilise almost four hundred thousand men. If Bulgaria again drew the sword, it was in a position to seriously damage the Allies. Bulgarian forces could strike Serbia in the back or come across the Greek border heading for the prize of Thessaloniki. Most critical for the gathering expedition was the possibility of facing a hundred thousand Bulgars coming in to save the Turks. Of course, that put Bulgarian history on its head, but revenge makes strange alliances possible.

The Turks had not been idle, as the Greeks had pointed out to Hamilton. Their forces defending the straits had been subordinated to the new 5th Army. On the European side, that included the III Corps and the fortress command of Gallipoli. They were joined by the 5th Infantry Division and a cavalry brigade commanded by the German Colonel von Sodenstern under the 5th Army. Commanding the recently assigned 19th Infantry Division was a dynamic young Turkish officer, Lieutenant Colonel Mustapha Kemal. His division was placed as a central reserve on the peninsula. On the Asiatic side, the XV Corps with the 3rd and 11th infantry divisions had been positioned. Commanding 5th Army was the formidable German general Liman von Sanders with his headquarters at the town of Gallipoli. Ever since the Turkish divisions had been brought up to war strength upon mobilisation they had been training rigorously. On 18 March a strong combined British–French naval force tried to force the straits, only to lose three battleships to mines. Turkish morale soared. Sanders, however, intensified training.

The only member of the British staff in Cairo to read one of the Greek reports was Second Lieutenant T. E. Lawrence, and it immediately caught his imagination. It was an analysis of the population of Eastern Thrace, the remaining European piece of the Ottoman Empire and the hinterland of Constantinople. It cited the 1910 Ottoman census that in all but one of the five districts, the Greeks formed a majority of the population – 362,000 Greeks against 294,000 Turks and 71,000 Bulgarians. Even in Constantinople the Christians of all denominations outnumbered the Turks. The statistics of the Ecumenical Patriarchate had a larger number of Greeks which supported the statements of the European experts who had actually conducted the census that the Turkish authorities had falsified the results by raising the number of Turks and lowering that of the Greeks and other Christian minorities.[26] He presented his idea to a sceptical Chief of Staff who passed it on to Hamilton.

Within a week Lawrence has slipped into Constantinople with the aid of a forged German passport and relevant documents. His blond hair and striking looks added to the deception: Turks were more than willing to give this archetypical German the benefit of the doubt. Lawrence was motivated by the knowledge. The Turks were systematically destroying all the Greek villages on the Gallipoli peninsula. He offered smiles to his unwitting Turkish hosts, but his luminous blue eyes were ice cold. Soon he had disappeared into Eastern Thrace to carry out his mission.[27]

The Landings at Enos, 25 April 1915

The final plan approved for the operation maintained the main Allied landings on the Gallipoli peninsula. Hamilton acceded to the strong Greek recommendations that their A Corps land at Enos, on the Saronic Gulf, a little town at the mouth of the Evros River. The river formed the boundary between the Ottoman Empire and the Bulgarian strip of Aegean coast it had won in the First Balkan War. There were fine sandy beaches and good open terrain to the east. Even the humiliating loss of three battleships had not altered Allied control of the sea. The Ottoman Navy was snugly out of the way in the Sea of Marmara, where it was going to stay. The nearest Ottoman Army unit was the independent cavalry brigade strung out over the eighty miles of the north coast of the Saronic Gulf. There was no opposition when the flotilla of Greek ships arrived off the town at dawn. With first light the guns of the fleet quickly destroyed the telegraph office. Covering fire from the Greek warships for the first wave of boats heading for shore drove off the few squadrons of cavalry that patrolled out of the town. The large number of small ships, many of them inter-island ferries, enabled the troops to get ashore quickly. Priority was given to the 1st and 3rd cavalry regiments, followed by the 1st and 2nd infantry divisions. The 13th Infantry Division was held in reserve on board ship.

The cavalry pushed off immediately to the east hoping to snap up the units of Turkish cavalry patrolling the coast. The next morning they were to be followed by the 1st Infantry Division, and then the 2nd Infantry Division the next day. Speed was vital. The trains would have to catch up as they could. Hurrying everything along was the A Corps commander, Lieutenant General Panagiotis Dangles. He had come ashore in the second wave determined to get things moving. There is nothing like being under the hard eyes of your corps commander to motivate a soldier. Venizelos had personally chosen him. His foreign military training had been in France; his background then balanced the pro-German sentiments on the General Staff. He has also been a military reformer and expert artilleryman. He had served as the Chief of Staff of the Army of Thessaly under then Crown Prince Constantine during the First Balkan War and had the king's confidence. He was also a political supporter of Venizelos's modernising policies. He was a sound choice. Now he was waving on an *Evzone* regiment, their kilts – like the British Army's Highland regiments on the Western Front – protected by a khaki wrap-around. The black tassels on their soft caps swung with the cadence of their march. As he rode in front of them, they shouted, '*Zeto Hellas, Zeto Hellas, Hellas Zeto!*'

('Live Greece, Live Greece, Greece, Live!') Standing in formation, waiting for their place in the march column, the Cretan Gendarme Battalion also lifted its shout. It was an incredibly heady moment. Greek soldiers had not trod this ground for 450 years, since the Turks had first tightened the noose on the hinterland of Constantinople. Now the Queen of Cities beckoned.[28]

At Gallipoli the Allies had run into a buzz saw. The landing beaches and shallows ran red with blood as the bodies piled up. They were finding out just how dangerous Johnny Turk could be when well trained and well led. Even when the Australians were on the point of winning, Kemal ordered his 57th Regiment to attack with the bayonet. They had no ammunition left. 'I do not order you to fight, I order you to die. In the time which passes until we die, other troops and commanders can come forward and take our places.' Every man of the 57th was killed or wounded, but the Australians were stopped.[29] General Sanders was pleased with the performance of his army; he would have been more pleased had the enemy been completely repulsed, but the enemy's crowded lodgments would be like slaughter pens as the Turks fired down into them. With the Enos telegraph down, and the Greek cavalry overwhelming the small detachments of the enemy's cavalry, Sanders did not hear of the landings that day.

Whilst Sanders's attention was fixed on the British landings, he was unaware of the Greek attack to the north-west. The news did not arrive until the small hours of the 26th that the Greeks were ashore and driving east in force. His closest unit was the 5th Infantry Division guarding the base of the Gallipoli peninsula and ready to repel landings at the eastern end of the Saronic Gulf. They had stood to all the day before as a large number of ships carrying the Naval Division hovered offshore while battleships and cruisers bombarded their emplacements. Another landing appeared imminent. He dared not send the 5th to stop the Greeks. His only reserve was the 19th Infantry Division, which had already been committed against the Australians. All he could do was send an urgent appeal to the 1st Army to come to his assistance. The problem was that the major railway in Thrace ran west from Constantinople to Edirne (Adrianople) near the Bulgarian border. That meant that any reinforcements able to reach the Saronic Gulf would have to march by road 120 kilometres from the nearest railway station. Enos was only eighty kilometres from the 5th Division, and the Greeks had covered at least thirty of that by now. They could be attacking the 5th Division in two days, he concluded. If the Greeks broke through, the entire Turkish force on the Gallipoli peninsula would be trapped. It would take 1st Army reinforcements at least six days to arrive. Too close, too close.

As Sanders pondered the awful prospect of encirclement, Hamilton was also possessed of the same idea. The news of the Greek success at Enos and the imminent arrival of the A Corps on the Turkish flank was far more than he had hoped for. At most he had hoped the Greeks would draw off some Turkish reserves. He realised now that the strategic equation had shifted. He stopped the French division from landing at Gallipoli and diverted them, along with the Naval Division, to land at Karachali at the eastern end of the Gulf along its wide sandy beaches on the 27th. Colonel von Sodenstern was not about to let this sizeable force organise and attack. He threw the 5th Division straight at the landing beaches. Waves of Turkish infantry shouting, '*Allah, Allah, Voll, Voll!*' ('Strike, Strike!') hit the French division beachhead, which only had half its force ashore. The first regiment was driven back onto the beach, and only the naval gunfire from the covering warships stopped the Turks, tearing great gaps in their ranks. The Naval Division's first brigade ashore moved to attack the Turkish flank and drove it back – the landings had been saved. By the time the Greek 1st Division arrived late on the 28th, the Turks had retreated into their prepared positions.

Meanwhile, to the north along the Edirne–Constantinople Railway a shadow play was taking place. During the night a party of men speaking Greek tore up tracks and set explosives under bridges and culverts. They were led by a small blond man whom they laughingly called, '*O Germanos*' (the German) for his cover. He was wearing a German uniform, which afforded him much deference among the Turks. His Greek was flawless if you were Socrates – the benefit of a classical education – but difficult if you were trying to communicate in modern Greek. Fortunately, enough of the Greeks understood the language of Homer, although the blind bard had never needed words for dynamite or blasting cap. Still, the idea got across. Lawrence and his crew had got together courtesy of Greek military intelligence. The Greeks were railway men. Anything requiring technical ability was usually heavily overrepresented by one of the Ottoman Christian or Jewish minorities.

'Aera!' and 'Voll!' – The Battle Cracks Wide Open

The day of 29 April saw the entire theatre in motion. The Greek A Corps had almost completely closed on the eastern end of the gulf while the French and Naval Division were positioning themselves to attack the 5th Division and cut off the rest of the Turkish 5th Army on the peninsula. The Greek B

Corps was within three days of landing just to the west of where the Naval Division had come ashore. The Turkish I Corps from Edirne should have been halfway to the coast by this time. Instead, it was stuck on the railway. Trains had been thrown off the tracks by loosened rails; others had ended in agonising crashes as the bridges under them blew up.

As Sanders read the telegram describing the delay of I Corps, he came to the bitter conclusion that his position on the peninsula was a trap that was closing inexorably on him. He would now have to conduct the most difficult of all military operations – retreat in the face of an enemy in contact. He waited one more day to see if there was any progress from I Corps. Nothing. He wired the Turkish government of his decision and received an adamant order not to retreat. Constantinople replied that every effort was being made to move I Corps to his assistance. Hamilton made all that irrelevant: he had come ashore the day before to be with the main attack against the 5th Division. While the French and Naval Division attacked from the front, the Greeks wheeled inland and came down on the Turks from the north capturing the town of Kavak. By 1 May, they had got behind the Turks, with one regiment reaching the straits. Sanders was cut off.

The 5th Division was broken by the weight of the Allied attack. Now four enemy divisions were sitting on his only escape route, itself only eight kilometres wide. The Greek 13th Infantry Division was due to arrive in a day or so to make the Allied barrier impregnable. But Sanders still refused to recognise the inevitability of surrender. Instead, with that inbred German determination to attack, he decided to break out. He chose Kemal to lead the effort with what remained of his division and the 7th Division. There was not enough time to pull out the guns. It would have to be with the bayonet.

In the early light of 7 May the hills to the north of the blocking positions of the Allied divisions seemed to be moving. The stillness was broken by a vast echoing shout of '*Allah, Allah, Voll, Voll!*' The sailors of the Naval Division had not put much stock in digging in and now paid for it. The Turks went down in droves, but their numbers told as they fought their way in among the British. The sailors died hard, but the centre of their line was broken, and the Turks surged through. The wings of the Naval Division unravelled as the Turks turned on the French on their right and the Greeks on their left whose own lines were also on the point of being swamped. Right behind the breakthrough came Kemal himself, leading the exploitation force. His men said he was a second Mehmet the Conqueror as they overran the enemy. The Greek 2nd Division refused its flank to let the

Turkish tide sweep by. The Naval Division had been all but destroyed, and the Turkish 5th Army was pouring through. Behind the attacking waves was much of the rest of the army. Only rearguards had been left in the hills above the beaches.

Hamilton's own headquarters was square in front of the point of the breakthrough. His own headquarters guard was barely a platoon of the 1st Battalion, the Lancashire Fusiliers. They fixed bayonets and stood to. He admired their coolness but not their chances. Captain Meinertzhagen was pacing back and forth with his knobkerrie in hand. As Hamilton's staff officers were on the point of bodily carrying their chief away, they heard the movement of many men coming from behind them. They were men in Greek kilts, bayonets fixed – the *Evzones*. They paused on command to ready their ranks, then with a shout of '*Aera!*' – the modern Greek battle cry – they rushed forward at the Turks.[30] Rushing up on their flank was a wave of big, formidable men in blue jackets. Their commander was a giant with a finely waxed black moustache. He stopped only long enough to shout, '*Thanatos tous Varbarous!*' ('Death to the Barbarians!') then rushed towards the fray. The Cretan Gendarmes were not about to let the *Evzones* take the lion's share of glory. The twentieth century seemed to melt away as the Greeks and Turks collided with cold steel. Meinertzhagen bellowed and joined the charge of the Gendarmes. For once he was not towering over everyone around him. Behind the Cretans was a regiment from the newly arrived B Corps, small where the Cretans hulked large. They were Arcadians, descendants of the short, stocky spearmen that filled eighty black ships to Troy, not so very far from this spot.

The men from the hard mountains of Crete and Arcadia were well matched by the men from the hard, bleak plateau of Anatolia. The mass roared and screamed in primal rage. Artillery from both sides fell into them. The Senegalese from the French Division rose to join the fray just as the host of Memnon the Ethiopian chieftain had come to fight alongside the Trojans. An officer on Hamilton's staff wrote, 'I fully expected to see a chariot emerge from the mass dragging a fallen chieftain behind it.'[31] Raging like a Homeric hero, Meinertzhagen cut a swathe through the Turks with his African club. Inside the mass two chieftains did indeed come across each other – the Cretan Gendarme commander fought his way to a Turkish officer. Their swords crossed but the big man beat down the other's guard as he fumbled for his pistol. A blow to the head felled him. A howl went up from the Turks around them. The heart seemed to go out of them. They broke for the rear, their fear racing ahead of them.[32]

Sanders after all accepted the inevitable and surrendered. With the death of Kemal and the failure of his attack in what was to be called the Battle of Karachalli, the game was over. He surrendered personally to Hamilton. Fifty-six thousand men went into the bag. The church bells rang throughout Greece. Constantinople was in chaos. In Sofia, so poised to join the Central Powers, the magnitude of the Ottoman defeat reversed the poles of geostrategy. British diplomacy, now with vast credit to its account, played its trump card. On 5 May Bulgaria declared war on the Ottoman Empire. The next day its army attacked towards Edirne. All thought of sending Turkish 1st Army Corps to the coast evaporated as it turned to fight the Bulgarians.[33]

Constantine had arrived with the B Corps to personally command the entire Greek force now designated the Army of Thrace. It headed north-east along the Sea of Marmara coast road towards the city. All along the way, Turkish military resistance evaporated as the roads were lined with Greek country people shouting, '*Zeto! Zeto!*' Shots fired by Turkish irregulars resulted in the burning of the nearest Turkish villages.[34] London, Paris, and Petrograd were aghast. The Greeks had cut loose from Hamilton. Although Gallipoli and its forts had surrendered, the Turkish forts on the Asiatic side of the strait had not; nor had the minefields been cleared. The Royal Navy, which could have won the race to Constantinople, was blocked.

Greek veterans would tell stories to the day they died of their first sight of the ruined walls of Theodosius, the ancient fortifications that had defended the city for a thousand years until smashed by the cannons of Mehmet the Conqueror. The city now fell without a fight. It was as if it welcomed home its conquerors. Constantine rode through the hoary Golden Gate of the emperors of Byzantium to the frenzied acclaim of the Greek inhabitants. The Turks stayed sullenly indoors or were crowding the docks to find passage across the Bosporus on anything that could float. The Cretan Gendarmes quickly established order.

The wooden doors of the Hagia Sofia Cathedral, on its last day as a mosque, were thrown open for the king. These were the same doors that had been hanging when the city had fallen centuries before. The only change had been the removal of the crossbar of the cross by the Turks. The king gazed up at the immense height of the dome, once glittering with gold mosaics. The marble columns and panelling still gleamed, if only dully through the grime of centuries. They would clean it of its Turkish excrescence and reconsecrate it. His troops filled the vast space shouting '*Axios, Axios, Axios!*' ('Worthy!') in his honour. Behind him, Venizelos wept.[35]

The Reality

The fate of Phocaea is true: the Turks began their ethnic cleansing of all Christian minorities in Anatolia as early as June 1914, beginning with the Greeks of the Aegean coast. That cleansing turned into genocide, not only of the Armenians but Greeks and Assyrians (Aramaic-speaking Arab Christians); the death toll has been estimated reliably at three to three and half million, of which perhaps over a million were Greek. The world remembers only the Armenians, however. It was indeed the precursor of the Jewish Holocaust, for when Hitler was writing *Mein Kampf* he brushed off the concerns of his followers that the world would not let that happen with his infamous line, 'Who remembers the Armenians?' The present author attended a NATO conference in which the Turkish delegate rolled out his talking point that there had been no Armenian genocide; then not thirty seconds later, he said, 'And besides they deserved it.' These barbarities have continued in the Turkish occupation of Cyprus in which two thousand Greek Cypriot civilians disappeared, their churches were desecrated, and even their classical ruins rendered into cement to erase the fact that their ancestors had been there since the Trojan War. In Turkey proper the few remaining Orthodox churches are vandalised as the Turkish government attempts through petty restrictions to drive the last Greek presence, the Ecumenical Patriarchate, out of Constantinople.

The chapter's point of departure is the vision of King Constantine. The story of his illness and the placing of the miracle-working icon by his bedside are true, but whether he actually had a vision is something he kept to himself. Venizelos did indeed resign. The country fell into rival royal and Venizelist camps provoking the 'Great Schism' in Greek politics. Constantine's neutrality was finally too much for the Allies and Venizelos. A military revolt led to Venizelos establishing a new government in Thessaloniki with the aid of the Allies, who forced Constantine to go into exile in 1917. He put Constantine's youngest son, Alexander, on the throne as a figurehead. Greece then entered the war actively on the Macedonian Front, fighting the Bulgarians as part of an Allied army.

With the collapse of the Ottoman Empire, Venizelos saw his chance to realise his dreams. The Treaty of Sèvres of August 1920 had given the Greeks Eastern Thrace and the vilyet of Smyrna though the Allies would not let the Greeks into Constantinople. A Greek Army had already landed at Smyrna in 1919 and quickly expanded its control of that part of old Asia Minor with the largest Greek population, defeating any Turkish resistance. Out of the ashes of the Ottoman Empire, Turkish nationalism was revitalised under the leadership of Kemal Mustapha. Then King Alexander I was bitten by his gardener's monkey and died within days of blood poisoning (you could not make this up!). At the same time Venizelos was defeated in new elections by a war-weary electorate that also voted for the return of Constantine. The newly returned king purged the army of those he thought loyal to Venizelos. Unfortunately, he rid himself of his best generals, which led to a great drawn-out battle outside Ankara. The British and French had blockaded the Aegean coast against any Greek reinforcement or resupply. The Greek supply lines failed, and the retreating army was routed, barely escaping through Smyrna. The vengeful Turks fell upon a Smyrna packed with Greek and Armenian refugees. The resulting slaughter can only be compared to the Rape of Nanking in its barbarity. The Greek defeat and the destruction of the Greek presence in Asia Minor has come to be known as the *Catastrophia*.

The returning Greek Army hanged six generals and cabinet officers. Venizelos was returned to power, and Constantine went into exile permanently, dying a few months later. Venizelos patched up a peace in the Treaty of Lausanne in 1923 which settled the modern Greco-Turkish borders. Each side expelled almost all of their respective minorities. Four hundred thousand Muslims were expelled from Greece and one and a half million Orthodox Christians from Turkey.[36] The result was the creation of two homogeneous countries. There were two exceptions to this exchange of populations: a hundred thousand Greeks were allowed to remain in Constantinople and a similar number of Turks in Greek Western Thrace. The Turks remain in Western Thrace, but almost a hundred years of pressure and pogroms, the latest officially sanctioned in 1955, have driven all but a few thousand Greeks out of Constantinople.

Winston Churchill put his finger on the tragedy of the *Megali Idea* when he wrote:

This story carried us back to classic times. It is true Greek tragedy, with Chance as the ever-ready handmaid of Fate. However the Greek race might have altered in blood and quality, their characteristics were found unchanged since the days of Alcibiades. As of old, they preferred faction above all other interests, and as of old in their crisis they had at their head one of the greatest of men. The interplay between the Greek love of party politics and the influence exercised over them by Venizelos constitutes the action of the piece. The scene and the lighting are the Great War; and the theme, 'How Greece gained the Empire of her dreams in spite of herself, and then threw it away when she awoke'.[37]

Notes

1 G. W. Prothero, *Anatolia* (London: H.M. Stationery Office, 1920). Phocaea was located in the vilayet (province) of Smyrna, named after its administrative centre. It was located in the south-west of Asia Minor including the ancient Lydia, Ionia, Caria, and western Lycia. It was described by the 1911 *Encyclopædia Britannica* as the 'richest and most productive province of Asiatic Turkey'. At the beginning of the twentieth century it reportedly had an area of 45,000 square kilometres (17,370 square miles). As of 1920, the vilayet had an 'exceptionally large' Christian population. The city of Smyrna was a vibrant cosmopolitan city and the commercial centre of the Ottoman Empire. Smyrna's largest population was half Greek, some 120,000 by 1920, but it also included *c*.80,000 Muslims, 20,000 Armenians and a sizeable Sephardic Jewish population. Yet the Greeks ran the economy. They owned 322 of the 391 factories in the city.

2 George Horton, *The Blight of Asia* (New York: Bobbs-Merrill, 1926), Chapter 6, available online at www.hri.org/docs/Horton/hb-6.html, accessed 10 October 2013.

3 Emre Erol, 'A Multidimensional Analysis of the Events in Eski Foça (Παλαιά Φώκαια) on the Period of Summer 1914', available online at http://ceb.revues.org/911, accessed 10 October 2013.

4 Dilys Powell, *The Villa Ariadne* (Pleasantville, NY: Arkadine Press, 2001), pp. 53, 58. Although this encounter between Venizelos and Evans is fictitious, the two men did know each other. Venizelos on a number of occasions showed respectful deference to Evans, who certainly believed, as one Cretan put it, 'After all he made Crete what it is now.'

5 Thessaloniki was founded by Cassander of Macedon in 310 BC. It has been known by various derivative names such as Salonica from the Greek colloquial Saloniki, the Slavic Soloun, and the Turkish Salonik.

6 'The Origins of the Ottomans', available online at http://home.comcast.net/~glennwatson550/worksheets/ottomans.html, accessed 10 October 2013. The first line refers to 'The City', by which the Greeks always meant Constantinople. With the coming of the Turkish Republic the name was changed to Istanbul, a seeming Turkish name. However, the origin of that name was simply the contraction of the Greek phrase *eis stin bolin* – 'to the city!'

7 Jon van der Kiste, *Kings of the Hellenes: The Greek Kings 1863–1974* (Stroud: Sutton Publishing Ltd, 1999), p. 89.

8 *Petros Zolintakis, *King Constantine I of the Hellenes, the New Nikephoros* (London: Charing Cross Publishers Ltd, 1936), pp. 178–9.

9 Van der Kiste, *Kings of the Hellenes*, p. 89.

10 Prince Nicholas of Greece, *My Fifty Years* (New York: Hutchinson, 1926), pp. 259–60.

11 Herbert Adams Gibbons, *Venizelos* (Boston: Houghton-Mifflin Co., 1920), p. 221.

12 Van der Kiste, *Kings of the Hellenes*, p. 92. The Virgin Mary is referred to in Greek as the Panayia, or 'All-Holy'.

13 *Spyridon Zacharopolous, *A Prophecy Fulfilled* (New York: Hutchinson Publishers, 1925), p. 88. The Virgin Mary had always been acknowledged as the patroness and special protector of Byzantine Constantinople.

14 Edward J. Erickson, *Gallipoli and the Middle East 1914–1918: From the Dardanelles to Mesopotamia* (London: Amber Books, 2008), pp. 51–5.

15 Eastern Thrace was at that time the only remaining European possession of the Ottoman Empire. Most of it had been lost to the Bulgarians in the First Balkan War but was recovered by the Turks in the Second Balkan War. Small as it is, it is modern Turkey's anchor in Europe today.

16 First Army (Ottoman Empire) structure, available online at http://en.wikipedia. org/wiki/First_Army_(Ottoman_Empire)#Order_of_Battle.2C_Late_ April_1915, accessed 13 October 2013.

17 *Robert Graves, *Lawrence of Thrace* (London: Blackfriars Publishers Ltd, 1925), p. 39. After the war Lawrence became fast friends with both the famous poet Graves as well as an unknown army officer, Basil Liddell Hart. Their correspondence has become famous.

18 *Richard Meinertzhagen, *Thracian Diary* (London: Roxbury Books Ltd, 1933) p. 22. Meinertzhagen's family was of German origin which earned him no end of scrutiny by guards examining his identification. He had been the intelligence officer on the disastrous Tanga expedition in German East Africa in 1914 and then been seconded to the British force assembling in Egypt.

19 *William Goddard, 'Planning for the Eastern Thrace Campaign,' *Royal Military Journal* XX (March 1942), pp. 89–91.

20 C. R. Ballard, *Kitchener* (New York: Dodd, Meade & Co., 1930), p. 272.

21 Gibbons, *Venizelos*, pp. 228–9.

22 Nigel Thomas and Dusan Babac, *Armies of the Balkans 1914–18* (Oxford: Osprey Publishing, 2001), p. 23.

23 Ibid.

24 Hellenic Army General Staff, Army History Directorate, *A History of the Hellenic Army 1821–1997* (Athens: Army History Directorate, 1999), pp. 126–9.

25 Erickson, *Gallipoli and the Middle East*, pp. 62–3.

26 Dimitri Pentzopoulos, *The Balkan Exchange of Minorities and its Impact on Greece* (New York: C. Hurst & Co., 2002). pp. 31–2.

27 *T. E. Lawrence, *In the Steps of Constantine the Great* (London: Trafalgar Press Ltd, 1928), p. 92. Before arriving in Constantinople, Lawrence had paid a visit to Athens, where he was briefed on conditions in Gallipoli and Eastern Thrace. He was also given contacts with Greek agents in Constantinople and Eastern Thrace.

28 *Theodoros Kolokotronis, *Aera! The Greek Army in the Thracian Campaign of 1915* (Athens: Acropolis Publishers, 1976), p. 72.

29 Edward Erickson, *Ordered to Die: A History of the Ottoman Army in the First World War* (Westport, CT: Greenwood Publishing, 2001), p. xv.

30 Historium, available online at http://historum.com/war-military-history/ 31183-bad-assed-battle-cries-history-5.html, accessed 14 October 2013. 'The Greek army battle cry is "Aera!", i.e. "[sweep them away like the] wind!".'

31 *Meinertzhagen, *Thracian Diary*, p. 232.

32 *Captain Meinertzhagen was to win the Victoria Cross for the carnage he inflicted that day, all by hand.

33 *Ian Hamilton, *The Campaign in Thrace* (London: Greenhill Books, 1993), p. 242. Greenhill carved an important niche in reissuing primary military works that had gone out of print such as Hamilton's important but largely forgotten memoir. Hamilton had remained under a cloud for what was perceived as his failure to stop the Greeks from seizing Constantinople. However, his deployment of his British forces northwards trapped the retreating Turkish 1st Army against the oncoming Bulgarians. The Australians and New Zealanders would fondly remember the subsequent pleasant summer of occupation in Thrace.

34 *Arnold Toynbee, *The Turkish Question in Great Greece* (New York: Hutchinson Publishers, 1924), p. 387. Toynbee rightly pointed out that the collapse of the Ottoman Empire generated the rise of a new Turkish nationalism that has proved a constant threat to Greek possessions in Asia Minor.

35 *Seraphim Zacharopoulos, *The Re-Hellinization of Constantinople* (London: Blakeny Press Ltd, 1928), p. 233. One result of the fall of Constantinople was the migration of large numbers of diaspora Greeks from the Russian shores of the Black Sea to the city. That and the departure of large numbers of Turks, gave the city a clear Greek majority.

36 It is thought that the majority of this number of Greeks had already fled in the face of massacres.

37 Winston S. Churchill, *The World Crisis: The Aftermath*, 1929, p. 379, cited in Michael Llewellyn Smith, *Ionian Vision: Greece in Asia Minor 1919–1922* (New York: St Martin's Press, 1975), p. xi.

5

Germania Delenda Est[1]
America Enters the War – 1915

Peter G. Tsouras

Liverpool, England, 10 September 1915

It was an act of gallant courtesy gone awry. The British were expecting the first American regiment to arrive in Liverpool since the United States had declared war on Germany in June and had gone through their military music library to find just the right piece to welcome their guests. As the men of the Georgia National Guard regiment began marching down the gangplank, they were stunned to be serenaded by a fine rendition of 'Marching Through Georgia'.[2] They took it well, though. When Oscar Wilde had said that the British and Americans were two peoples separated by the same language, he was on to something. American overstatement would collide with British understatement all too often.

That collision was all the more frequent in the intemperate person of the commander of the American Expeditionary Force (AEF), Lieutenant General Frederick Funston. At barely five foot five inches, 121 pounds, he was a bantam rooster of a man. In addition to a brilliant, even ruthless combat record in the war with Spain and the Philippine Insurrection, he was a good friend of President Theodore Roosevelt, who had personally selected him to lead the AEF. To say that he was an impulsive man was putting it mildly. Incendiary would be a better descriptor. His comments on what should be done to those who opposed American policy in the Philippines almost ignites on its own:

82

I personally strung up thirty-five Filipinos without trial, so what was all the fuss over Waller's 'dispatching' a few 'treacherous savages'? If there had been more Smiths and Wallers, the war would have been over long ago. Impromptu domestic hanging might also hasten the end of the war. For starters, all Americans who had recently petitioned Congress to sue for peace in the Philippines should be dragged out of their homes and lynched.[3]

Theodore Roosevelt and the Road to War

Theodore Roosevelt's victory in the 1912 election at the head of a united Republican Party would be looked upon by future historians as a decisive factor in the coming Great War. Roosevelt was an Anglophile to the bone. He and the then Prince of Wales, the future Edward VII, had led the rapprochement of their two countries that had sunk to a nadir because of Britain's all-too-painful preference for the Confederacy in the Civil War. Roosevelt realised that the unity of blood, language, history, and culture as well as Britain's conduct in international affairs made the two countries natural allies. Had not the Iron Chancellor himself, Otto von Bismarck, remarked that 'The most significant event of the 20th century will be the fact that the North Americans speak English?'[4] Roosevelt could therefore write the following to Prime Minister Asquith on 22 January 1915:

> To the crux of the situation has been Belgium. If England or France had acted toward Belgium as Germany has acted I should have opposed them, exactly as I now oppose Germany. I have emphatically approved your action as a model for what should be done by those who believe that treaties should be observed in good faith and that there is such a thing as international morality. I take the position as an American; who is no more an Englishman than he is a German, who endeavors loyally to serve the interest of his own country, but also has endeavored to do what he can for justice and decency as regards mankind at large and who therefore feels obliged to judge all other nations by their conduct on any given occasion.[5]

He had given immediate and forceful opposition to the German violation of Belgian neutrality. That his remonstrations to the German government had been met with a feckless argument for the iron law of necessity had only accelerated his natural desire to weigh into the fight. He was a naturally combative man, and the German response, as well as the horror stories of German atrocities, convinced him that America needed to be in this war. Unrestricted German submarine warfare and the sinking of the British liner *Lusitania* by a German submarine on 7 May 1915 with the loss of 128 American lives, mostly women and children, had given him all the ammunition he needed. The photos of babies washing up on the Irish shore stunned the nation. This followed the widespread revulsion at the first use of poison gas by the Germans at Ypres in late April. The stories of the attack on their Canadian cousins struck a strong chord with the American public. Roosevelt now acted while the American anger was white hot. At night on 1 June, 'armed cavalry restrained a seething multitude outside the Capitol, while in front of a subdued Congress, with a packed gallery listening, the President delivered his war message. The Supreme Court justices were present. They and most of the Congressmen wore small American flags in their lapels.' The House of Representatives voted with near unanimity. The United States was now at war with the German Empire and an ally of the Entente.[6]

Despite his determination to enter the war and his revulsion at German conduct, Roosevelt retained a residue of respect and even affection for the German people. He had acquired it in a five-month visit to Dresden as a fifteen year old when he learned to speak passable German. He would later write, 'I gained an impression of the German people which I never got over. From that time to this it would have been quite impossible to make me feel that the Germans were foreigners.' He recalled that his stay had 'made a subconscious impression upon me which . . . is very vivid still forty years later'.[7]

The immediate result of the declaration of war was the almost complete cut-off of the foreign trade that was slipping through the British blockade of Germany, almost all of which had been carried in American bottoms, almost four hundred ships since the war had begun less than a year before. As Captain B. H. Liddell Hart observed, 'No longer was the grip of the naval blockade hampered by neutral quibbles, but instead America's cooperation converted it into a strangle-hold under which the enemy must soon grow limp, since military power is based on economic endurance.'[8]

Huge loans to the Allies followed, as did vast orders to American industry which was already straining to meet those placed since the previous August. The United States could produce many things, but it was not tooled up to manufacture the weapons of war. That would take time. The army had fewer than four hundred thousand of its excellent M1903 Springfield rifles, produced by the Springfield Arsenal, in reserve. Private American factories, such as Remington, Winchester, and Midvale Steel were already under contract with the British and Russians. The British Secretary of State for War, Field Marshal Lord Kitchener had placed an order for two million Enfield rifles which had soaked up most of American private capacity without yet producing many weapons. Private industry simply had no excess capacity. The decision was made to issue Springfield rifle stocks first and produce what they could at the Springfield Arsenal. It was hoped that then production would catch up. Events would prove that hope was not a strategy. The only fallback was to issue the stocks of half a million inferior Krag-Jorgensen rifles, which the M1903 had replaced. Similar problems existed for the production of artillery and machine guns. The result was that soldiers could be conscripted and trained faster than they could be armed. British and French production was in similar throes of expansion and could not even support their own requirements.

Unfortunately, time was the element that could not be accelerated. That was especially true in the creation of the necessary expeditionary force that would dwarf the entire Union Army in the Civil War. Socrates had put his finger on the problem when he had observed that 'a disorderly mob is no more an army than a heap of building materials is a house.'[9]

In 1915 the US Army numbered 255,000 men. The National Guard added another quarter million. There were also 10,000 marines. There would have been fewer than 190,000 regulars had it not been for the military preparedness programme Roosevelt had pushed through in his first year in office. The programme also paid for a quadrupling of the General Staff from fifty-five to two hundred officers. Ford Motor Company was producing a specially designed robust truck for the army. The Signal Corps had been upgraded with equipment and its air component expanded to two hundred aircraft, with intensive training of pilots based on growing experience of the war in Europe. An interesting innovation was the establishment of a reserve officers' training programme at a large new camp near Plattsburg, New York, that was turning out several thousand second lieutenants a year. A few were accepted on active duty, more went into the National Guard, but the large majority went back to civilian life, willing to be recalled in a national emergency. The hardest part of the reform was to subordinate the traditionally autonomous army bureaus directly to the Chief of Staff. Roosevelt had to marshal all the powers of the bully pulpit and cash in a lot of political favours to generate public support. Even after this immense effort, the Military Preparedness Bill of 1913 had barely passed the Congress. But it had passed.[10]

Roosevelt had done more than push through this bill. He had appointed Lieutenant General Leonard Wood to a second term as Chief of Staff. They had met during the Cuban campaign of 1899, and Roosevelt, then commanding his own regiment of the Rough Riders, had been immensely impressed with the army physician, the only one ever to rise to the position of Chief of Staff. He had been a champion of military preparedness himself, and Roosevelt and he found natural allies in each other. Early in his administration, the president had ordered Wood to begin planning for a major expansion of the army in time of war. He agreed with Wood's recommendation to also begin planning for conscription to man this new army. In late August 1914, Roosevelt further instructed Wood to begin planning for sending that army to Europe to fight on the side of the Allies. The newly expanded General Staff found an immense task set before it.

Roosevelt drew on the men he had met in the war with Spain. Funston was one of them. Another was Brigadier General John J. Pershing, who had commanded a troop of the black 10th Cavalry Buffalo Soldiers at St Juan Hill. Roosevelt's Rough Riders and the Buffalo Soldiers attacked together up the hill. He remarked that Pershing 'was the coolest man under fire I ever saw'. As president he jumped the then Captain Pershing to the rank of brigadier general over 882 senior officers.[11] Now, as he appointed Funston to command the AEF, he promoted Pershing to major general and designated him to command the first US division (1st Infantry Division) to arrive in France.

The Yanks Are Coming

Within two weeks of the declaration of war, Funston and his AEF staff had set sail for Europe. He had surrounded himself with the army's best and brightest, men who knew how to get things done and had the drive to do it. The US Army's excellent school system had prepared them for just this crisis.

They arrived in Liverpool on 21 May and almost immediately Funston's lack of discretion set a jarring note. The French and British were attacking in Artois but had suffered heavy losses for little gain in the face of a well-prepared and tenacious German defence. Funston commented tactlessly that the US Army would have carried the German positions easily. That immediately got the British backs up and served only to confirm opinion of Americans as ill-mannered boors. Funston's meeting with the king was therefore not as cordial as George V had wanted it to be; his meeting with the Secretary of State for War, Field Marshal Lord Kitchener, was downright frosty.

Funston continued to break diplomatic crockery after landing in France despite the studied efforts of his hosts to be gracious and accommodating. Frantic cables from the American ambassadors in London and Paris alarmed the president enough to do what he had wanted to do in the first place. On 10 June he embarked for Europe on board a fast cruiser. It was a typically bold move that shattered precedent. No president of the United States had ever left the country during his time in office. Accompanying him was his distant cousin, Franklin D. Roosevelt. The dashing young politician's progressivism had been influenced by the older man. Theodore had given away his niece, Eleanor Roosevelt, to young Franklin at their wedding in 1904, joking, 'Well, Franklin, there's nothing like keeping the name in the family.'[12] So, he found it easy to change parties after a successful term in the New York State senate to accept the president's offer of the position of Assistant Secretary of the Army. The president had a role for Franklin. He was to remain in France and rein in Funston's tongue.[13]

The president's visit was a great success. His magnetic personality and engaging Anglophilia wiped away the irritation caused by Funston. His meeting with George V had gone superbly well, prompting the king to say, 'It has always been my dream that the two English-speaking nations should some day be united in a great cause, and to-day my dream is realised. Together we are fighting for the greatest cause for which peoples could fight. The Anglo-Saxon race must save civilisation.'[14] The king had inherited this belief in the natural affinity of the English-speaking peoples from his father, the late Edward VII. The occasional jibe at the French was made with that sort of knowing look that presupposed that the Americans shared the traditional British disdain for their Gallic allies, not realising the bond of affection between the United States and France dating back to the War for Independence. Attempts at humour at the expense of the French usually fell flat, such as the one made by British general, 'If [you Americans serve] with the French, you would probably want your own food supply also.'[15]

The British assumption that Americans were only slightly removed Britons did not take into account the creation of the American character and that almost half of the American people were not of British origin by this time. The Americans of Irish and German origin were a significant proportion of the population. Irish-Americans were largely descendants of the refugees of the Great Famine, and many nursed a hatred of Britain as a cherished legacy. The process of Americanisation, though, had created a new identity that, in this time of national crisis, had trumped the past. The engine of assimilation had created an American nationality whether the name was Keyes, Kelly, or Keller.

Thus, the president was highly conscious of American national interests and would go only so far as to accommodate the Anglo-Saxon theme pushed by the British. When Prime Minister Herbert Asquith recommended that the American forces be associated with the British in a special arrangement, Roosevelt made it emphatically clear that the United States would not play favourites among its allies. Needless to say, when he repeated his position in Paris, it was enthusiastically greeted. That did not stop the French from trying to establish their own special relationship with the Americans based upon the cherished memory in the United States of the French aid during the War for Independence. Funston remarked that he would be a rich man if he got a nickel for every time the French brought up the name Lafayette.

Roosevelt turned the charm campaign back upon the French when he laid a wreath on the tomb of Lafayette in Picpus Cemetery in Paris. He noted that the soil that covered the grave had been brought from Bunker Hill, that Lafayette had been the only man ever granted American citizenship by Congress, that Washington loved him like a son, and that his memory was beloved to the nation. He ended his speech, saying, 'America has joined forces with the Allied Powers, and what we have of blood and treasure are yours. Therefore it is that with loving pride we drape the colors in tribute of respect to this citizen of your great republic. And here and now, in the presence of the illustrious dead, we pledge our hearts and our honor in carrying this war to a successful issue. Lafayette, we are here.' The ovation from the huge French crowd broke like a thunderclap.[16]

Settling Down in France

The British referred to their appearance as the 'Fred and Franklin Show' – an arrangement that would never have happened in their own armies. That Funston needed a minder only lessened their opinion of him. Franklin Roosevelt, on the other hand, only gave the best impression, a self-assured aristocrat with deadly charm and a first-rate temperament.

The first American force to land in France was the 1st Infantry Division composed of regular regiments. In the regular regiments, however, at least half the men were new recruits. Pershing worried about the impression they would make when the French invited a contingent to march in the Bastille Day parade. Despite their lack of smart uniforms and drill, the French crowds went wild.

The view from Berlin was dismissive. The Chief of the German General Staff, General Erich von Falkenhayn, did not think much of the Americans. His impression had been fixed by the opinion of the late genius of the wars of German unification, Field Marshal Helmut von Moltke (the Elder). He had sniffed at the American experience in their Civil War as nothing more than the collision of armed mobs. Falkenhayn had no doubt that the German Army would make short work of the new generation of these new armed mobs that were assembling so slowly in France. The minuscule size of the regular US Army and the unmilitary nature of the Americans simply reinforced his opinion that any expansion could only result in an incompetent force. His optimism was buoyed by the German success in defeating every Allied attack in the West and in the crushing blows that had sent the Russians reeling on the Eastern Front.

The German chancellor, Theobald von Bethmann-Hollweg, was of a different mind. He was burdened by his role in helping to create the conditions which forced the British to declare war on Germany. Now he fretted that just another such mistake had led to America's entry into the war. He was not as dismissive of the Americans as Falkenhayn. He was much more aware of their economic power and huge population. The foreign ministry papers on American potential had been more than revealing – they had been alarming. He realised that Falkenhayn had missed the forest for the trees. Yes, the Americans were indeed not a military people – uniforms and parades did not impress them – but their history showed clearly that when provoked they were a very warlike people. In this they had much in common with the Australians, whose valour was being thrown away at Gallipoli. Bethman-Hollweg's attempts to caution Falkenhayn were wasted.

The Chief of the Imperial General Staff was becoming obsessed with a way to break the stalemate on the Western Front. He concluded that although the British were the more dangerous enemy, their front offered no good purchase for decisive action. The French on the other hand, he believed, were near exhaustion. If he could entice them into desperately trying to hold onto something that their national pride would not let them relinquish, Falkenhayn was convinced he could bleed them white. He would turn that battle into a killing machine. Verdun was the perfect point for the attack.

He had assured the Kaiser that the superiority of the German Army was such that, in either attack or defence, it would inflict three casualties for every one it suffered. His strategy was sure to bring the enemy to their knees. The Kaiser retorted, 'Attrition is the absence of strategy! Go back to work and figure something else out.'[17]

By December only four American divisions had arrived – 1st and 2nd infantry divisions and the 26th and 42nd infantry divisions of the National Guard. Each American division numbered 28,000 men, with four large infantry regiments in two brigades, about the size of a European corps. In addition, the Marine Corps provided a brigade (5th and 6th marines), commanded by Colonel John Lejeune. Pershing had so impressed Funston that the latter had quickly promoted him to command the new I Corps (1st and 42nd infantry divisions). The II Corps included the remaining two divisions. The Marine Brigade remained an army-level reserve. By December Funston was ready to stand up the 1st Army, and he gladly handed the command to Pershing.

In January, German intelligence reported that the American 1st Army was about to take over part of the Verdun sector from the French. Two more divisions arrived and went into training in the rear. Falkenhayn had been stung by the imperial rebuke. He was shortly offered a solution. Where before he had seen the Americans as relatively unimportant, he now saw the Americans as an opportunity.

Funston was like an excited terrier as his divisions moved into the trenches, often going in with the first battalions to personally observe. Pershing had argued fruitlessly that he had enough to worry about without having the commander of the American Expeditionary Force roaming the forward trenches like a second lieutenant.

On 15 January Funston decided to accompany one of the leading platoons of the 18th Infantry Regiment (1st Infantry Division) as it took over the front-line trenches from the French. He had refused a large escort and ordered the regimental commander to get on with his duties. Little did he know that Falkenhayn had planned a welcoming present for the Americans. The German had instructed Crown Prince Wilhelm, whose army group included the 5th Army facing the Americans, to carefully note their arrival in the trenches. Just as Funston was peering over a parapet, with his aide pleading for him to get down, the Germans dropped a barrage over just that part of the trenches in the shape of an isolating box of exploding shells. From carefully cut holes in the wire, German *Stosstruppen* (assault troops specially trained for trench raiding) dashed forward, tossing grenades into the trenches and dropping down into them to spray left and right with their machine pistols. The aide had jumped in front of Funston to take the bullets. Shielded by the dying lieutenant, Funston pulled his own .45-calibre pistol and dropped the first German and then the one behind him. Within seconds the trench around him was a seething mass of men in grey and brown locked in hand-to-hand combat.

It was an uneven contest. The elite German raiders outnumbered the defenders and were better trained and equipped for the bloody work. But Funston had not been known as a killer for nothing. He had faced Spanish bayonets and Filipino bolos before. His pistol empty, he picked up an entrenching tool, one side sharpened for just such a moment. He caught the first German in the corner of the neck and nearly decapitated him. Another swipe sent a German screaming with his face slashed open. Funston drew back his arm to strike the next man when suddenly the entrenching tool slipped from his fingers, and he simply fell into the mud. The Germans trod over his body as they cleaned out the rest of the Americans in that isolated part of the trench and hustled their prisoners back across no man's land.

Pershing's prediction was borne out when he received an urgent telephone call from the Chief of Staff of the 1st Division, Lieutenant Colonel George C. Marshall. Funston had been killed in a German trench raid. He had not gone easily. His body was found near those of his aide and escort, surrounded by four dead Germans. Strangely there was no mark on his body. An autopsy would show that he had died of a massive heart attack.

Pershing immediately assumed temporary command of the AEF, a measure which was immediately confirmed by Franklin Roosevelt. Funston's death stunned Washington, alarmed the Allies, and greatly amused the Germans. They thought it a good omen. Falkenhayn pinned a *Pour le Mérit* on the commander of the raid. He was more than pleased with himself. His thinking had been confirmed.

Verdun

Funston's death had sent a shock wave through the Allies. For one thing, it had become rare in this war for a general officer to fall in battle. Far more significant was the moral effect of killing the commander of the new ally. The British and French generals with whom he had worked were actually relieved and somewhat enjoyed the American comeuppance. Funston had been a hard man to like. Their other ranks volunteered the names of some of their own generals they would like to see go the same way. The Americans, on the other hand, were out for revenge. The Germans, once they discovered whom they had killed on the raid, were both astounded and amused. It contributed to their growing contempt of the Americans as a serious enemy.

Secretary of War Newton D. Baker immediately travelled to Europe to sort out the new command and inspect the AEF, now grown to half a million men, most of whom were in advanced training in north-eastern France. In contrast the British had 1,210,000 men in France.[18] The 1st Army was still only seven divisions strong with the arrival of the 3rd Infantry Division. Baker was relieved to receive a glowing report on Pershing from Franklin Roosevelt. Pershing brought to his attention in no uncertain terms the critical failure to supply his growing army with basic firearms. 'Mr Secretary, you can build an army of ten million men, and it won't mean a damn if you can't put a rifle in the infantryman's hands.' The production of rifles and other small arms had been very slow. At the beginning of the war, Kitchener had ordered two million Enfield rifles from American producers, but at a Parliamentary inquiry in early June he would admit that only 480 had actually been delivered.[19] The British in particular were experiencing their own shell shortage at the time and could spare nothing for the Americans in that regard. The French were in better shape, but what they could provide the new American divisions was limited.

Pershing continued, 'At this rate, Mr Secretary, the supply of Springfield rifles we had at the beginning of the war will only allow us to equip ten divisions here in France, given the training requirements at home, even if we use all the Krag stocks. I am already receiving thousands of men who have had no musketry training whatsoever. I have had to ensure that only the infantry is issued the Springfield; all other troops requiring a rifle – engineers, signals, guards behind the lines – are being issued Krags.' Baker could only promise him that every effort would be made to accelerate production of small arms.[20]

Pershing had more than enough problems in ensuring that the 1st Army was ready and able to hold its new sector. And it was very bad one, thought Lieutenant Colonel Marshall. The sector formed a shallow salient that was bisected by the Meuse River, which at this time was rain swollen to a mile in width, effectively cutting the east and west banks off from mutual support except by artillery. Joffre had attached a colonial corps to 1st Army to occupy the west bank of the Meuse but retained command of the fortress complex in French hands. But at the same time, at Marshal Joffre's insistence, the forts had been stripped of most of their garrisons and guns.

Not only were the defenses of Verdun in poor condition but the salient was poorly served by roads and railroads, a situation which was to make logistical support difficult. Two standard-gauge railroads entered the city, one from the south and the other from the west. The former had been cut by the enemy at St. Mihiel, and the latter was within German artillery range. There was a narrow gauge line from Bar-le-Duc, but it had a very limited capacity. Fortunately, the highway from Bar-le-Duc had recently been improved.[21]

Crown Prince Wilhelm was relieved at Falkenhayn's change of mission. He had been as aghast as his father at the proposed killing machine Falkenhayn wanted to unleash on the French. The machine worked both ways, he reasoned, and he was solicitous of the lives of the men he commanded. Although he had had little command experience before the war, he had learned quickly from his skilled army group General Staff. As Winston Churchill would later comment, 'It may also be said that no group of German armies was more consistently successful than his; and that there is evidence that this personal influence – whatever it may have been – was often thrown into the right side of the scales.'[22] He had come to realise along with Falkenhayn that trench warfare had made fortresses that could not be bypassed or stormed. But the Americans, Falkenhayn concluded, would by their very inexperience be the exception. The 5th Army's mission was then to smash in the Americans and break through to open country, to restore movement to the war, a skill in which the Germans excelled.

In a masterful concentration of forces in January and February, the German Army massed over 1,200 guns including 542 'heavies', among which were thirteen of the 420-mm and seventeen of the 350-mm howitzers that had crushed the Belgian forts in the first month of the war. Ten new rail lines were laid and ten stations built to handle the concentration. With the guns came mountains of shells carefully hidden in huge underground bunkers. Four new corps of ten highly rated divisions reinforced the 5th Army's nine divisions. The Germans would strike a zone of eight miles of the American front with one division and 150 guns per mile. The initial barrage was to be so crushing that 'no line is to remain unbombarded, no possibilities of supply unmolested, nowhere should the enemy feel himself safe.' The blow was named Operation Gericht (Judgement). Falkenhayn had every expectation that it would, indeed, be Judgement Day for the Americans.[23]

French intelligence correctly identified the build-up and its intended target. Joffre and the French General Staff dismissed it as a deception. Pershing, however, did not. In a series of savage trench raids, nicknamed 'Funsties', the Americans brought back enough prisoners, augmented by a deserter or two, for them to confirm the conclusions of French intelligence.

Pershing arrayed his forces with this in mind. The 1st Army had the French 3rd Army on the left and the 2nd Army on the right. His I Corps (1st and 41st infantry divisions) was on its left at Brabant sur Meuse. Next came II Corps (26th and 32nd infantry divisions), and to its right was the III Corps (2nd and 42nd infantry divisions) with its right at Gussainville on the Orne River. The 1st Army front ran twenty-two miles. In reserve was the Marine Brigade and the 3rd Infantry Division, which was pulled early out of advanced training. All in all the entire AEF had half a million men in France, but fewer than half were 1st Army. By this time, the entire prewar stock of Springfield rifles has been distributed, but production was only up to three thousand a month, barely enough to equip one infantry regiment.[24]

In the Verdun sector, recently promoted Colonel Marshal recommended that, considering the weight of the oncoming attack, the front lines be thinned considerably with only enough troops to delay the Germans. The Americans then discovered how seriously the forts defending Verdun had been denuded of men, guns, and ammunition. The 66,000 men in the garrisons had been reduced to caretaker staffs with 237 guns and 647 long tons of ammunition removed. The smashing of the Belgian forts by German heavy artillery had convinced the French that their own forts were far too vulnerable. Only the heavy guns in the retractable gun turrets remained. In a stormy meeting with Joffre, Pershing demanded and finally received control of the Verdun forts. He immediately began transferring troops in training camps, primarily artillery and engineers, to man them. The French caretaker troops remained to train the Americans on the functioning of the forts.

Trench raids by both sides reached a crescendo in mid-February. Encounters between raiding parties in no man's land were becoming common. The *Stosstruppen* were surprised at the sheer aggressiveness of the Americans. Their first raid had made the Germans overconfident. They would have been shocked to learn that the dashing Chief of Staff of the 42nd Infantry Division, Colonel Douglas MacArthur, personally led trench raids armed with only a riding crop. It was his raid that brought back the prisoner that told them of the date of the attack.[25]

Judgement Days

Dawn had not yet brightened the horizon on 21 February when the first German gun symbolically sent a round into the fortress complex. 'Three hours later the real bombardment began. For over twelve hours the . . . German guns fired 100,000 shells per hour into a small area, a bombardment of unprecedented ferocity.'[26] The Germans did not plan to throw masses of men at the enemy. They intended their artillery to smash the enemy; their infantry would pick up the pieces. Their plans for overcoming any surviving defences were subtle and well-thought out. At 1715 the cry went up along the German trenches, '*Raus, Raus!*' as a wave of specialised groups emerged to advance over the 650 to 1200 yards of no-man's land. One German would write:

> Each troop had a specific task, with an objective of limited breadth and depth. Before taking hold of it, a wave of scouts was sent forward to test the destruction by the artillery fire. If the destruction were not thorough the scouts retired and further artillery preparation was organised. The attack took place in waves about 80 meters apart. First came a line of pioneers and men with bombs. Then came the main body in single file. Then followed a reserve section carrying up ammunition, tools, sandbags, and filling up the gaps in the first wave. A second line followed in the same order, passing through the first line, supporting it if checked and renewing the assault on their own initiative. The attack should now proceed by encircling movements, utilizing cover and passing along ravines. Thus the centres of resistance would fall one by one. Shell fire would support the advance continually. On no account should troops attempt to overcome resistance which has not been broken up by artillery fire. Units, when held up, must wait for fresh artillery action.[27]

The lightly manned forward trenches were indeed smashed. A hundred thousand men were advancing on an eight-mile front to the east of the Meuse. Suddenly flares shot up from the centre of no man's land. Now it was the turn of the American artillery to respond, joined by the concentrated French batteries to the west of the Meuse. The German scouts were in advance of the fire, but it caught the pioneers and grenade men and the main body out in the open and did terrible slaughter.

The scouts were surprised to find almost no one in the smashed forward trenches. Yet with the enemy artillery dicing through no man's land, it was difficult to report the situation. The main body eventually forced its way through the artillery with some loss, only to find that the scouts had nothing to report. There was no enemy except a few dead bodies and the occasional stubborn machine-gun crew. The terrain was hilly with ravines running south-west, which tended to direct the Germans in that direction to run up against the rain-swollen Meuse instead of due south at Verdun. The German attacking waves were now bunching up as they overran the wrecked trenches, making an even greater meal for the American and French guns. By the time the scouts had been sent forward again, it was the morning of the 22nd.

The Germans repeated their tactics that day against the new American main line of resistance, but this time their fires were less effective. They were also hit by brigade-level counterattacks delivered with an élan and fury that they had not seen since 1914. Yet such courage was costly. The Americans paid a heavy price against their more experienced enemies. The battle see-sawed across the smashed forward trenches. In places the Americans pushed the Germans back to no man's land, only to be driven back in turn by the inevitable German counterattacks. In the swirling, confused fighting, 2nd Brigade of 41st Division found itself cut off and surrounded. The Germans seized advantage of the sudden gap in the American line, pressing forward past flimsy defences. They drove the 1st Infantry Division back towards the Meuse near Samogneux.

The American I Corps was now assailed by elements of the German VII Reserve and XVIII Corps threatening to cut it off. Colonel John Lejeune, commanding the Marine Brigade, made an epic march to throw his two regiments at the German XVIII Corps flank, driving it in and re-establishing contact with 1st Division. The Germans had not seen such bayonet attacks since the opening days of the war. By all odds the assault should have failed in the face of concentrated rifle and machine-gun fire, but the Germans were not prepared for how swiftly and effectively the marines crossed the beaten zone to fall upon them. The price to save I Corps was an appalling 2,500 casualties. Yet, the Germans had gained a great respect for the marines, calling them *Teufel Hünde* (Devil Dogs), a battle honour that the marines would add to their ever-growing list. Pershing immediately appointed Lejeune to command the badly shaken 41st Division. Renewed German attacks the next day forced I Corps to pull back south-eastwards. On that day the isolated American brigade tried to break out but was held in tight by follow-on German units.

It was like this all along 1st Army's front. The Americans would be driven back only to turn on their heels and deliver sharp, though often unskilled and costly, counterattacks. They were being pressed back from west, north, and east towards the fortress belt of Verdun. On the fourth day, the line of the Meuse from just east of Cumiéres to just west of Charny – a distance of almost three miles – had been reached by the Germans. They immediately began bridging the rain-swollen river. Once across they would be in open country. Pershing committed his last reserve, the 3rd Infantry Division. Its 15th and 38th infantry regiments hammered the German bridgehead until it collapsed, then defended the river line for a brutal night and next day as the Germans repeatedly tried to cross. By then Joffre had committed his XXX Corps to close up to the Meuse and put paid to any German chance to bounce the river. For their stand on the river, those two regiments earned their division the title 'Rock of the Meuse', bestowed by Joffre himself.

On the fifth day the Germans, too long enfiladed by French artillery on the west bank of the Meuse, attacked from the north to clear it of the French VII Corps. The Crown Prince was not sanguine about the situation. The Americans had not broken, and he said, 'We have hammered them into a position we will never get them out of.' German losses had been heavy. They had learned that the Americans were resilient, and their counterattacks, though costly, were to be feared. Their accurate and rapid rifle fire reminded the survivors of 1914 of the British regulars. There had been too few prisoners as well, and that isolated brigade remained obstinately defiant. French reinforcements were also converging on Verdun. The Americans, on the other hand, were in a bad mood at having given up so much ground. Their baptism of fire had been painfully brutal. However, the Germans were the best of teachers, and their students quick to learn. At home the country held its breath as the greatest battle in American history unfolded.

Falkenhayn was not holding his breath. He was busy stripping more troops from the armies facing the British to reinforce the battle to break the Americans as they settled into the trench system connecting all the forts around Verdun. The storm of German artillery now fell on the old forts. To everyone's amazement, unlike the Belgian forts, they held. The most important and largest of the nineteen forts was Douaumont at the northern apex of the complex.

Built between 1885 and 1903, the fort covered thirty thousand square metres and was four hundred metres long. A steel-reinforced concrete roof twelve metres thick, resting on a cushion of sand, protected two underground levels. The fort was armed with a 155-mm and a 75-mm gun in individual rotating/retractable gun turrets. Four more 75-mm guns were placed in flanking casemates that swept the intervals with machine-gun turrets. Hotchkiss anti-personnel revolving guns at each corner prevented entry into the surrounding moat.

The fort was a magnet for the Germans. A raiding party of the 24th Brandenburg Regiment (6th Infantry Division) led by Pioneer-Sergeant Kunze, slipped through the American strongpoints outside the fort and approached the moat. The weather was so bad that they were mistaken by American machine-gunners as a returning patrol. Kunze wanted to press forward but could see no access. His men refused to go any further. They were easily driven away by one of the fort's machine guns. Another group of Brandenburgers led by reserve officer Lieutenant Radtke approached the fort from another direction, but were massacred by the alert garrison as they tried to cross the moat.[28]

The battle ground to a stalemate despite repeated German attacks. The Crown Prince had been right. The Americans had been hammered back into the defences of Verdun, a much shorter front, which could be far more easily defended. Now that his front had been shortened so much, Pershing was able to rotate his divisions between the front and rest areas in the rear to prevent them from being burned out. Falkenhayn, in contrast, simply reinforced his committed divisions. Morale fell as the men realised that the battle had become a death sentence. Heavy rains simply worsened conditions for the attackers. On the American side reinforcements and supplies could only be forwarded by the single road and light rail from Bar-le-Duc. In the sort of organisational and logistical efforts for which the Americans had a special talent, almost all the huge fleet of tough Ford trucks in the AEF were devoted to keeping the 1st Army alive and fighting. Looking south from Verdun at night, the road was one solid chain of head lights. The troops dubbed it Henry Ford Drive.[29]

Falkenhayn continued to strip away these reinforcements from the army group facing the British and throw them into the grinding fight at Verdun. The German concentration was much more vulnerable to the massed American and French artillery. The French 3rd Army fought off the German attempt to clear them from the west bank of the Meuse and continued to sweep the German rear with enfilade fire, disrupting their attempts to supply and reinforce their forces.[30]

By the middle of March, it was clear to both Joffre and Pershing that the German attack had passed its culminating point, that time in the process of a battle when losses far outweighed any possible gains. It was a defining moment, such as when the French General Staff saw the gap opening between the German 1st and 2nd armies in the Battle of the Marne in 1914 and an

1-1. Kaiser Wilhelm II. The German Emperor's common sense led to German victory.
1-2. General Helmuth von Molkte, Chief of the German Army General Staff, a man inadequate for his responsibilities.
1-3. Russian mobilisation was slower than Germany's, allowing the Germans to assemble an overwhelming mass of manoeuvre for the battles of 1914.

1-4. Russian POWs taken during the roll of German victories in 1914.

2-1. German heavy howitzers in action. These guns had a devastating effect on the British defences at Gheluvelt, 1914.

2-2. (*Above, left*) Brigadier-General Charles FitzClarence VC. His tragic death removed any hope of stemming the tide of the German advance.

2-3. (*Above, right*) General Max von Fabeck. His meticulous preparation for the assault on Gheluvelt ensured that the Germans achieved a decisive breakthrough.

2-4. (*Below, left*) British and German troops locked in murderous combat at the Battle of Gheluvelt. The outnumbered British defenders were ultimately overwhelmed at the point of the bayonet.

2-5. (*Below, left*) Battle-worn French infantry during the harrowing retreat from Flanders, November 1914.

(*From top, left to right*)
3-1. Field Marshal Earl Kitchener of Khartoum and Broome in 1914.
3-2. Lieutenant General Sir Ian Hamilton, commander of the Constantinople Expeditionary Force.
3-3. HMS *Doris*, the light cruiser whose cheeky raid on Alexandretta emphasized its weakness.
3-4. Indian lancer cavalry in the drive on Aleppo.

3-5. Machine-gunners of the Indian Corps at the Battle of Alexandretta.

3-6. 2nd Australian Light Horse from the ANZAC Mounted Division with thousands of Turkish prisoners taken in the drive on Aleppo.

4-1. Venizelos and the Great Idea: A map of Great Greece with Venizelos's portrait in the left corner.

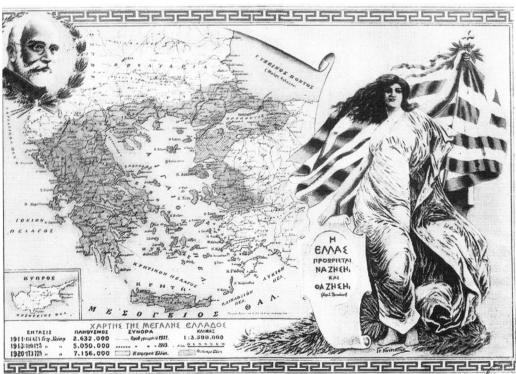

4-2. (*Above, left*) Venizelos and Constantine I, King of the Hellenes.
4-3. (*Above, right*) Colonel Mustapha Kemal, commander of the Ottoman 9th Infantry Division at Gallipoli.

4-4. Greek soldiers of A Corps fighting to cut off the Turkish 5th Army in Gallipoli.

4-5. (*Above, left*) General Liman von Sanders, who commanded the Turkish 5th Army at Gallipoli.
4-6. (*Above, right*) Constantine I and the Greek Army of Thrace on the march to Constantinople.
4-7. (*Below*) The Hagia Sophia before its reconsecration as an Eastern Orthodox cathedral after the Greek capture of Constantinople.

4-8. Greek troops marching in the Allied victory parade in Paris.

5-1. Former President Theodore Roosevelt visiting Kaiser Wilhelm II in 1910. His happy childhood experience in Germany tempered the Allied terms for a defeated Germany.

5-2. General Frederick Funston was selected by President Roosevelt to command the American Expeditionary Force.

5-3. The brilliant American Assistant Secretary of the Army, Franklin D. Roosevelt, President Theodore Roosevelt's proconsul in Europe.

5-4. Fort Douaumont, the key to the fortress complex of Verdun.

5-5. The marine counterattack at Verdun.

5-6. King George V decorates an American soldier armed with the American Enfield, the US modification of the famed British rifle.

6-1. Admiral Sir John Jellicoe aboard his flagship HMS *Iron Duke*. His deft handling of the Grand Fleet ensured a major British victory at Jutland.

6-2. Admiral Reinhard Scheer. His ambitious plan to ambush a portion of the Grand Fleet at Jutland was fatally compromised by British signals intelligence.

6-3. British battlecruiser HMS *Lion* in action at the Battle of Jutland, 1916.

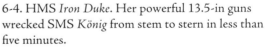

6-4. HMS *Iron Duke*. Her powerful 13.5-in guns wrecked SMS *König* from stem to stern in less than five minutes.

7-1. Pyotr Stolypin, the Russian defence minister, who brought order to the chaos of Russian command.

7-2. General Aleksei Brusilov, the genius behind the Russian victory that won the war.

7-3. General Nikolai Nikolaevich Yudenich, a proven commander, was transferred from the Caucasus Front to command the North-West Front against the Germans.

7-4. General Franz Ferdinand, commander of the Austro-Hungarian 4th Army which collapsed on the first day of the Brusilov Offensive.

7-5. Cossack cavalry overrunning an Austro-Hungarian artillery battery during the exploitation of the Russian breakthrough of the Brusilov Offensive.

7-6. British Lanchester armoured cars armed with a Vickers machine gun in the turret, part of the British Armoured Car Expeditionary Force in Russia that found itself on the plains of Hungary.

8-1. Sir Henry Seymour Rawlinson: the cautious commander (1864–1925). His methodical approach minimized British casualties at the Battle of the Somme at the cost of missing opportunities for a decisive breakthrough.

8-2. British night bombardment at the Battle of the Somme. Relentless British bombardment was the key to Rawlinson's 'bite and hold' approach.

8-3. British infantry in the attack at the Battle of the Somme. Rawlinson had ordered that advances be kept to strictly limited objectives.

8-4. Vanishing villages: Beaumont Hamel, 1916. The fighting to consolidate the captured villages and woods was prolonged and bloody.

9-1. A damaged British tank at the Battle of Arras, April 1917. Arras was a brutal proving ground for the armoured branch, but the lessons learned here laid the foundations for a decisive victory later that year.

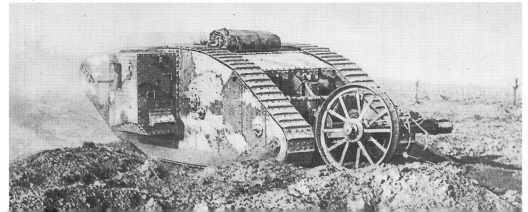

9-2. Light tanks in action at the Battle of St Quentin, 1917. The original caption erroneously describes the tanks as Whippets. They are actually French RT tanks.

9-3. A British tank smashing through a German trench at the Battle of St Quentin. The defenders were powerless to resist the onslaught of the 'Thousand Tank Army'.

9-4. British heavy tanks pushing forward into open country following the breakthrough at the Battle of St Quentin, 1917.

10-1. Alfred Charles William Harmsworth, 1st Viscount Northcliffe.

10-2. German Gotha GV, heavy bomber, June 1917.

10-3. 'End of the Baby Killers!' – British poster showing the destruction of a German airship in a bombing raid over London.

10-4. Prime Minister David Lloyd George, whose murder led to the Northcliffe dictatorship.

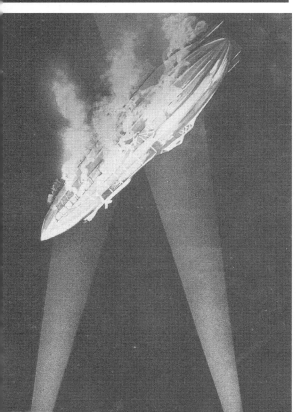

officer had exclaimed, 'They have presented us their flank!' Opportunity beckoned. Joffre and Pershing were of one mind. The opportunity had potential far beyond the immediate battle. Intense pressure was put on Field Marshal Haig, commander of the British Expeditionary Force (BEF) to cooperate. Haig insisted the British were not ready, but the pressure was only elevated to the ministerial level and higher. Franklin Roosevelt, who had become essentially the American proconsul in Europe, personally met with Kitchener, Asquith, and the king, speaking directly for the president. Haig was finally budged, but not as far as Joffre and Pershing wanted. He had been planning for a major attack in the Somme for the beginning of July. The only help he could offer would have limited goals. Good enough, said Joffre.

Operation Drumfire began on 10 March. General Philippe Pétain's heavily reinforced tough 2nd Army attacked directly into the German left flank. On 12 March Pershing sent the 1st Army into the attack just as the Germans had shifted their local reserves to meet Pétain's offensive. Newly promoted Major General MacArthur, now commanding the 42nd Division, and Brigadier General Lejeune, commanding the 41st Division, ruptured the first German line despite heavy losses. MacArthur fell at the head of the last attack to the intense grief of his men.[31] Falkenhayn's response was to pull more troops from the armies facing the British. As soon as this became evident to the Allies on 15 March, Haig launched a series of attacks with limited goals. The weakened German front unexpectedly cracked, and the British quickly reinforced this success.

It was clear to almost everyone in the German higher commands that the great crisis of the war on the Western Front had arrived – everyone but Falkenhayn. It was left to the Crown Prince in a direct appeal to his father to demand that the offensive be called off. The Kaiser rose to the logic of the occasion and dismissed his Chief of the General Staff. General Paul von Hindenburg, the commander of German forces on the Eastern Front, replaced him. It took all his unflappable steadiness and the genius of his alter ego, General Erich Ludendorff, to jury rig repairs to a collapsing Western Front as spring arrived. The 5th Army withdrew to its starting point and was even driven back across the Orne. It was then bludgeoned by Pershing and Pétain's joint attack, which pushed dangerously close to Metz and the railways that supplied most of the German armies to the west.

To the north the situation was even more desperate. The Germans had been pushed out of their defences that had multiplied their combat power in the past. The Hindenburg–Ludendorff repairs unravelled. The unexpected break in the German front allowed the British cavalry corps, ably supported by armoured-car detachments, to fan out in the German rear. The German armies there fought stubbornly where they could, but the front was no longer a single fortress line. It had been ruptured. Almost a hundred thousand prisoners were taken as the BEF surged forward. It became increasingly futile to shift reserves to ward off a relentless cascade of blows. The final blow was the fall of Metz to the Americans and the French in Operation Lafayette on 30 May. The railway network supplying the German armies to the West was thereby severed. Church bells rang across both France and America. In desperation for a victory the Germans sallied their High Seas Fleet for a showdown battle with the British Grand Fleet. The resulting Battle of Jutland was a decisive defeat for the Germans on 1 June. On the Eastern Front, three days later the Russian Brusilov Offensive erupted and went on to break the back of the Austro-Hungarian Army, forcing Vienna to sue for peace. There could be no reinforcements from the disintegrating Eastern Front. Defeat upon defeat crushed the hope of an increasingly hungry German people.[32]

In the bitterest day of his life, the Kaiser authorised Bethmann-Hollweg to seek an armistice at the beginning of July. The queen of the Netherlands offered her good offices, and commissioners met in The Hague to hammer out the truce that threw silence over the armies on the first day of August. Theodore Roosevelt's outsized personality gave him a prominence in the fashioning of peace. Now his nature as a peacemaker eclipsed that of the soldier. It was his influence that prevented a ruinous peace from being imposed on Germany.

As the diplomats and generals said their goodbyes after the peace had been settled, a member of the French delegation, the white-maned Georges Clemenceau, responded to a German complaint that his country had been treated unjustly. The old man bristled with a fierce look. 'Do not complain, Boche. You should kiss that American's arse. Had you fought on, and had it been in my power, I would have fastened upon you such a Carthaginian Peace that you would never have risen again – *Germania delenda est*.'

The Reality

The point of departure for this chapter was the election of Theodore Roosevelt in the 1912 election, where, in fact, he had been defeated by running as leader of a third party against Republican President Howard Taft and Democrat

Woodrow Wilson. He had actually picked Taft to succeed him in the 1908 election. Thereafter Taft and he had had a falling out that led Roosevelt to organise and run on the ticket of the new Bull Moose party. By splitting the Republicans, Roosevelt handed the election to Wilson. Roosevelt's actions in this story are fully in accord with his attitudes and statements. He was eager to get the United States into the Great War on the side of the Allies. His distant cousin, Franklin Roosevelt, was appointed by President Wilson as Assistant Secretary of the Navy, a position in which he excelled. It led to a lifetime love for the navy. During the Second World War, Chief of Staff of the US Marshal, General George C. Marshall, pleaded with President Franklin Roosevelt to stop referring to the navy as 'us' and the army as 'them'.

General Frederick Funston was a friend of Roosevelt and the most prominent American commander. He was actually picked by Secretary of War Baker and President Wilson to lead the AEF. He died of a massive heart attack just before the appointment could be made. Pershing, who had been serving under Funston in the expedition against Mexico at the time, was then selected.

American intervention in mid-1915 would have come at a time when American production of weapons and the other materials of war had not had time to tool up as it had by the time the United States entered the war in mid-1917. There would have been a very large bottleneck in equipping the expanding US Army because the Allies themselves were in the process of expanding their production in that first year of the war. That alone would have limited the number of American divisions that could actually be equipped for combat. Nevertheless, by late 1916 the American economy would have been fully tooled and able to support a multi-million-man AEF, a full two years before America's actual entry into the war in April 1917. The disparity in numbers and resources most likely would have peaked far earlier than it did in reality because a large part of the German Army was still committed to the Eastern Front.

In reality, in 1917 American weapons producers had already tooled up for producing the British Enfield rifle, despite the contracts being cancelled in June 1916. The decision was made to concentrate on producing an Enfield modified to take American ammunition. It was designated the M1917 Enfield or the 'American Enfield'. During the war, 2,193,429 American Enfields were produced. It was issued to 75 per cent of the AEF and was the weapon with which Sergeant Alvin York earned the Medal of Honour. In the Second World War the British bought 618,000 of these weapons, which were delivered in the summer of 1940.

Falkenhayn concluded that the Western Front was a fortress that could not be turned. Instead he planned the Battle of Verdun to be a killing machine, convinced that he could force the French to bleed their army white and break the morale of the French people at an acceptable cost in German lives. That was one of the greatest miscalculations in military history. He had thought that he could inflict three French casualties for every one German. Instead, it turned out to be almost one to one. In this story, the presence of a new and inexperienced American army inserted into the line at Verdun invalidated those calculations and made a complete rupture of the front a real possibility to him.

Sergeant Kunze and Lieutenant Radtke were actually responsible for capturing Fort Douaumont by entering through undefended casemates left unmanned by Joffre's insistence on stripping the forts of their garrisons. The officer who came much later to take over command of the fort sent the report of its capture. He was the one awarded the *Pour le Mérit*, Germany's highest medal, by the Kaiser. It certainly seemed fitting, for the man was a Prussian officer whose family name was preceded by 'von', the mark of the historical German social and political elite. Neither Kunze nor Radtke were recognised during the war. Only when the official histories were written after the war were their deeds discovered. Kunze was a police officer then and received a quickly advanced promotion to inspector. Radtke was given an autographed photo of the deposed Crown Prince. *Sic transit gloria mundi.*[33]

Notes

1 In the years leading to the third Punic War (149–146 BC) in which Rome destroyed Carthage, the Roman statesman, Cato the Elder, frequently ended his speeches in the Senate even when they had nothing to do with foreign policy, with the sentence, 'Carthago delenda est' ('Carthage must be destroyed').

2 The Civil War song 'Marching Through Georgia' was sung by Union troops under General William T. Sherman as they burned a swathe through Georgia sixty miles wide, from Atlanta to the sea, in 1864.

3 Stuart Creighton Miller, *Benevolent Assimilation: The American Conquest of the Philippines 1899–1903* (New Haven: Yale University Press, 1982), pp. 234–5.

4 http://en.wikiquote.org/wiki/Talk:Otto_von_Bismarck, accessed 14 November 2013. He also said, a 'special Providence watches over children, drunkards, and the United States', *Harper's New Monthly Magazine*, December 1856.

5 'Letter from Theodore Roosevelt to Sir Edward Grey,' available online at http://wwi.lib.byu.edu/index.php/Letter_from_Theodore_Roosevelt_to_Sir_Edward_Grey, accessed 13 June 2014.

6 S. L. A. Marshall, *World War I* (New York: American Heritage Press, 1971), p. 271. *See also Edward M. House, *He Kept Us Out of War: An Alternate History of the Presidency of Woodrow Wilson* (New York: Simpson & Sons, 2009), p. 22. This popular alternate history speculates on the twentieth century without American intervention in the Great War, particularly how the neutrality of a fictitious Wilson administration, elected twice in 1912 and 1916, allowed the victory of the Central Powers in 1918 and the subsequent naval war between the United States and Germany, 1928–9.

7 H. W. Brands, *TR: The Last Romantic* (New York: Basic Books, 1997), p. 43.

8 B. H. Liddell Hart, *The Real War 1914 to 1918* (Boston: Little, Brown, & Co., 1930), p. 313.

9 Peter G. Tsouras (ed.), *Warriors' Words: A Quotation Book* (London: Arms & Armour Press, 1992), p. 184.

10 *Joseph McPherson, *Roosevelt and Military Preparedness* (New York: Warner & Bros, 1922), pp. 89–92.

11 Laurence Stallings, *The Doughboys: The Story of the AEF* (New York: Harper & Row, 1961), p. 30.

12 Brands, *TR: The Last Romantic*, p. 521.

13 *James Weathers, *Franklin Roosevelt in the Great War* (New York: Black, Hutton & Co., 1948), p. 44. Franklin Roosevelt's role as Assistant Secretary of the Army led to a permanent identification with that service. During his own presidency, the Chief of Naval Operations was at pains to remind the president not to refer to the army as us and the navy as them. See also James MacGregor Burns, *Roosevelt: The Soldier of Freedom: 1940–1945*, Francis Parkman Prize Edition (New York: History Book Club, 2006), p. 349.

14 John J. Pershing, *My Experiences in the Great War* (New York: Frederick A. Stokes, 1931), vol. 1, p. 48.

15 John S. D. Eisenhower, *Yanks: The Epic Story of the American Army in World War I* (New York: The Free Press, 2001), p. 17.

16 *John Winthrop, 'Theodore Roosevelt as War President', *American Historical Review* (March 1943), p. 38. Roosevelt actually cribbed these lines from one of Funston's staff officers who accompanied him to the ceremony – Colonel Charles E. Stanton, a nephew of Lincoln's Secretary of War, Edwin Stanton.

17 *Oscar E. Steinhaus, *Der Kaiser im Krieg und Frieden* (Frankurt: Bettelman & Söhne, 1923), p. 246.

18 C. R. Ballard, *Kitchener* (New York: Dodd, Mead & Co., 1930), p. 327.

19 David Burg, *Almanac of World War I* (Lexington: University Press of Kentucky, 2010), p. 120.

20 Leonard G. Shurtleff, 'The Doughboy's Rifle: It Wasn't Necessarily a Springfield', The Doughboy Center, The Story of the American Expeditionary Forces, www.worldwar1.com/dbc/dbrifle.htm, accessed 10 November 2013.

21 Thomas Dodson Stamps and Vincent Joseph Esposito, *Short Military History of World War I* (West Point, NY: United States Military Academy, 1950), pp. 163–4.

22 Winston S. Churchill, *The World Crisis 1916–1918, Part I* (London: Thornton Butterworth Ltd, 1927), p. 87.

23 John Keegan, *The First World War* (New York: Alfred A. Knopf, 1999), p. 279.

24 *Dwight D. Eisenhower, *American Arms Production in the Great War*, Leavenworth Monograph Series (Fort. Leavenworth, KS: US Army Command and General Staff College, 1935), p. 34. Production did in fact spike during the summer of 1916. Still it would be a minuscule rate compared to the production of the America Enfield when it was expected to go into full production in the later part of 1916.

25 *Jonathan T. Miller, *American Hero: MacArthur of the 42nd Division* (Boston: Houghton, Mifflin Co., 1922), p. 110.

26 Stamps and Esposito, *Short Military History of World War I*, p. 164.

27 Ibid., p. 165.

28 Alistair Horne, *The Price of Glory: Verdun 1916* (New York: Harper Colophon Books, 1967), pp. 109–16.

29 *Louis Davout, *France's Crown of Thorns: The Battle of Verdun* (New York: William Morrow and Co., 1935), p. 97. In this richly imagined alternate history, the point of departure is the delayed American entry into the war in 1917 and Falkenhayn's pursuit of his original idea of launching a battle of attrition to kill so many Frenchmen that the morale of France would collapse.

30 *George C. Marshall, *Verdun: America's Greatest Battle* (Garden City: Doubleday, Doran & Co., 1919), pp. 280–2.

31 *Miller, *American Hero*, p. 291. MacArthur was awarded the Medal of Honor which President Roosevelt presented to his mother at a ceremony at West Point where a new cadet barracks was named after him.

32 *Winston S. Churchill, *Spring of Victory: 1916* (London: John Murray, 1920), pp. 322–5. As commander of the 6th Royal Scots Fusiliers at the time, his eyewitness accounts of the breakthrough and pursuit of the German armies captured the heady excitement of victory.

33 Horne, *Price of Glory*, pp. 120–1.

6

Britannia Rules the Waves

The Battle of Jutland, 1916

Spencer Jones

The Challenge

On 15 June 1888, the twenty-year-old Kaiser Wilhelm II was crowned emperor of Germany. Although capable of moments of brilliant insight, Wilhelm II was infamous for his obnoxious arrogance, uncontrollable temper and erratic decision making. Intensely Anglophobic, he despised the British Empire and felt that Germany was being denied 'a place in the sun' by a conspiracy of British and French interests. Wilhelm II was determined to redress this balance.

Germany began to build its colonial empire in the 1890s using a handful of warships, but Wilhelm II dreamed of creating a fleet that would one day topple the Royal Navy itself. In 1897 he appointed Konteradmiral Alfred von Tirpitz as Secretary of the Imperial Navy Office. Tirpitz shared Wilhelm II's naval ambitions and had the political skill to steer the proposals through the Reichstag. Within a year, Germany had passed the First Naval Bill, which called for the construction of nineteen battleships by 1904. In 1900, Tirpitz used the pretext of strained Anglo-German relations as a result of the Boer War to increase the provision of battleships to thirty-eight vessels.

The gauntlet had been thrown down to Britain. For almost a century the Royal Navy had been the undisputed master of the oceans. Lord Horatio Nelson's legendary victory at the Battle of Trafalgar in 1805 had established such an overwhelming sense of British naval superiority that no other major power had dared to challenge it – until now.

The British government quickly perceived that German naval building was not merely a danger to the empire, but, by virtue of Germany's geographic position, represented a grave threat to Britain itself.[1] The Royal Navy responded to German construction in kind. The first great arms race of the twentieth century had begun.

In 1906 the Royal Navy changed the terms of the contest with the launch of the revolutionary battleship *Dreadnought*. This vessel was faster, better armoured and more heavily armed than any ship then afloat. *Dreadnought* was so advanced compared to her rivals that from that point on battleships would be classed either as modern dreadnoughts or outdated pre-dreadnoughts.

Some strategists in Britain hoped that the launch of *Dreadnought* would convince the Germans that they were beaten and thus end the ruinously expensive contest. They had reckoned without the determination of Wilhelm II and Tirpitz. Germany saw the launch of *Dreadnought* as an opportunity, for although the new ship had rendered the German fleet obsolete, it had also done the same for the vast majority of existing British battleships. The balance sheet was cleared and it would now be a contest to see who could build dreadnoughts fastest. The arms race intensified in the years that followed as both sides strained to manufacture ever greater numbers of modern warships.

From *Dreadnought* onwards, each successive class of ships was bigger, faster, and more powerful than the last. Covered in thick steel plate, driven by the largest and most powerful engines available and carrying the heaviest guns it was possible to mount, the modern battleship was the most powerful weapon system in the world. The dreadnoughts were supported by battlecruisers, formidable vessels of comparable size that were built to emphasise speed and armament at the expense of armoured protection. In addition, both navies constructed numerous light cruisers, destroyers, and torpedo boats to support the heavy ships.

The naval race strained finances to the limit, but it was Britain which emerged as the clear leader. By the outbreak of war the Royal Navy had launched twenty dreadnoughts, with another twelve under construction, compared to thirteen German dreadnoughts, with seven being built.[2]

Germany now faced a serious strategic problem. During the arms race, Tirpitz had deluded himself with the hope that the fleet would be a deterrent weapon that would intimidate Britain and convince it to stay neutral in the event of war. At its heart the policy was a bluff – and the bluff was abruptly called in August 1914. The German Hochseeflotte (High Seas Fleet) now had to consider how to overcome the numerically superior Royal Navy.

The Balance of Power

Although heavily outnumbered, the High Seas Fleet had some advantages over the rival Grand Fleet. The most obvious was that it was concentrated in the North Sea. Whereas the British had to provide vessels to police the imperial trading lanes, the Germans could focus all their attention on the main theatre of operations. The expectation of operating in the North Sea had influenced German ship design. The vessels of the High Seas Fleet tended to be less heavily armed but more heavily armoured than their British counterparts. This trade-off was considered viable given Germany's numerical disadvantage. Each vessel was precious and therefore survivability was of foremost importance.

There was no doubt that the German ships were highly resistant to damage. However, this fact was well known to the British Admiralty, and during the naval arms race a number of measures had been taken to nullify the German advantage in armoured protection. The British had increased the calibre of their heavy guns so that their latest vessels mounted mighty 15-inch batteries. More importantly, the British had also given serious thought to the design and effectiveness of their armour-piercing shells. Firing exercises had discovered numerous flaws with existing British ammunition. The most serious was the tendency of the shells to burst against armour plating rather than tearing through the steel and exploding in the interior of the enemy ship as they were intended. The problem was traced to a combination of inadequate fuses and unreliable explosive.[3]

Director of Naval Ordnance and future commander of the Grand Fleet John Jellicoe was at the forefront of demanding improvements in ammunition. Although promotion soon took him away from his role with the ordnance department, he continued a vigorous campaign for better shells.[4] The Admiralty reacted with the tardiness typical of large bureaucracies but Jellicoe refused to let the matter rest. The reform of the design, testing, and procurement process for new shells was painfully protracted but on the very eve of the war a new type of armour-piercing shell was finally accepted. Jellicoe was well pleased with the improved ammunition, claiming that it 'certainly doubled' the effectiveness of the Grand Fleet's big guns.[5] However, production delays caused by the demands of war meant that it took until mid-1915 for the fleet to be fully equipped with the new shells.

At the same time that ammunition was being improved, a fierce and often ill-tempered debate was raging over the best methods of fire control. At the heart of the issue was the firebrand Captain Percy Scott, who campaigned for centrally directed fire control and a wholesale reform of gunnery training. An abrasive and arrogant character, Scott nevertheless drove his reforms through and conclusively proved the value of his methods during gunnery trials. Admiral Sir John Fisher offered a blunt assessment of Scott: 'I don't care if he drinks, gambles and womanises; *he hits the target*.'[6]

A particularly important reform pioneered by Scott was the adoption of a 'double salvo' system of fire. Under this system a capital ship would fire two quick salvos spaced several hundred yards apart. The fall of shot would be observed and appropriate corrections made: for example, if one salvo fell short and the other went over the target then the distance clearly lay in the middle and could be quickly calculated. Once the double salvo had acquired the range the guns would switch to rapid fire and smother the target with shells. The advantage of double salvo was that it allowed guns to zero in far quicker than if the range was determined using a single salvo.[7]

The combined effect of these reforms was considerable. The Grand Fleet possessed more numerous and noticeably heavier guns than the High Seas Fleet. It was clear that in a fleet encounter the mighty broadsides of the British ships would prove decisive. As a result, Germany planned to fight a *klienkrieg* – a 'small war' – using mines and submarines. These subtle weapons would whittle away at the Royal Navy's numerical preponderance until the number of British capital ships was so reduced that a fleet action could be fought on even terms.

Unfortunately for Germany, the strategy was bankrupt from the very beginning. The Royal Navy instituted a distant blockade based on closing the exits of the North Sea and refused to charge recklessly into German waters which were teeming with undersea hazards. For their part, the Germans limited their efforts to some commerce raiding and the occasional 'tip and run' bombardment of British seaside towns. However, the latter operations were abandoned after the German battlecruisers of the 1st Scouting Group barely escaped from a bruising encounter with their British opposites at the Battle of Dogger Bank on 24 January 1915.

Forbidden by order of Wilhelm II from taking undue risks, the High Seas Fleet spent the rest of 1915 in a state of inertia. Meanwhile, the British blockade slowly tightened. Rationing was introduced in Germany in early 1915. The German nation was in the grip of a British stranglehold and only the navy had the power to break it.

The Ambush

In early 1916 a new commander, Admiral Reinhard Scheer, took charge of the High Seas Fleet. Scheer recognised that the naval situation was intolerable for Germany. Its attempts to use submarines to attack British commerce had succeeded only in alienating the United States. By contrast, Britain's surface blockade was unrelenting and would remain so as long as the Grand Fleet was still afloat.

Scheer proposed a new strategy. The High Seas Fleet would take the fight to the British by returning to 'tip and run' attacks and aggressive operations designed to lure the Grand Fleet into an unfavourable battle. Scheer hoped to inflict stinging losses by ambushing isolated squadrons of the Royal Navy and escaping before retribution followed. The High Seas Fleet would work alongside submarines and minelayers to draw the British into ambush zones.

Yet unbeknownst to Scheer, the strategy had a fatal flaw – the British knew his every move. In August 1914 the German cruiser *Magdeburg* had run aground in the Baltic and been captured by the Russians. Onboard were three copies of the German naval signals book and cyphers.[8] The Russians shared a copy with the British, and by November the Admiralty had established a dedicated naval cryptography department codenamed Room 40. By 1916, Room 40 could decode virtually all German naval signals traffic. Relevant information was swiftly passed to Jellicoe and the Grand Fleet.

Ignorant of these developments, Scheer spent May 1916 planning an ambush for the British. The fast battlecruisers of the 1st Scouting Group would draw out the British battlecruisers and lead them on a chase that would ultimately carry them into the arms of the German battleships. Locally outnumbered, the British would be destroyed before reinforcements could arrive.

It was a simple and effective plan that may well have worked – but the British knew of it before it had even begun. In the small hours of 31 May, before Scheer had even set sail, the entire Grand Fleet had left port and was steaming towards the ambush area. Jellicoe planned to turn the tables on the Germans. His battlecruisers, under the command of flamboyant Vice-Admiral David Beatty, would 'allow' themselves to be drawn into Scheer's trap. However, as soon as the German battleships appeared, Beatty was to turn about and lead them into a head-on collision with the awesome force of the entire Grand Fleet. The trap was set.

The Chase

The Battle of Jutland started in unassuming fashion. Beatty's vessels were cruising in the region of anticipated German activity but the disappointing absence of enemy ships was in danger of dampening the mood. At 2.20 p.m. the light cruiser *Galatea* noticed a small tramp steamer blowing off an unusually large amount of steam, an action consistent with suddenly being forced to stop. Curious, the *Galatea* turned away from her sister ships and approached the civilian vessel. It was a minor incident in what had so far been an uneventful sweep.

As she approached the steamer, *Galatea* observed two unknown ships approaching from the opposite direction. Several pairs of binoculars snapped onto the newcomers and less than a minute later the signal 'ENEMY IN SIGHT' was flying from her yardarms and an urgent message had been whisked down to her wireless station. Seconds later she fired the first shot of the great battle, hurling a 6-inch shell at the approaching German ships.

The signal had an electrifying effect on Beatty's squadron of six battlecruisers – *Lion, Princess Royal, Queen Mary, Tiger, New Zealand,* and *Indomitable*. With Beatty's flagship *Lion* in the lead, the battlecruisers swung around towards the approaching enemy. The call 'Action Stations!' was sounded and dense smoke poured from the funnels of the fast, sleek ships as they worked up to their fearsome top speed of some twenty-seven knots. Following close behind were the four battleships of the 5th Battle Squadron – *Barham, Valiant, Malaya,* and *Warspite* – under the command of Rear-Admiral Hugh Evan-Thomas. Ships of the *Queen Elizabeth* class, they were known as 'super dreadnoughts' due to their cutting-edge combination of armour, guns, and speed. Due to their high top speed of twenty-five knots the *Queen Elizabeth* class were the only heavy units capable of operating alongside battlecruisers; however, in any prolonged chase they would inevitably start to lose ground.

Fortunately for the British, Beatty had taken account of 5th Battle Squadron's lower top speed and had kept the ships close to his battlecruisers so that they would not be left behind in any sudden change of course.[9] Both battleships and battlecruisers now turned to the south-east, increasing speed and clearing the decks for action. Union flags were hoisted at the main mast and numerous white ensigns were run up the yardarms. *Malaya* raised the flag of the Federated States of Malaya. Ten formidable warships were now surging through the sea to meet the Germans head on.

Their opponents were the five battlecruisers of Rear-Admiral Franz von Hipper's 1st Scouting Group – *Lutzow, Derfflinger, Seydlitz, Moltke,* and *Von der Tann.* A German gunner onboard *Derfflinger* recorded the approach of the British ships: 'even at this great distance they looked powerful, massive . . . It was a stimulating, majestic spectacle as the dark-grey giants approached like fate itself.'[10] However, Hipper remained calm. His task was not to engage in a stand-up fight but instead to lure the British into reach of Scheer's battleships. As Beatty and Evan-Thomas bore down on him, Hipper reversed course and began to race away to the south-east. The chase was on.

The range steadily decreased as the British closed in on the fleeing Germans. Beatty's battlecruisers had reached twenty-five knots, with Evan-Thomas's ships straining to keep up behind him. British and German destroyer flotillas rushed into the 'no man's land' between the capital ships, prows bursting from the sea as they raced along at thirty-five knots. The tension was almost unbearable. A stoker in *New Zealand* remembered an 'incredible thrill' at hearing the order 'All guns load!' being relayed through the internal telephone system.[11]

It was the Germans who began the firing. The broadsides of their battle-cruisers rippled with flame as their sent out their first salvo at approximately 18,500 yards range – and closing fast. The British immediately returned fire. A crewman on *Malaya* remembered: 'It was the most glorious sight and I was tremendously thrilled.'[12] Incoming shells 'appeared just like big bluebottles flying straight towards you, each time going to hit you in the eye; then they would fall and the shell would either burst or else ricochet off the water and lollop away above and beyond you; turning over and over in the air.'[13]

But shells soon began to smash home. Visibility favoured the Germans and they exploited their advantage to the full. *Tiger* was set ablaze and a direct hit on *Lion* blew the roof off a forward turret and started a dangerous fire that threatened to detonate the magazine – and with it the entire ship – until the chamber was flooded by order of the fatally injured Major Francis Harvey, who won a posthumous Victoria Cross for his action. Most seriously of all, the *Indomitable* was simultaneously struck by almost every shot of a salvo fired from *Von der Tann*. The damage was catastrophic: ablaze from stem to stern, *Indomitable* turned away from the action and tried to open the range, but within a minute she was engulfed in a huge explosion and disappeared beneath the waves.

The British battlecruisers returned fire furiously but their gunnery was wayward, for their crews were not as thoroughly trained as their Grand Fleet comrades. However, the big guns of the 5th Battle Squadron were a different proposition. A German crewman recalled of the *Queen Elizabeth*s: 'There had been much talk in our fleet of these ships . . . Their speed was scarcely inferior to ours but they fired a shell more than twice as heavy as ours. They opened fire at portentous ranges.'[14]

The effect was swift. Fifteen-inch shells plunged down around the German ships, causing devastation wherever they struck. All of Hipper's ships felt the force of this fire, but *Von der Tann* was hit particularly hard. Shells wrecked her superstructure and caused serious flooding below decks. One crewman recalled that the 'tremendous blow' of being hit by a 15-inch shell made the 'hull vibrate longitudinally like a tuning fork'.[15]

Although visibility favoured Hipper's ships, the greater weight of British fire began to tell on the 1st Scouting Group. German vessels shuddered beneath high-calibre-shell hits that sliced through steel plate as though it were paper. Soon Hipper's battlecruisers were cloaked beneath the smoke of the numerous fires that raged aboard. *Von der Tann* was so heavily damaged that she could scarcely fire a single gun, but her captain courageously kept her in the line so that the British could not concentrate fire on her sister ships.[16] German fire slackened as the 1st Scouting Group adopted a zigzag pattern to try and throw off the aim of the British ships.

However, Hipper could endure such punishment as long as he could fulfil his part of the German plan. Every minute of the chase brought the British closer to Scheer's battleships. The trap was about to be sprung.

The Run to the North

At approximately 4.35 p.m. a barrage of signals burst from Beatty's advanced light cruiser screen. The most important was 'Have sighted enemy battlefleet SE. Enemy course north.' Scheer and his battleships were on the way.

However, Beatty had been prepared for this due to the information relayed by Room 40. Wasting no time, at 4.40 p.m. he ordered his squadron to swing about and begin its own race to the north. In a role reversal, Hipper's ships turned and now became the pursuers, whilst Scheer and his dreadnoughts increased their speed and strained to bring their heavy guns to bear.

Fortunately for the British the turn away from Scheer was executed with skill. The 5th Battle Squadron fell into line behind Beatty's battlecruisers and the two squadrons raced north. The battle against Hipper's ships continued, and the 5th Battle Squadron exchanged long-range fire with the van of Scheer's battlefleet. A British sailor remembered that 'their salvos began to arrive thick and fast around us at the rate of 6, 8, or 9 a minute.'[17] Visibility once again favoured the Germans, but both sides scored hits. By now the 1st Scouting Group was feeling the effects of an hour of fierce combat. At around 5 p.m. *Von der Tann*, listing and ablaze, suffered a serious hit to her engine room that brought her to a shuddering halt. Down at the bows and crippled beyond repair, she sank within the hour.

Scheer was prepared to accept these losses if he could catch and destroy Beatty's force. Unfortunately for the Germans, every minute brought them closer to the British trap. Beatty was sending a steady stream of positional reports to the rapidly approaching Jellicoe, who was well informed as to the German course, speed, and bearing.[18] At 4.51 p.m. Jellicoe had felt sufficiently confident to send a tantalising signal to the Admiralty: 'FLEET ACTION IS IMMINENT'.[19]

Jellicoe had a little longer to wait. It was not until around 5.40 p.m. that Beatty made contact with the advance elements of the Grand Fleet. At this point Beatty made an important and decisive manoeuvre, turning his ships on a north-easterly course and cutting across the German vessels that were running parallel to him. This caused the Germans to turn onto a similar course themselves to avoid Beatty 'crossing the T' and being able to concentrate the fire of his entire squadron on the first ship in the German line. A German officer later commented that this was 'an excellent tactical manoeuvre', for it blinded Scheer to the approach of the Grand Fleet until it was far too late.[20]

Concealed from German view and with the element of surprise on his side, Jellicoe gave orders for his massive fleet to change from cruising formation to a battle line. This was a decision that could have momentous consequences. If Jellicoe got the manoeuvre wrong his ships would blunder into battle in a state of disorganisation and possibly be defeated as a result.

The stakes were enormous. In Winston Churchill's memorable words, Jellicoe 'was the only man on either side who could lose the war in an afternoon'.[21]

If the gravity of the situation weighed on Jellicoe's mind, his ice-cold demeanour did not betray the fact. His orders were clear and his crews thoroughly trained. With a smoothness that belied the complexity of the manoeuvre, twenty-four dreadnoughts deployed into a compact fighting line approximately six miles in length. Years after the battle, the famous fighting admiral Sir Andrew Cunningham remarked: 'I hope I would have the sense to make the same deployment that JJ did.'[22]

The Tables Are Turned

Scheer was about to receive the shock of his life. A fellow officer on the bridge of the *Friedrich der Grosse* noted that Scheer did not have 'the foggiest idea of what was happening'.[23] The German fleet of sixteen dreadnoughts and six pre-dreadnoughts was heading directly towards the massed broadsides of the Grand Fleet. Beatty's sharp turn had blinded the Germans to the danger which they were about to face.

Hipper's battered vessels were the first to feel the force of the British guns. Localised fog had descended across part of the seascape and Hipper was surprised when several fresh British battlecruisers – the vanguard of the Grand Fleet – suddenly emerged at medium range. Both sides opened fire immediately but the British gunnery was exceptionally good. *Invincible* rained shells on the German ships, prompting her captain to inform his gunnery officer: 'Your fire is very good. Keep it up as quickly as you can. Every shot is telling!'[24] The punishment proved too much for Hipper's flagship *Lutzow*, which staggered away from the action with mortal damage below the waterline. Hipper transferred his flag to a torpedo boat but was unable to get aboard a capital ship for the remainder of the battle, thus removing his dynamic leadership from the German fleet.

However, this short, violent clash of battlecruisers was only a precursor to the main event. At around 6.20 p.m. 'the veil of mist was split across like the curtain at a theatre' and Scheer's battlefleet was confronted with an image of Armageddon.[25] One officer recalled that all he could see on the horizon was 'the belching guns of an interminable line of heavy ships, salvo followed salvo almost without intermission.'[26]

The results were devastating. Jellicoe's flagship *Iron Duke* singled out the *König* and fired forty-three shells at her in less than five minutes, scoring hit after hit. Shell splinters ripped through the armoured compartments, gun turrets were torn asunder, and an officer recalled being knocked off his feet as a result of 'several violent concussions in the forepart of the ship' that produced a drastic list to port. More hits followed until the *König* suddenly lurched over and capsized.

Elsewhere the courageous battlecruisers of the 1st Scouting Group finally met their nemesis. The gunnery officer of *Derfflinger* recalled: 'Several heavy shells pierced our ship with terrific force and exploded with a tremendous roar which shook every seam and rivet.'[27] With her lower compartments flooded, her funnels shot away and her gun turrets reduced to burning wreckage, *Derfflinger* finally disappeared beneath the deluge of fire. Her sister ships *Moltke* and *Seydlitz* only escaped a similar fate by retreating into the mist, concealed by smoke from the uncontrolled fires that raged aboard. The 1st Scouting Group had effectively been destroyed. *Seydlitz* would sink later that night and *Moltke* was lucky to be able to limp home with severe damage.

Scheer had a single chance to save his fleet. With shells plunging down around his ships and the *König* vanishing beneath the waves, Scheer ordered a *Gefechtskehrtwendung* – a sudden, simultaneous turn away – to take his ships away from Jellicoe's punishing fire. It is a testament to the quality of German training that the manoeuvre was carried out comparatively successfully, although Scheer's lead ships were subjected to a hail of shells that inflicted further damage. Turning his back to the British, Scheer led his vessels away into the darkening mist.

Jellicoe was not in a position to observe the manoeuvre and was initially perplexed as to what had happened. Expecting Scheer to re-emerge from the fog at any moment, Jellicoe steered his fleet to the south to close in on his quarry. At this point, Scheer made a fatal mistake. As the firing died out, he reasoned that if he were to reverse course again then he would pass in the wake of the Grand Fleet, effectively slipping behind them while they fruitlessly cruised south. This done, he would be able to escape into the dusk and retreat to safer waters.[28]

However, Scheer had miscalculated. Instead of slipping behind the Grand Fleet, he mistimed his turn and led his ships right into the middle of the southbound British line. The position was even worse than during the initial clash. The German line was in a state of disorganisation, many ships were struggling to put out fires caused by the earlier encounter with Jellicoe, and the 1st Scouting Group had been forced to withdraw from the action, leaving the High Seas Fleet partially blind. Visibility decisively favoured the Grand Fleet: British ships were partially concealed in the North Sea mist, but German vessels were silhouetted against the horizon and presented a perfect target.

The German situation was dire. Scheer's vessels were closely bunched as a result of their earlier sharp turns. The congestion at the head of the fleet was so severe that some ships were forced to stop to avoid collisions with their sisters.[29] One officer described the situation as an 'absoluten Wurstkessel!'[30] A tornado of British fire swept through the German line. Salvo after salvo shrieked in from the east, with the source only visible from the constant gun flashes that illuminated the horizon.

With the 1st Scouting Group gone from the battle, the British were able to concentrate every available gun on Scheer's dreadnoughts. The damage was catastrophic. A shell smashed into the engine room of the *Markgraf* and exploded with dreadful force. A survivor recalled: 'The terrific air pressure resulting from [an] explosion in a confined space roars through every opening and tears through every weak spot. Men were picked up by that terrific air pressure and tossed to a horrible death among the machinery.'[31] *Grosser Kurfurst* was struck by a 15-inch round that blew a thirty-foot-wide hole below her waterline and caused her to list sharply to port. A shell ripped through a casemate gun battery aboard *Kaiser* and ignited stored ammunition, causing a huge gout of flame to erupt from the side of the ship.

With his battleships reeling under the remorseless guns of the Grand Fleet, Scheer desperately ordered a second *Gefechtskehrtwendung*. But the manoeuvre was no easy matter under heavy fire, with the High Seas Fleet dangerously bunched and forced to steer around the crippled *Markgraf*. In the confusion *Kronprinz* and *Prinzregent Luitpold* collided, with both ships suffering severe damage as a result. Attempting to buy time, Scheer ordered his torpedo boat flotillas to rush the Grand Fleet and launch a mass torpedo attack.

The small vessels raced towards the Grand Fleet, braving a barrage of fire from the secondary batteries of the battleships. Jellicoe responded by steering his ships away from the oncoming attack, causing many of the torpedoes to run out of range well short of his battle line. The few that reached the battleships were easily avoided. The manoeuvre was a 'skilful dodge' that left Jellicoe's line undamaged and fully formed.[32]

However, the turn away had broken contact with Scheer's ships, which had disappeared into the gloomy twilight, leaving behind only the stricken

Markgraf, which was swiftly 'blotted out' by a hail of heavy shells. Steering towards Scheer's last position, Jellicoe's ships sporadically opened fire at dim sightings in the mist, but the fading light prevented a renewal of battle.

The darkness saved the High Seas Fleet from complete destruction, but the German fleet experienced a harrowing night. On several occasions the picket lines of light cruisers and destroyers brushed against one another, prompting sudden, savage skirmishes in which both sides lost ships. More seriously for Scheer, British destroyer flotillas slipped through the German cruiser screen to launch daring torpedo attacks against his battleships. In the confused engagement that followed, the German pre-dreadnought *Pommern* was hit and sank with all hands.

As the night wore on, Scheer planned his escape route. He guessed that the British would be steaming south to try and cut off his retreat. He hoped to slip behind them and take his surviving ships home to Wilhelmshaven via the Horns Reef. He reasoned Jellicoe would be unlikely to pursue for fear of running into hidden German minefields.

But Room 40 was a step ahead. At 10.10 p.m. they had decrypted a signal from Scheer which asked for zeppelin reconnaissance over Horns Reef at first light. The message was in Jellicoe's hands by 10.30 p.m. and he altered the Grand Fleet's course to intercept Scheer at first light. This was not a simple manoeuvre and involved a great deal of what Commodore Reginald Tyrwhitt described as 'groping in the dark'.[33] Tensions were high and the night was punctuated by sudden bursts of gunfire at real or imagined targets.

Both British and German officers anxiously scanned the horizon as the grey dawn began to break over the North Sea. However, it was the weather – the ultimate arbiter of naval warfare – that would define the engagement of 1 June. The sea around Horns Reef was shrouded with dense fog that gradually broke up into thick clouds of drifting mist. Visibility was poor and information sketchy.

In places the mist suddenly cleared and short, sharp actions broke out. These engagements proved fatal for several damaged German vessels. The most serious loss was the *Prinzregent Luitpold*. The ship was already listing due to severe damage below the waterline as a result of her earlier collision when she was suddenly engaged at long range by *Benbow*. *Prinzregent Luitpold* was hit several times in the brief exchange of fire that followed, causing further flooding and forcing her crew to abandon ship.

However, there was to be no general engagement on 1 June. Visibility was poor and although Jellicoe was aware from sighting reports that he was in rough proximity to the southbound High Seas Fleet, he was increasingly concerned that he was in danger of leading his vessels into one of the many German minefields in the area. Ultimately, a fresh Room 40 decrypt informed Jellicoe that Scheer was in the region of Heligoland to the south. The High Seas Fleet had slipped away in the mist. Jellicoe was disappointed and afterwards criticised himself for not pressing the retreating Germans harder, but he was comforted by a letter from Beatty in which the latter reminded his commander, 'When you are winning, risk nothing.'[34]

Nevertheless, it was clear that the Royal Navy had won a striking victory. The High Seas Fleet had been mauled, losing four battlecruisers in the form of *Lutzow*, *Seydlitz*, *Derfflinger*, and *Von der Tann*, five battleships – *König*, *Kaiser*, *Grosser Kurfurst*, *Markgraf*, and *Prinzregent Luitpold* – as well as the pre-dreadnought *Pommern* and a considerable number of lighter ships. In addition, unbeknownst to the British the battleship *Ostfriesland* struck a mine on its way home and sank.[35]

The Battle of Jutland was over. The triumph was not quite on the scale of Trafalgar, but it was a great victory for the Royal Navy all the same.

The Fruits of Victory

The Grand Fleet returned home in a jubilant mood. They had inflicted a heavy defeat on the Germans and suffered few casualties in return – *Indefatigable* was the only British capital ship lost during the fighting. Jellicoe was the hero of the hour and was lauded by press, public, and navy. Beatty also received lavish praise, although he was heard to grumble that without the efforts of his battlecruisers the battle would never have occurred, much less been won. After almost two years of difficulties and setbacks on the land front, the British public savoured the moment of triumph. The 'spell of Trafalgar' had been recast.

The Admiralty soon sought to capitalise on the victory. There was bold talk of withdrawing the Royal Naval Division from the Western Front and using it in an amphibious assault against one of the small islands that dotted the German North Sea coast. Daring attacks on Heligoland and Borkum were proposed as a precursor to a landing on the coastline of Germany itself. However, the painful lessons of Gallipoli were still fresh in British minds and there was little appetite for another risky amphibious operation. Furthermore, such naval adventures would needlessly place elements of the Grand Fleet at risk and allow the Germans to extract some measure of revenge for Jutland.

Nevertheless some of the bolder officers of the Royal Navy saw merit in making feints against the German coast. They reasoned that the psychological effect of 'demonstrations, raids, and harassment' in enemy waters would be considerable. The inability of the High Seas Fleet to prevent such operations would be revealed, thereby harming public morale and perhaps even persuading the German General Staff to transfer additional army resources to defend the coast.

Over the course of 1916 the Royal Navy launched several raids against German coastal islands and associated shipping. The highly trained Harwich Force and its dynamic commander, Commodore Roger Keyes, were at the forefront of these operations. Although the attackers were at risk from mines and submarines, they were secure in the knowledge that the battleships of the cowed High Seas Fleet would not emerge to destroy them. Germany's coastal defence forces consisted of small or obsolete vessels that were no match for the modern destroyers and light cruisers of Harwich Force. Several German ships were intercepted and sunk during raids in June and July. In August, Harwich Force took advantage of a captured map that revealed the swept channels in the German minefields and carried out a daring bombardment against shore installations on Heligoland. One of the shells struck an overstocked magazine and caused a huge explosion that was visible on the German coastline. The incident sparked alarm amongst the civilian population, who feared that it was a precursor to a British invasion. As a result, the army sent additional forces to Hamburg and invested considerable effort in improving Germany's coastal defences.[36]

The most important consequence of the Battle of Jutland was the tightening of the Allied blockade. Although the naval cordon was already formidable, there were some weaknesses that allowed neutral powers to continue trade with Germany. For example, Norway had continued to trade materials such as coal, copper ore, and nickel on the basis that they were not classed as contraband under the terms of the London Naval Conference of 1909. However, the dominance of the Royal Navy after Jutland allowed Britain to pressure Norway and other neutrals into ceasing maritime trade with Germany altogether.

In addition, the victory had altered the balance of power in the Baltic. Russian and German vessels had sparred with one another throughout 1915, but Russian efforts were hampered by concerns that Germany would deploy the High Seas Fleet to the east and overwhelm Russia's Baltic defences. Jutland removed this fear and allowed Russia to adopt a more aggressive naval strategy. Encouraged by Britain, Russia targeted Germany's iron-ore trade with neutral Sweden.[37] Although the delicate nature of Russo-Swedish relations made it impossible to halt the trade entirely, the efforts of the Russian Navy greatly diminished the flow of the precious raw material.

In combination, these changes applied a deep chokehold on Germany's economic windpipe. The pressure steadily mounted in the second half of 1916 and the effects would be severely felt the following year.

Recriminations and Consequences

In Germany, the search for a scapegoat began scant hours after the battered remnants of the High Seas Fleet had limped into Wilhelmshaven. On hearing news of the disaster Wilhelm II worked himself to such a pitch of fury that witnesses feared for his health.[38] The worst of his wrath fell upon Scheer. Citing the example of Admiral John Byng, a British officer executed by firing squad in 1757 for 'failing to do his utmost in battle', the Kaiser demanded that Scheer be placed on trial for his very life. The demand met with concerted opposition from officers and men of the fleet – including its new commander, Franz von Hipper – as well as from ministers and politicians.

Wilhelm II ultimately backed down in the face of threats of resignation and mutterings of mutiny in the fleet. Soon, his mood had changed from anger to despair. Depressed over the fate of his beloved navy, he refused to visit the remaining vessels of the High Seas Fleet and lost all interest in naval matters. The Kaiser's apathy hurt the survivors of Jutland deeply, contributing to a precipitate decline in morale that would fester into open mutiny by early 1917.[39]

The Naval Staff remained detached from the post-battle recriminations and devoted their efforts to formulating a new strategy. The possibility of an Allied landing against the German coast was studied in depth. Although the exploits of Harwich Force caused a degree of concern, the Germans judged that the British were unlikely to risk capital ships in mine-infested coastal waters. Nevertheless, the Naval Staff gratefully accepted the offer of army support and the construction of heavy-gun emplacements on the North Sea coastline.

A much more serious problem was the remorseless and intensifying blockade. Planners warned that the German economy would be brought to its knees in 1917 unless the stranglehold was broken. But how was this to be achieved? There was no prospect of defeating the Grand Fleet in battle. In the view of many key naval officers the only hope lay in the submarine. In late June, Admiral Henning von Holtzendorff produced a controversial memorandum arguing that a return to unrestricted U-boat warfare was Germany's only hope of victory. This was a risky proposal, for a new submarine campaign would bring the United States into the war on the side of the Allies. Holtzendorff's case rested on the belief that submarines could inflict such severe damage on maritime trade that Britain would be forced to seek terms within six to eight months. Britain would thus be defeated long before America had fully mobilised. The plan was a huge gamble, but it offered the tantalising prospect of victory.

On 1 September 1916 Germany announced the resumption of unrestricted submarine warfare. Despite initial successes the policy would prove disastrous. Neutral opinion was enraged and the United States declared war in November. Worse still, Britain was ultimately able to overcome the submarine menace through introducing the convoy system and assigning large numbers of destroyers from the Grand Fleet to serve as escorts. The full and terrible consequences of Germany's policy would become apparent in 1917.

The Reality

The Battle of Jutland is one of the most studied naval engagements of all time. The debate still continues as to which side 'won' the battle. The Germans inflicted heavier losses, sinking the battlecruisers *Indefatigable*, *Queen Mary*, and *Invincible* and only losing the battlecruiser *Lutzow* in return. But ultimately the High Seas Fleet fled from the engagement damaged and in disorder. The experience was sufficient to convince Scheer that future surface engagements were best avoided. As a result the German Navy would not seek battle in the North Sea for the remainder of the war. After casting about for a solution for several months, Germany finally returned to submarine warfare in February 1917. The High Seas Fleet languished in harbour and was wracked by mutiny in November 1918.

There are innumerable 'what ifs' around the Battle of Jutland, many of which focus on the contrasting personalities and decisions of Beatty and Jellicoe. Much of the interest of Jutland centres on how close the British came to a crushing victory. Historically, the British had a tremendous advantage in the form of Room 40 and possession of the German code books. As described in the story, British intelligence on Scheer's movements was so good that the Grand Fleet actually set sail before the High Seas Fleet had left port. Such accurate intelligence placed the initiative firmly in the Royal Navy's hands. Beatty managed to lead the unsuspecting High Seas Fleet into range of Jellicoe's guns and Scheer's ships were in mortal danger, particularly when they blundered into the Grand Fleet for the second time. However, Jellicoe lost sight of the enemy by turning away to avoid a torpedo attack and was unable to regain contact in the evening gloom.

In this scenario the main change to the history is technical rather than tactical. A fundamental problem for the Royal Navy was the inadequacy of their armour-piercing shells. A detailed study of damage at Jutland discovered that British armour-piercing shells managed to penetrate heavy armour and explode internally on just one occasion (a 15-inch hit from *Revenge* on *Derfflinger*).[40] Historically, Jellicoe was aware of the problems with British shells as early as 1910, but made little effort to make changes.

In the story these problems are corrected by Jellicoe prior to the war. I have assumed the Royal Navy are equipped with the improved shells that appeared in 1917–18, making British gunnery far more powerful. I have also had the navy adopt the 'double salvo' system prior to the war; historically it was introduced post-Jutland to speed up gunnery, but there is no reason why it could not have been introduced earlier.

The main tactical change in the scenario is Beatty's performance in the opening of the battle. In reality, Beatty made a serious tactical error by leaving the 5th Battle Squadron too far behind his battlecruisers, thus denying himself their powerful support in the engagement against Hipper. Here I have assumed he handles his forces with more skill and keeps the *Queen Elizabeth* class close. This would have dramatically changed the nature of the fighting and probably saved the *Queen Mary* from destruction. Finally, I have introduced the Room 40 decrypt that revealed Scheer was heading to Horns Reef, thus allowing the Grand Fleet a few parting shots. Historically, it remains a mystery why this message was never passed on to Jellicoe.

I am very grateful to Dr Philip Weir for his assistance in researching this scenario.

Notes

1 V. E. Tarrant, *Jutland: The German Perspective* (London: Brockhampton Press, 1999), p. 11.
2 Ibid., p. 18.
3 Andrew Gordon, *The Rules of the Game: Jutland and British Naval Command* (London: John Murray, 1996), p. 505.
4 *Philip Weir, *Feed the Guns: The Reform of British Naval Gunnery 1905–1914* (London: Oaken Press, 2012) p. 145.
5 Gordon, *Rules of the Game*, p. 506.
6 Keith Yates, *Flawed Victory: Jutland 1916* (Annapolis: Naval Institute Press, 2000), p. 30.
7 Norman Friedman, *Naval Firepower: Battleship Guns and Gunnery in the Dreadnought Era* (Annapolis: Naval Institute Press, 2008), pp. 103–4.
8 Paul G. Halpern, *A Naval History of World War I* (Annapolis: Naval Institute Press, 1994), pp. 36–7.
9 *Weir, *Feed the Guns*, p. 150.
10 Gordon, *Rules of the Game*, p. 108.
11 Ibid., p. 108.
12 Ibid., p. 109.
13 Ibid., p. 110.
14 Ibid., p. 115.
15 Tarrant, *Jutland: German Perspective*, p. 88.
16 Ibid., p. 107.
17 Gordon, *Rules of the Game*, p. 411.
18 *R. B. Cartwright, *Beatty and Jellicoe: A Dynamic Partnership* (London: Castle Press, 2001).
19 Gordon, *Rules of the Game*, p. 419.
20 Ibid., p. 32.
21 Winston Churchill, *The World Crisis 1911–1918* (London: Odhams Press, 1931), vol. 2, p. 1015.
22 Gordon, *Rules of the Game*, p. 441.
23 Ibid.
24 Ibid., p. 450.
25 Ibid.
26 Ibid., p. 452.
27 Tarrant, *Jutland: German Perspective*, p. 133.
28 Scheer's thought processes at this moment remain the subject of much debate. See Gordon, *Rules of the Game*, p. 458.
29 Ibid., p. 459.

30 Ibid. Literally, an 'absolute sausage boiler!'

31 Tarrant, *Jutland: German Perspective*, p. 37.

32 Gordon, *Rules of the Game*, p. 461.

33 Halpern, *Naval History*, p. 331.

34 Ibid.

35 *Mark Randleman, *Naval Statistics of the Great War* (London: Hodder, 1937), pp. 212–15.

36 *C. D. Stoneman, *Raiders! British Operations in German Coastal Waters 1916–1918* (London: Castle Press, 2007), pp. 45–56.

37 Halpern, *Naval History*, pp. 206–17.

38 *Jonathan Myles, *The Kaiser's Court* (London: E. Arnold, 1956).

39 *Owen Prytherch, *Red Fleet: The Mutiny at Wilhelmshaven 1917* (Cardiff: Triumvirate Press, 2009).

40 John Campbell, *Jutland: An Analysis of the Fighting* (London: Conway, 1999), p. 222.

7

The Brusilov Offensive, 1916
Russia's Glory

Peter G. Tsouras

Kiev Opera House, 14 September 1911

The sparkling overture to Rimsky-Korsakov's *The Tale of Tsar Saltan* had just concentrated every eye in the Opera House away from Tsar Nicholas II and his two eldest daughters, the Grand Duchesses Olga and Tatiana. In the stalls was Pyotr Stolypin, forty-nine, the former prime minister. Stolypin had resigned only a few months before, but the tsar wanted to show there was no bad feeling and had made the opera a command performance for his former minister.

Using his badge as a member of the Okrana, the Russian secret police, an armed Dmitri Bogrov was able to approach Stolypin, who had refused to wear his armoured vest even though the police had warned him of an assassination plot. Bogrov shot him twice in the arm and once in the chest. As the assassin was dragged away, Stolypin opened his coat to reveal a blood-soaked shirt. Looking up at the stunned Nicholas in his box, he made the sign of the cross and announced in a firm voice that he was happy to die for the tsar. He was rushed to the hospital, where the doctors were only barely able to save his life. A very long recovery was diagnosed. The tsar came to Stolypin's hospital bed and humbled himself as he begged, 'Forgive me.'[1]

Verdun, 21 February 1916

At first light 1,201 German guns erupted to hurl a continuous crushing fire on the three French divisions defending an eight-mile sector protecting the French fortress complex at Verdun. Two-thirds of the guns were heavy or mediums, the former stripped from the rest of the German armies on the Western Front. Thirty-three ammunition trains a day would be needed to feed the guns as the reinforced 5th Army attacked. It was an offensive designed by the Chief of the German General Staff, Erich von Falkenhayn, to burn out the French Army. Winston Churchill would write of it:

> It was not to be an attempt to 'break through.' The assailants were not to be drawn into pockets from which they would be fired upon from all sides. They were to fire at the French and assault them continually in positions which French pride would make it impossible to yield. The nineteen German divisions and the massed artillery assigned to the task were to wear out and 'bleed white' the French Army. Verdun was to become the anvil upon which French military manhood was to be hammered to death by German cannon. The French were to be fastened to fixed positions by sentiment, and battered to pieces by artillery.[2]

French pride, however, did not preclude them from strenuously asking the Russians for help as more and more of their own divisions were committed to the slaughterhouse of Verdun. The French were desperate for the Russians to launch offensives that would force the Germans to reinforce their eastern front from forces fighting it out in the great battle in the west. The Russians promised to help, but they had memories of the last time they had made such vows – at the opening of the war they had charged into Prussia with two field armies, only to have one utterly destroyed and the other gutted.

Russian High Command of the Army, Mogilev, 25 February 1916

Defence Minister Stolypin shivered despite the warmth of the fireplace in his study. The import of the French demands for help was not lost on him. The war was consuming Russia. The previous year had been one of disaster. The Russian Army had been driven out of Poland and suffered two million losses – 1916 promised to be even worse.

His wound suffered five years ago in the assassination attempt ached all the more in the cold weather. It had taken him years to recover, and it was only last month that the tsar had asked him to take up the burdens of defence minister.[3] It was an easy decision for Nicholas to make. After all, the tsar bore an enormous sense of guilt for the attempt on Stolypin's life, having put him in harm's way by requesting his presence at the opera. The tsar had every reason to feel remorse. Stolypin had been the finest of his ministers. His agricultural reforms to break up the peasant collectives into individual farmsteads had begun to establish an independent peasantry to be a bulwark of the throne. Now more than ever that throne needed support.

Nicholas's incompetence as a war leader, after he had assumed command of the armed forces, had done much to discredit the monarchy. His only talent seemed to be the ability to make the wrong decision. It was a feast for a host of revolutionaries whom Stolypin had so effectively curbed, before his wounding, by ruthlessly employing what a Duma member had termed, 'Stolypin's efficient black Monday necktie' – the gallows. Stolypin had reason to hate them: a bomb had killed his fifteen-year-old daughter and wounded his three-year-old son. One of the revolutionary leaders, Vladimir Lenin, from his exile in Switzerland, had said it was Stolypin's agricultural policy that was the greatest threat they faced in seizing power. The imbecilic decision at the beginning of the war to abolish the military police corps had allowed the revolutionaries a priceless opportunity to sow sedition, repeatedly fertilised by endless reverses.

What had cleared the way for the tsar's decision, besides the universal recommendation of his ministers and the Russian Orthodox Church, was the murder of his chief enemy, the depraved but hypnotic monk Gregori Rasputin. Stolypin had warned the tsar about Rasputin's antics, but Nicholas had ignored it because of the tsarina. Alexandria believed Stolypin was evil for his opposition to Rasputin, and to her that threatened the life of her only boy, her beloved Aleksei, the heir, fatally afflicted with haemophilia. Only Rasputin had been able, through what she believed was his spiritual power, to bring him back from death's door as his body began to bleed uncontrollably. That opposition had been swept away by Prince Prince Felix Yussupov and Duma member Vladimir Purishkevich when they lured Rasputin to the former's palace, and with great effort, murdered him in December 1915. Luckily, the tsarevich had not had an attack since the monk's death. Stolypin lit a new candle in church every day to pray that the tsarevich remained in good health and that his mother continued to dote on her son rather than direct her venom at him. He also kept his fingers crossed. He knew that sooner or later the boy's affliction would kill him, and he did not need the imperial family consumed in grief or the political shock waves that would come from the death of the heir. That would leave Grand Duchess Olga next in line of succession. It occurred to him that Russia had not done too badly when a woman had sat on the throne.

As to his ability to save that throne and Russia, Stolypin thought it was probably too late. War production had not been able to properly equip and sustain the army. There had not been enough rifles for the hundreds of thousands of men being called up to replace the staggering losses, not enough ammunition of all kinds. The only serious victories had been against the Austro-Hungarians whose empire, a patchwork of fractious nationalities, had proved especially brittle. Had it been only a war between Austria and Russia, the tsar's armies would by now have occupied Vienna. But it was the Germans who were the serious enemy – efficient, professional, well-supplied, and brilliantly led at every level. The German Army proved remarkably resilient and its combat effectiveness had actually improved as the war had continued. It was their remorseless and deadly offensives that inflicted the worst damage on the Russians. Furthermore, German reinforcements and their increasing operational control of the Austro-Hungarians had saved them from being mortally savaged by the Russian bear. The Germans had soon learned to treat their Austro-Hungarians with a well-deserved contempt. Early in the war the German representative on the Austro-Hungarian General Staff had wired Berlin presciently, 'that we are shackled to a corpse'.

That appraisal was cold comfort to the Russians now. Stolypin, in his recuperation, had stayed abreast of events and personalities that the war had raised up. His first requirement was for capable men. That was why his cousin's husband, General Aleksei Brusilov, was sitting beside him in front of the fireplace. He had not seen him for years, but the man did not seem to have changed. Despite his sixty-three years, he remained slim and energetic at an age when Russian generals so often turned to fat. There was a sharp intelligence in his blue eyes which made you realise why he was considered the finest of Russia's generals, the man who had repeatedly beaten the Austro-Hungarians. It was not by brute force but by his high leadership skills, his thoroughness, and above all by his ability to innovate and adapt. The men of his 8th Army had been better trained and cared for than in any other command, and they had given him victories.

'Aleksei Alekseyevich, Forgive me for not rising to greet you,' Stolypin said. He had never fully recovered from that bullet wound, 'but . . .'

'No need, Pyotr Arkadyevich. Soldiers understand. Your injuries were suffered in service to Russia as much as any soldier's on the battlefield.' They had both used the familiar first name and patronymic that bespoke a deep friendship. They exchanged pleasantries as a servant brought in steaming glasses of tea, which only Russians seem to be able to hold without burning themselves.

When the doors shut, Stolypin turned to the matter at hand. 'I must speak candidly. Tell me, have we lost the war?'

'Yes, we have.' He paused, then added, 'If things are allowed to go on without any serious changes in the command of the armies.'

Russia needed a giant like Peter the Great or even Nicholas's father, Alexander III, a real autocrat with the ability to carry it off. Instead, they had 'Nicky', as his German and English cousins called him, a man who had been born on the name day of 'Job the Sufferer', which had not been lost on a pious Russia. Peter and Alexander must be rolling in their graves. Before he had been shot, an incredulous Stolypin had written in his diary of the tsar's words to him. 'I have a premonition. I have the certainty that I am destined for terrible trials, but I will not receive a reward for them in this world . . . Perhaps there must be a victim in expiation in order to save Russia. I will be this victim. May God's will be done!'[4]

Stolypin's immediate problem was guiding the tsar, who seemed to be even more the resigned and passive martyr; since he had declared himself commander-in-chief of the armed forces, he had not thought to actually take command. With Rasputin out of the way, Stolypin was able more and more to influence Nicholas, who seemed be almost relieved to leave decisions on the war to such a strong, capable personality.

Brusilov was too tactful to criticise the tsar to his defence minister, family or not, but he took aim right below him, at the Chief of Staff of the Russian Army, General Mikhail V. Alekseyev. He said, 'Alekseyev is not up to the job. He is conscientious but gets lost in the details and has no strategic vision. Nor can he enforce his will on the front commanders who run to the tsar and bring up their social connections every time he tries to force them to exercise common sense and good judgement.' Stolypin agreed with Brusilov's description of the Stavka (army high command) and Alekseyev.

'And the front commanders?' Stolypin asked.

'Evert is stubborn, cautious, and does not cooperate, even on Alekseyev's orders. Kuropatkin is indecisive and incapable of organising his forces. His performance is no different than in the war with the Japanese twelve years ago. What did Voltaire say? Learned nothing and forgotten nothing.' Stolypin nodded at the assessments of the commanders of the North-West and Northern Fronts, Generals Aleksei Evert and Aleksei N. Kuropatkin.

'And your own front commander?' he asked.

Brusilov did not hesitate. '[Nikoalis L.] Ivanov is just worn out and used up. He has no more to give. The demands of modern war are beyond him. He has become an old ninny.'

'Whom would you recommend to replace them?'

Headquarters, Ober-Ost, 10 March 1916

Field Marshal Paul von Hindenburg was not happy with Falkenhayn's obsession with Verdun. Already, the plan to wear the French down was a double-edged sword. German soldiers in that maelstrom were starting to call him the 'blood miller of Verdun'. Hindenburg, the Ober-Ost, commander of the four German armies fighting the Russians, thought German resources would be better used in a major offensive in the east to knock the Russians out of the war. Already he had them on the ropes. He chafed that he did not control the German troops sent to reinforce the relentlessly incompetent Austro-Hungarian armies south of the Pripet Marshes. This vast natural barrier formed the boundary between the German and Austro-Hungarian armies.

Falkenhayn and Hindenburg did agree that the Austro-Hungarian obsession with their new offensive against the Italians was draining strength from their armies facing the Russians. The Austro-Hungarian Chief of Staff, Franz Conrad von Hötzendorf was, to say the least, not well thought of by his German allies. Conrad's missteps would have earned him a brutal dismissal in any other army, yet the fecklessness of Austro-Hungarian politics kept him in place. Now his determination to punish the Italians for joining the Allies against their former dual-monarchy allies was making him oblivious to the Russians. By February Conrad planned to transfer three of his divisions from the Russian front and asked for German troops to backstop them. Falkenhayn and Hindenburg turned him down flat. Falkenhayn had already transferred eight German divisions from the east to Verdun. Not only would there be no German support, but if there was a Russian build-up opposite Hindenburg's armies in the north, German troops supporting the Austro-Hungarians would be recalled.

Conrad was unfazed. He withdrew four division in March for the offensive planned to begin in May. He further weakened these armies by withdrawing numerous individual battalions, often the most experienced, as well as fifteen batteries, almost all the heavy artillery in the four armies facing the Russians. For example, on 14 February, the 3rd Infantry Division, made up of ethnic Austro-Hungarian Germans with a good combat record, transferred to the Tirol. It was replaced by the 70th Honved (Hungarian Reserve) Division, which had absolutely no combat experience. Conrad reasoned that the preponderance of Russian forces faced the Germans while only 600,000 Russians faced 570,000 Austro-Hungarians along their 450-kilometre front. Against the Germans they had a definite numerical superiority. That is where the Russians were expected to attack. He wrote in late March that under conditions of parity on his own front, 'a Russian attack would have to be considered pointless.'[5]

The incapacity of the Russians had just been proved by their disastrous performance at the Battle of Lake Naroch on 18 March. In response to the French pleas for offensive action to take some pressure off their forces at Verdun, the Russians had attacked the Germans in the southern approaches to the Baltic with 350,000 men of the Russian 2nd Army against the 75,000 men of the German 10th Army – twenty divisions against four and half. For once there were enough artillery shells to feed the almost one thousand guns. It was a disaster. The Russians staggered off after having lost a hundred thousand men to the fewer than twenty thousand German casualties. No account had been taken of the spring thaws that made the ground a morass that sucked up artillery shells. There was no artillery reconnaissance, and most of the huge shell expenditure was wasted. Senior leadership had been wretched. Alekseyev wrote of one general commanding a group of corps, 'It seems unlikely that he will be able to manage the bold and connected offensive action or the systemic execution of a plan that are needed. Still, he could not relieve him because of his social connections as it was alleged, "some old granny still has fluttering about the heart when his name comes up."'[6] Lake Naroch was the death knell of the old Russian Army. It remained to be seen if a phoenix would rise out of the ashes.

Russian High Command of the Army (Stavka), Mogilev, 14 April 1916

Stolypin's increasing control of the tsar and the war effort was like a fresh wind blowing through the army. The war itself had already done its own winnowing. Men who knew how to get things done were increasingly filling critical positions. One of them was General Anton Ivanovich Denikin. Brusilov had praised him to the heavens as just the sort of outstanding combat leader the army needed. Under Brusilov, he had commanded first the famed Iron Brigade and then the 48th Division with an intelligent aggressiveness that made it famous and lethal. He was quickly advanced to command the VIII Corps in Brusilov's 8th Army.

Another officer was twenty-three-year-old Captain Mikhail Nikolayevich Tukhachevsky, an officer of the Semyenovsky Guards Regiment,[7] who had said as the war began, 'I am convinced that all that is needed in order to achieve what I want is bravery and self-confidence. I certainly have enough self-confidence . . . I told myself that I shall either be a general at thirty, or that I shall not be alive by then.' In the space of the first six months of the war he was decorated five times for valour. Unfortunately, he had been captured early in 1915 and sent to the German POW camp at Ingolstadt for being an incorrigible escapee. He succeeded on his second attempt to cross the German–Swiss border and returned via the United States and the Trans-Siberian Railway, just in time to be assigned to Brusilov's staff. He quickly showed that he was brilliant. Brusilov paired him with Denikin as his deputy operations officer. The two hit it off famously and made a great team, with the young man fully taking over the job as operations officer. It quickly became clear that the young Tukhachevsky had a ruthless streak. He did not suffer fools. Neither did Denikin. They would have their hands full.[8]

Stolypin astounded the Russian Army by sacking Evert and replacing him with General Vasily Iosifovich Gurko, fifty-four, to command the West Front's three armies. The former commander of the 2nd Army and the man who had reorganised the Guards Corps after its heavy losses, Gurko had been a major advocate of military reform before the war. In a private interview Stolypin told the astounded Gurko that it was Brusilov who had enthusiastically recommended him. Stolypin explained, 'I have promoted you because we need to sweep away the habit of defeat. You know, of course, that you have made an enemy of every general you have jumped over. Most of them need to be jumped over. I give you the authority in the tsar's name to remove any officer you think not up to the job and to promote any you think have talent.' Stolypin was accelerating the already growing rise of capable men in the Russian Army. The anvil of war had hammered away many a phony reputation, but there were unfortunately many left.

Kuropatkin was dismissed at the same time. His replacement to command the North-West Front was the fifty-four-year-old General Nikolai Nikolayevich Yudenich who had repeatedly beaten the Turks on the Caucasus Front. His latest success was to capture the city and fortress of Ezerum in eastern Anatolia in January just in time to take the bloom off the Turkish victory at Gallipoli. Stolypin decided to keep Alekseyev who now received rational and firm direction through the tsar from Stolypin, who was closely advised by Brusilov. With Brusilov, Denikin, and Yudenich now commanding the three Russian fronts, Alekseyev would find his team easy in the traces. He also reasoned that it was one change too many for Nicholas to lose someone who was such a committed defender of the monarchy, something Stolypin was in full accord with.

The power arrangement was clear when Stolypin sat in on the first meeting of Alekseyev and his three new front commanders, an unprecedented intrusion into military affairs by a civilian minister. No one complained. He simply listened. The British and French were asking for a strong Russian offensive to take the pressure off them in France, and the meeting was ostensibly about how to address that. Alekseyev began by recommending that another attack by the West and North-West Fronts against the Germans would be the most effective. 'We are capable of a decisive attack only on the front north of the Pripet.' He went on to explain that when the new conscript classes arrived, they would have a superiority of 745,000 men north of the Pripet and only 132,000 south of it in Brusilov's South-West Front.[9] Enough rifles, artillery, and ammunition of all sorts was now starting to be received from Russian industry as well as Allied shipments to the Arctic ports and along the Trans-Siberian Railway from Vladivostock. For the first time, there would be adequate ammunition and enough rifles. Men would not have to be told to pick up the weapons of the fallen.

Brusilov spoke: 'Gentlemen, the unfortunate strategic truth is that we are simply not going to beat the Germans in the field, this year at least, by directly attacking them.'

Gurko stood up, visibly angry, 'Are you saying the war is hopeless? I refuse to accept that we cannot defeat them.'

'I did not say we could not defeat them, general. I said we could not beat them in the field. There is a difference. The Germans have an Achilles heel, gentlemen, but it is not anywhere along their front. The vulnerability is their alliance with Austria. If it had been a war just between Russia and Austria, the tsar would have been dictating terms in Vienna last year. The only thing that holds the Austro-Hungarian front together is the stiffening of a few German divisions and the ability of the Germans to reinforce them. The Austro-Hungarian Army is a shell. If it collapses, Vienna must sue for peace and drop out of the war. The Germans simply do not have the forces to cover the entire war in the east. To defeat the Germans, we must attack them indirectly.'

He also pointed out that, unlike the German Army which was ethnically homogeneous, the Austro-Hungarian armies were patchworks of nationalities, most of whom could not speak German, the command language of the army. In '1906, out of every 1,000 enlisted men, there were 267 Germans, 223 Hungarians, 135 Czechs, 85 Poles, 81 Ruthenians (or Ukrainians), 67 Croats and Serbs, 64 Romanians, 38 Slovaks, 26 Slovenes, and 14 Italians.' Almost half of that thousand (422) were ethnic Slavs of one kind or another, many of whom would be inclined to identify with their fellow Slavs, the Russians. The ruling Germans and Hungarians numbered 490, not even half of the force. The remainder were the Italian and Romanian Latins whose homelands were outside the empire, and in the case of Italy, were at war with the Hapsburgs.[10]

'This is what I propose. You – Gurko and Yudenich – will pitch into the Germans and hold them tight so that they dare not send any reinforcements to the Austro-Hungarians. I will attack the Austro-Hungarians with my front. The Austro-Hungarians will shatter, we will pursue them through the passes in the Carpathian Mountains and into the plains of Hungary. We have fifty cavalry divisions we can unleash into that perfect country for horsemen. No matter what the Germans do they will not be able to establish a line.'

Everyone was silent as they drank in the ramifications of what Brusilov had just outlined. Alekseyev spoke first. 'Unfortunately, we learned from Lake Naroch that even plentiful artillery ammunition was not enough to break the German lines.'

'General, there is nothing like incompetent execution to ruin a good idea. We will deal with the incompetence and waste no more Russian lives because of it. The Germans are due for a surprise.'

South-West Front, April–May 1916

Brusilov's innovations at the South-West Front became a school for the rest of the army. Staffs and commanders from the other two fronts rotated frequently through to observe and take note and to implement those models on their return to their own commands. Brusilov was keenly aware that the Germans had good intelligence of what was going on behind the Russian lines. The movement of large forces spotted by German reconnaissance aircraft was always a key indicator of Russian intentions. For that reason, Brusilov asked only for a few reinforcements but those were in specialised units such as engineers, signals, some heavy artillery, and aeroplanes. The latter's chief role was in reconnaissance of the Austro-Hungarian Army positions opposing the South-West Front.

It became clear that the Austro-Hungarians 'were concentrating on construction rather than on any active defence against the Russians. Recruits sent to the Russian Front as replacements for the veteran troops diverted to the Tirol were put to work extending and strengthening the positions established . . . in September 1915.' The emphasis was on strength of the forward positions with very little depth. This was done at the expense of combat training and active defence. What training they did receive consisted of rifle drill, parades, and snow shovelling. There was no live fire or close-combat training. 'This had the dual effect of tiring the troops and establishing non-military activity as the "norm" of the front lines.' Those forward defences were intended to consist of three groups of three lines each, but as late as the beginning of June the Austro-Hungarians had only completed the first element along most of their front. Aerial reconnaissance kept Brusilov fully informed of the extent and layout of these defences.[11]

The Austro-Hungarian forces had been reinforced with about thirteen thousand German troops, interspersed among several of the Hapsburg armies. The northernmost was Army Group Linsingen commanded by the highly capable German colonel, General Alexander von Linsingen. The German element was Group Gronau (German XLI Reserve Corps) of Guards Cavalry, 5th Cavalry and 65th and 81st infantry divisions. This force blocked the southern part of the Pripet Marshes, and were not directly opposed to the Russian South-West Front. They faced the West Front's 3rd Army. The Austro-Hungarian 4th Army was nominally under the command of Linsingen, but the fact that its commander, Archduke Josef Ferdinand, was the godson of Emperor Franz Joseph allowed him to escape the usual German domineering attitude when commanding Austro-Hungarian forces.

The following table shows the Hapsburg forces, with attached German divisions, from north to south. They numbered eight cavalry and 37 infantry divisions of which two were German. All units are Austro-Hungarian unless identified as German.[12]

Austro-Hungarian Order of Battle Opposing the Russian South-West Front 4 June 1916

4th Army, HQ Lutsk, Commander: Archduke Josef Ferdinand
Cavalry Corps
Polish Legion (9th KD, 11th HID)
    Corps Fath (26th and 53rd ID)
    Corps Szurmay (7th and 70th ID)
X Corps (2nd ID, 37th HID)
II Corps (4th ID, 41st HID)

The following 1st and 2nd Armies formed Army Group Böhm-Ermoli.

1st Army, HQ Ziechov, Commander General Paul Puhallo von Brlog
XVIII Corps (7th KD, 25th and 46th ID)
Group Marwitz (7th and 48th German ID, 22nd and 107th ID)
2nd Army, HQ Brody, Commander General Eduard Freiherr Böhm-
    Ermoli
Group Kosak (4th, 17th, 29th ID)
V Corps (31st ID)
IV Corps (14th and 33rd ID)
Südarmee, HQ Brzesany, Commander General Count Felix von Bothmer
IX Corps (19th and 32nd ID)
Corps Hofman (54th and 55th ID)
48th German Reserve ID
7th Army, HQ Kolmea, Commander General Karl von Pflanzer-Baltin
VI Corps (12th and 39th ID)
XIII Corps (2nd KD, 15th and 36th ID)
Group Hadfy (6th KD and 21st ID)
Group Benigni (3rd, 5th and 8th KD, 30th, 42nd and 51st ID)
XI Corps (5th, 24th and 40th ID)

Brusilov was keen to bring any useful innovation to the attack and drew creatively from the experiences of the Russo-Japanese War and the lessons learned by the French on the Western Front. He was eager to accept the French instructors who taught the concept of the 'Joffre Attack' developed in Champagne the previous year. 'There the French had forsaken the doctrine of concentration of forces in favour of preparation, creating holding areas for the reserves close to the German lines to reduce the time between the artillery bombardment and the infantry assault.' The bombardment was short but intense, what the Germans called 'drumming fire'. Brusilov had already adopted these tactics in his 8th Army a month before he was promoted to command the front.

Brusilov's emphasis was on thorough preparation since he knew that few reserves were available. To some degree large numbers of reinforcements would be a liability since their movement to the front would reveal to the Germans that a large offensive was coming. Therefore, Brusilov ordered that the reserves of each army be brought into the forward lines and put to work digging the *place d'armée*, trenches 300 by 90 metres, from which the Russians would mount their assault. Since this was happening all along the front, the Austro-Hungarians had no indication where the main blow would fall. The next step was to dig forward trenches towards the enemy lines from which the attack would be made. Brusilov wanted them no more than a hundred metres from the enemy lines and preferably only sixty, or even less.

At the same time the Russians were conducting a thorough reconnaissance of the Austro-Hungarian positions. Of particular importance was aerial photography which put special emphasis on the location of Austro-Hungarian artillery. The resulting diagrams were more accurate than the enemy's maps of their own positions. Brusilov ensured this information was shared with his own gunners. Based on this intelligence each army commander in consultation with Brusilov selected the main breakthrough point on his front. Once this was done, models of the Austro-Hungarian positions were built, and the hand-picked assault troops, called *Shturmavye Otriady*, practised taking them over and over again.

Attack groups were to be no larger than five divisions, with the attack broken into four waves. The first wave equipped with hand grenades, was to push into the enemy's front trench and take out any flanking guns the artillery had missed. The second wave would follow 200 paces behind and then attack the second line of trenches directly. Once the breach was secured, the third wave would bring the Russian machine guns forward and set about expanding the gap along the line. The fourth wave was to secure the flanks of the gap, allowing the Russian cavalry to pour through and into the enemy rear.

Brusilov fully integrated his artillery into these techniques. Commanders carefully selected their own targets, and Brusilov brought in experienced French and Japanese officers to train them properly for these new missions. The drumming fire would last only ten to twelve minutes. First the light artillery would blow open 4–5-metre gaps in the wire and then shift to knock out enemy machine guns. Then they would shift again to concentrate on the Austro-Hungarian infantry in the forward trenches and the heavy artillery within range. At the same time the Russian heavy guns would be destroying the enemy's communication trenches before shifting to join the light artillery in hitting the Austro-Hungarian infantry.

Brusilov had another resource that the Austro-Hungarians did not have – *autopolemetaye* (armoured-car) platoons (AAP), that he specifically ordered held back for the exploitation phase of the offensive. Each platoon was equipped with three armoured cars.

Armoured-Car Platoons, South-West Front 4 June 1916[13]

26th AAP	II Corps	7th Army
20th and 32nd AAP	XXXII Corps	8th Army
15th AAP	XXXIX Corps	8th Army
31st AAP	XVIII Corps	11th Army
19th AAP	VI Corps	11th Army
34th AAP	VII Corps	11th Army
18th and 2nd AAP	XXXIII Corps	9th Army
17th AAP (under repair)		9th Army

Reinforcing these Russian armoured-car platoon were Belgian and British armoured-car units. The Belgian Expeditionary Force in Russia (*Corps Expéditionnaire des Autos-Canons-Mitrailleuses Belges en Russie*) had been very effective in the Flanders battles of 1914, but the static front that followed gave them nothing to do until Nicholas asked King Albert of the Belgians for their loan. The corps, 333 men and thirteen armoured cars strong, arrived in Russia in October 1915, fought well in Galicia on the South-West Front in February 1916, and were mentioned five times in dispatches. The British Armoured Car Expeditionary Force (ACEF) of twenty-eight armoured cars and 566 men arrived in Russia in January 1916 and was specifically requested by Brusilov for use in his offensive. They arrived just in time for the offensive. In all Brusilov would be able to deploy seventy-one armoured cars and their highly trained crews.[14]

Despite the Belgian and British contingents, the South-West Front was a true reflection of the Russian Empire. Four of its cavalry divisions and two of the brigades were made of Cossacks from the Orenburg, Don, and Terek Cossacks. There were four Finnish infantry divisions, a division from Turkestan, and four of Siberians from the Transamur region. In all, the front numbered ten cavalry and forty infantry divisions, only five more than the Austro-Hungarians facing them, despite a Russian advantage of 132,000 men.[15] This was due mostly to the wave of new conscripts that he had integrated and intensively trained into his existing divisions.

Brusilov chose his old command, the 8th Army, to carry the main thrust of the attack. If there was to be a weak link, it was the leadership of the 8th Army's commander, General Aleksei M. Kaledin. Brusilov had to make frequent visits to his headquarters to keep him from having a nervous breakdown. With Stolypin's backing he relieved Kaledin and put Denikin in his place. The 8th Army was the elite formation of the South-West Front. Brusilov had trained it hard and led it well. Many of its officers were men of talent whose promotion and placement had been due to their success in battle rather than the cronyism that dogged other Russian units. Brusilov knew his old army would be up to the task now that it was in the hands of a first-class soldier. Since 8th Army would carry the primary assault of the front, this was not a minor consideration.

Berdichev, South-West Front Headquarters, 1 June 1916

In his mind's eye Brusilov could picture what was happening to the north. The half light of dusk had barely fallen when two thousand Russian guns on the West Front opened up on the German trenches. At exactly the same time, another fifteen hundred guns on the North-West Front lit up the gathering darkness. Gurko and Yudenich's troops had been well trained in the Brusilov method. By the next morning they had made serious penetrations into the enemy trench networks. The Germans were indeed

Order of Battle of the Russian South-West Front
4 June 1916

Front Reserve (Placed under 8th Army for the offensive)

12th KD

4th Finnish ID

Heavy Artillery Division

8th Army, HQ: Rovno, Commander: General Anton I. Denikin
    V Cavalry Corps (Orenberg Cossack KD and 11th KD
    XX Corps (71st, 80th and 100th ID)
    XXXIX Corps (102nd and 125th ID)
    XL Corps (2nd and 4th Rifle Divs)
    VIII Corps (14 and 15th ID)
    XXXII Corps (101st and 105th ID)
    7th KD

11th Army, HQ: Volochisk, Commander: General Vladimir V. Sakharov
    XVII Corps (3rd and 35th ID)
    VII Corps (10th and 34th ID)
    VI Corps (4th and 16th ID)
    XVIII Corps (23rd and 37th ID)
    Transamur KD

7th Army, HQ Guzyatin, Commander: General Dmitrii G. Scherbatschev
    XXII Corps (1st and 3rd Finland ID)
    XVI Corps (41st and 47th ID)
    II Corps (26th and 43rd ID
    3rd Turkestan ID
    II Cavalry Corps (Composite Cossack KD, 2nd Don Cossack Cavalry
        Brigade, Composite Cossack Cavalry Brigade, 9th KD)
    V Caucasian Corps
    1st Ind Cavalry Brigade
    2nd Finland ID

9th Army, HQ: Kaments-Podolsk, Commander: General Platon A.
    Letschitski
    XXIII Corps (1st and 2nd Transamur ID)
    XLI Corps (3rd and 74th Transamur ID)
    XI Corps (11th and 32nd ID)
    II Corps (12th and 19th ID)
    Composite Corps (82nd and 103rd ID)
    III Cavalry Corps (1st Don Cossack KD, Terek Cossack KD, 10th KD)

surprised. The accuracy and volume of Russian artillery was unprecedented. Right behind came the *Shturmavye Otriady*. These were not the conscript masses, so often fodder for the German machine guns. They were well-trained deadly small groups advancing behind a hail of grenades and the spurting glare of flamethrowers. Ober-Ost was shocked when a German division simply disintegrated, losing four thousand of its men as prisoners. By the second night, Hindenburg was authorising the commitment of theatre reserves. His famous equanimity was not disturbed, but his volatile Chief of Staff, Erich Ludendorff, was calling this attack the crisis of the war in the east. With Hindenburg's permission he notified Falkenhayn that reinforcements might be necessary. Brusilov counted on just that reaction. The attention of the Germans was now firmly fixed on their own front as their reserves were sucked into the fighting.

Meanwhile, the relative lull that had settled on the Austro-Hungarian front was about to be shattered. There the senior officers of the dual monarchy were relishing – with no little *Schadenfreude* – the distress of the Germans. It had not been lost on them for some time that an offensive was building up against them. Brusilov was glad that they had not missed the obvious. He simply overwhelmed them with his efforts at deception, what the Russians called *maskirovka*. Since all the Russian armies were making identical preparations along the entire front, the Austro-Hungarians could not pinpoint where the main attacks would be. To add to their confusion, Brusilov cluttered their analysis with false signals, documents, and deserters primed with misleading information. They could gain no coherent picture of the Russian plans, but they comforted themselves by believing the Russians would fight in the same old way and could be easily repulsed in the same old way. They had fallen into the trap laid by all great strategic surprises. Their complacency caused them to 'make the wish father to the thought'.

The next day Brusilov's air reconnaissance began to report the movement to the rear of the two German divisions attached to the Austro-Hungarian 1st Army and Südarmee. In addition several of the German divisions in Group Gronau covering the Pripet Marshes at the boundary of West and South-West fronts were observed to be moving to the rear. The offensive to the north had done its job, and the Austro-Hungarians were now left without the shield of German protection.

HQ, South-West Front, Berdichev, 4 June 1916

At one in the morning Brusilov gave the order for the offensive to begin in three hours. He announced, 'It is time to drive out this dishonourable enemy.' At four the Russian artillery commenced firing along the front and for three hours hammered the enemy. At seven the Russian guns paused to check the damage done. In that time, the Austro-Hungarians rushed their reserves to the forward trenches and unleashed their own artillery into an empty no man's land where they thought the attacking Russian masses would be swarming. They were relieved that their own losses had been minimal, reinforcing their belief that the coming Russian attack could be easily fended off. By now, they had correctly concluded that the Russian 8th Army would lead the primary attack. Brusilov had stacked 8th Army with half of his front's guns, the foreign armoured-car units, and enough forces to give Denikin at least a fifty-thousand-man advantage over the Austro-Hungarian 4th Army commanded by Archduke Ferdinand. Brusilov, like Alexander the Great, was lucky in his enemies. If the Macedonian had Darius, Brusilov had Ferdinand. The archduke, although a career soldier, was so manifestly incompetent that he remained preoccupied with the sixtieth birthday party he was hosting for Conrad even as the artillery duel of a major battle was underway. The fact that 8th Army's infantry did not follow up its barrage drew the eyes of the Austro-Hungarian commanders further south.

There the Russian Army's artillery preparation had made a shambles of the trenches of the Austro-Hungarian 2nd Army. An Austro-Hungarian observed that 'there was drum-fire of hitherto unequalled intensity and length which in a few hours shattered and levelled our carefully-constructed trenches . . . Apart from the bombardment's destruction of wire obstacles, the entire zone of battle was covered by a huge, thick cloud of explosive-gases, which prevented men from seeing, made breathing difficult, and allowed the Russians to come over in thick waves into our trenches.' The Austro-Hungarian artillery was either silenced or expended its ammunition in initially firing into the empty no man's land.[16] The pauses in the Russian fire unnerved the troops, who kept to their bunkers. The sudden appearance of thirteen Russian armoured cars of 11th Army deep in their position along the Tarnopol–Lemberg railway sowed confusion and panic. Behind them, the Russian assault troops had breached the enemy's second line. To the north Russian attacks wiped out the Austro-Hungarian 1st Army's bridgehead over the Ikvanie River. But it was in the south, on the fronts of the Südarmee and 7th Army, where the Austro-Hungarians felt most secure, that disaster fell upon them.

The disaster was least expected because 7th Army was made up largely of Hungarians and loyal Croats. The army commander, however, had put the untested 79th Honved Infantry Brigade in the front line, not realising that he was cramming the Hungarians into positions meant for only half their numbers. One of those pauses in the Russian fire caused them to boil out of the confining shelters, only to be caught rushing out into their trenches by a resumption of the enemy guns. The slaughter was so great that the survivors were stunned. The next morning the Russian assault troops of 9th Army hit them. The Hungarian brigade disintegrated, losing 4,600 of 5,200 men. The rest of the day was spent driving the Austro-Hungarians back from one position until by nightfall the Russians were through to open country, having taken thousands of prisoners.

Forward Trenches, Russian 8th Army, Dusk, 5 June 1916

Senior Lieutenant Vladimir Golitsyn looked back in the gloom and could barely make out the faces of the first few men in his assault group. Despite the aristocratic name, he had been a clerk in Tula when he had enlisted in 1914. The old Russian Army had made him a sergeant. The new Russian Army had recognised his leadership abilities and made him an officer. He knew his job, and he took care of his men. Now they were all waiting for the moment they had repeatedly rehearsed.[17]

There it was – the thunder of the guns! The earth shook because the shells were falling only sixty yards ahead of them into the Austro-Hungarian trenches. The Russian guns were tearing gaps in the wire directly in front of them. In all the guns cleared fifty-one gaps in 8th Army's front. In twelve minutes the guns fell silent, and Golitsyn bolted forward out of the trench, not even looking back to see if the men followed. They were right behind and dashed through the gap in the wire and into the first enemy trench and its smashed machine guns. They had been so close to the enemy trenches, just as Brusilov wanted, that they were into them before the Austro-Hungarian troops began to emerge from their bunkers to man their positions.

Golitsyn and his men were running down an empty trench when a man in Austro-Hungarian field grey appeared out of the entrance to a bunker. Golitsyn shot him with his revolver, and the men behind him threw in half a dozen grenades. Screams. Then smoke, and the choking words in Italian and German, 'We surrender, comrades.' Over fifty men stumbled out with their hands up, but Golitsyn and most of his men were already gone, blasting out more bunkers and taking more prisoners. Behind the *Shturmavye Otriady* came the next waves, tasked with gathering up the prisoners and following up the success by overrunning the next trench line. By the time the Russian follow-on infantry arrived, the trenches were full of dead and wounded; the survivors simply surrendered. Such was the fate of the 70th Honved Infantry Division, the poorly trained Hungarian reservists. Almost 7,000 out of a strength of 12,200 surrendered without a shot.

With the collapse of the Hungarians, the *Shturmavye Otriady* were able to penetrate quickly into the third enemy line and turn against the flanks of adjoining divisions of the Austro-Hungarian X Corps. By nightfall that corps had lost 80 per cent of its men, and the third and last position had fallen. Austro-Hungarian troops, especially the non-Germans, had begun surrendering everywhere. In the first two positions 85 per cent of Austro-Hungarian casualties had been caused by the artillery and rifles. In the third line the garrison surrendered en masse.[18]

By the next morning Denikin was driving the enemy back across open ground. He was right behind the advance elements, a place rarely seen by general officers in this war. At this point, he unleashed his Belgian, British, and Russian armoured-car units and his cavalry divisions. The armoured cars raced ahead, machine-gunning the masses of fleeing Austro-Hungarians, further disintegrating what little cohesion they had left. As the survivors scattered, the Cossacks rode in amongst them, sabring and lancing. That same day the Russians closed on the railway hub of Lutsk and captured it with another five thousand prisoners to add to the fifty thousand men and seventy-seven guns they had already taken. One Austro-Hungarian corps commander wailed, 'the whole of IV Army has really been taken prisoner . . . It's a complete debacle, we can do nothing with the troops.' By the end of the day, 4th Army, reduced to fewer than 27,000 men from its original strength of 100,000, no longer existed as a serious military force. Truly, as Homer wrote, panic was brother to blood-stained rout. One captured Austro-Hungarian staff officer said, 'They moved so fast that every attempt to reform was shattered by the armored cars. The Russians had brought lightning to the battlefield, they were so swift.'[19]

The Russian cavalry divisions of 8th Army rode deep into the Austro-Hungarian rear, reaping the fruits of victory in the pursuit – prisoners, ammo and food dumps, wagon trains and truck convoys. By the evening of the 7th they were forty-five kilometres west of Lutsk, snapping up what was left of the Austro-Hungarian line of communications. The armoured cars that had not broken down kept pace by refuelling from captured petrol stocks. Of even greater importance was all the captured railway stock. It was immediately put to use by Russian railway troops, easing the problem of supplying their advancing infantry. That in turn was made even easier by the vast amounts of food stocks and artillery ammunition captured by the Russians. So much Austro-Hungarian artillery ammunition was captured that the Russian factories that had been devoted to producing shells for captured guns received emergency orders to shift back to making Russian shells.[20]

Ober-Ost, 9 June 1916

All the news stank of disaster. Ludendorff was so anxious that it took all of Hindenburg's granite calm to keep him from becoming hysterical. Their armies were locked in a death struggle with the Russian West and North-West Fronts. They had never seen the Russians fight so effectively. German intelligence had reported the appointment of two new generals to command the two fronts, but both Hindenburg and Ludendorff underestimated them. Gurko was new to front command, and Yudenich had only fought against the Turks. There was no doubt that the Germans could eventually contain the Russian attacks, but there was not a man in reserve to spare. That was why their real concern was for the collapsing Austro-Hungarian armies. Each new message only added to the scale of the disaster. Instead of being able to send reserves and senior commanders to brace up the Austro-Hungarians, Ober-Ost had to request, in the strongest terms, reinforcements from the Western Front. So serious was the unfolding situation that Falkenhayn actually broke off the Verdun offensive to send troops east.

Until then there was only one German division available anywhere to help stem the Russian advance: the 48th Reserve Division that had been withdrawn from Südarmee before the Russian offensive. It was now turned around at Kovel in order to help defend that vital communications centre. Linsingen's Group Gronau had been fixed in place by attacks of West Front's 3rd Army and could not support the 48th. The last message Ober-Ost received stated that the division had been surrounded with scattered remnants of 4th Army there. That meant the Russians had advanced a hundred kilometres since the offensive began. The major communications centre and fortress of Brest-Litovsk was only another 160 kilometres from Koval. Group Gronau was now threatened by the Russians from the south as well as the east and began to disengage to prevent encirclement. That day the Germans and the Austro-Hungarians received the shocking news that Romania had entered the war. The dramatic Russian victories convinced the Romanians that this was the golden opportunity to be on the winning side. Though their combat effectiveness was low, their attack against the right flank of the retreating Austro-Hungarian 7th Army pinned them long enough for the pursuing Russian 9th Army to hammer them to pieces. By then the Russian 11th Army was within twenty kilometres of Lvov, 120 kilometres from its start point. Russian cavalry and armoured cars were ranging far ahead of their infantry, running down or bypassing what remained of Südarmee.

Stavka, Mogliev, 23 June 1916

Jubilation ran through the headquarters at the news that Brusilov's forces had entered the Lupkov, Volovets, Veretsky, and Delatyn passes over the eastern Carpathian Mountains with little or no opposition. Brest-Litovsk had fallen the day before. The Hapsburg armies seemed to have simply collapsed. Troops were surrendering everywhere. Divisions frantically transferred from the Italian front arrived piecemeal, only to be swept up in the panic. Only some of their ethnic German and Hungarian regiments kept together and fought, but they fought to escape.

On the 26th, Cossack patrols of 7th and 9th armies descended from the passes through the Carpathian Mountains into the Kingdom of Hungary. There was no resistance. Ahead of them, though, were a few Lanchester armoured cars that entered the town of Munkacs. The British crewmen thought it strange to see so many Hasidic Jews, not realising it was the only city in the Austro-Hungarian Empire with a Jewish majority. Lieutenant Clyde Sutherland walked into an empty police station, paused, and said, 'I say there, anyone at home?' With not a single member of the police or administration remaining, he ended up accepting the surrender of the city from the chief rabbi. The telegraph office was open, and he sent a telegram to the Austro-Hungarian emperor that the city of Munkacs had surrendered to the forces of His Majesties, George V and Nicholas II. The latter he included out of courtesy to their Russian Army translator. Of course, the Cossacks were announcing their arrival elsewhere with plumes of smoke from burning towns and villages.[21]

Budapest panicked at the news, and Vienna was stunned. That night Emperor Franz Joseph died in his sleep. The next morning his heir, Archduke Karl, summoned the cabinet and ordered them to sue for peace without informing Berlin. The Germans found out in two days; their outrage had nowhere to go. They calculated the odds, and began a strategic withdrawal from their most advanced positions in France to concentrate forces desperately needed in the east. Those reinforcements only succeeded in occupying Bohemia and Moravia to prevent any threat to south-eastern Germany. The British and French, noting the sudden withdrawal of the Germans, launched an immediate pursuit. For the first time in two years, the fighting was in open country as the Germans fought a stubborn retreat.

The Russians demanded that Vienna immediately order the cessation of hostilities and then sever its alliance with Germany. Vienna conceded with shameless haste. With the Hapsburg Empire not only out of the war but on the point of collapse, the Ottomans also realised the war was hopeless. Austria-Hungary's capitulation severed German munitions and military support, without which the Turks simply could no longer fight on. They also sued for peace; the Bulgarians quickly followed. That immediately opened the Dardanelles sea route to Russia's Black Sea ports for Allied aid. This truly was the handwriting on the wall for Berlin. Germany could fight on, but to what end? A rational observer could see only inevitable defeat in Germany's future. It would only be a matter of time.

Berlin asked the Argentine government to offer its good services to broker a peace. In the end Germany did not come badly out of the Peace of Buenos Aires. Almost everyone did well because the prostrate Hapsburg state provided plenty of pickings. The Russians took all of Galicia and recovered most of their Polish lands. The Germans swallowed that by swallowing Bohemia and Moravia. The Romanians were awarded Transylvania, not so much for their feeble military contribution but for their timing. Serbia got a slice of southern Hungary and Bosnia-Herzogovina. Italy got the Italian populated parts of the Tyrol and Trieste. By the end, the Austro-Hungarian Empire was reduced to its German provinces of Austria, the remnants of Hungary, and faithful Croatia and Slovenia. France and Great Britain had to be satisfied with the evacuation of Belgium, Luxembourg, and France as well as a handful of German colonies in Africa. The status of Alsace-Lorraine was to be subject to a plebiscite. Britain was able to force a reduction in the

German Navy since its recent drubbing at Jutland. Of course, there were pickings in the Ottoman Empire as well. Britain took Palestine, and France, pressing its ancestral claims, was ceded Syria. Russia took all of traditional Armenia in eastern Anatolia.[22]

The liturgy of thanksgiving for Russia's victory was held fittingly in Christ the Saviour Cathedral across the Moscow River from the Kremlin. The cathedral glittered with thousands of candles reflecting off its brilliant frescoes, marbles, and mosaics; it was scented with clouds of fragrant incense and echoed with chants that seemed the voices of angels. It was only fitting that the celebration be held here. The cathedral had been built with the pennies of the Russian people in thanks for their deliverance from Napoleon. Now it celebrated a new saviour of Russia, in the place of honour next to the imperial family – Marshal of Russia Aleksesi Brusilov. Three rows back, behind the last of the imperial relatives and the senior generals sat Pyotr Stolypin. He had a new portfolio now. His mind was not distracted by the sensory feast around him. It ran into the future, and the reforms that would secure the Romanov dynasty for another hundred years.

The Reality

To this day a staple of Russian intellectual speculation has been what would have happened to Russia had Pyotr Stolypin not been assassinated in 1911. This chapter follows one path in that tradition. The presence of a figure with the ability and reputation of Stolypin to advise and influence Nicholas II would have been crucial in the events leading up to the Brusilov Offensive.

That offensive was planned as a supporting attack for the main effort to be made by Evert's West Front and Kuropatkin's North-West Front. In fact, both Evert and Kuropatkin were loath to make the effort. They were supposed to have attacked first, but to Brusilov's rage they did not. Brusilov had correctly seen that knocking the Austro-Hungarians out of the war was the most feasible plan for the Russians, yet the overwhelming strength of the Russian armies continued to face the Germans. Nevertheless, with the resources he had, he broke the back of the Austro-Hungarian armies facing him, taking 350,000 prisoners. However, Evert and Kuropatkin's continued failure seriously to attack the Germans meant that Hindenburg could send reinforcements from his front and Falkenhayn could send more from the Western Front in France to brace up the Austro-Hungarians. The Germans sent not only divisions but senior commanders who essentially took over the Hapsburg armies. Eventually, Brusilov's offensive was ground down in the face of German control of the now-braced Austro-Hungarian armies, suffering half a million casualties by the time it was called off. That was the last serious Russian opportunity to achieve victory on the Eastern Front. What was overlooked in this spoiled victory was that Brusilov had originated an early form of the stormtrooper tactics the Germans would develop later in the war for their 1918 offensives. Also overlooked was the use of armoured cars for exploitation of Russian penetrations of the Austro-Hungarian front, a year before the British first used tanks at Cambrai.

With the coming of the Bolshevik Revolution and the Civil War, Brusilov threw in his lot with the Reds, reasoning that governments come and go but that Russia endured and must be served. He was not forgiven by the émigré Russian community which has clouded his reputation in the minds of many. Yet he was by far Russia's finest commander in the First World War and a great captain by any standards.

The mad monk Rasputin was a mortal enemy of Stolypin, and it is not inconceivable that the minister's streak of ruthlessness in dealing with the enemies of Russia might – if mentioned in the right ears – have resulted in the Russian equivalent of: 'Will no one rid me of this meddlesome priest?' Thus Rasputin's murder was advanced in time to remove his opposition to the Brusilov Offensive. Lieutenants Golitsyn and Sutherland are the only fictional characters in the story.

Notes

1 The Russian prime minister was shot during festivities to mark the centenary of the liberation of Russia's serfs on 14 September 1911: www.historytoday. com/richard-cavendish/pyotr-stolypin-assassinated-kiev, accessed 4 October 2013. Bogrov's motivations to this day remain murky. He was playing a double role as both a revolutionary and an agent of the Okrana. His motive as a Jew could have been revenge for Stolypin's support as interior minister of the Jewish pogroms of 1903. As a revolutionary he would have seen Stolypin's reforms as a prime threat to any hope for the violent overthrow of the monarchy. As an Okrana agent he could have been acting for the conservative elements in the government who had detested his reforms. Since Stolypin was no longer prime minister at the time of the attempt on his life, the latter motive seemed to have been overtaken by his departure from office.

2 Winston S. Churchill, *The World Crisis 1916–1918, Part I* (London: Thornton Butterworth Ltd, 1927), pp. 84–5.

3 *Aleksei P. Apraxin, *The Life of Pyotr Stolypin* (St Petersburg: Imperial Russia Press, 1933), p. 192.

4 'Orthodox in the District: Living the Ancient Faith in the Nation's Capital', http://ryanphunter.wordpress.com/tag/tsarina-alexandra-romanova, accessed 28 September 2013.

5 Timothy C. Dowling, *The Brusilov Offensive* (Bloomington: Indiana University Press, 2008), pp. 50, 54.

6 Norman Stone, *The Eastern Front 1914–1917* (New York: Charles Scribner's Sons, 1975), p. 228

7 The Semyenovsky Guards Regiment was established by Peter the Great and had precedence over all other regiments in the Russian Army except for the Preobreshensky Guards, which was also established by Peter. It was a very prestigious regiment.

8 *Mikhail N. Tukhachevsky, *My Adventures in the World War* (London: Blackfriars Press Ltd, 1944), p. 118. Tukhachevsky and Denikin formed one of the great, though brief, command teams of the war. Their bond was so close that the young officer married Denikin's daughter. He wrote his memoirs of the World War just before his retirement as Chief of Staff of the Imperial Russian Army in 1945.

9 Stone, *Eastern Front*, p. 234.

10 G. Rothenburg, *The Army of Franz Joseph* (West Lafayette: Purdue University Press) p. 83.

11 Dowling, *Brusilov Offensive*, pp. 53–4.

12 Ibid., pp. 64–5.

13 http://landships.activeboard.com/t49402890/brusilov-offensive-armored-car-oob, accessed 2 October 2013.

14 http://en.wikipedia.org/wiki/Belgian_Expeditionary_Corps_in_Russia; www.philatelicdatabase.com/postal-history/wwi-belgium-armoured-car-division-in-russia; www.wio.ru/tank/for-rus.htm; http://landships.activeboard.com/t5106674/armoured-car-of-the-russian-army-1914-1917, accessed 2 October 2013.

15 Dowling, *Brusilov Offensive*, pp. 43, 65, 71. Dowling provides the only order-of-battle table available for the South-Western Front. He states that the Russians had fifteen cavalry divisions, but his own order of battle lists only ten. Elsewhere the description of divisions and corps in the text often does not follow the order of battle. The author of this chapter has attempted to make what sense was possible from these contradictions.

16 Stone, *Eastern Front*, p. 249.

17 *Vladimir I. Golitsyn, *Diary of an Assault Soldier*, War Studies Autobiography Studies No. 39 (Fort Levenworth: Command & General Staff College, 1933), p. 99.

18 Stone, *Eastern Front*, p. 250.

19 *Major George S. Patton, US Army (ret), *Lightning War: The Russian Development of Deep Operations in the Great War* (Fort Knox: U.S. Armor School Press, 1945), p. 286.

20 Stone, *Eastern Front*, p. 250.

21 *Simon B. Forrester, *With the Armored Cars in Russia* (London: Charing Cross Publishers Ltd, 1926), p. 311.

22 *Friedrich von Boettecher, *The Peace of Zurich and the New European Order* (New York: Empire State Books, 1928), pp. 322–4. All the Western Slav, Italian, and Romanian minorities were lost to the rump of the Austro-Hungarian Empire, making it a more cohesive state. The only colony that German retained in Africa was Deutsche Ost Afrika, because of its gallant and successful defence by General Paul Lettow-Vorbeck.

8

The Somme Steamroller

Stuart Mitchell

The tide of the First World War turned at 7.30 a.m. on 1 July 1916. Over one and a half thousand artillery pieces lifted their fire onto the next line and nineteen divisions of British and French infantry rushed towards the German positions. This was the first day of the Battle of the Somme and would prove to be the British Army's greatest victory since the war began.

Four Months Earlier . . .
17 March 1916: Chateau de Querrieu, Querrieu, France

General Sir Henry Rawlinson was sick with influenza. He had only moved the headquarters of his 4th Army to the lofty, lush surroundings of Chateau de Querrieu on 24 February and now he had been forced to depart for two weeks to the south of France. In the meantime his able Chief of Staff Brigadier General Archibald Montgomery set to work formulating the plan for what would be the largest attack in the history of the British Army.

Rawlinson, or 'Rawly' as he was known, was a tall, slender, upright man. The thin, moustached face and warm – sometimes toothy – smile masked a ruthless, devious streak. His unbridled ambition had led some to dub him 'the Cad', but he was serious and analytical about his profession. His military education had taken him from the fields of Sandhurst to the kopjes of South Africa; he attended the Staff College at Camberley and toured the battlefields of the Franco-Prussian War of 1870–1. He understood the principles and realities of modern war, the value of combined arms, the importance of 'moral' fortitude and the danger of modern firepower, especially machine guns and quick-firing artillery. It was no surprise that at the outbreak of the Great War he rose rapidly through the ranks, from a War Office staff position to command of IV Corps, all in a matter of months. In January 1916 he took charge of the newly created 4th Army, and by the end of February he had been entrusted with command of the planned assault on the Somme. Before the sickness took hold he had thoroughly inspected the front line and outlined his intentions to Montgomery. The offensive would have to take the form of a calculated bite-and-hold attack. This method had two intertwined elements. First came the 'bite': overwhelming artillery fire would neutralise a limited portion of the German defences, allowing the British infantry to seize and consolidate the position. The second element was the 'hold': when the Germans launched their inevitable counterattacks, they would be met by dug-in British infantry and devastating artillery fire. In theory, bite-and-hold allowed the British to capture a position relatively cheaply, and then inflict stinging casualties on the Germans when they counterattacked across open ground.

Despite demanding caution in planning, Rawly was optimistic: 'It is capital country in which to undertake an offensive when we get a sufficiency of artillery, for the observation is excellent and with plenty of guns and ammunition we ought to be able to avoid the heavy losses which the infantry have always suffered on previous occasions.'[1]

Refreshed and rejuvenated, Rawlinson returned at the end of March. He found Montgomery's plan to his liking. The idea was to launch a limited attack on the German line, encompassing a wide frontage between Serre and Mametz, after a prolonged bombardment of four or five days. Once this line was taken, and the German counterattacks repelled, the artillery would be brought forward and the second line would be assaulted in the north between Serre and Combles within a matter of days, using the same bite-and-hold techniques. Step by cautious step, 4th Army would blast holes in the enemy defences and repel all attempts to strike back. The process of attrition would favour the British, for they would use firepower as an answer to manpower. The Germans would lack this luxury, and every repulsed counterattack would cost them in blood. Over time the German infantry would be bled white until finally it would be unable to resist. After this calculated, methodical destruction was wrought and the Germans had cracked, the British would swing south and roll up the line. Territory was no longer an end in itself but merely a means of causing as many German casualties as possible. It was to be a battle of pure, remorseless attrition.

Meanwhile . . .
British General Headquarters, Montreuil-sur-Mer, France

Douglas Haig was under pressure. The BEF's commander-in-chief had to contend with politicians in Westminster still reluctant to give the commitments needed to win a continental war. He also faced problems with his French allies, who were under immense strain after the German assault on the fortress town of Verdun began on 21 February. Amidst all this he had to oversee and coordinate the preparations for a combined attack in line with the agreements made at the Chantilly conferences in December 1915 and February 1916. Haig was not yet confident this force was up to the task. He confided in his diary: 'I have not got an Army in France really, but a collection of divisions untrained for the field.'[2] In spite of these problems, the German attack against Verdun distracted attention from the British section of the line, and provided Haig with an opportunity to strike a serious, unexpected blow when the time was right. Haig was cautiously optimistic about his chances.

The Rawlinson–Montgomery plan left Haig conflicted. On the one hand he knew that the plan to 'kill Germans' was fundamentally 'correct' but it took little account of the needs of the French army. Inter-Allied relations were fragile and dangerous.[3] Any British action had to relieve the pressure on its ally and every day of fighting at Verdun curtailed French commitment a little more. French plans for the Somme dwindled from a grandiose assault using three armies to crush the German defences, into a single army operating in a subsidiary capacity to the British. The French commander-in-chief, General Joseph Joffre, maintained the hope that under sustained, violent assault the entire Western Front might shatter. His optimism fuelled Haig. The 4th Army must be more ambitious. Three or four kilometres of ground and a heap of dead Germans were not enough: 'I think we can do better than this by aiming at getting as large a combined force of French and British across the Somme and fighting the Enemy in the open!'[4] Haig wanted the first and second line assaulted on the same day. He wanted a short bombardment. Thus began a tortuous process of planning, Rawlinson compromising with Haig, and Haig compromising with Joffre.

Back at Chateau de Querrieu . . .
April 1916

Rawlinson knew what was coming. He knew Haig had grander ideas: 'I daresay I shall have a tussle with him over the limited objective for I hear he is inclined to favour the unlimited with the chance of breaking the German line.'[5] When Haig's comments came back pushing for deeper objectives, a wider front, and a short bombardment, his expectations were fulfilled. The idea of taking the first and second lines in one bound was 'alluring', but Rawlinson knew from bitter experience that to stand any chance of success he must concentrate his artillery on a single line, pulverise the German positions and give his infantry the best cover possible. This put him in a tricky position. One did not simply ignore 'the chief', but he knew anything more ambitious than the first line risked abject failure.

The terse thought bluntly shot through Rawlinson's head: 'I owe this man. He saved my career.' Haig had shielded him from dismissal the previous year, when Rawlinson's devious streak had got the better of him: in a moment of scandalous weakness, Rawlinson had pinned the blame for his own failings at the Battle of Neuve Chapelle on his poor subordinate Joey Davies, commanding 8th Division. But that was over a year ago. He had to focus on the here and now; he had to convince his superior that bite-and-hold was the best method. They had always had a strong working relationship and Rawlinson knew what the British Army's manual, *Field Service Regulations Part I*, said of planning: the commander could set the object of the attack but the method of attaining it was up to him.[6] Rawlinson simply did not have the means to achieve the goals Haig set him, so he restated his rationale behind the first plan. The German second line was too far away to assault before enemy reserves arrived; it was sited on a reverse slope, making observation and wire-cutting extremely difficult; and the green troops of the New Armies would find it hard to maintain coordination at such distances. Rawlinson knew this would not be enough, so he offered a fig-leaf compromise: he would extend the line of attack down to Maricourt and include the town of Montauban in the initial objectives. This would link the attack up with the French and aid their assault north of the Somme. Cavalry would be assigned to the assault corps and would be held in readiness to exploit any sudden disintegration of the German defences. The guns would also be brought forward immediately to support a rapid advance on the second line if the enemy was found to be in disarray. Despite this, on the final issue of bombardment there could be no such rapprochement. Rawlinson knew he did not have the guns, the ammunition, or the gunners skilled enough to deliver a short hurricane bombardment of sufficient intensity to cut the wire and neutralise the defenders. In any case, what surprise and 'moral' impact that could be gained would surely be sacrificed by the French, who planned a long bombardment. Rawlinson stood firm on his plans. Time would tell if he was justified.

May–June 1916: GHQ, Montreuil-sur-Mer

Haig began to wonder whether he should have left Edmund Allenby, 3rd Army's intimidating commander, in charge of the operation. After all, he originally held that section of the line before he was forced to send a British Army to relieve the French 10th Army outside Arras. It was too late now to change. Clemenceau, the French prime minister, met with Haig on 4 May 1916 and impressed upon him the dangers of a premature offensive, for defeat risked inflicting irreparable harm on French civilian morale. Yet there was also time pressure, for the bloodletting at Verdun continued unchecked. The French could not be expected to continue to shoulder the burden of the fighting. The British must play their part.

Joseph Joffre doubted that the British would be willing to take their share of the war. He was not alone. His fears were shared by his Army Group commander, Ferdinand Foch, who felt a French commitment was the only way to ensure the British would be drawn into a major battle. He would attack and it would be methodical, limited, and crushing, and they would do this arm-in-arm with the British.

The strain of Verdun was showing. Mutual suspicions flared. But Haig kept a cool head. He saw the wisdom in conducting an attack in line with his allies and using similar methods. Speed and surprise remained important, but with the French demanding action and the plans set down across the line for a limited attack, Haig accepted that Rawlinson should be allowed to use his bite-and-hold approach.

Haig knew what it would mean if he got this decision wrong: 'I am responsible and must bear the blame, not General Joffre!' he told Clemenceau. Alliance concerns dominated, and by the end of the month he spelt it out to William Robertson, Chief of the Imperial General Staff at the War Office, 'we *must* march to support the French.'[7] Haig still felt that a breakthrough of the German lines was possible but accepted, as Joffre had, that this would only come after a succession of significant blows. Meanwhile, Rawlinson's 4th Army was put to work organising the artillery plans, preparing the ground, and setting the tactical plans.

Tactical Choices . . .
May 1916: Chateau de Querrieu, Querrieu, France

These troops were green and Rawlinson knew it. The large expansion of the army had meant that officers and commanders were generally inexperienced in their roles. It was his duty to help in whatever way he could and so he began drawing up his *Tactical Notes*: a short pamphlet giving practical guidance to his subordinates. By May the memorandum was ready to be sent to his formations. Rawlinson spelt out the importance of setting objectives that took account of the effective range of the artillery and the physical endurance of the men. In combat he urged his infantry to use a steady pace all the way to their objectives and attack simultaneously along the length of the line. Rawlinson knew that selectively breaking from this doctrine might turn the tide of battle, and thus he approved of lightly equipped elements rushing forward to tackle certain enemy features. That was not the end of it. The memorandum also recommended that units take a parallel position to the target objective to help keep direction; consolidating captured positions using strongpoints with supports linked by robust communications with the rear; and the employment of Stokes mortars and Lewis light machine guns to suppress troublesome enemy small-arms fire. Much advice that might have been dangerously irrelevant in a broad breakthrough attack was pertinent to men tasked with a genuine bite-and-hold attack. The *Tactical Notes* were the product of Rawlinson's reflection on the conduct of limited attacks, where coordination, order, and cohesion trumped speed and surprise. Effective consolidation and the use of the infantry's firepower was the key to inflicting serious losses to the German counterattacks.

Yet in Rawlinson's notes lay the seeds of controversy and disappointment. His desire for structure and order, driven by a pessimistic view of the fitness, capabilities, and robustness of the new citizen army, pushed him to advise his subordinates that 'each body of troops must be given a definite objective to attack and consolidate.' This short, innocuous sentence, indicative of the rigidly defined approach, would cast a shadow across the achievements of 4th

Army long after the guns had fallen silent.[8] In the postwar world Winston Churchill and David Lloyd George became the chief prosecutors in the courtroom of public opinion. Politicians led a crusade to separate themselves from the bloody costs of victory, while Haig and Rawlinson were condemned as the timid generals guilty of letting a great victory slip from the nation's grasp. But all of that was yet to come.

Flogged by Hail of Leaden Balls . . .
24 June–1 July 1916: Serre to Maricourt, the Somme, France

On 24 June a wall of flame, steel, and shot engulfed the German positions between Serre and Maricourt. For the next seven days the British guns brutally and methodically undertook their violent work. The 4th Army's 182 heavy guns and 245 heavy howitzers attended to the systematic obliteration of the skeletal remains of once-idyllic French villages. Beaumont Hamel, Thiepval, Ovillers, La Boiselle, Fricourt, and Mametz were reduced to ruins and scattered brickwork. Field howitzers and trench mortars of all sizes launched their deadly projectiles into the German lines, splintering, smashing, and collapsing whole sections and their supporting revetments. Meanwhile the field guns launched clouds of shrapnel into the thick banks of barbed wire, shifting and slicing significant gaps. Elsewhere, quick firing 18-pounders raked the communication routes with a hailstorm of projectiles day after day and night after night. The bombardment was devastating and altered the landscape beyond recognition. All that remained after the war was a desolate, pock-marked strip of land scarred by war, with its detritus scattered all around. The haunting image of the barren, cratered hill upon which Beaumont Hamel once stood was typical of the entire twenty-thousand-yard front.

The British infantry were in good spirits. 'Oh there is no doubt about it, Germany is finished,' one Scotsman wrote home. Others remarked upon the 'days of terror for the enemy' living under the 'tumult of rage' coming from the guns.[9] Official reports took a terse tone, only noting that the fire was having a 'good effect. The enemy trenches much knocked about. Remaining wire was all cleared. Hostile enemy artillery was observed registering his own trenches.'[10]

The infantry were not mere bystanders to this bombardment. Every night, patrols and raids were conducted to assess the damage; they probed the line looking for strongpoints and areas that remained untouched by the persistent shelling. Areas where the German defences were stiff were reported to the artillery for further attention. But broadly, the enemy defence was feeble and laboured, as would be expected of troops forced to endure incessant bombardment, and whose supply and communications had been severed. Nightly, British infantry would patrol no man's land and sweep rear areas with machine-gun fire. The constant pressure made no man's land a no-go area for the Germans. All the while, overhead, the buzz of British and French aeroplanes constantly reminded the defenders that they were materially outmatched.

The German *Frontsoldaten* suffered terribly under the thunderous bombardment. The *trommelfeuer* (drum-fire) was unrelenting, pummelling the hapless defenders who were deprived of rest, support, and resources. One soldier spoke of the 'hail of leaden balls [that] whistled through the air and the leaves of the trees and flogged into what was left of the village of Beaumont Hamel.' By the end of the bombardment one surviving German recalled how 'it seemed like our end had come.' Their wire was flattened, the trenches reduced to 'shallow hollows' and their deep dugouts, which offered the only protection in this fire-swept wasteland, had their exits blown in. For the unlucky few whose dugouts did not have multiple exit points their havens became their tombs. On 26 and 27 June the British released poison gas, and while the overall effect was limited it served to compound the misery of the German soldier.[11]

The bombardment was due to end on 29 June, but poor weather hampered observation and delayed the assault by two days. The density and intensity of the fire, its relentless thumping of the German lines and the deprivation it caused left the front-line garrisons tired, hungry, and concussed. Yet they were not a broken force. Despite the overwhelming material superiority of the Allies, the desire for revenge was awoken: 'You made a good job of it, you British! Seven days and nights you rapped and hammered on our door! Now your reception was going to match your turbulent longing to enter!' Seven days had passed, one and a half million shells had been fired and now it was the moment of truth: would Rawlinson's limited approach be vindicated?

Into Battle!
1 July 1916, 7.30 a.m. Onwards . . .

In the north the attack began well. The left and centre divisions (31st and 4th) of Hunter-Weston's VIII Corps soon seized the German front-line trenches. The bombardment had flattened the defensive positions and progress was swift. The left flank was covered by a thick barrage of smoke and shrapnel. But the 'bite' was only the first part of the battle. VIII Corps was up against strong, well-trained German regiments – 66th on the flank to the north, 161st opposing the 31st Division, and 121st against the 4th Division – who responded with immediate counterattacks. These hit the British before they had chance to consolidate their gains. The battle degenerated into localised fighting centring on strongpoints like the town of Serre, and the heavily fortified Quadrilateral Redoubt, known to the Germans as the *Heidenkopf*.

Although there was no tactical prescription – some battalions had attacked in waves and others in column – the two divisions of VIII Corps maintained cohesion and were able to repel the determined German counterattacks and push onwards towards their final objectives. By the end of the day, the 31st Division held the first two lines of trenches and had established themselves along the north and western perimeter of Serre. The village itself remained in German hands, as did Pendant Copse. Unfortunately, the counterattacks had taken much of the impetus out of their assault, and German artillery fire made reinforcement difficult. To their right the 4th Division had overcome the vicious resistance at the Quadrilateral Redoubt and pushed on to the Redan Ridge. Their progress was then stalled by the failure to take Serre and Beaumont Hamel to the south, and the formidable Munich Trench, running from the southern edge of Serre, remained in German hands.

The story of VIII Corps' right division, the 29th, was more tragic. Attacking along a valley overlooked by German observation posts, the British launched themselves against the enemy positions surrounding Beaumont Hamel. To ease their passage, 4th Army had approved the detonation of a bomb that been placed under Hawthorn Redoubt by mining companies. At 7.20 a.m. this was blown. The eruption flung debris skywards, cleaving a huge hole in the ridge. As the assault progressed, both sides occupied opposing lips of the crater. Bullets thudded into the broken earth as each side furiously tried to win the fire-fight. Artillery and trench mortar shells thudded into the shattered terrain, churning the already broken ground. All attempts to evict the defenders from their makeshift positions ended in bloody failure and the attack was halted. Further down the line 'Y Ravine' posed a problem; concealed German positions that had avoided detection during the bombardment took a heavy toll on the attacking 87th Brigade and the British attack stalled, unable to progress beyond the captured front line.

The trenches around Y Ravine remained in British hands, but over the coming days bloody localised bombing battles erupted as the infantry sought to make further inroads. These small, piecemeal close-quarter battles took their toll on the 87th Brigade and their relieving 88th Brigade, but, fighting downhill, gains were gradually made. For the VIII Corps the day was a mixed affair: initial optimism was soon replaced by sombre disappointment as German counterattacks, concentrated defensive barrages, and fire from remaining strongpoints took their toll. The Germans had held onto Beaumont Hamel and Serre, but lost some important positions. However, while their hold on VIII Corps' front had been significantly weakened, it was far from broken.

Things went better for X Corps. On the left of their line the 36th (Ulster) Division had advanced early and taken position in no man's land whilst the bombardment was still in progress. Once the guns had lifted, the division stormed the positions north and south of the Ancre. German shellfire made communications difficult but within a few hours the Ulstermen had taken all of their objectives and established themselves in the formidable Schwaben Redoubt. The concentrated British artillery bombardment had obliterated any German resistance and, while some enfilade fire was taken from the north around Beaucourt and Thiepval in the south, the division remained cohesive enough to hold their gains. A battery of French artillery equipped with quick-firing 75-mm guns further bolstered the density of the 36th Division's artillery and did much that day to protect the flank of the division.[12]

To their right, 32nd Division faced the fortified town of Thiepval and the adjacent Leipzig spur. German machine guns with overlapping fields of fire made any approach extremely dangerous. The 32nd Division had made an extensive reconnaissance of the town: buildings were counted and of the sixty-six identified, thirteen were picked out for significant attention from the artillery. Those with deep cellars were subjected to the heaviest shelling. During the preliminary bombardment the buildings that remained were flattened in a hail of howitzer and trench mortar fire. This careful preparation greatly facilitated the advance of the division. The two leading brigades adopted a similar approach to the 36th (Ulster) Division and waited out the barrage in no man's land. The idea originally stemmed from the 97th Brigade's wily commander, James Jardine, who had witnessed the Japanese 'hug' the barrage and storm the Russian entrenchments in the Russo-Japanese War of 1904–5.

The results were initially spectacular. On the left the 96th Brigade, facing the north-western edge of the village, swept through the trenches and drove onwards, taking advantage of the defenders' disorder. The subsequent waves struggled to mop up some of the German front-line dugouts, whose garrisons emerged after the first assault had passed, but these defenders had suffered heavy losses and were no match for the reinforcements now flowing into their lines. Prisoners streamed back towards the British positions, in some places suffering casualties where their own patchy counter-barrage fell. As the rear of Thiepval was reached, the supporting battalions of the 14th Brigade were committed and each trench, ruin, and cellar was fought over with bomb and bayonet until the village was in British hands.

On the right the 97th Brigade assaulted the Leipzig spur. The maze of trenches along this jutting ridge line was crowned by two strongpoints: the *Wundwerk*, 'Wonder Work' to the British, in the rear and the Leipzig Redoubt at the tip. Before the assault the two leading battalions crept forward until they were a mere fifty yards from the bombardment; once the guns lifted, the Scotsmen stormed the position. The khaki-clad figures of the 16th and 17th Highland Light Infantry smashed into the German lines, overwhelming the dazed defenders. Some immediately surrendered, others fired distress flares and scampered rearwards; a few remained motionless in their dugouts, cowed by the ferocity of what they had experienced over the last seven days. The Scots ploughed on while 'moppers-up' poured in behind to take their place. The deep dugouts may have held firm against the mightiest of shells but they offered no protection against explosives rolled down the steps. Phosphorous grenades burned men out of their catatonia – another horror of industrial war.

The leading units took the first and support lines before the 97th Brigade's supporting battalion was committed to the fray. By end of the day the village and accompanying spur had been taken. The achievements of the 36th (Ulster) Division, and the flanking fire provided against the village, greatly aided the progress of the 96th Brigade, while the 97th Brigade's innovative tactics gave the attack a rapid tempo leaving the defenders impotent. Nevertheless, casualties were heavy especially for the families of Salford and Glasgow, whose Lancashire Fusiliers and Highland Infantry Battalions had led the charge. For many the news of the achievements would offer little consolation for the loss of a father, husband, brother, or son.

Sir William Pulteney's III Corps attacked with two divisions, the 8th and 34th. Advancing against Ovillers and La Boiselle, they made slow but steady progress. The 8th Division was over-extended and committed all three brigades to the attack, leaving itself no local reserve. Nevertheless, despite the broad front, the attack was limited to taking Ovillers and the trench line protecting the Nab valley. The defences here were less formidable than further north, but the width between the British lines and the German positions meant that much more was riding on the success of the bombardment in neutralising the defensive positions. When the attack opened, the men advanced over the obliterated front lines pushing up the Nab valley. The speed and rushes of the X Corps could not be repeated by the 8th Division, who were attacking along a bend in the line. In particular, the 70th Brigade had the unenviable task of having to make a left wheel to attack the *Nordwerk* strongpoint in the German reserve trench. The slower pace of the advance helped keep cohesion but meant that the infantry had to spend longer in the open. Fortunately, the Royal Artillery carried out splendid work on this front, concentrating fire on the German reserves and *Nordwerk* positions and subduing the defenders, allowing the 8th Division to achieve their goals. German counterattacks were frequent, but the observation provided by the captured Leipzig spur allowed the artillery to engage them as they amassed in the valley below. Elsewhere, the 34th Division employed two mines in this heavily cratered area; both were blown at 7.28 a.m., allowing the troops to take advantage of the disorder. Hard fighting took place in this narrow front, but by the end of the day the salient at La Boiselle was in British hands.

To the south of La Boiselle sat the villages of Fricourt and Mametz. The plan here was for XV Corps' two divisions, 21st and 7th, to progress either side of Fricourt, converging on the German third line of trenches. The right brigade of the 7th Division would fight alongside the XIII Corps' 18th Division and take Mametz. The bombardment was particularly effective on this front. Mines were used on the strongpoints in front of Fricourt and the 21st Division took their objectives to the north of the village. But the surviving German defenders reaped a heavy toll on the division and the frontal attack by the 50th Brigade (attached from 17th Division) blundered into the assault in piecemeal fashion. Enemy soldiers could be seen standing brazenly above the parapet, pouring fire into the oncoming Tommies. Machine guns raked the lines, causing considerable losses to the leading companies. Still the Yorkshiremen came, pressing forward with courage and tenacity. It was not enough and the men of this brigade were massacred.

The 7th Division's 22nd Brigade fared better. The German positions were far weaker on this front and in some places the defensive works had not been completed before the bombardment started. Although the brigade suffered heavily from German fire from Fricourt, they managed to push forward methodically, infiltrating the German trench line, driving beyond the village and threatening its flank. The German garrison was left with no choice but to evacuate towards Fricourt Wood. They left behind them a scene of devastation, German and British bodies were strewn among the shattered brickwork and trench lines. The attackers had fought well. The pursuing British infantry established a contiguous line of defence encompassing Fricourt, Fricourt Wood, and the German reserve trenches. The success at Fricourt was down to a combination of positioning, bombardment, and circumstance.

The right of the 7th Division progressed in an equally satisfactory manner. Mametz offered stern resistance but the relentless pummelling it had taken from the predatory bombardment had fatally weakened its defenders. Advancing under a novel curtain of artillery shells, a creeping barrage, the 7th Division swept across no man's land. Their objectives were taken with few losses. Both 21st and 7th Division 'joined hands' along their final objective. The attackers had accomplished their task and heavy losses had been inflicted on the Germans. Moreover, the two divisions maintained enough strength to repel all counterattacks.

The greatest success of the day came on the XIII Corps' front where the 18th Division and 30th Division captured Pommiers Redoubt and the town of Montauban. As with other successes, the way was paved by the gunners, who had shattered the German defences with a maelstrom of shells. The metronomic clatter of artillery provided the percussion accompaniment to a soundtrack whose high notes were hit by the rattle of distant machine guns. In a final crescendo the attacking infantry swept aside the stunned and disorganised defenders, and all objectives were quickly taken.

The success of the British advance in this sector presented a tantalising opportunity. On the left Fricourt, Mametz, and Montauban had fallen, whilst to the right the French were progressing apace. All German counterattacks were hurled back in disarray. The German defences were in danger of collapsing on a wide front and Joffre's dream of shattering the Western Front with one great blow was on the brink of becoming reality. Patrols pushed out over the next two days penetrated two miles through the fractured German lines.

In the coming years Rawlinson and Haig would be vilified for their rigidity in planning. David Lloyd George, the Secretary of State for War during the battle, bemoaned his generals' lack of impetus:

A general must have vision, imagination and initiative – he must show untiring assiduity, must exercise constant oversight and command of great battles, must possess the driving force to carry the activity through to the very end and see that no blow goes unstruck. Haig and Rawlinson showed no such flair for conducting the great fight, on the Somme they were content to use only a broadsword when a rapier was required.[13]

Lloyd George had a point, Rawlinson's approach did prevent the British from seizing this opportunity, despite the plan accommodating a rapid follow-up. His cautious, rigidly defined objectives allowed little scope to immediately push beyond the gains of 1 July. A determined drive with fresh reserves would have certainly taken a significant chunk of the German second line in the south, and possibly threatened the incomplete defences beyond. But no offensive could restore mobility in one blow and across the whole line the 4th Army was disorganised. The fog of war had descended rapidly and while patrols hinted at localised possibilities for a rapid advance the commanders knew the German reinforcements would be speeding their way from quieter sections of the line. Communications were intermittent and there were still doubts about the successes in the north and centre. It would be three days before the dust settled and Rawlinson realised the severity of the blow that he had struck against the German Army.

In the north the VIII Corps had been stopped just outside of Serre, while Beaumont Hamel remained stubbornly in German hands. The Corps found itself dangerously exposed in a salient and localised battles raged to improve their position. The neighbouring X Corps to the south fared better. The 36th Division swept forward astride the Ancre, taking important strongpoints and pushing outposts out beyond the final objective. The 32nd Division took the fortified town of Thiepval and the prominent Leipzig spur. Thanks in part to the efforts of the X Corps, William Pulteney's III Corps escaped comparatively lightly. The Germans were pushed out of the *Nordwerk* strongpoint, while Ovillers and La Boiselle both fell. XV Corps on the right flank of III Corps ejected the enemy from Fricourt and the eponymous wood beyond but the belligerent defence of the town took a grave toll. The 21st Division suffered 3,994 casualties, the worst of any British division that day. The greatest laurels rested with the XIII Corps whose rapid assault smashed the defences around Montauban and destabilised the front ahead of them for two miles. The neighbouring French had played their part but much credit has to go to the 18th and 30th divisions, whose well-executed and meticulous assault ensured success in this portion of the line.

At the close of the first day on the Somme the British casualties totalled 26,609, of which 5,424 were killed. In return the Germans lost 32,109 across the combined British and French fronts, which amounted to nearly a third of the German strength in this sector. When the French gains are also considered, 1 July was a devastating blow and truly was 'the muddy grave of the German field army'.[14] They had lost key tactical positions and almost all of their first-line system from Beaumont Hamel to Fay in the French sector, with only Serre and Beaumont Hamel remaining in German hands.

Aftermath

Truly 1 July 1916 was a defining moment of the First World War. The German Army had been dealt a vicious blow. The pressure of fighting the British on the Somme and the French at Verdun was unbearable. The German Chief of the General Staff, Erich von Falkenhayn, reacted swiftly. On 2 July all planned offensive action at Verdun was halted and divisions were diverted to the Somme sector. Meanwhile back in Germany political support was growing for Paul von Hindenburg to replace Falkenhayn.

In the days that followed the guns were brought forward to new positions in the old British front line. Patrols were pushed out by the advanced divisions but key tactical points remained unoccupied, later to be bitterly contested. Places that would become the site of notorious bloodletting in the days that followed – Bernafay Wood, Trones Wood, Delville Wood, Contalmaison, and Longueval – may have fallen with little cost in those precious forty-eight hours after the initial assault. A more experienced army may have seized the initiative and captured them without instructions; as it was, the battalion, brigade, divisional, and corps commanders all proved reluctant to stray from the parameters of Rawlinson's battle plan. As the shaken German divisions were reinforced, replaced, or regrouped, the Somme front began to stabilise. Consolidation and preparation for the next attack proved to be far more prolonged and bloody than Haig, Rawlinson, or Montgomery had expected.

The second great 'bite' came on 14 July. This was another tremendous hammer blow, albeit this time on a far smaller scale. In one swift night attack the German second-line positions south of Pozières along the Bazentin Ridge were swept away. High Wood remained a formidable obstacle halting the swift conquest of Flers and Martinpuich, while Pozières itself loomed like a spectre over the British gains. Furthermore, this methodical operation was followed by another bitter struggle to consolidate the gains and capture surviving strongpoints. The fighting cost thousands of lives on both sides of the wire. This was the limitation of 'bite and hold'. It was not a universal panacea to the problems of trench warfare. Rawlinson's rigid planning undoubtedly saved lives in the assault, but the costly localised battles that raged on in woods and ruined villages exacted a heavy toll on the British Army.

The British achieved their greatest success with the first two offensives on 1 July and 14 July. There were further 'bites', but the army's teeth were becoming worn and each successive advance achieved a little less and suffered a little more. Rawlinson has been rightly criticised for failing to recognise the unflinching grip the law of diminishing returns had upon the Western Front. The difficulty of maintaining supply over a shell-ravaged battlefield, the baleful effect of wear on gun barrels which caused a reduction in artillery support, and the sheer speed with which the German Army was able to fortify new positions all contributed to the loss of offensive impetus. August, September, and October were bloody months. The battles for the heavily entrenched villages of Grandcourt, Warlencourt, Le Sars, and Gueudecourt scorched their names into the national psyche.

The fact that the final line came to rest along the axis of Puisieux, Irles, Gueudecourt, and Le Transloy was a testament to the limitations of Rawlinson's method. As the battle became bogged down it was ever harder to make significant gains. Each operational pause to bring guns, munitions, men, and supplies forward gave the Germans enough time to prepare new and formidable defensive positions.

Credit should also be given to the German Army, which did not stay static in its defensive approach. After each successive British blow the Germans adapted their tactics accordingly. By the end of the battle the German method placed little emphasis on holding the front line, relying instead on deep interlocking defensive positions and carefully concealed artillery that would hold its fire until it could inflict maximum damage on the attackers. The speed, intensity, and effectiveness of German counterattacks increased, and they proved capable of inflicting significant casualties on surprised British infantry. These experiences towards the end of the Somme, brought on in part by the need to swiftly improvise defences, were a precursor of what would become standard German practice in 1917. When the battle was closed down in October, the German army, although battered and bloody, could nevertheless claim some credit for having fought the British to a standstill.

Yet for all the criticism that has been heaped upon the generals for embracing caution and attrition so unflinchingly, the first day of the Battle of the

Somme was the vicious opening blow in a campaign that would wrest the strategic initiative firmly away from the Central Powers. The campaign led to a marked decline in the quality and morale of German troops and, despite tactical improvements, they would never quite recover. A testament to the Somme's importance was given by Basil Liddell Hart who, in his best-selling *The Real War* recognised 1 July as a moment of triumph for the 'steady, meticulous and limited approach to battle. No position of strength can be rendered so strong that it could resist well-coordinated artillery and infantry attack.'[15]

It created a military crisis for the German Army. On 18 July, four days after the second British attack, with consistent French pressure in the south and a major counteroffensive in Verdun, Falkenhayn was removed. Paul von Hindenburg was installed in his place and immediately ordered construction on a new heavily fortified position – the *Siegfriedstellung* – that would allow the Germans to withdraw from the Somme and shorten the Western Front by twenty-five miles. Although the immediate crisis passed, the cumulative damage was considerable. With troops being funnelled into Verdun and the Somme, the Eastern Front became a further source of serious concern, and only Russian political instability rescued the Germans from major losses. The following year they faced further crises, when a combination of Plumer's methodical and effective offensive around Ypres and 3rd Army's surprise tank attack at Cambrai broke the stalemate of the Western Front. Despite revolutionary fervour bubbling over in Russia, the provisional government did enough to tie down German forces in the East. Attrition had worked, the cumulative losses of the Somme, Verdun, Third Ypres, and Cambrai had shattered the manpower and morale of the German Army in the West. On 25 December 1917 an armistice was declared.

The Reality

In reality, 1 July was not a great triumph of arms, although the planning process certainly established the potential for it to be a success. It is easy to criticise after the event and ridicule the incompetence that led to certain decisions being taken, but it has to be remembered that in 1916 there was no consensus on what it would take to win the war and there was no established formula for success in battle.

This scenario explores what may have happened had Rawlinson's 'bite-and-hold' method been implemented. Rawlinson's limited approach may have led to greater initial success, fewer casualties, and it could well have averted the greatest single day of bloodshed in the British Army's history. This should not be underestimated or downplayed. But 'bite and hold' was not a panacea to the problems of the Western Front. Given the technology, logistics, and organisational strength of the German Army it is almost inconceivable that the battle would have brought an end to the war in 1916. The BEF simply did not have the means to fight a war at the speed and tempo needed to overcome a modern European army like the Germans had at that time. A more successful attack in July 1916 may have accelerated the learning process for the British Army but there would be a lot further to go before it could culminate in success for the Entente.

In reality the Somme struck a heavy blow to German morale, but it was not terminal and it recovered fairly quickly; in this alternative reality something similar would have been the case. The involvement of British 'pals' battalions in the battle proved pivotal in creating a powerful local heritage and commemoration; this too would have remained although there may have been a greater variety of dates on the village memorials to the lost. Perhaps the most profound impact of the Somme has been upon the reputations of the generals who commanded it. In France Joffre, Foch, and Fayolle have been saved from the stigma reserved for Haig, and to a lesser extent, Rawlinson. The fact they were fighting a war of national survival with a self-evident military objective contrasts with the murky, disputed reasoning for Britain's entry into the conflict. This would always have led to questions being asked of why and how the war was fought. Haig and Rawlinson may have shortened the war considerably by their actions in 1916 and 1917 but it is difficult to see how they would have escaped the snide, scathing, sometimes-satirical finger-pointing of later decades. Thankfully, in that alternative world there were also historians whose revisions might have challenged such simplistic notions.

Notes

1 National Army Museum, 5201-33-18, Rawlinson Papers, Rawlinson to Wigram 27/2/1916; also quoted in Robin Prior and Trevor Wilson, *Command on the Western Front: The Military Career of Sir Henry Rawlinson 1914–1918* (London: Blackwell, 1992) p. 139.

2 Gary Sheffield and John Bourne, *Douglas Haig: War Diaries and Letters 1914–1918* (London: Weidenfeld & Nicolson, 2005), 29 March 1916, p. 183.

3 The National Archives (TNA), WO 158/233/7, Plan for Offensive by Fourth Army, 3 April 1916; see also William Philpott, *Bloody Victory* (London: Little, Brown, 2009).

4 TNA, WO 158/233/7, 5 April 1916, p. 184.

5 Churchill College, Cambridge, Rawlinson Diary RWLN 1/5, 4 April 1916; also quoted in Prior and Wilson, *Command on the Western Front*, p. 141.

6 General Staff, *Field Service Regulations Part I: Operations* (London: HMSO, 1909), p. 23.

7 Sheffield and Bourne, *Douglas Haig: War Diaries*, 4 May 1916, p. 185; 25 May 1916, p. 187.

8 Brigadier General James Edmonds, *Military Operations: France and Belgium 1916, vol. 1 Appendices* (London: Imperial War Museum/Battery Press, 1993 or 1932), Appendix 18: Fourth Army Tactical Notes, pp. 131–47.

9 Quoted in Philpott, *Bloody Victory*, p. 174; Gary Sheffield, *The Somme* (London: Cassell, 2003), p. 57.

10 *TNA, WO 95/2375, 32nd Division CRA, 24/6/16–30/6/16 (although not the exact phrasing, similar sentiments can be found in this file).

11 Christopher Duffy, *Through German Eyes: The British and the Somme 1916* (London: Weidenfeld & Nicolson, 2006), pp. 124–7.

12 Cyril Falls, *The History of the 36th (Ulster) Division* (London: Constable, 1922), p. 56.

13 *David Lloyd George, *War Memoirs* (London: Odhams Press, 1933), p. 607.

14 Captain von Hentig, quoted in Edmonds, *Military Operations: France and Belgium 1916, vol.1*, p. 494.

15 *Basil Lidell Hart, *The Real War* (London: Cassell, 1930), p. 331

9

'From Mud, Through Blood to the Green Fields Beyond'

The Great Allied Tank Offensive of 1917

Spencer Jones

Prologue: The Battle of Paardeberg, South Africa, February 1900

Major General Horace Smith-Dorrien could not believe what he was seeing. Throughout the scorching South African summer day the British infantry had been ordered into reckless frontal assaults against an entrenched Boer position. The task had been hopeless. The famous Afrikaner marksmen had gunned down the attackers time and again. The dusty *veld* was carpeted with khaki-clad bodies that revealed the futility of the British tactics. But now, yet another attack was being formed up in the early evening light.

Watching through binoculars, Smith-Dorrien looked on in dismay as the British line rose from cover with a roar and moved forward at the double. A crash of rifle fire burst from the Boer line in response. Officers leading the advance with swords drawn were prime targets and were swiftly picked off. The British line convulsed as bullets ripped through its ranks. Gaps appeared. Survivors bunched together, pushing forward, stepping over the fallen of earlier assaults. The Boers concentrated fire on these heroic pockets and mowed them down. Within minutes it was all over. The attack had simply been destroyed.

171

The attack left a deep impression on Smith-Dorrien. He remembered after the war: 'It was a gallant charge, gallantly led, but the fact that not one of them got within 300 yards of the enemy is sufficient proof of its futility.'[1] No amount of heroism could overcome the effects of modern firepower. Surely there had to be a better way of making war?

The desire for a 'better way' would plant a seed in Smith-Dorrien's mind that would finally bear fruit in the First World War – but first, the solution had to be devised.

Necessity is the Mother of All Invention

In December 1903 the visionary science fiction author H. G. Wells published his story 'The Land Ironclads' in the *Strand* magazine. The prescient tale took place during a thinly disguised reimagining of the Boer War, where an army representing the British became deadlocked by the trenches of their opponents. After a month of stalemate, a bold new weapon takes to the field – the land ironclads of the title, mechanical behemoths one hundred feet in length, studded with guns and guided by huge searchlights. The mechanical monsters prove invulnerable to the rifle fire of the enemy and crush the defences with ease. In years to come, Wells would look back with pride on his prediction of armoured warfare.[2]

Unfortunately for the British Army, the technology described in the story still lay in the future. Working with the equipment that was available, a number of officers proposed the use of bulletproof, man-portable shields that could be carried or rolled across the ground.[3] Numerous experiments took place in Britain and India. Disappointingly, all work with the shields proved unsatisfactory. The devices were heavy and unwieldy, and it was soon found that they were only mobile on firm, flat ground.

However, an unorthodox and intriguing design emerged in 1912. After several uncomfortable experiences driving trucks over rough terrain, Australian inventor Lancelot de Mole designed a caterpillar-tracked transporter that could carry heavy loads across battlefields. Although he envisaged a transport rather than a fighting vehicle, de Mole suggested that his machine would be capable of crossing trenches and sufficiently armoured to withstand enemy fire.[4] De Mole forwarded his proposal to the British War Office. In a stroke of good fortune, the design was brought to the attention of General Sir Ian Hamilton. Earlier in his career Hamilton had favoured the use of super heavy artillery and had been intrigued by the idea of using steam traction engines to haul it into battle.[5] Hamilton used his influence to attract interest in de Mole's design, prompting the Royal Engineers to carry out a feasibility study on the vehicle. The resulting report was issued in early 1914 and drew a very favourable conclusion.[6] Unfortunately, the scandal of the Curragh incident[7] in March and command reshuffle that followed distracted the authorities and the report was largely forgotten.

The outbreak of war in August 1914 came with armoured technology still beyond reach. Instead, the British Expeditionary Force marched into battle relying on suppressing fire, use of cover, and extended formations to keep its infantry safe. These methods served well enough in the defensive battles of August 1914. But the casualties suffered attempting to storm the German trenches at the Battle of the Aisne in September gave a stark warning that the killing power of modern weapons now far exceeded those that had been used in the Boer War. Defenders occupying earthworks could inflict severe losses on any attacker whilst suffering comparatively few in return. This imbalance between attack and defence led to the trench deadlock that took hold of the Western Front at the end of 1914. The lines ran from the Channel coast to the Swiss border. There were no flanks to turn, no room for manoeuvre, and seemingly no way through the barbed wire, machine guns, and artillery fire of the defenders.

The British Army cast about for solutions to the impasse. Amongst the many officers drawing up proposals was the official war correspondent Ernest Swinton. An intelligent and imaginative man, Swinton remembered a conversation with a friend who had once suggested that civilian tractors running on caterpillar tracks might have some military application.[8] In October, Swinton had passed his thoughts on to his friend Colonel Maurice Hankey, who was working as an assistant to the prime minister.

On 28 December 1914, Hankey issued a paper of military ideas known as the 'Boxing Day Memorandum'. Amongst various suggestions for the conduct of the war there was a paragraph that spoke of the future. Hankey suggested the use of 'Numbers of large heavy rollers, themselves bullet proof, propelled from behind by motor-engines, geared very low, the driving wheel fitted with a caterpillar driving gear to grip the ground, the driver's seat armoured and a Maxim gun fitted. The object of this device would be to roll down the barbed wire by sheer weight, to give some cover to men creeping up behind and to support the advance with machine gun fire.'[9]

This paragraph had an electrifying effect on Winston Churchill, then serving as First Lord of the Admiralty, who immediately wrote to the prime minister urging that the proposal be pursued.[10] The vehicle that would ultimately become known as the tank had a powerful supporter. Science fiction was about to become reality.

Design

Armoured cars had served with some success in 1914 but the idea of creating a tracked fighting vehicle was a new concept within the British military. It was such a radical idea that it was not clear who should have authority over the design. Should it be developed by the navy, which had more experience with steel and engines, or by the army, who would actually use it in battle? Without a firm hand to guide the project, the proposals could easily have become lost amongst the papers of the overworked War Office and disappeared from view, or else have languished in forgotten obscurity on the cluttered desks of important figures.

Fortunately for the British the vehicle had two enthusiastic champions. Churchill had immediately seen the potential in the device and supported it throughout its creation, but his influenced waxed and waned with the fortunes of his political career. However, his enthusiasm was shared by the Chief of the Imperial General Staff, Sir Douglas Haig. Haig had been promoted to the post of CIGS during the hasty command reshuffle that took place in the aftermath of the Curragh incident of early 1914.[11] Although desperately disappointed to be denied a combat command, he overcame his frustration by absorbing himself with his work. He proved to be a determined and energetic CIGS. Convinced that the war could only be won by defeating Germany on the Western Front, Haig was an enthusiastic supporter of new technologies that promised to break the deadlock. His fascination with innovative weapons was sometimes to his detriment, and at one point he was even taken in by a charlatan who claimed to have invented a death ray.[12] However, when it came to the development of armoured vehicles, Haig's instincts were correct. He saw the tank as a decisive weapon and used the strength of his position to ensure that the work was fully funded and pursued with vigour.[13]

The British had another major advantage in their early design work. Although it had been overlooked for the better part of a year, the feasibility study on the de Mole vehicle was suddenly remembered. The report gave the wartime designers a crucial head start.[14] Driven by Churchill's enthusiasm and Haig's determination, work on an armoured vehicle began in early 1915 and the project progressed rapidly. Debate followed as to its ideal size, weight, armour, and armament. Numerous tests and rigorous trials took place. The process was further complicated by the need for absolute secrecy so that the Germans would have no time to develop countermeasures.

The first fully functional prototype was ready for trials in August 1915.[15] It was a caterpillar-tracked, rhomboid-shaped vehicle with room for heavy weapons in side sponsons and machine guns in its central hull. It was a slow-moving and somewhat crude machine, but it was also a revolutionary weapon. Having passed its trials, the tank was demonstrated to senior government and military figures. Ernest Swinton remembered: 'it was a striking scene when the signal was given and a species of gigantic cubist steel slug slid out of its lair.'[16] The display was impressive. One observer commented, 'wire entanglements it goes through like a rhinoceros through a field of corn.'[17] There was one burning question that was raised by the army representatives: 'How soon can we have them?' The Ministry of Munitions thought it could have fifty tanks ready by early 1916 with more to follow.

Yet armoured innovators, including Swinton and Churchill, urged that the army should be patient and not launch a premature attack with a handful of machines. It would be better to build up the armoured branch until it was powerful enough to strike a decisive blow against the German line. Their views found favour with Field Marshal Sir Horace Smith-Dorrien. Smith-Dorrien had been promoted to full command of the British Army in France in mid-1915 and he had been searching for innovative ideas for breaking the deadlock ever since.[18] The development of the tank had enormous promise. However, Smith-Dorrien knew that the matter could not be rushed. Earlier in the war he had criticised the hasty deployment of undertrained infantry. He would not see the same mistake made with the new armoured branch. Time was needed to train the crews and devise tactics for the vehicles. Although the temptation to deploy them immediately was very great, Smith-Dorrien made the bold decision to hold back the tanks until they were adjudged to be battle ready.

The vehicles were assigned their own organisation that could coordinate command, training, and operational planning. To maintain secrecy, the tanks were formed into the Heavy Branch of the Machine Gun Corps. In the meantime designers, crews, and commanders worked feverishly on all aspects of the new arm. Tactics had to be devised entirely from scratch and crews had to be trained in the use of the new machine. The designers tested and refined the MK I tank, correcting problems, adding features, and producing improved versions. There was also some interchange of ideas with the French, who were working independently on their own tank designs.

In September 1916 an agreement was reached between the British and French armies: neither side would deploy their tanks until the other was ready, thus ensuring that their combat usage came as an unpleasant surprise to the Germans. The decision would have important consequences.

April 1917: Allied Plans

April 1917 was to be a critical month in the Allied war effort. The German retreat to the fortifications of the Hindenburg Line, although strategically sound, also revealed that the battles of 1916 had inflicted serious damage on the German Army. After a relative lull during the bitterly cold winter months, the dawning of the spring signalled that it was time for the British and French to renew the offensive and hurl the invader back to his own borders. To do this, they would deploy their carefully prepared secret weapon.

Tanks had been gathering behind Allied lines throughout late 1916. Officers had the chance to inspect them, and tank commanders had the opportunity to work with the infantry that they would be supporting in battle. Every effort was made to maintain secrecy during this assemblage. Tanks were concealed in aircraft hangars, in wooded areas and even in disused railway tunnels to keep them from the prying eyes of German reconnaissance aircraft. Despite the best efforts of the British, the Germans gathered some inkling of the new machines. Remarkably, this information had virtually no influence on their military planning. General Erich Ludendorff paid them no heed, prompting Churchill's postwar assessment that when it came to tanks, 'the ablest soldier in Germany was blind'.[19] At the front line there were vague warnings that the Allies were preparing 'land cruisers' for their next offensive.[20] However, what these machines looked like or were capable of remained a mystery, and the Germans were taken completely by surprise when the tanks finally attacked.

It was decided that April would be the month when the tanks were to be unleashed on the enemy. The French intended to deploy their own vehicles in support of their massive offensive against the Chemin des Dames. The British had agreed to play their own role in supporting this operation by attacking around Arras. There was an optimistic hope that if both British and French attacks broke through then they would drive onwards to link up deep in German-occupied territory, outflanking the Hindenburg Line at a stroke. More realistically, the British attack would draw in German reserves and distract attention from the heavy French assault.

The German position around Arras was anchored on the dominating heights of the Vimy Ridge to the north and on the sophisticated defences of the Hindenburg Line at Bullecourt to the south. The trench lines were constructed in depth and the position stretched back some ten thousand yards. Faced with these strong defences, the British had assembled approximately five hundred battle-ready tanks. The majority of the vehicles were MK I and MK II tanks, little changed from the first prototype that had been demonstrated in September 1915. However, a significant proportion of the force consisted of the more sophisticated and reliable MK IVs which had only recently rolled off the production lines.[21]

The Battle of Arras would be defined by surprise. Unlike earlier battles, which had been characterised by bombardments lasting a week or more, the Arras attack was to be preceded with a short but intense bombardment of no more than forty-eight hours.[22] As soon as the barrage lifted, the tanks would lead the assault on the German line, crushing any unbroken wire beneath their tracks and making a path for the infantry. Surviving German strongpoints would be destroyed by the 6-pounder guns carried by the 'male' versions of the tanks, whilst the machine-gun-armed 'females' would mow down any German counterattacks.[23] The British infantry would surge forward to consolidate the ground and continue the advance. The Battle of Arras represented a remarkably ambitious plan and its reliance on an entirely untried weapon was unprecedented in the history of warfare. The Heavy Branch was about to receive its baptism of fire.

First Blood

The British attack had originally been planned for 9 April but the assault was delayed for three days due to unusually poor weather. It was bitterly cold when the battle began on 12 April and many accounts recalled the sudden snow flurries that swept across the area.

As planned, the Royal Artillery had opened the fighting with an intense bombardment. After forty-eight hours of constant shelling the fire reached its crescendo, the gunners labouring feverishly to work their guns, with many stripped to the waist despite the unseasonable cold. As its final act, the artillery smothered the German position with a mixture of dense poison gas and choking black smoke, blinding the defenders to ensure that they would not see the approach of the tanks until it was too late.

Tanks were carefully concealed all along the British line and their commanders nervously counted down the minutes until zero hour. Although thoroughly trained, none of the crews had any real idea what to expect. Some crewmen had battle experience in other arms of service, but this was the first time any had seen actual combat from the inside of their vehicles. One veteran recalled a tank commanded by a young second lieutenant who had 'never seen a shot fired in his life' but who was determined to 'attack Germany all on his own' by 'shooting at every living thing he saw'.[24]

At zero hour the tanks lurched forward from the British trenches. The advance seemed painfully slow. Some tanks failed to move from their start positions due to engine failure or the driver 'missing the gears'. Others lumbered forward a short distance before experiencing similar breakdown or else becoming stuck in soft ground. The ironclad line was ragged in places. The clouds that blinded the German defenders would not last forever. Infantrymen strained to get forward and ahead of the slow-moving machines, not wanting to be caught in no man's land when the Germans recovered their wits.

Yet, although it was slow, the tank attack had a relentless quality. The vehicles clambered through shell holes and over battlefield detritus. Suddenly, they had reached the wire belts – already thoroughly mangled by the British bombardment – and crashed through the steel defences without pause. One crewman remembered the sound as his tank crushed the obstacle: 'It screeched against the hull . . . snapping and scraping, snapping and grating, it eventually fizzled out and we had got ourselves through.'[25]

Peering through the thick lenses of their gas masks, the German infantry in the front line witnessed an amazing – and appalling – sight. Dark, mechanical shapes were emerging from the smoke. The growl of their engines and the grinding of their tracks were audible even above the din of battle. As the machines approached, their hulls were suddenly lit with flashes as their numerous guns opened fire. The dreaded *materialschlat* – the 'battle of equipment' – had taken on a new and terrible form.

The defenders were stunned. A British officer recalled with quiet understatement: 'The Germans . . . were too staggered at the sight of the tank to make much resistance.'[26] Many surrendered on the spot, and those who did not were powerless to resist the tanks and the infantry that followed close behind. The tanks rumbled over the trenches and beyond, leaving behind small parties of infantry to mop up in their wake.

Yet not all the defenders were numbed by the experience. Runners sprinted down communication trenches to warn the rear areas of the approaching metal monsters. Infantry officers snatched up field telephones, bellowing for immediate artillery support to stop the fabled 'land cruisers'. At the other end of the line, the German gunners gritted their teeth against the brutal British counter-battery fire and responded with every gun they had.

The tanks pushed forward, moving even deeper into the German position. Shells began to burst around them. Shrapnel from near misses rattled against the hull. Direct hits proved fatal, igniting the vulnerable fuel tanks and reducing tanks to burning wrecks. German machine-gunners fired entire belts of ammunition at the tanks, hoping to find a weak point. Although most bullets bounced off the armour, these bursts of fire shattered vision periscopes, rendering the crew effectively blind. Even worse was the previously unknown effect of 'splash': bullet impacts on the exterior of the tank caused interior armour to flake, hurling tiny pieces of hot metal into faces of the crew. A tank commander remembered 'a smash against my flap at the front caused splinters to come in and the blood to pour down my face. Another minute and my driver got the same.'[27] In places German infantry assaulted isolated tanks directly, attempting to tear open the crew hatches, thrusting bayonets through vision slits and jamming grenades between the tracks.

The attackers steadily lost vehicles, some knocked out by enemy action, others suffering breakdowns, or ditching in shell holes. But the remaining tanks ploughed forward, pressing ever deeper into the German defensive system. In the skies overhead Royal Flying Corps observation aircraft watched and reported on the advance. Vimy Ridge fell to the triumphant Canadians, whilst the Australians captured Bullecourt with the aid of dozens of tanks. With the flanks secure, the British attack drove deep into the central German position. The haul of prisoners was immense.

However, the attack gradually lost its momentum. Although the tanks could pass through German shelling to an extent, their supporting infantry and cavalry were not so fortunate. As a result leading tanks became isolated and were either forced to fall back or else be overrun by German attacks. As evening approached it was clear that the attack was petering out and it was decided to consolidate the gains and prepare for a renewed advance the following day.

The British Army had made the deepest advance against a German position since the dawn of trench warfare, with some spearheads reaching the very last of the defence lines before they were forced to stop. Key positions had been taken at a comparatively low cost in lives. Thousands of German prisoners had been captured. For the first time in the war, church bells were sounded across Britain to signify a great victory.

But the battle was not over. The shock and surprise of the first day was fading and the Germans rushed in counterattack divisions to seal the breach. The British position was strung out and in many cases beyond the protective umbrella of its artillery. Furthermore, the Heavy Branch was exhausted. The Battle of Arras had been a brutal proving ground for men and machines. The crew compartment was atrociously hot in battle and the interior air was thick with carbon monoxide from the poorly ventilated engine. Surviving crewmen were left exhausted by the experience and many required at least thirty-six hours' rest to recover. In other cases the crew no longer had a functioning tank to operate. The hours of darkness were filled with curses as crewmen tried to repair damaged vehicles or extract their machine from the mud. Few were successful before renewed fighting disrupted their work. Of some five hundred tanks committed to the fighting on 12 April, fewer than two hundred were reported as ready for action on the following day. The number continued to decline as the battle continued. The sound of church bells would prove to be premature.

The Battle of Arras is remembered as a flawed victory. The British renewed their attacks in the days that followed, hurling the remaining tanks into action once more. Local advances were made, but the momentum of that first day could not be recreated. As more and more tanks were disabled the fighting assumed the character of so many other First World War battles: a remorseless, attritional struggle over a muddy landscape swept with artillery. German counterattacks crashed into the British line and clawed back some of the lost ground. Both sides fought themselves to a standstill until the battle ended through mutual exhaustion. Elsewhere, the French offensive on the Chemin des Dames had similarly achieved a notable initial success with its armour, only to have the advance peter out amidst mud and shellfire. French casualties were high but all agreed that they would have been far worse without the advantage gained by the surprise use of tanks.

In the following weeks the Allies licked their wounds and pondered the future. Nowhere was this truer than the Heavy Branch. Its performance in battle had earned it the title of the Royal Tank Corps. Its official motto was 'Fear Naught', but it took pride in its unofficial saying of 'From Mud, Through Blood to the Green Fields Beyond'. The latter slogan proved hugely popular with officers and men. The unofficial motto encapsulated the Tank Corps' dogged outlook and reaffirmed its determination to smash through the German lines and reach the open country. Although there was disappointment and frustration in the aftermath of the Battle of Arras, there was also a learning process that would ultimately lead to a greater success.

Reinforcements

Despite the heavy loss of tanks at Arras, the devastating opening attack had convinced even the most stubborn doubters in the War Office that the vehicles were much more than ironclad novelties. As a result vehicle design and production accelerated exponentially. Long-term champion Winston Churchill – now serving as minister of munitions – was delighted by the performance of the branch and used his authority to increase production of new vehicles. His optimistic message for the Tank Corps was: 'the resources are available, the knowledge is available, the time is available, the result is certain'[28] and 'we are standing by to put new weapons in their hands . . . let there be no misunderstanding therefore but only confidence and full steam ahead.'[29] Churchill planned to provide not only replacements for battlefield losses but also entirely new models of tanks.

Combat experience had revealed the strengths and weaknesses of the armoured branch. The lessons of the Battle of Arras would inform design and manufacture of the next generation of tanks. The old MK I and MK II models were found to be vulnerable to German SmK bullets – armour-piercing rounds used against the steel-covered loopholes favoured by snipers – but the more advanced MK IVs were effectively immune to infantry fire. Nevertheless, the numerous injuries suffered as a result of internal 'splash' necessitated the issue of chainmail masks and protective goggles for crewmen.

The majority of tanks had been disabled by mechanical breakdown or becoming stuck in shell holes. The necessity for an improved engine and transmission system was obvious. Fortunately, the solution was at hand in the form of a newly designed 150-hp engine that entered large-scale production in early 1917. This was a major improvement on the 105-hp engines used by the first generation of tanks. It would first be used in the MK V tank that began to reach the front in mid-1917. The British had also begun manufacture of a new class of tank – the Medium Mark A, better known as the 'Whippet'. Smaller and faster than existing British vehicles, the Whippet was designed to exploit the breaches made by its heavier cousins and harry retreating German infantry.[30] Herculean industrial and organisational effort was placed on the production of Allied armour, even at the expense of other war industries. By the latter part of 1917 the new machines were arriving in considerable numbers.

Whilst the Allies were improving their tanks, the Germans were instituting a crash programme of anti-tank weapons. Engineers inspected the wrecked and captured vehicles that had been abandoned at Arras. Fortunately for the Allies, the only intact machines that the Germans were able to capture were some of the older MK I models. Nevertheless, the Germans quickly devised short-term solutions. Provision of armour-piercing SmK bullets was increased and specialist anti-tank artillery units were formed. In parts of the line the trenches were widened to make it impossible for tanks to cross without falling in. The technological race between Allied tank design and German anti-tank measures would continue throughout the summer.

The tanks had caught the public imagination and were featured prominently in press stories and propaganda features. Having entered the war in the same month as the Battle of Arras, the United States Army took a special interest in armoured warfare. A US Tank Board was immediately founded and several 'hell bent' observers were rushed to the Western Front to gather information. As a result of their observations it was decided that the US would equip its fledgling tank branch with two thousand light French tanks and two hundred heavy British tanks. A thirty-two-year-old cavalry captain with a bright future – George S. Patton – was made head of the American Expeditionary Force's Light Tank School.[31]

Readying the Hammer

As the American forces mustered, the British and French were preparing their next hammer blow. The Tank Corps repaired its damaged machines, rested its weary crews, and received a steady stream of reinforcements. At headquarters there was very little time to rest. Smith-Dorrien had been sufficiently impressed with the performance of the tanks that he asked the Tank Corps to take a leading role in drafting plans for its next operation.

Much of the planning fell to Major J. F. C. Fuller, an erratic yet brilliant staff officer. Fuller understood that the biggest impediment to the tanks had been the muddy, shell-cratered landscape and offered an innovative solution: the usual pre-battle bombardment would be abandoned and tanks would attack without warning. The armour would smash the barbed-wire screens and allow the infantry to storm the German position. For this daring operation to work, speed, surprise, and good terrain were absolutely essential. Ultimately the plan was too radical even for the open-minded Smith-Dorrien, who approved the basic principles but insisted on incorporating artillery support. Fortunately, the Royal Artillery proposed a solution. The gunners had been perfecting new methods of 'firing from the map' which would allow them to call down a storm of accurate fire at a moment's notice. Artillery support for the Tank Corps did not need to take the form of a preparatory bombardment that gave notice of the impending attack and devastated the landscape, but would instead be a sudden deluge of shells that fell without warning.

Confident in this knowledge, Fuller proposed an armoured assault against St Quentin, which lay in the centre of the Hindenburg Line. The defences here were formidable but the gently rolling slopes and flat valleys made it ideal tank country and a significant breakthrough would rupture the entire Hindenburg position. However, St Quentin marked the borderline between British and French sectors and any operation here would require direct cooperation. Fortunately, it was soon found that the French commander opposite St Quentin, Franchert d'Espery, was enthusiastic about the idea of an Anglo-French tank attack. With cooperation ensured, Fuller planned an armoured assault employing a combination of heavy and light tanks that aimed to shatter the Hindenburg Line in one dramatic blow.

Planning and preparation began immediately. The British were already involved in heavy fighting around Ypres that kept the Germans occupied. The French mounted subsidiary operations at various points along the Western Front to keep the Germans guessing. Great efforts were made to ensure secrecy on the St Quentin front. Allied aircraft flew hundreds of sorties to keep German reconnaissance flights away from concentration areas. Tanks were concealed under specially made camouflage netting and their tell-tale tracks were obscured with brushwood and straw. Artillery inched into position and infantry quietly assembled opposite the front. Certain innovative preparations were made, including the provision of supply tanks to carry fuel and ammunition to the fighting line once battle began, and the deployment of tanks carrying field telephones and wireless to provide battlefield communications. Other novel methods included the use of tank-carried fascines that could be dropped to fill in wide German trenches and allow them to be crossed with ease. Finally, a number of 'dummy' tanks, constructed of wood and fabric, were placed near the German front at Cambrai to give the false impression an attack was brewing here. The combination of secrecy and deception meant that the Allies achieved complete surprise when they finally attacked.

After a delay imposed by the wait for greater numbers of the new Whippet and light French Renault RT tanks, the Anglo-French force was ready for action on 30 September 1917.

Smashing the Hindenburg Line

The St Quentin position was truly formidable. The approach to the line was choked with dense barbed-wire belts and covered by numerous hidden machine-gun nests. The St Quentin canal had been incorporated into the defensive works. A handful of bridges were left intact to allow German forces access to the far bank, but each was heavily defended and rigged to be blown if threatened with capture. The centrepiece of the position was the six-thousand-yard-long Bellicourt tunnel, through which the canal ran. The German garrison slept inside the tunnel on specially converted canal boats. In the event of an attack the defenders would rush to their positions on the surface using strategically placed stairwells.

The Bellicourt tunnel was a marvel of engineering – but it was also a weak point in the face of a tank attack. The tunnel provided a natural bridge that a rapid assault could cross. This was important, as tanks were normally unable to cross canal lines until engineers had constructed a bridge. There was also a second weakness in the German position – the very strength of the defences had bred complacency. The position was thinly held by weak reserve divisions only considered capable of garrison duty. Compared to the battle zones at Ypres, Arras, and the Aisne, the sector had been quiet for months. Wild flowers bloomed in no man's land and the barbed-wire belts were turning brown with rust.

The tranquillity was about to be shattered. The press would subsequently term the British assault force as 'the thousand tank army', but in reality there were 850 vehicles ready for action, with a similar number available to the French to the south.[32] The Allies had learned the value of keeping a reserve of tanks and around 250 machines were held back for second-day operations. The attack would be supported by several corps of infantry and a cavalry corps, all covered by the guns of the Royal Artillery. The gunners had secretly ranged their weapons on the Hindenburg Line – a process greatly aided by the fortuitous capture of a complete German map of the position during a trench raid in August[33] – and now awaited the signal to begin.

A cold mist blanketed no man's land on the morning of the attack. The German defenders were going about their usual daily routine when they were struck by a 'cyclone of fire' from the concealed British artillery. A veteran remembered: 'We had seen bombardments before, but this was something new in its intensity.'[34] Following close behind the shells was a steel horde of tanks, grinding across the open ground and crashing through the decaying barbed wire. Stunned German outposts barely had time to release their distress flares before they were overrun. Alarm bells rang throughout the Bellicourt tunnel, summoning the defenders to man their positions. Such was the accuracy of British artillery fire that some Germans emerged only to find smouldering craters where their machine-gun nests had once stood. Future panzer commander Heinz Guderian described the events that followed: 'Suddenly indistinct black forms could be discerned. They were spitting fire and under their weight the strong and deep obstacle line was cracking like matchwood . . . the troops hastened to their machine guns and tried to put up a defence. It was all in vain! . . . The tanks appeared not one at a time but in whole lines kilometres in length!'[35]

The British attack came on quickly. The ground was good and the tanks were not impeded by shell craters. An armoured wedge converged on the Bellicourt tunnel, driving upwards, guns thundering as the crews engaged their targets. One veteran remembered being ordered 'to put all guns into action, to blaze our way forward. The noise was terrific; two 6-pounders going and our machine guns.'[36] The defenders fought back with armour-piercing bullets and hurled grenade bundles that were capable of tearing open tank hulls. In some places the Germans had dragged field artillery guns up to the front and used them as improvised but effective anti-tank weapons.

The battle for control of the ridge was ferocious, described as 'like Dante's *Inferno*' by one crewman.[37] But the tanks could not be stopped. Guderian recalled: 'The German infantrymen were pinned down and unable to withstand the mighty material superiority of the British. The only alternatives were death or surrender . . . [nobody] could hope to survive under this fire.'[38] Advancing remorselessly, the tanks crushed German positions under their tracks. Stunned defenders were overrun or else they stumbled back in confused retreat. One German gunner recalled meeting a bloodied, retreating infantry officer who gasped out '*Sturmwagen*! It is terrible; we cannot do anything. The front is broken!'[39]

The Bellicourt tunnel had been overwhelmed by mid-morning and the attackers drove deeper into the German position. The defenders were so surprised that the Allies were able to seize several intact canal bridges. Royal Engineers rushed forward to secure them and build additional crossing points to allow wider exploitation. Fierce fighting continued as the tanks assaulted the German second line. To the south, the French attack had met with similar success.

Pockets of German resistance stubbornly fought on but the momentum of the advance could not be stopped. As the main attack paused for consolidation, Whippet tanks and cavalry pressed forwards, 'leap-frogging' through the front line, past columns of prisoners and crowds of cheering British infantry. The assistance of light tanks meant that for the first time in the war 'the cavalry went through', causing chaos in the German rear areas and managing to capture an entire train loaded with reinforcements. By the end of the day the Allied victory was clear. The heart of the Hindenburg Line had been smashed in a single day and the linchpin of the German defences on the Western Front was compromised. The attack continued in the subsequent days, using the reserve tanks and widening the breach.

The Germans launched ferocious counterattacks to try and stem the Allied tide, but this had been expected. Tank battalions had been kept in reserve to be used as an armoured counter-punch against German advances. The relatively nimble Whippet tanks proved highly effective in this role, bursting from cover like 'savage rabbits' and smashing German infantry spearheads before they could gain ground. The battle see-sawed back and forth throughout October, but in contrast to the Battle of Arras, the Germans could not claw back the ground that they had lost. The best that they could manage was to slow Allied forward progress. However, rather than becoming involved in a fruitless war of attrition for which the tanks were ill-suited, the Allies consolidated their gains in the centre and instead launched fresh tank operations on the flanks, widening the breach in the German position. By the end of the year the Hindenburg Line was well and truly broken and the initiative lay firmly in Allied hands.

End Game

The Battle of St Quentin removed a cornerstone of German strategy. The General Staff had previously had complete confidence that the Hindenburg Line was unbreakable. That confidence was now shattered. Even though Russia had been defeated in late 1917, the prospects for 1918 suddenly looked bleak. The Germans could expect to face further tank attacks on the Western Front. The growing strength of Allied war industries meant there would be more vehicles of increasingly effective design. Furthermore they would be supported by the arrival of the American Expeditionary Force with its fresh divisions and newly formed armoured branch.

Even worse, morale amongst the German infantry was dangerously low. The front-line soldiers were exhausted by the intense fighting and dispirited by the clear evidence of Allied material superiority. By the end of 1917 insubordination, desertion, and localised mutiny had become common.[40] With the Hindenburg defences broken and the army close to mutiny, the grim but realistic prediction of the General Staff was that Germany could only delay the Allied advance for a few months before a total breakthrough occurred. They recommended seeking a way out of the war with honour intact.

On the other side of the front, the Allies were in a bullish mood. Their strength was increasing with greater tank production and American reinforcements, and the front seemed ripe with possibilities for further attacks. A series of armoured hammer blows were planned for spring 1918, with the British organising an attack against Cambrai whilst the French and Americans planned to pinch out the St Mihiel salient. Prime Minister David Lloyd George was confident enough to publicly express belief that victory would occur before the end of the year.

Lloyd George would be proved correct. With the tanks at the forefront, a rain of blows fell on the German lines in early 1918. The Germans defended with desperation and the fighting was intense, but the end result was inevitable. Germany had no answer to the ever-growing numbers of Allied tanks, and, as the Battle of St Quentin had proved, even its strongest positions could be breached.

Epilogue: The Victory Parade, London, 1919

Alongside King George V and Prime Minister Lloyd George, Earl Smith-Dorrien watched with immense pride as the parade passed the viewing podium. Enormous crowds thronged the parade route, cheering every regiment that passed by.

The biggest cheer of the day signalled the arrival of the Royal Tank Corps. The tanks rumbled through, resplendent in fresh paint and a far cry from the battle-scarred beasts that had broken the Hindenburg Line. Hatches were thrown open and commanders proudly saluted their chief as they passed the podium.

Returning the salute, Smith-Dorrien let his mind drift back to the battle nineteen years earlier in South Africa. It had taken bitter experience and the loss of many lives, but the British had finally found a better way of making war in the form of the tank. The wonder weapon had proved its worth.

The Reality

This story takes its cue from Winston Churchill's claim in *The World Crisis* that Britain could have had three thousand tanks in the field in early 1917 and so could have launched a major armoured offensive months before it actually did so at the Battle of Cambrai in November 1917. Given the existing demands on British wartime industry the figure of three thousand tanks is a piece of classic Churchillian bombast. However, there were certainly opportunities for Britain to have accelerated the pace of armoured development.

In this scenario I have given the army a headstart through its early interest in Lancelot de Mole's advanced proposals (which were sadly ignored in reality) thus placing armoured development several months ahead of its historical pace. However, a great problem for tank development was the novelty of the technology and the lack of a definite War Office champion in the early months of design. Historically, Douglas Haig was one of the greatest supporters of the tank but his position in France limited his influence on design and production. In this story I have made Haig Chief of the Imperial General Staff, placing him in a position where he can drive forward development.

The biggest change to the history is the decision to employ tanks en masse in early 1917. In reality, the decision to deploy a handful of tanks in September 1916 remains the source of much controversy. Contemporaries, including Swinton, Churchill, David Lloyd George, and J. F. C. Fuller, condemned the deployment as premature. The French had asked the British to wait until both sides could attack simultaneously with a mass of tanks, but this request was declined. Critics argue that it alerted the Germans to the existence of the weapon and achieved no great military advantage. By the time the Allies were ready to deploy massed armour in late 1917 the Germans had developed several anti-tank countermeasures. Defenders of the decision to commit the tanks early point out that combat experience was essential to provide a basis for crew training and vehicle design. However, whether these could have been developed with more thorough work at home remains a point of debate.

It is intriguing to consider what a mass of armour may have achieved in early 1917. The novelty of the weapon would have undoubtedly had a shock effect on the Germans, but the inexperience of the tank crews and lack of practice working alongside infantry would have been detrimental. However, an early and reasonably successful commitment of tanks would probably have provided fresh impetus to design and procurement. This is the basis for the latter half of the story, which sees advanced designs that historically debuted in 1918, such as the MK V and the Whippet, introduced much earlier in the war, and an Anglo-French tank attack taking place in late 1917. Historically, Fuller abandoned his plan to attack St Quentin as he could not secure cooperation from the French army, which was recovering from the mutinies of April 1917. In this scenario I have assumed that the surprise use of massed tanks turns the Chemin des Dames offensive into a relative success for the French, thus allowing them to launch renewed attacks in the autumn.

Historically, the tank was a valuable part of the Allied arsenal, particularly in the more mobile conditions of 1918, but it never became the decisive weapon that its champions had hoped. Technical limitations, political wrangling, and production problems delayed its appearance in numbers, whilst the novelty of the tank made devising tactics for it a problem.

Notes

1 Horace Smith-Dorrien, *Memories of Forty Eight Years' Service* (London: J. Murray, 1925), p. 154.

2 J. P. Harris, *Men, Ideas and Tanks* (Manchester: University of Manchester Press, 1995), pp. 1–7.

3 Major G. H. J. Rooke, 'Shielded Infantry and the Decisive Frontal Attack', *Journal of the Royal United Service Institute*, 58(1), pp. 771–83.

4 John Glanfield, *The Devil's Chariots* (Stroud: Sutton Publishing, 2001), pp. 266–7.

5 Spencer Jones, *From Boer War to World War* (Norman: University of Oklahoma Press, 2012), p. 123.

6 *The National Archives, WO 426/86/11, 'Study of a New Form of Tracked Transporter'.

7 The Irish Home Rule Bill was due to come into force in 1914 despite the fierce opposition of the paramilitary Ulster Volunteers. Fearing a civil war in Ireland, the British government considered using the military to suppress the Ulstermen. News that the army might be used against British citizens prompted a miniature mutiny with several officers refusing to obey the order and others choosing to resign. The government backed down but the incident led to a reshuffle of command in the army.

8 Ernest D. Swinton, *Eyewitness* (London: Hodder & Stoughton, 1932), pp. 31–2.

9 Harris, *Ideas and Tanks*, p. 16.

10 Ibid., pp. 16–17.

11 *Henry Wilson, *Curragh Chaos: A Personal Memoir* (London: E. Arnold, 1920), p. 331.

12 Gary Sheffield, *The Chief: Douglas Haig and the British Army* (London: Aurum Press, 2011) p. 371.

13 *Basil Liddell Hart, *The Great Tank War* (London: J. Murray, 1931), pp. 45–50.

14 *Lancelot de Mole, *Tanks: The Memoirs of a Pioneer* (London: Harman, 1929), p. 14.

15 *Tank Museum Archives, 'Report on Test of Armoured Land Cruiser Prototype'.

16 Swinton, *Eyewitness*, p. 196.

17 Christy Campbell, *Band of Brigands: The Extraordinary Story of the First Men in Tanks* (London: Harper, 2008), p. 104.

18 *Smith-Dorrien had replaced Sir John French after French fell seriously ill with pneumonia.

19 Winston S. Churchill, *The World Crisis 1911–1918* (London: Odhams Press, 1931), vol. 2, p. 1220.

20 Campbell, *Band of Brigands*, p. 225.

21 *Andrew Southall, *British Tank Production in the First World War* (London: Magic Press, 2010), p. 11.

22 J. P. Harris, *Douglas Haig and the First World War* (Cambridge: University of Cambridge Press, 2008), p. 302.

23 British heavy tanks came in two types: 'males' were armed with a 6-pounder gun in each side sponson and 'females' replaced the two 6-pounders with four heavy machine guns.

24 Campbell, *Band of Brigands*, p. 185.

25 Ibid., p. 330.

26 Ibid., p. 187.

27 Ibid., p. 191.

28 Glanfield, *Devil's Chariots*, p. 215.

29 Campbell, *Band of Brigands*, p. 308.

30 Ibid., p .294.

31 Ibid., p. 304.

32 *J. F. C. Fuller, *The Thousand Tank Army* (London: E. Arnold, 1928), pp. 75–88.

33 Peter Hart, *1918: A Very British Victory* (London: Weidenfeld & Nicolson, 2008), p. 449.

34 Ibid., p. 325.

35 Heinz Guderian, *Achtung-Panzer* (London: Cassell, 1999 reprint), p. 81.

36 Hart, *1918*, p. 345.

37 Ibid., p. 346.

38 Guderian, *Achtung-Panzer*, pp. 81–2.

39 Campbell, *Band of Brigands*, p. 332.

40 Alexander Watson, *Enduring the Great War* (Cambridge: Cambridge University Press, 2008) pp. 167–8.

10

German Strategic Raiding, the Murder of David Lloyd George, and the Rise of Lord Northcliffe

James Pugh[1]

Members of both the House of Commons and the House of Lords had assembled in the Royal Gallery of the Palace of Westminster with express instructions to be in their seats for 10.50 a.m. Attendance was to be mandatory, and whether for reasons of duty, fear, or in appreciation of the historic significance of the event, no member was absent. It was at precisely 10.59 a.m. that James Lowther, the Speaker of the House of Commons, rose to his feet to begin proceedings. His instructions of 'order, order' were, on this occasion, entirely unnecessary, as an atmosphere of hushed anticipation had been prevalent in the hall since the first peers and MPs had made their way into the building. The presence of a battalion of Coldstream Guards, including armed personnel stationed inside the hall itself, served to punctuate the need for silence, reverence, and awe.

As he cast his eyes across the rows of seats, Lowther could not help but reflect on the extraordinary events that had led to this moment, and he recognised in the faces of those staring back at him that each member was asking of himself the same question. Such thoughts filled the Speaker with a plethora of emotions: anger, confusion, sadness, and, most of all, guilt: 'How did we let this happen?' Nonetheless, Lowther was duty-bound to see proceedings through. He inhaled deeply and, before continuing, let out a barely audible groan, a sigh of collective pain for the death of democracy: 'My Lords, and Right Honourable Members of both Houses, pray silence for the Prime Minister of Great Britain, Lord Northcliffe.'[2]

Northcliffe strode towards the lavishly appointed lectern and surveyed Britain's political elite, shifting his gaze to examine the portraits of the British monarchs and prime ministers that adorned the walls of the gallery: an illuminated history of the leadership of the British Empire. He was now of their number. He had reached the summit, and his power and influence were all-pervading. His brief time for reflection over, Northcliffe set his feet and allowed his body to relax a little into the lectern, for this would be an address of some length. Never a comfortable or prodigious public speaker, Northcliffe cleared his throat with a gentle cough, took a sip of water, and began his address:

'My noble Lords, and Right Honourable Members of the Commons, as you will have no doubt read in *The Times* and the *Daily Mail* – the only remaining bastions of a free and trustworthy press – my government received representations from Germany and the Central Powers during the course of the previous day. In leading the delegation, the German government noted their desire for a cessation of hostilities. Issuing the Central Powers with our terms of surrender, negotiations were swiftly and decisively concluded and, as of 11 a.m. this morning, the Great War of 1914 to 1918 has come to an end. The British Empire and Her Allies are victorious: a victory for the good and righteous nations of the globe that secures Britain's position as a shining beacon of justice and integrity.

'This, however, has been a costly and divisive conflict that has shaken the very fabric of British society to its core. The incompetent and frankly corrupt nature of Britain's political leadership in the years up to 1917 has meant that the British people have been compelled to shoulder a heavy and almost crippling weight. Of course, as you will all recall, it was during the unprecedented crisis of 1917, when Britain faced the prospect of total paralysis as Germany launched a murderous campaign of aerial raiding against civilian targets in this country, resulting in the murder of the then prime minster, Mr David Lloyd George, that I was persuaded, against my natural instincts, to assume the reins of power and guide Britain and Her Empire through the most difficult period in its history. With the support of the much-pressed Royal Family I was able to provide this glorious Empire with stability and strong leadership; a duty that I alone could bear.

'After changing our military policy, and adopting a holding strategy on the Western Front, we were able to devote our resources to building a massive and powerful aerial fleet, which, through a concentrated and decisive campaign against the German homeland, has seen the British Empire and

Her Allies march relentlessly, effectively, and efficiently to victory. It has been with some regret that this campaign has seen the deployment of aerially dropped chemical ordnance against targets in Germany. However, when I was persuaded to shoulder the heavy burden of providing leadership in such a time of crisis, I made it plain that all political, strategic, and military options had to be considered. In this vein, and, as another consequence of the unprecedented nature of the crisis facing Britain, there was the need to pass emergency legislation that served to reform the ineffective system of political leadership in Britain, circumventing the painfully inefficient culture of committees: a culture that served to stifle and paralyse decisive leadership. Moreover, given the nature of the death of my predecessor, Mr Lloyd George, some equally decisive steps were needed to protect the British people from certain violent elements amongst their number. Such measures are, of course, temporary in nature, and it is hoped that, in time, it will be possible to repeal some aspects of this emergency legislation. Quite obviously, this time has not yet been reached, but the British people can rest assured that I will review the status of such legislation on a regular basis, returning the governance of Britain to its more "conventional" foundations as soon as I am able.'[3]

Northcliffe paused and took a sip of water. His eyes focused on the only empty chair amongst the audience, a chair marked with the crest of Marlborough. That this chair remained in the gallery served to send a powerful reminder to those who would dare to question the authority of Northcliffe and his regime. Outspoken on one too many occasions, Mr Churchill, former First Lord of the Admiralty, had been unwilling to support the emergency legislation that Northcliffe deemed a necessary prerequisite to the successful prosecution of a war against Germany. Rumours persisted as to Churchill's whereabouts, and *The Times* and *Daily Mail* had managed to find evidence to suggest that the former First Lord had been passing secrets to the Central Powers and was now, in fact, hidden away in a *Schloss* in southern Germany.[4] Sitting behind Northcliffe, Lowther, a graduate of Eton, King's College London, and Trinity College, Cambridge, a true and honest custodian of British democracy, reflected on the nightmarish situation unfolding before his eyes. Catching the gaze of one of the tall and alert Guardsmen, Lowther could not help but focus on the soldier's Lee Enfield rifle, his mind returning to that one burning question: 'How did we let this happen?'

Alfred Harmsworth, as Lord Northcliffe was known before his elevation to the peerage, began building his media empire in the 1890s.[5] Important steps on this journey included the creation of the *Daily Mail* in 1896, and his acquisition of *The Times* and *The Sunday Times* in 1908. Other publications that were created or owned by Northcliffe during this period included the *Daily Mirror*, the *Evening Post*, and the *Observer*. By the outbreak of war in 1914, the Northcliffe press controlled 40 per cent of morning, 45 per cent of evening, and 15 per cent of Sunday newspaper circulation.[6] Northcliffe's power and influence stemmed from the wide range of publications he owned, which 'reached all classes of the nation'.[7] The *Mail* was the highest-selling, non-illustrated morning newspaper within the UK, and, in 1914, the *Mail*'s circulation in London alone was 950,000 copies.[8] The extent of this portfolio meant that, in the words of Beaverbrook, '[Northcliffe's] power was so considerable that it was of the utmost importance in all matters of public interest to secure his assistance or at any rate his neutrality.'[9] As a consequence, Northcliffe was given regular access to Britain's political and military elites, and by 1914 he could include Churchill, Lloyd George, Andrew Bonar Law, Sir John French, and Sir John Fisher amongst those with whom he corresponded.[10]

There was also something uniquely personal about the manner in which Northcliffe ran his media empire. He was able to fashion 'his proprietorship into a super-editorship'.[11] As Northcliffe himself was to write in private correspondence with one of his journalists, '[i]f you read "The Times" and the "Daily Mail" leading articles, you will see very plainly what my views are. I write most of the "Daily Mail" articles myself, and have a good deal to do with the concoction of those in "The Times".'[12] Viewed as possessing 'a supernatural sensitivity to the popular mood', Northcliffe was a much-feared presence in Britain's political landscape in 1914.[13] Such a process was only heightened during wartime, as the print media had little competition with regard to the delivery of information: 'Northcliffe, already a force to be reckoned with before 1914, became the chief beneficiary of the wartime intensification of press influence.'[14]

Given the close control that Northcliffe exerted over the content of his newspapers, particularly the *Daily Mail*, it is unsurprising that he chose to focus on matters of deep personal interest. One of the most important was his somewhat neurotic belief in the strategic vulnerability of the British Empire, particularly the British Isles, which was evidenced by his 'extraordinary outburst' directed at the editorial staff of the *Daily Mail* on the outbreak of war in 1914. Fearing that the deployment of an expeditionary force to the continent would leave Britain in an acutely vulnerable position, Northcliffe exclaimed, 'What about invasion? What about our own country? Put that in the leader. Do you hear? Not a single soldier will go with my consent. Say so in the paper tomorrow.'[15] Northcliffe's feelings of vulnerability were only heightened in the prewar period as relations between Britain and Germany continued to deteriorate, a process aggravated to a considerable degree by the increasingly hostile anti-German position adopted by the *Daily Mail* and *The Times*.[16] The decision of the Northcliffe press to focus on Germany's military progress and preparations before 1914, juxtaposing such efforts against Britain's seemingly pedestrian attitude to such matters, set an important precedent, and Northcliffe used his press empire to harass and criticise the British government in relation to its national defence policies. For example, on 31 July 1914, the *Daily Mail* declared that, '[t]he failure to arm and organise the British nation so as to meet the conditions of Europe has left us dependent on foreign allies.'[17]

Such criticism dovetailed neatly with another of Northcliffe's personal fascinations. He possessed 'a boy's interest' in new technologies, particularly aviation.[18] In fact, the *Daily Mail* was a leading force in promoting the development of aviation in the United Kingdom, offering prizes for various aeronautical achievements.[19] When a French aviator, Louis Bleriot, crossed the Channel and landed in Britain in 1909, Northcliffe was heard to remark that England was 'no longer an Island', reflecting that the historic protection afforded to the British peoples by the sea was being eroded.[20] In attempting to promote the development and proliferation of aviation in Britain, Northcliffe became increasingly alarmed by the progress made in Germany, particularly in relation to the growing fleet of airships possessed by both the German Army and German Navy. Northcliffe was to warn important figures in the government about Britain's 'truly pathetic' position in relation to aviation.[21] Thus, at the outbreak of war, Northcliffe felt that Britain was acutely vulnerable to aerial attack by a fleet of German aerial craft.

In many respects, Northcliffe was right to be concerned. The air defence of the United Kingdom was a responsibility over which Britain's two service departments – the Admiralty and War Office – fought a bitter battle in the prewar period. The battle was, in many respects, an extension of the more general inter-service rivalry that characterised Admiralty–War Office relations during this period.[22] However, whilst the Admiralty made at least some provisions to assist in the air defence of Great Britain, the War Office, which effectively possessed sole responsibility for the security of the UK from aerial attack, had made absolutely no provision for such duties at the outbreak of war.[23] In fact, by September 1914, the Secretary of State for War, Lord

Kitchener, made a formal request to Churchill and the Admiralty to assume responsibility for the air defence of Britain.[24]

It was with a sense of some anticipation that Northcliffe waited for the first German air raid against the British mainland. For example, the sensationalist headline, 'Zeppelin bomb havoc in Antwerp', was how the *Daily Mail* chose to highlight a German aerial raid against the Belgian coast.[25] Northcliffe continued to warn of the threat posed by German aerial raiding during the autumn of 1914, and when the first serious Zeppelin raid took place during the middle of January 1915, the excitement recorded in the pages of the *Mail* was almost palpable: 'Zeppelin at last!'[26] On the following day, the *Mail* noted that, whilst the raid was relatively minor in character, German airships had been unopposed. The government was urged to make its intention clear with regard to air defence policy, ensuring that future raids were met with a warm reception.[27] The effects of early German airship raiding, whilst extremely limited in terms of the material damage inflicted, sent shock waves through the Admiralty.[28] During an already difficult period for Churchill, particularly given the situation in the Dardanelles, the First Sea Lord, Sir John Fisher, offered his resignation on two occasions, citing the threat of Zeppelin raiding and noting that he felt the Admiralty would be blamed for the ensuing massacre.[29]

Criticism of British air defence policy reached its first crescendo in the summer of 1915, as a German airship raid struck Hull and Grimsby on 6 June 1915. Up to this stage, German raiding was generally directed against targets in southern England, where Britain's limited air defence network was concentrated. However, by attacking further north, German airships were able to circumnavigate such defences and strike at undefended targets.[30] As the official historian was to conclude, press criticism of the Admiralty led to the appointment of the famous gunnery expert, Sir Percy Scott, to take command of the air defences of London.[31] His appointment did not escape comment from the *Mail*, although it treated the news with a large degree of cynicism. Rather than to develop an effective air defence system, the *Mail* suggested that Scott's position served to screen the government from the 'indignation of the citizens'.[32] The tone of the *Mail* then shifted into a higher gear, and its criticism of the Admiralty and government was put in blunt terms: '. . . the whole question of the air defence of London is in a state of chaotic muddle, and the only plan so far apparent of fighting off the air assassins consists in hoping that they will not come, or, if they do come, of trying to believe that they do not accomplish anything.'[33]

Such criticism was the result of wider public feeling, itself a product of the genuinely slow progress made by the government with regard to improving Britain's air defences. The more serene tones of the *Mail*, a partial feature of the summer of 1915, were replaced by increasing anger and frustration during the autumn and winter of 1915–16. In mid-October 1915, in a well-attended meeting organised by the *Globe*, the *Mail* noted with approval the resolutions passed during the gathering that criticised government policy over air defence and called for reprisals against Germany.[34]

Keen to rid itself of an increasingly burdensome responsibility, the Admiralty was able to force the War Office to fulfil its air defence responsibilities, although not without an extended bureaucratic battle that lasted throughout the winter of 1915–16.[35] On 7 February 1916, the *Mail* recorded that Sir John French and the War Office were to assume control of air defences, with confirmation printed on 11 February.[36] The appointment of Sir John did not immediately placate the *Mail*. Its gentle criticism, which focused on French's health and the already extensive remit of his post as Commander of Home Forces, captured wider feelings that the government did not realise the 'gravity of the air problem'.[37] That the *Mail* treated the subject with such restraint is surprising, given the nature of air defence developments in the opening months of 1916. Another round of airship raids had been launched against Britain during January 1916. This was statistically the most intense period of strategic raiding during the conflict.[38] The culmination was the raid of 31 January 1916, in which German airships reached as far north as the Midlands. Such penetrative raids were juxtaposed against the performance of the defenders, in which, of the fourteen aircraft dispatched, seven were damaged, with three pilots injured, two fatally.[39] Fierce criticism followed in the *Mail*, and comments focused on the convoluted management of Britain's air defences and the 'inertia, slackness, lack of prevision and provision' displayed by the government.[40]

Whilst there were some improvements in Britain's air defence system during 1916, Northcliffe felt compelled to offer direct and personal criticism of British air defence policy. As his secretary noted, Northcliffe rarely made public declarations under his own name, and his decision to do so in the field of air defence reflected the gravity with which he viewed the subject.[41] In an extremely rare address to the House of Lords, Northcliffe selected air power as the subject for his comments.[42] His speech was driven by the perceived failures in the British government's handling of its air power resources. Northcliffe also published a printed volume during 1916 that detailed his views on various aspects of the war. His thoughts on air power were well developed, and he offered a stark warning regarding the vulnerability of the British Isles to air attack.[43]

Northcliffe's criticisms of the British government extended far and wide during 1916, and his press played a central role in the collapse of the Asquith government in the winter of 1916.[44] His power and influence growing, Northcliffe felt compelled to warn Asquith's successor, David Lloyd George, that '. . . if I hear he has been interfering with strategy . . . I shall break him.'[45]

In fact, by the winter of 1916, Britain's air defences had, with the allocation of increased resources and the accumulation of precious operational experience, improved to such an extent as to overcome the German airship threat.[46] Success against the attacking airships was widely praised in the *Mail*, and, reflecting the journalistic truism that 'good news is not news', air power matters, which had been a significant aspect of the *Mail*'s reporting, appeared less frequently during the latter half of 1916.[47] Of course, as recorded by the *Mail* at the end of November 1916, the appearance, during daylight, of a lone German aircraft over London (dropping some 60 kg of bombs) established a worrying precedent, and foreshadowed the devastating events that would unfold during the summer and autumn of 1917.[48]

Going largely unnoticed by the Northcliffe press, the running down of Britain's air defences was a feature of the first half of 1917. Facing sustained pressure on the Western Front, maximum resources were required to help the Royal Flying Corps (RFC) through the most challenging period it faced during the course of the First World War. In fact, reporting in the Northcliffe press during this period demonstrated a very significant shift in focus, and the government was criticised for not providing sufficient support to the RFC in France.[49]

This was to change as Germany launched tentative daylight raids using aircraft – the infamous Gotha strategic bomber – instead of airships during May 1917. This period had an 'impact disproportionate' to the attacking forces involved and ordnance delivered, and saw perhaps the most sustained and agitated criticism of British air defence policy by the *Mail*.[50] Importantly, the shock of such raiding seemed all the more profound, given that Britain's air defences had become more effective during 1916. In addition, the very nature of daylight raiding, with well-drilled formations of German bombers making 'serene progress' in the skies, was a highly visible image of the failure of the air defences around London.[51]

The fraught reaction of the public and press fed off one another, and feelings of anger and resentment toward both the raiders and the inadequate provisions of the British government grew swiftly. In many cases the frightened and frustrated public reacted with rioting, targeting shops with German-sounding names. At one stage the disturbances were so out of hand that soldiers at Chelsea barracks were brought to readiness to quell the riots.[52] Such reactions added to what was already a troubled climate. Heavy casualties on the Western Front, severe losses at sea at the hands of a reinvigorated U-boat campaign and increasingly aggressive labour disputes all piled concerns on top of Lloyd George and his government.[53] This context drove the government into a veritable frenzy of activity.

The British inability to halt the German raid of 13 June 1917 prompted a barrage of criticism in the press. In response, the government discussed air power matters with senior military officials at a meeting of the War Cabinet on 20 June.[54] The conclusions of the Cabinet included instructions to redeploy two fighter squadrons from the Western Front to air defence duties. No. 56 Squadron, a unit known for its fighting reputation, was duly dispatched to the UK, but, as the official history notes, 'after an uneventful fortnight the [squadron] rejoined the British Expeditionary Force.'[55] As one of its pilots remarked, '[t]he defence of London was quite a secondary affair. The things of real importance were squadron dances . . . The squadron stood by, gloriously idle.'[56]

It was with the most unfortunate timing possible that, on 7 July 1917, only hours after No. 56 Squadron returned to France, the Gothas struck their most devastating blow against London.[57] The *Mail's* response was even more forthright than usual, matching the level of public indignation at the ineffectiveness of Britain's defences.[58] The raid resulted in fifty-seven civilian deaths and prompted further anti-German rioting. In many respects, the Northcliffe press was responsible for creating a moral panic amongst the British public.[59]

With Britain teetering on the edge of violent civil unrest, a process that drove high-level strategic planning to use soldiers to suppress any uprisings, Lloyd George felt compelled to take action. A special Cabinet meeting of the afternoon of 7 July ordered the dispatch of two fighting squadrons from France to strengthen the air defences around London, whilst a third squadron, forming for overseas service, was to be kept back for defensive duties.[60] Moreover, in keeping with the dominant committee culture of the period, Lloyd George established a two-man inquiry under his chairmanship, with the South African General Jan Smuts being tasked to explore how to, first, improve Britain's air defences, and second, to develop plans to launch aerial raids against Germany.[61] To develop effective plans took time, and Smuts and Lloyd George were not able to offer any respite to the much-pressed citizens of the East End of London. German bombing in September and October 1917 had resulted in the citizens of London making use of the underground railway stations as shelters.

As German night raiding continued into October, the War Cabinet continued to express concerns regarding the role of the press. On 2 October 1917, the War Cabinet recorded that the 'poorest classes, whose tenements are often of the flimsiest description', were the most likely to 'give way to panic' during raids.[62] Such panic, the War Cabinet alleged, was driven by the press, who published 'detailed descriptions and photographs of casualties caused and damage done'.[63] Lloyd George was tasked with speaking to the editors of the principal newspapers involved, asking them to refrain from publishing such material. In addition, they were told to stress the very limited casualties that German raiding inflicted, which included making overt comparisons to statistics for road traffic accidents.[64] The role of the press during this period was of significant concern to Lloyd George, and it may well explain his decision, after the War Cabinet meeting of 2 October 1917, to visit some of London's 'poorest classes' in the East End. As reported in the *Mail* on the following day, Lloyd George, when addressing the 'local poor', had remarked that: '[w]e'll give it them all back. We'll give them hell. And we'll give it them back soon. We shall bomb Germany with compound interest.'[65]

Of course, it was whilst delivering this very speech that German raiders struck their most provocative and devastating blow against London. Penetrating British airspace at low level, a flight of Gothas flew on a direct course for Buckingham Palace, scoring several hits on the Royal residency. Simultaneously, a much larger formation of Gothas, operating at high altitude, dropped their bombs indiscriminately over the East End. It was in close proximity to Lloyd George's location that a direct hit was achieved against a school in Bonner Street, Bethnal Green, resulting in the deaths of 103 children and three of their teachers. Rescue efforts were hampered as a final squadron of German aircraft dropped a high concentration of chemical ordnance, creating swirling clouds of toxic gases that swept across the poorest parts of London.[66]

As the subsequent Home Office investigation noted, it was whilst attempting to evacuate the prime minister from the affected area that Lloyd

George and his security detail encountered a rioting mob.[67] Lloyd George was no stranger to such situations, having been lucky to escape with his life during a riot in Birmingham in 1901.[68] However, on this occasion, good fortune abandoned the prime minister. Whilst his bodyguards were able to hold back the crowd for several minutes, the sheer number and ferocity of the rioters, incensed by the hollow ring of Lloyd George's speech, was overwhelming, and Britain's thirty-sixth prime minister, along with six members of Special Branch, his private secretary, and his parliamentary secretary, were murdered in cold blood.[69]

As reports filtered back to Whitehall of the prime minister's death, a series of emergency plans were brought into operation. The most significant of these, driven by the knowledge that German raiders had deliberately targeted the Royal Family, and that violence and unrest were growing in London, saw Britain's senior military and political officials focus on ensuring the safety of King George and his family. In line with a well-established protocol, King George, Queen Mary, and their children were driven across country to a remote naval base on the West Coast of England to be evacuated to Canada, seeing out the crisis in the New World. However, the king made heated protests, stating that he 'would not abandon Britain in her hour of need'.[70] Whilst George V refused to leave British soil, the king's decision to stay in Great Britain did little to help stabilise the anarchic attitude of the civil population of his kingdom. Violence and unrest multiplied exponentially, resulting in three nights of unparalleled rioting and looting throughout the major cities of Britain.

The Northcliffe press began playing a double-handed game. Whilst the edition of 4 October 1917 called for calm and restraint, the *Mail* could not help but cause further alarm by noting that Britain was drifting helplessly without political leadership, and remained vulnerable to further attack from German strategic raiding.[71] In an editorial penned by an unknown hand, Lord Northcliffe's prophetic insights into air power and the vulnerability of the British Isles were highlighted. The piece closed with a call to appoint a bold and decisive leader, who possessed expert knowledge of 'aerial matters', and who would be able to steer Britain through its present crisis.[72] Similar editorials and stories, repeated in editions of *The Times* and *Daily Mail* on the following days, seemed to strike a chord with the British people, particularly after further German raiding took place on 7 October 1917, pushing the already volatile atmosphere in Britain to a tangible crescendo.[73] The morning of 8 October saw massive rallies in Printing House

Square and outside Carmelite House, where Lord Northcliffe's two most important offices were located. Placards and banners urged Northcliffe to seize control of the situation, whilst the crowds chanted for the peer to be made prime minster.

The level of support had reached a critical mass by 11 October, as the crowds outside the Northcliffe offices continued to swell, with similar demonstrations held outside Parliament and Whitehall. Whilst *The Times* and *Daily Mail* urged for restraint amongst the British people, they continued to push for the appointment of a 'bold and decisive' leader to save Britain in its hour of need.[74] Lord Northcliffe was not seen in person throughout this period, although reports indicated that he did not leave his office in Carmelite House for nearly a week, working long into the night with his editorial teams. On the afternoon of 11 October, the War Cabinet, including Andrew Bonar Law, Lord Milner, Lord Curzon, and Arthur Henderson, met in a final attempt to address the leadership situation. One of Lloyd George's great skills had been to hold together a potentially disparate coalition, but since his death the four men that constituted the inner War Cabinet had achieved little, their discussions bogged down in party political considerations. In spite of the deployment of significant numbers of troops throughout the UK, and of government statements calling for calm, the situation continued to deteriorate. The four men were at least able to agree that Britain sat on the edge of total anarchy.[75] It is frustrating to the modern historian that the records of this meeting have not survived, but what is evident is that, after a discussion that lasted several hours, Lord Northcliffe was invited to meet with the War Cabinet. Even George V, who viewed Northcliffe with a great deal of mistrust, was to tell his private secretary that 'in light of the revolutionary fervour spreading across Europe, including here on our own shores, it might be time for Britain to search out a more *authoritative* leader [emphasis added].'[76]

On the morning of 12 October, *The Times* and *Daily Mail* ran with a joint exclusive headline, 'Lord Northcliffe to be Prime Minster', and, by the afternoon of the same day, Northcliffe had been unveiled as the thirty-seventh prime minster of Great Britain. Demonstrating decisive leadership, Northcliffe's first measure was to publish amendments to the Defence of the Realm Act of 1914. These far-reaching and 'temporary' amendments included the power for the prime minster to circumvent the typical law-making channels during times of emergency, including the ability to temporarily dissolve both Houses, the suspension of *Habeas Corpus*, the suspension of elections, the institution of a nationwide curfew, and the banning of non-government-approved media outlets. As a government statement accompanying these amendments made clear, such measures were a necessary evil given the crisis facing Great Britain and Her Empire, and, quite obviously, the more draconian amendments to the Act would be repealed at the first available opportunity.[77] Such measures proved too much to bear for some members. Winston Churchill, then minister of munitions, felt compelled to openly criticise Northcliffe and resign from his position. As noted, it was shortly after making these statements that both *The Times* and *Mail* commented upon the disappearance of Churchill, who, it was alleged, had been passing secrets to Germany.[78] Comments in the press praised Northcliffe for the boldness of his leadership, whilst figures who criticised the new prime minster were subjected to vitriolic campaigns that drove them underground.[79]

Whilst Northcliffe's ascension to office did much to stabilise the mood of the nation, it was the consequences of the Smuts inquiry, commissioned by Lloyd George, that resulted in a significant improvement in Britain's air defences. It was also extremely fortuitous that there was a prolonged break in German raiding due to bad weather in the winter of 1917–18, providing the British with a much-needed opportunity to marshal their defences. An experienced RFC officer, E. B. Ashmore, was appointed to oversee London's defences, and, with the approval and drive of Northcliffe, a separate Air Ministry was created, headed by his brother and fellow media mogul, Lord Rothermere.[80] This resulted in the creation of the Royal Air Force (RAF), the world's first independent air service, and a prioritisation of air power resources to strike directly against Germany. In the guise of the newly developed Handley-Page V/1500 strategic bomber, and the 3,000-kg mustard-gas bomb, both developed with the enthusiastic approval of Northcliffe, Britain possessed the ability to devastate the German homeland. As the commander of the newly formed RAF, Sir Hugh Trenchard, noted in his first address to the personnel of his bomber fleet, 'Germany has sown the wind, and they are now going to reap the whirlwind.'[81] After only three heavy raids against the German capital, in which tens of thousands of casualties were inflicted, the Central Powers felt compelled to seek terms with the British and their allies. It was on the following day that Northcliffe delivered his victory speech at the Royal Gallery.

The Reality

During the First World War, Germany undertook a total of 103 air raids against the United Kingdom (fifty-two by aeroplane and fifty-one by airship), dropping a total of 270 tons of bombs, inflicting some 4,830 casualties (including 1,414 deaths), and causing damage worth almost £3 million.[82] To offer a telling comparison with the Second World War, during only one daylight raid over London in September 1940, the *Luftwaffe* dropped an estimated 316 tons of high-explosive bombs.[83] It is difficult not to accept Ferris's conclusion that the 'first battle of Britain scarcely affected the outcome of the First World War'.[84]

Nonetheless, German raiding against the United Kingdom caused significant headaches for the British government, with the Northcliffe press playing a central role in criticising British air defence policy throughout the course of the conflict.[85] The ability of Lord Northcliffe to influence the British public, whether real or imagined, became a significant factor in British politics during the First World War. Lloyd George felt compelled to tread a careful path with the peer, and, after the decision was taken to create an Air Ministry, a result of pressure from the press and public alike, Northcliffe was offered the position as Secretary of State for Air. In an open letter to Lloyd George, published in both *The Times* and the *Daily Mail*, Northcliffe rejected the offer out of hand, and with it, his chance to attain a ministerial position.[86] After chaffing and harassing the government on air power policy throughout the war, it seems strange that, when presented with the opportunity to help rectify the perceived shortcomings in Britain's provision and application of air power, including air defence policy, Northcliffe was so abrupt in refusing Lloyd George's overtures. This was all the more curious given that, at times, editorial pieces in the *Mail* made both overt and thinly veiled calls for Northcliffe to be appointed Secretary of State for Air.[87]

Northcliffe's reasoning, detailed in his letter of 16 November 1917, reflected his consistent vision that he felt most useful to Britain's war effort by maintaining his freedom to criticise the government.[88] Northcliffe's pronouncement forced Lloyd George's hand, and it is difficult not to view the decision to appoint Northcliffe's brother, Lord Rothermere, to the post as a further effort to appease the owner of the *Mail*. Even without a ministerial position, Northcliffe and his publications brought pressure to bear on the British government, pressure that played no small part in ensuring that, by the close of the war, Britain possessed the most sophisticated air defence system the world had ever seen. As Ferris notes, this model became the foundation for all air defence systems that followed.[89]

Notes

1 The author is extremely grateful to the editors, Dr Spencer Jones and Lieutenant Colonel (Ret'd) Peter Tsouras, for their helpful criticism on an early draft of this chapter.

2 *Lord Northcliffe's victory address, a full transcript of which appeared in *The Times*, 3 February 1918.

3 *Ibid.

4 *The Times*, 14 September 1918; *Daily Mail*, 14 September 1918.

5 On Northcliffe, see J. Lee Thompson, *Politicians, the Press, and Propaganda: Lord Northcliffe and the Great War, 1914–1919* (Kent, OH: Kent State University Press, 1999); J. Lee Thompson, *Press Baron in Politics, 1865–1922* (London: John Murray, 2000); R. Pound and G. Harmsworth, *Northcliffe* (London: Cassell, 1959).

6 Lee Thompson, *Politicians*, p. 2.

7 J. McEwen, 'The National Press during the First World War: Ownership and Circulation,' *Journal of Contemporary History*, 17:3 (July 1982), p. 472.

8 Ibid, p. 468; C. Seymore-Ure, 'Northcliffe's Legacy', in P. Caterall, C. Seymore-Ure and A. Smith (eds), *Northcliffe's Legacy: Aspects of the British Popular Press, 1896–1996* (London: Macmillan, 2000), p. 10. Only the *Daily Mirror*, originally established by Northcliffe, sold more copies.

9 Lord Beaverbrook, *Men and Power, 1917–1918* (London: Hutchinson, 1956), p. xxii.

10 The British Library (BL), St Pancras, London, Northcliffe Additional Manuscripts (NAM).

11 S. Koss, *The Rise and Fall of the Political Press in Britain, Volume II: The Twentieth Century* (London: Hamish Hamilton, 1984), pp. 253–4.

12 See BL, NAM, 62206: Correspondence with H. Fyfe (Correspondent for the *Daily Mail*), ff. 114–16. Letter, Northcliffe to Fyfe, 11 May 1915.

13 Koss, *Rise and Fall*, p. 117.

14 Lee Thompson, *Politicians*, p. 2.

15 T. Clarke, *My Northcliffe Diary* (New York: Cosmopolitan Book Corporation, 1931), pp. 52–4.

16 A. J. Morris, *The Scaremongers: The Advocacy of War and Rearmament, 1896–1914* (London: Routledge & Kegan Paul, 1984), p. 70.

17 *Daily Mail*, 31 July 1914.

18 Clarke, *My Northcliffe Diary*, p. 3.

19 'The New *Daily Mail* Prizes', *Flight*, 14:5 (5 April 1913), p. 393.

20 Pound and Harmsworth, *Northcliffe*, pp. 300–1; L. Owen, *The Real Lord Northcliffe: Some Personal Recollections of a Private Secretary* (London: Cassell, 1922), p. 24. More generally, see A. Gollin, *No Longer an Island: Britain and the Wright Brothers, 1902–1909* (London: Heinemann, 1984).

21 Pound and Harmsworth, *Northcliffe*, pp. 353–4.

22 A. Gollin, 'A Flawed Strategy: Early British Air Defence Arrangements', in R. J. Adams (ed.), *The Great War, 1914–1918: Essays on the Military, Political and Social History of the First World War* (London: Macmillan, 1990), pp. 31–7.

23 J. Pugh, 'The Conceptual Origins of the Control of the Air: British Military and Naval Aviation, 1911–1918' (PhD thesis, University of Birmingham, 2012), chapters 2, 3, and 6.

24 The National Archives (TNA), Air Ministry File (AIR) 1/2314/22/6: Memo, Churchill to Cabinet, Air Defence, 22 October 1914.

25 *Daily Mail*, 27 August 1914.

26 *Daily Mail*, 20 January 1915. See also H. A. Jones, *The War in the Air: Being the Story of the Part Played in the Great War by the Royal Air Force, Volume III* (Oxford: Clarendon Press, 1931), pp. 90–1.

27 *Daily Mail*, 21 January 1915.

28 On air defence during this period, see J. Ferris, 'Airbandit: C3I and Strategic Air Defence during the First Battle of Britain, 1915–18', M. Dockrill and D. French (eds), *Strategy and Intelligence: British Policy During the First World War* (London: Hambledon Press, 1996); C. Cole and E. F. Cheesman, *The Air Defence of Great Britain, 1914–1918* (London: Putnam, 1984).

29 A. J. Marder, *Fear God and Dread Nought: The Correspondence of Admiral of the Fleet Lord Fisher of Kilverstone, Volume III: Restoration, Abdication, and Last Years, 1914–1920* (London: Jonathan Cape, 1959), p. 124. Letter Fisher to Churchill, 4 January 1915.

30 Jones, *War in the Air, Vol. III*, p. 103.

31 Ibid., pp. 121–2.

32 *Daily Mail*, 22 October 1915.

33 Ibid.

34 *Daily Mail*, 15 October 1915.

35 Jones, *War in the Air, Vol. III*, pp. 153–7.

36 *Daily Mail*, 7 and 11 February 1916.

37 *Daily Mail*, 11 February 1916. See also *Daily Mail*, 8 February 1916.

38 Jones, *War in the Air, Vol. III*, pp. 135–44.

39 Ibid., pp. 146–7.

40 *Daily Mail*, 2 February 1916.

41 Owen, *The Real Lord Northcliffe*, pp. 46–7.

42 Lord Northcliffe, Speech to House of Lords, 23 May 1916, *Hansard Parliamentary Debates*, 5th series, vol. XXII, May 1916, cols 124–6.

43 Lord Northcliffe, *At the War* (London: Hodder & Stoughton, 1917), p. 46.

44 Lee Thompson, *Politicians*, pp. 112–16.

45 Pound and Harmsworth, *Northcliffe*, pp. 508–9. For Northcliffe's recollection of the event, see BL, NAM, 61260, Correspondence with P. Sassoon, Secretary to Sir Douglas Haig, ff. 45–8. Letter, Northcliffe to Sassoon, 18 October 1916.

46 S. F. Wise, *Canadian Airmen in the First World War: The Official History of the Royal Canadian Air Force, Volume I* (Toronto: University of Toronto Press, 1980), pp. 239–42.

47 For example, see *Daily Mail*, 25 September 1916.

48 *Daily Mail*, 29 November 1916.

49 For example, see *Daily Mail*, 3, 9, and 13 April 1917.

50 T. Davis Biddle, *Rhetoric and Reality: The Evolution of British and American Ideas about Strategic Bombing, 1914–1945* (Princeton: Princeton University Press, 2002), p. 30.

51 For contemporary intelligence reports of these raids, see TNA, AIR 1/2319/223/30/14 – 'Air Raids, 1917, Report IA, 25 May–13 June. Intelligence Section, GHQ, HF, Sep 1917; TNA, AIR 1/2319/223/30/15 – 'Air Raids, 1917, Report II, July. For the reaction of the *Mail*, see the editions of 28 May, 14, 15, 18 June, and 8 July 1917.

52 P. Panayi, 'Anti-German Riots in London during the First World War', *German History*, 7:2 (August 1989), pp. 200–1.

53 Davis Biddle, *Rhetoric and Reality*, pp. 32–3.

54 H. A. Jones, *The War in the Air: Being the Story of the Part Played in the Great War by the Royal Air Force (WIA), Volume V* (Oxford: Clarendon Press, 1935), pp. 29–32.

55 Jones, *WIA, Vol. V*, p. 32.

56 C. Lewis, *Sagittarius Rising* (London: Greenhill, 2007), p. 187.

57 For War Cabinet discussions of these raids, see TNA, Cabinet Papers (CAB) 23/3 – War Cabinet Minutes, 7 July 1917.

58 *Daily Mail*, 8 July 1917.

59 B. Holman, 'The Next War in the Air: Civilian Fears of Strategic Bombardment in Britain, 1908–1941' (PhD thesis, University of Melbourne, 2009), pp. 270–2.

60 TNA, CAB 23/3 – War Cabinet Minutes, 7 July 1917.

61 The second, and most far-reaching, Smuts report can be found in TNA, CAB 24/22 – G.T. 1658 – 'Committee on Air Organisation and Home Defence against Air Raids. Second Report', 17 August 1917. The first Smuts report, which dealt exclusively with improving the provision of localised air defence, can be found in TNA, CAB 24/20 – G.T.1451, 'Committee on Air Organisation and Home Defence against Air Raids. First Report', 19 July 1917.

62 TNA, CAB 23/4 – War Cabinet Minutes, 2 Oct 1917.

63 Ibid.

64 Ibid.

65 *Daily Mail*, 3 October 1917.

66 *Daily Mail*, 3 October 1917.

67 *TNA, Home Office Papers (HO) 38/7 – Home Office Report into the Murder of Mr David Lloyd George, 7 December 1917.

68 H. Du Parcq, *Life of David Lloyd George, Volume II* (London: Caxton, 1912), pp. 292–3.

69 *TNA, HO 38/7.

70 *Ibid.

71 *Daily Mail*, 4 October 1917.

72 *Ibid.

73 *The Times*, 5, 6, and 7 October 1917; *Daily Mail*, 5, 6, 7, and 8 October 1917.

74 *The Times*, 11 October 1917; *Daily Mail*, 11 October 1917.

75 *Parliamentary Archives, Private Papers of Andrew Bonar Law, Appointments Diary, September–November 1917.

76 *P. O'Boyle, *The Life of Lord Stamfordham* (Birmingham: Monkey Tree Publishing, 2011), p. 183.

77 *Government statement, copy printed in *The Times*, 13 October 1917.

78 *The Times*, 16 October 1917.

79 *The Times*, 13, 14, 15, and 17 October 1917; *Daily Mail*, 13, 14, 15, 16, and 17 October 1917.

80 E. B. Ashmore, *Air Defence* (London: Longmans, Green & Co., 1929).

81 *A. Boyle, *Bomber Trenchard: The Life and Legacy of Sir Hugh Trenchard* (London: Collins, 1952), p. 38.

82 For statistics of German air raids during the First World War, see H. A. Jones, *The War in the Air: Being the Story of the part played in the Great War by the Royal Air Force, Appendices* (Oxford: Clarendon Press, 1937), p. 164: 'Appendix XLIV – Summary Statistics of German Air Raids on Great Britain, 1914–1918'.

83 TNA, AIR 41/15 – Air Historical Branch Narrative, *The Air Defence of Great Britain, Vol. II: The Battle of Britain*. See Appendix 17: 'German Estimate of

Tonnage (Metric) Dropped in Attacks on London, September, 1940'. The example cited is the daylight raid of 7 September 1940.

84 Ferris, 'Airbandit', p. 23.

85 It was not until August 1918 that the *Mail* was prepared to declare that Britain's air defences were 'ready for the enemy'. *Daily Mail*, 7 August 1918.

86 *The Times* and *Daily Mail*, 16 November 1917.

87 For a not so subtle example, see *Daily Mail*, 3 February 1916.

88 *The Times* and *Daily Mail*, 16 November 1917.

89 Ferris, 'Airbandit', p. 56.